Amazing Gracie

To, Deirdre

with best wishes,

Lisa Jane Weller

x

Amazing Gracie

Lisa Jane Weller

First published in 2006 by Troll Boy Books
106 Bladindon Drive, Bexley, Kent, DA5 3BW

Distributed by Gazelle Book Services Limited
Hightown, White Cross Mills, South Rd, Lancaster, England LA1 4XS

All characters and events in this book are fictitious and any resemblance to real persons, living or dead, is purely coincidental.

British Library Cataloguing in Publication Data
A catalogue record for this book is available from the British Library.

ISBN 0-9551346-0-9
ISBN 978-0-9551346-0-9

Typeset by Amolibros, Milverton, Somerset
This book production has been managed by Amolibros
Printed and bound by T J International Ltd, Padstow, Cornwall, UK

For Mum, Dad and James

Acknowledgements

Firstly, huge thanks to everybody who helped and encouraged me throughout the writing of this novel – especially Emma, Harry, Carol, and the entire Caritas crew.

To Hilary Johnson, for her invaluable advice, provided far beyond the call of duty.

To Miss Hancock, who let me indulge my creative side even when the assignment didn't call for it. It's true what they say; you never forget a good teacher.

And finally, very special thanks go to the three people who provide unwavering love, support, help and encouragement in everything I do.

To Mum, Dad and James – here's looking forward to novel number two!

Chapter One

My name is Gracie Parker. I'm twenty-four years old. I have a job that I hate. I have no boyfriend. Oh, and I live at home with my parents.

Okay, so I know that must sound really desperate, but things weren't always this way. Honest. I mean, I had a life once. A really good life. I used to quite enjoy my job. I had a lovely flat that I shared with my fiancé (we were going to get married).

And then everything fell apart.

It all happened nearly three months ago – on Valentine's Day actually, if you can believe the irony of it…

❄ ❄ ❄

'Well, Gracie? What do you think?'

It was Valentine's Day. And I had quite contentedly been getting ready for perhaps the most romantic evening of my life, when who should knock at the door but my mother.

'Lovely,' I smiled, though inwardly cringing.

My mother, Ellen Parker, stood in front of me –

correction, twirled in front of me – wearing a recently-purchased and most certainly very expensive red dress.

'Are you sure, darling?' she asked, before – thank God – stopping her twirling. 'You don't think it makes my calves look fat?'

I just stared at her.

'Mum, you're fifty-two years old.'

She looked at me indignantly.

'What's that got to do with anything?'

'Nothing,' I sighed.

Six months ago, my mother joined the local gym. She didn't need to of course, because she's always had one of those figures that are just so. You know, like those models you get draped over sports cars in dirty magazines. The ones with all the right bits in all the right places. You know the ones I mean.

Anyway, in her younger days at least, my mother could have been one of those girls. Still, lately she had become unnaturally obsessive about her body. I think she may have been having some sort of sexual awakening.

And now she was standing in front of me, adjusting the front of her dress to seemingly show as much cleavage as humanly possible. I couldn't help it. I just had to say something.

'So are *Baywatch* actually hiring again, or is this all for Dad's benefit?'

'I just want to look nice for your father,' Mum replied haughtily.

Apparently satisfied that her dress was now in place, she began preening her hair instead.

My mother's hair was the same honey-blonde colour it had always been. But was it still natural? I didn't dare ask. As always though, it looked perfect. Which shouldn't have been surprising, as Mum wouldn't leave the house with so much as a single hair out of place. Or without her make-up on.

'It might be news to your generation,' Mum continued, shooting a withering glance in my direction, 'but some people do like to make an effort with their appearance, you know.'

I flinched. My mother had never been the most tactful person around. In fact, she could be pretty thoughtless sometimes. And although I had learnt from experience not to take her comments to heart, this time she seemed to have struck a nerve.

'I haven't finished getting ready yet,' I mumbled, as I wandered off into the bedroom.

'Well you'd better hurry,' Mum said, following me into the room, 'David will be home from work soon.'

Mum watched as I examined my appearance in the bedroom's full-length mirror. It was no wonder she had always been critical of the way I looked – because although I was pretty (or so David always insisted), I had inherited none of her features.

Whereas my mother had always been well-proportioned, petite and graceful, I had spent most of my formative years as a slightly gangly tomboy. And although I had since filled out a little, I knew that very same awkward and clumsy teenager was still alive and well. I knew this because she always seemed to make an appearance whenever my mother was around.

'And when David gets home,' I turned to face my mother, hoping she would take the hint, 'do you plan on still being here?'

'Honestly, Gracie!' Mum sniffed. 'You can be awfully rude sometimes!'

'I just meant…'

'No, no. That's okay,' she said, pretending to be insulted. 'I know when I'm not wanted.'

I knew from past experience that she was just looking for some sympathy. And she knew from past experience that she would get it.

'Mum, don't be silly,' I said, in my best soothing voice, 'of course you're wanted. You're very welcome here – you know that.'

'Well, perhaps I need to hear it just a little more often.'

I couldn't resist the urge to roll my eyes, so I turned away to do so. Glancing back in the mirror, I pushed a lock of brown hair out of my face, tucking it behind my right ear. It was a nervous habit I had developed many years before and was one that – to my mother's great annoyance – I had never been able to break.

'How does my hair look?' I asked, turning back to face my mother.

'Short,' she replied, eyeing it critically.

'Mum, we've been through this,' I sighed, tired of the same old argument. 'I'm going to grow it back out again.'

'You should never have had it cut in the first place,' Mum scolded me. 'All that pretty long hair lost – it's such a waste.'

I didn't know what to think. I'd never been particularly

fond of my long hair, and a few weeks ago had decided it was time for a change. I'd had my doubts about whether or not the cut would suit me of course (who doesn't get nervous before a visit to the hairdressers?), but ultimately I'd been pleased with the result.

David, however, had hated my new look. At first, he'd said nothing, but I'd known all the same – and eventually he'd admitted it. Meanwhile, my mother, not surprisingly, had demonstrated her dismay at the change somewhat more vocally.

And so I had set about growing my hair out again. It was already long enough to brush the top of my shoulders, but apparently even that wasn't good enough for Mother.

'You know,' Mum said, smiling at me sympathetically, 'men do prefer women with long hair.'

'Thanks Mum,' I replied, scowling, 'that's really helpful.'

'I'm just saying!' she protested, sounding wounded. 'No need to shoot the messenger!'

I bit my tongue to avoid saying something I'd regret. Luckily, I didn't get the chance – as suddenly, and to my great relief, the telephone rang.

My mother immediately perked up a little. She has a thing for telephones, you see. She would spend all day and all night gossiping over the phone if she could. My father once said that if they ever made an Olympic sport out of talking on the telephone, Mum would win a gold medal hands down. And I have to say I agree with him.

'I'll get it!' she cooed, before grabbing for the receiver. I tried to get there first – to no avail. 'Hello?'

A moment, then: 'David!' she squealed. 'How are you?' Another pause.

'Mum –' I began, and reached for the receiver. She batted my hand away.

'Well you really must come over for dinner sometime,' she said into the phone. 'Richard and I haven't seen you for ages. And Gracie just keeps telling me how busy you both are.'

A moment, then: 'Yes, you certainly do sound exhausted,' she laughed huskily. 'I can't quite imagine what Gracie must be doing to wear you out so completely…'

'Mum!'

Annoyed, I reached out and snatched the receiver from her grasp, watching her pout as I cradled it against my ear. 'Hi, David.'

'Gracie, hi! Listen, I can't talk for long.'

'Why not?' I frowned. 'You're on your way home from work, right?'

'No, I'm not,' David sighed apologetically. I knew what was coming next. 'Gracie, I'm sorry –' he began.

'Don't even say it.'

'Gracie –'

'No, David. Today is Valentine's Day. We were supposed to spend a romantic evening together, remember?'

'I remember.'

'Good. So you're coming home then.'

'Gracie, I can't. I'm sorry, but we're completely snowed under here. I'm going to be working through most of the night.'

'One of the pitfalls of dating a successful lawyer, darling,'

Mother chirped over my shoulder, making no attempt to disguise the fact that she was listening to my conversation. I could feel my temper rising.

'Mum!' I glared at her, doing my very best not to shout. 'Do you mind?'

Amazingly, she took the not-so-subtle hint.

'I'll just step outside for a minute,' she said, then smiled as she did so, closing the door halfway behind her.

Once she was gone, I turned my attention back to my fiancé, still hanging on the other end of the phone.

'David?'

'Gracie, you know the drill,' he began. 'I work this hard now, it pays off in the future. *Our* future. You know I hate letting you down, but I really have no choice.' I fell silent for a moment, contemplating this. 'Gracie?'

'I know,' I sighed. 'I know you're only doing what's best for us.'

'I promise you we'll have our evening another time,' David said sincerely, 'but I really have to go now. I have so much work to get through.'

'Okay. Well, I guess if you have to go you have to go, right?'

'I have to go. I do love you, Gracie.'

'I love you too.'

Quietly, I hung up the phone and looked towards the door. Although I couldn't see my mother standing, listening, on the other side of it, I knew she was there. 'You can come in now!' I called out to her. The door didn't open for a few moments.

This, of course, was one of my mother's favourite tricks

– pretending she had moved a polite distance away from the room and consequently had to make her way back to it. Eventually she reappeared though, her curious expression masking the fact that she already knew all that had been exchanged between David and me.

'Is everything okay?' she asked tentatively.

'No, Mum, everything is not okay,' I said. 'In fact, everything is looking pretty crappy right about now.'

'Well, there's no need for that sort of language,' my mother said. 'Now why don't you calm down and tell me what's wrong?'

'I am calm!' I replied angrily. 'And you already know what's wrong.'

'Well, it's not the end of the world now, is it?' Mum said breezily.

'It may as well be,' I said, watching her. 'I'm now the only person I know who doesn't have a date for Valentine's Day!'

'That's not true,' Mum replied, trying to be helpful. 'Your brother doesn't have a date.'

'Of course he doesn't!' I exclaimed. 'He has the social skills of a skunk!'

Warren, my little brother, had never been the cleanest person around.

'There's no need to resort to name calling, Gracie,' Mum said sternly. 'And if you must know, Warren has been making much more of an effort with his appearance lately. I think it has something to do with a girl at college he wants to impress.'

My mother frowned, as if something had suddenly occurred to her. 'Oh, that's right,' she said, remembering, 'he's taking her out to the movies tonight.'

'So everyone really does have a date but me,' I said glumly. 'God, even you're going out tonight!'

'And so are you,' my mother said.

As I stood watching, Mum made her way over to my wardrobe and began rummaging around inside, eventually emerging with my best jacket in her hands.

'Here.' She passed the jacket to me.

'What am I supposed to do? Go out and get a table for one?'

'No,' she smiled. A smile that said she had made up her mind and there was nothing I could do to change it. 'You're coming out to dinner with your father and me.'

❄ ❄ ❄

Two hours later, and I found myself trailing along behind my parents as they entered what was perhaps the trendiest restaurant in town – and definitely the most expensive. I wondered if they had won the lottery but neglected to tell me because, in my mother's own words:

'Gracie just can't be trusted with money!'

'Booking for the name of Parker,' my father, Richard, said to the smartly-dressed young man at the door.

Oh God. I called him a young man. A sure sign that I am getting old and that, when I do, I will undoubtedly turn out like my mother. I try not to think about it.

'Table for two?' the young man asked my father, raising his eyebrows inquisitively in my direction. I could already feel myself blushing with embarrassment.

'Plus one,' my mother added, smiling sweetly. 'That won't be a problem, will it?'

'I'm sure we can fit her in,' the young man (who I am disliking more every second) replied, looking at me with disdain.

'I'm not sure this was such a good idea,' I mumbled. 'I think I'll just go home.' I turned to leave. Mum grabbed my arm, firmly pulling me back.

Damn. Not quick enough.

'Don't be silly, darling,' she said.

She leant towards the young man as if to whisper a secret – then spoke loud enough so that everyone within about fifty feet could hear her. 'Poor thing, she didn't have a date tonight. On Valentine's Day of all days! So I very generously suggested that she accompany us. Wasn't that nice of me?'

I watched her as she smiled at the young man, pretending she'd committed such an act of goodwill that she was on a par with Mother Teresa or something. He smiled back at her, clearly taken in.

'Let me show you to your table,' he said, then offered my mother his arm – which she accepted with a smile – and began escorting her across the restaurant.

I looked at my father for his reaction to this turn of events. He raised his eyebrows at me, in a look which said he wasn't in the least bit surprised, and then offered me his arm in an exaggerated take on the young man's gesture.

'Shall we?'

'We shall.' I smiled and took his arm, letting him lead me across the restaurant after Mother and her new toy, thinking that perhaps this evening wouldn't be quite so bad after all.

Of course, I could always be wrong.

We reached the table. A small table; clearly designed for two. And guess how many chairs were at that table? That's right – just two. The young man took our coats and, while Mum and Dad sat down opposite each other at the table, he smiled patronisingly at me.

'I'll just find you a spare chair.' With that, he departed, and I was left standing there like an idiot, wondering how many people had noticed I was playing third wheel on my parents' date. I needn't have wondered.

'Who needed the extra chair?' I heard a few minutes later – a question shouted so loudly that it may as well have been broadcast over the restaurant's PA system. My mother looked up.

Oh God. I knew what was coming next.

'Over here, please!' she called out, pointing to me as the recipient of said extra chair. Meanwhile, everyone turned to look at the sad specimen of a human being so pathetic that she was spending Valentine's night with her parents.

'I'm just nipping to the loo,' I mumbled, then, with head down and not daring to look anyone in the eye for fear of total and utter embarrassment, I made my way as quickly as possible towards the sanctuary of the ladies' bathroom.

I stepped inside silently and stopped in front of a mirror, reaching into my bag and hoping I had remembered to bring along a paper bag, a Halloween mask, or some other way of hiding my face from the world. I found nothing but a different shade of lipstick. But I figured it couldn't hurt. Maybe people wouldn't recognise me wearing Pink Sorbet rather than Rose Petal?

Then, just as I was about to put my plan of disguise into action, I heard a noise coming from one of the cubicles behind me. A noise that didn't seem quite right somehow. And as I studied the only taken cubicle in the mirror, I suddenly saw something shoot out from under the door.

I turned around to see a shoe lying on the floor. A very pretty black stiletto with an eye-catching red flower attached to the front. I moved closer to examine the shoe, and something else caught my eye. What looked like a little black dress, discarded on the cubicle floor.

Suddenly there was a loud crash, as something hit the cubicle door from the inside, making it shake. I jumped. Then I heard that noise again; louder this time. The cubicle door shook once more and I heard…

Groaning. Loud, excited groaning.

And I realised.

Hastily putting my lipstick back into my bag, I hurried out of the bathroom – the sound of two people in the throes of passion still ringing in my ears. I quickly made my way back to the table where my parents were waiting, and sat down on the extra chair, trying to look as composed as possible. Mum looked at me curiously.

'Are you alright, dear? You look a little flushed.'

'I'm fine,' I said, not looking her in the eye. 'Shall we order?'

❄ ❄ ❄

Half-an-hour later, and my parents were enthusiastically tucking into their meals. Meanwhile, I was approaching mine with slightly less enthusiasm, having strangely lost my appetite. Mother noticed.

'Gracie, don't play with your food, darling,' she said disapprovingly (between mouthfuls of food, of course – my mother has always been big on table manners). 'You're not a child, for goodness sake.'

'Sorry,' I said, not meaning it. Then I cast another glance behind me, towards the ladies' bathroom – once again annoyed that having my back to the scene of the crime had prevented me from seeing who'd perpetrated it.

As I turned back, I saw a man in a chef's uniform moving down our row of tables, stopping at each one for just a moment. He reached our table a few minutes later, where he stopped once more and smiled at my parents.

'Is everything okay with your meals?' he asked, obviously not expecting them to say anything but 'yes'.

'Lovely, thanks,' my father got in, before Mum could finish her mouthful of food and strike up a conversation with the newcomer.

The chef smiled and went to move away, but was stopped by a young waiter, who was holding a plate of food.

'The customer has asked for some gravy on this,' the waiter told the chef. 'Shall I just go ahead and do it?'

The chef looked at the contents of the plate, confused.

'It's fillet steak,' the chef commented. 'Why would he want gravy with fillet steak?'

'He said that's the way he likes it,' the waiter shrugged.

'Philistine!' the chef muttered, shaking his head. 'Well, go ahead and do it then,' he finally added for the waiter's benefit, and they both moved away.

Once they were gone, Mum looked at me.

'Gracie, isn't that strange?' she said. 'There's somebody else out there who likes gravy with fillet steak. That's David's favourite as well, isn't it?'

'Yes, it is,' I murmured, as I watched the waiter emerging from the kitchen with the fillet steak dish (now including gravy), and followed him with my eyes in order to ascertain his destination.

He carried the plate towards the very far corner of the restaurant, eventually disappearing from my sight behind a large decorative pillar.

My attention aroused, I stood up and made my way past the rows of tables until I could clearly see the couple sitting at the table behind the pillar. A couple that looked very familiar indeed.

'Gracie?' Mum called, but I didn't answer. I just carried on walking across the restaurant, towards the table behind the pillar.

The man was in his late twenties, the woman somewhat younger. The woman had hair so blonde it was almost white. It spilled in waves over her shoulders and down her back. Her eyes were green and held a cat-like cunning; her fingernails sparkled with icy polish. The man had neatly-trimmed, sandy-blond hair and the most beautiful blue eyes you will ever see. His hands were large but gentle; his lips soft and extremely kissable.

I couldn't see all this from where I was standing, of course.

But then, I didn't need to. I had seen it all before. I knew this couple – one of them very well indeed.

'Hello, David,' I said loudly, coming to a stop in front of the table.

The man at the table, David McAllister – my fiancé – looked up. And saw me.

'Gracie!' he spluttered in complete shock. 'What – what are you doing here?'

'I could ask you the same question,' I replied frostily.

He looked at the woman sitting across the table from him, and then looked back at me guiltily. 'I – we were just –'

'We were just having dinner, Gracie,' David's companion chipped in. I turned to look at her as she gave me a sickly-sweet smile. 'Purely innocent, of course.'

'Nothing you do is ever innocent, Lorna,' I replied, before turning back to David. 'I can't believe this!' I exclaimed. 'You told me you had to work late. And here you are – out with her, of all people.'

And I really couldn't believe it. David knew just how much I hated Lorna Spence, his dinner companion. And I usually don't hate anyone.

Lorna was a colleague of David's. Her father owned the law firm where they both worked, where, being the boss' daughter, Lorna knew she could get away with murder – something she frequently took full advantage of.

Just over a year ago I'd walked into David's office and, standing just out of sight, had witnessed Lorna trying to seduce my fiancé. To my great relief, David had rejected her advances, declaring his love for me. But he'd later admitted to me that it wasn't the first time Lorna had done such a thing.

I'd ended up confronting Lorna about the whole situation, but had eventually kept the peace for the sake of David's career. However, I still hadn't forgiven Lorna, who hadn't once apologised and didn't seem at all sorry for what she'd done.

David knew just how much I hated Lorna Spence. And yet here he was – having dinner with my worst enemy.

'Honestly, Gracie. Don't tell me you're still mad about that little disagreement we had,' Lorna simpered. 'That was positively ages ago.'

'Actually, yes, I am –' I began, and then abruptly stopped, my mouth unable to form words while my brain was occupied elsewhere.

'Gracie?' David asked.

'Oh God.'

I couldn't think. I could only stare down at Lorna's feet. At what she was wearing on them. Pretty black stilettos with eye-catching red flowers attached to the front. My mind raced. All I could see were those shoes. All I could hear were those sounds. The sounds of my fiancé making love to Lorna Spence.

Suddenly, my mind cleared. I looked up at David angrily. 'You had sex with her!'

I shouted it. I didn't care who heard.

'Gracie, I –' David fumbled.

'You had sex with her in the ladies' bathroom!' I shouted at him angrily. I wanted to shake him. Shake him until he begged me to stop.

'It was her idea…' David stammered.

'Her idea?!' I exploded. 'How old are you? Five?'

Suddenly, the young man from the front of the restaurant appeared beside me. 'Excuse me, Miss, but could you please take this outside?' he asked politely.

'Yes, Gracie, let's go outside,' David said pleadingly, standing up and attempting to take my arm. I snatched it away from him.

'No, David. Let's not go outside!' I shouted. 'Let's stay here and let everyone know what a complete bastard you've been!'

'Miss –' the rather worried-looking restaurant employee began.

'What?!' I whirled on him, annoyed.

Scared out of his wits, he stumbled backwards – practically hiding behind my parents, who'd come over to see what all the commotion was about.

'Gracie, you're causing a scene,' Mum scolded me. 'Please, let's go outside and sort this out.'

I looked around. She was right. I *was* causing a scene. Every single person in that restaurant had stopped what they were doing and focused their attention on me. The whole room was deathly silent as they stared, waiting to see what I would do next. I turned back to David.

'Gracie –' he began quietly.

'I can't believe you would do this to me!' I said, this time to David only, with tears welling in my eyes.

And with that, I made my way hurriedly out of the restaurant, feeling the eyes of the other diners burning into me as I passed.

❄ ❄ ❄

David didn't bother following me out of the restaurant that night. The next time I saw him was later that evening, when I was back at the flat, packing up my things to leave.

'Gracie?' David asked, entering the flat. 'Are you here?'

I was in the bedroom, grabbing my clothes from the wardrobe and stuffing them into a suitcase.

'Not for much longer,' I called out to him, as I tossed a pair of trainers into the case. This was definitely not my best packing ever, but I didn't care. All I wanted was to get out of there as quickly as possible.

Finally all of those late nights I'd spent alone in this very bedroom, while David was supposedly hard at work at the office, made complete sense to me.

I had believed David's lies because I knew how dedicated he was to his work. In fact, it was because of David's job that the two of us had met.

My father had been the one to introduce us (no doubt he regretted that now). Dad was an accountant and, nearly four years ago, a former client had taken him to court for providing 'unsound' financial advice. David had represented my father – doing a very good job of it too (as he'd pointed out, it was a ridiculous case and shouldn't even have made it in front of a judge). My mother, meanwhile, had immediately taken to David, inviting him over to dinner and to family get-togethers, and our relationship had developed from there.

Mother had always wanted me to marry a doctor or a lawyer. Guess I should've gone for the doctor.

'Gracie, I am so sorry,' David said, as he cautiously entered the bedroom.

'You didn't sound sorry in the ladies' bathroom,' I told him, still packing furiously. 'In fact, you sounded like you were having a great time!'

My words shocked David into silence and for that I was glad. I was finding it hard enough to keep my composure as it was, without having to listen to him protesting his innocence. At that moment, I was torn between bursting into tears and pummelling my fist repeatedly against the bedroom wall. Or against David's head – because if that just happened to get in the way, then so be it.

'Tell me,' I instructed David, 'when you proposed to me – did that mean nothing to you?'

'Of course it meant something!' David replied. 'I loved you, I –'

'Oh, you *loved* me,' I repeated. 'So you don't anymore?'

'Gracie, please – just listen to me for a minute,' David requested.

I stopped what I was doing and looked at him, wondering if he was about to beg my forgiveness and ask me to stay. I should've known better.

'You weren't supposed to find out like this,' he told me.

'I wasn't supposed to find out at all,' I replied.

'I was going to tell you about Lorna and me,' David insisted. 'It was just never the right time.'

'How long has it been going on?' I asked him, before quickly changing my mind. 'No, wait – I don't want to know.'

'I've been seeing Lorna for the past four months,' David told me.

I glared at him.

'What part of "I don't want to know" did you not understand?' I asked him.

On the inside though, I was screaming. Four months?? He'd been sleeping with Lorna for four months and I hadn't realised? I wanted to throw up, but decided not to give David the satisfaction of seeing me do so.

'Was the sex that good?' I finally asked him. 'Was it really worth throwing away a loving three-year relationship for?'

'You don't understand,' David told me sadly. 'It wasn't just about sex. I love Lorna.'

'You what?!' I nearly choked.

'I love her,' he repeated. 'And I'm sorry if I've hurt you, Gracie, but I can't help the way I feel.'

My whole world came crashing down around me. And as it fell, I laughed. There was nothing else I could do.

David stared at me like I'd gone completely insane. 'Gracie?' he asked.

I abruptly stopped laughing. Slamming my suitcase shut, I grabbed it from the bed.

'Well, good luck to you both,' I said, before sweeping out of the room.

I made it as far as the front door before I burst into tears.

❄ ❄ ❄

That night, I returned home. But don't believe for one minute I was happy about it. Moving back in with my parents wasn't my favourite option. It was simply my only option.

I'd read a book once, written by a life coach, which said you should never move backwards in your life – only forward. Only there *was* no forward for me anymore.

And so I had no choice but to go back. Back to where I'd grown up – to where I'd always felt safe. Back to my trusty old bedroom. The bedroom that contained my cuddly toys, posters of my one-time crushes, all of my childhood things. Except, as I soon found out to my horror, that bedroom no longer existed.

'Mum!' I yelled. 'What's happened to my room?!'

My mother appeared behind me, looked inside what used to be my beautiful bedroom, but what now more closely resembled a rubbish tip, shrugged and said: 'Warren moved in here about a month ago.'

She looked at me for my reaction, and then added: 'If you came to see us a bit more often you would've known that.'

I just stared into the room in astonishment.

'Somebody actually sleeps in here?'

Though I'm not quite sure why I was surprised. Warren had always been a slob.

'You can have Warren's old room,' Mum said, moving down the hallway towards the smallest bedroom in the house. 'All your old things are in there already.'

I reluctantly followed her down the hallway and watched as she opened the bedroom door. She was right – inside were all of my old things. And barely enough room to move. Sighing, I picked up my bags and entered the room.

'Thanks Mum.'

It was to be the beginning of a brand new nightmare for me.

Chapter Two

'My mother is driving me insane!' I said, as I hung up the phone. 'If she calls me one more time to remind me about tonight, I swear I'm going to kill her.'

Sitting at the desk opposite mine, Cleo Armstrong – my very best friend in the whole world – grinned at me in reply.

'Well, I won't stop you,' she said. 'In fact, I'll lend you the rat poison.'

And she wasn't lying. Saying that Cleo and my mother didn't get along was an understatement. Mum thought Cleo was a bad influence. Cleo thought my mother was an overbearing witch and, during one particularly heated argument about the best way to help me get over David, had told her just that. Cleo was still banned from our house.

'Sometimes you disturb me,' I told her, meaning every word.

Was my mother right? Was Cleo a bad influence? Probably – but she was also the most loyal person I had ever met.

The past three months had been anything but pretty. Getting over David was the hardest thing I'd ever had to do. But Cleo had pulled me through, dragging me kicking and screaming when necessary, and I had made it out the other side. Without her, I'm not sure what I would have done.

'I'm glad I disturb you,' Cleo replied breezily. If there was one thing Cleo really enjoyed, it was shocking people.

Which probably explained why Cleo currently had her foot perched on her desk and was painting her toenails, despite the fact that she was sitting right in the middle of the office in which we both worked.

'Should you be doing that?' I asked her.

'What? You don't like the colour?' she enquired, missing my point entirely.

I shrugged, resigned to the fact that Cleo would do whatever she liked, whether it was a good idea or not.

'No, it's nice,' I had to admit, 'matches your hair.'

Which, given that the nail polish was a metallic blue colour, was more than a little strange.

In the time I had known Cleo – which was coming up for three years now – she had changed her hair colour no less than five times. Her latest experiment was a jet-black rinse, streaked with royal blue highlights that were only one shade darker than her eyes. It looked fantastic on Cleo. On anyone else – including me – it would have looked disastrous.

'So what's happening tonight?' Cleo asked me.

'Warren's bringing his girlfriend home to dinner,' I explained. 'And of course Mum's making a huge deal out of it.'

Putting the finishing touches to the last of her toenails, Cleo screwed the top back onto her bottle of polish and gave me her full attention.

'Warren has a girlfriend?' she asked, clearly confused.

I nodded in reply. 'Some girl from college,' I told her. 'I think her name's Amy.'

'So what is she?' Cleo grinned. 'Blind, deaf or dumb?'

'Probably all three if she's dating Warren,' I replied.

'You haven't met her?'

'None of us have – I was beginning to think she didn't exist.'

'Well I guess tonight you'll find out,' Cleo teased. 'Aren't you the lucky one?'

'Yeah,' I replied, rolling my eyes, 'lucky me.'

In case you were wondering, Cleo and I *were* at work. Granted, we weren't doing much work, but we were there all the same – putting in the hours.

The recruitment agency with which Cleo and I were employed wasn't a favourite place to be for either of us. In fact, the only thing I really had to thank the agency for was introducing me to Cleo. Apart from that, my job was an ocean of tediousness – one that was slowly drowning me. It was strange how I'd never noticed this while I was with David. I guess that's what being happy does for you.

Since the collapse of my relationship though, my job had lost all meaning for me – and my output into the general running of the office had seriously dwindled. Cleo, meanwhile, hadn't really made any effort in the workplace for some time. But then as someone having secret romantic (well, okay – sexual) liaisons with the man ultimately in charge of the whole agency, she really didn't have to.

And so, bored with our lives and our jobs, Cleo and I sat and gossiped.

'I had a dream about David last night,' I confided in her.

'Gracie!' Cleo cried. 'It's been three months! I thought you were finally over him!'

'I am!' I protested. 'I can't control what I dream about!'

Cleo studied me, suspicion clear in her eyes.

'I know what you mean,' she finally conceded. 'Like last night I dreamt that Jason and I were skinny-dipping in a lake of chocolate.'

'Okay,' I frowned, 'that sounds like some perverse sexual fantasy that I don't need to hear about.'

'Yeah, but then Jason disappeared,' Cleo continued, 'and I started eating all the chocolate.'

Cleo had a serious chocolate addiction – one she was currently counteracting with lollipops. Oh, and lots of sex.

I watched as Cleo opened her desk drawer and pulled out a strawberry lollipop, which she unwrapped and popped in her mouth.

'You need help,' I told her.

'I need Jason,' she confessed, mumbling the words out over the lollipop. 'Just about the only time I don't think about chocolate is when we're having sex – and even then it's touch and go.'

'Again,' I said, cringing at her analogy, 'too much information.'

'Sorry,' Cleo apologised. 'So what was your dream about?

And if you mention David and sex in the same sentence I will beat you over the head with my in-tray.'

I shook my head. 'It wasn't *that* sort of dream,' I told her. 'It was weird.'

'Weird is good,' Cleo said. 'Go ahead – tell me everything. I'll analyse it for you.'

'I didn't exactly write it down,' I told her. 'All I remember is that I had David tied to a chair –'

'Kinky!' Cleo interrupted, grinning at me over her lollipop.

'It wasn't like that,' I protested, shooting her a dirty look. 'He was strapped down to a chair and I was cutting his hair. And if I remember it right, I wasn't doing such a great job of it either – I was just grabbing huge chunks of his hair and hacking it off.'

'It's symbolic,' Cleo told me, nodding wisely, 'a metaphor.'

'So what does it mean?' I asked her.

'It means you want to castrate him,' she shrugged. 'And who can blame you? It's more than he deserves, after all.'

'You know,' I said, not sure that Cleo's explanation was entirely accurate, 'I don't think that's what it means.'

'Why don't you ask your mother at dinner tonight?' Cleo suggested, a wicked glint in her eye. 'I'm sure she'll agree with my theory.'

'I think she'd rather serve dinner naked than agree with *your* theory,' I told Cleo.

'Now wouldn't *that* make dinner interesting?' Cleo grinned.

'Yes, it would,' I agreed, already dreading the evening ahead. 'It's just a shame that nothing else is going to.'

Which just goes to show you how wrong I could be.

❄ ❄ ❄

'Well don't you look handsome?' Mum said, as Warren came downstairs. 'Like a mini version of your father!'

Warren scowled in response.

'Thanks a lot.'

'Hey, if anyone should be insulted by that, it's me!' my father said jokingly, as he joined the rest of us in the hallway.

Looking between my father and brother I realised that, for once, Mum was right. Warren and Dad did look quite alike.

Like me, Warren had inherited Dad's dark hair and brown eyes – and his height (for which I was very grateful). But while my father's now slightly-greying hair was cut short and tidy, Warren's was nothing more than an unruly mop that, to his great displeasure, had always had a tendency to form into ringlets.

'Why are you so cheery tonight?' I asked my father, suspicious. He had even dressed up for the occasion, which was quite unlike him. Meaning he had probably done so at my mother's insistence.

'Are you kidding?' Dad asked. 'My son is bringing home his very first girlfriend – I couldn't be prouder!'

Dad patted Warren on the shoulder enthusiastically, before disappearing into the kitchen – no doubt to see if there was any food on offer prior to tonight's dinner. Dad had never been a big fan of waiting for food.

Meanwhile, Warren and I exchanged a look. We both

knew Amy wasn't his first girlfriend. In fact, Warren had been a little heartbreaker from the age of about fourteen or so. Amy just happened to be the first girl he'd ever brought home.

However, there was no reason for my father to know this, and so I kept quiet. Besides, it was always something I could blackmail Warren with later.

'Look at these lovely curls,' Mum said, fingering Warren's hair. 'Just like when you were a baby.'

'Mum!' Warren complained. He batted her hand away.

'Don't worry,' I told Warren, smiling at his misfortune, 'she'll save the most embarrassing comments for when Amy gets here.'

Mum scowled at me in response, but didn't reply as, at that moment, the doorbell rang.

'I'll get it!' she cried, before hurrying to the front door.

'Don't you want to answer the door?' I asked Warren.

'I don't care,' Warren shrugged.

Mum swung the front door open. Standing on the doorstep was a girl of about seventeen. She had long, wavy, auburn hair and was wearing a dress that matched her green eyes. She smiled warmly at my mother – big mistake.

'You must be Amy!' Mum immediately cooed, putting her arm around the girl and ushering her into the house. 'It's so nice to finally meet you!'

I felt sorry for Amy already. She looked shell-shocked – like a deer caught in the headlights of a speeding car. And I can't say I blamed her. My mother could be pretty scary sometimes.

'It's nice to meet you too,' Amy replied.

Mum immediately began fussing over the girl.

'Let me take your coat,' she insisted, smiling encouragingly.

As Amy obediently took off her jacket, Mum took a step towards the kitchen. 'Richard!' she called. 'Amy's here!' There was no answer from the kitchen.

Mum smiled at Amy before trying again, louder this time. 'Richard!'

My father suddenly emerged from the kitchen, discreetly chewing on something. Mother noticed.

'Richard, I hope you're not eating?' Mum asked him, her voice bearing a teasing tone that she used only when we had company. 'You wouldn't want to spoil your dinner now, would you?'

'Oh no,' my father said, smiling back, 'I wouldn't want that.'

Catching my eye, he winked at me and I couldn't help but smile.

Meanwhile, Mum took Amy's jacket from her and began making her way upstairs.

'Make yourself at home,' Mum instructed Amy. 'I'll just go hang this up and then I'll be right back.'

Once Mum had disappeared upstairs, Dad nipped back into the kitchen, leaving me alone with Warren and Amy.

'Thanks for coming,' Warren told Amy.

'No problem,' Amy smiled, though she was beginning to look like she regretted the decision.

Amy looked at me questioningly, so I decided to introduce myself. It was clear, after all, that Warren wasn't going to do the honours.

'Hi, I'm Gracie,' I smiled at her. 'I'm Warren's big sister.'

'Hi,' Amy smiled back. 'Warren didn't tell me he had a sister.'

I glared at Warren, who just shrugged in response. Why wasn't I surprised?

'So how long have you two been going out?' I asked Amy.

'Six weeks,' Amy replied – at exactly the same time as Warren said:

'Three months.'

I looked from Amy to Warren. 'So which is it?' I asked, more interested in their difference of opinion than in the answer to the question.

'We've been going out for six weeks,' Warren said, 'but we've known each other for three months.'

'That's right,' Amy agreed, as my mother came back downstairs.

'Now then,' Mum said, looking at each of us in turn. 'Who would like some dinner?'

'Love some,' Warren replied, quickly ushering Amy into the dining room.

I watched them go, more than a little confused. Warren excited about Mum's cooking? That was a definite first.

Why did I get the feeling that something strange was going on here?

❄ ❄ ❄

Dinner had been surprisingly pleasant so far. At least, it

had been for me. For poor Amy, however, it had been something akin to a cross-examination.

My mother had spent the last half-an-hour firing question after question in Amy's direction, eager to learn all about the girl who had 'won her son's heart' (her words, not mine). Amy had answered each of these enquiries as politely and concisely as possible, but I could tell she was beginning to tire of my mother's constant attention.

'What do you plan to do after college?' Mum asked Amy, continuing her career-related line of questioning.

Having just put a forkful of food into her mouth, Amy had to hurriedly chew and swallow before she could answer my mother's question.

'I haven't really decided yet,' Amy eventually replied. 'Maybe something to do with graphic design though.'

'Lovely,' Mum said. 'Is that what you're studying at college?'

'Yes,' Amy confirmed, nodding.

The poor thing was trying to eat her dinner and failing miserably. Every time she attempted to take a bite of food, Mum threw a new question at her.

And as if on cue, Mum opened her mouth to speak again. This time, however, my father jumped in first with a question of his own.

'Did you have a good day at work today, Gracie?' Dad asked me, attempting to steer the conversation away from Amy for a while.

'Same as usual,' I sighed, unable to summon up any more enthusiasm than that for my job. 'Same as every day this week.'

'What do you do?' Amy asked me, seemingly eager to discuss someone other than herself.

She looked interested in my answer, though I guessed she was just attempting to be polite and didn't really care what I did for a living. After all, I knew politeness was the only reason for which I ever asked that question.

'Gracie's a recruitment consultant,' Mum replied, before I could even open my mouth.

God, I hated it when she did that. It wasn't like I couldn't speak for myself.

'No, Mum,' I corrected her. 'If I was a recruitment consultant, I'd be earning a lot more money than I do right now.'

I turned to smile at Amy. 'I work for a recruitment agency,' I told her. 'I'm in charge of the agency's website, where all the current job vacancies are advertised. Which basically means that I get to input all of the jobs onto our database and then upload them to the site.'

'Sounds interesting,' Amy offered. This time she was definitely only being polite.

'Not really,' I told her. 'In fact, I think I might have to start keeping a closer eye on the vacancies coming in – just in case anything exciting turns up.'

'For one of your clients you mean?' Mum asked.

'No,' I replied, deciding it was easier not to remind my mother that I didn't actually have any clients, 'for me.'

As soon as the words tumbled out of my mouth, I realised I'd made a huge mistake.

'For you?' Mum asked. 'Since when are you looking for a job? You already have a job.'

Her voice sounded taut and high-pitched. I could tell she wasn't happy. I had to be really careful of what I said next.

'I know,' I told her, attempting to sound nonchalant. 'I just thought it would be worth looking around. You know, see what else is out there.'

Looking across the table, I caught Warren's eye. He smiled wickedly and made a choking gesture at me, obviously very amused by the turn the conversation had taken. I fought the sudden urge I had to poke my tongue out at him.

'I thought you liked your job?' Mum asked sorrowfully.

She seemed to be taking this awfully personally – as if any negative comments I'd made about my job had also been directed at her. That wasn't a good sign.

'I used to,' I admitted. 'But I've been doing it for nearly three years now and, to be honest, it's starting to bore me.'

'Yes,' Mum said, 'but that doesn't really matter, does it? I mean, do you think your father likes his job?'

'Well, actually –' Dad began, but Mum didn't give him a chance to finish.

'Of course he doesn't!' she said. 'But he does it anyway because he knows he has a family to support.'

'I don't have a family to support,' I reminded her.

'That's not the point,' Mum said. 'Tell her, Richard.'

She looked at my father, silently urging him to speak.

I felt incredibly sorry for my father right then, as I knew just how much he hated getting stuck in the middle of arguments between Mother and me. Or between Mother and anyone, come to think of it.

'I think what your mother's trying to say,' my father said, attempting to be as diplomatic as ever, 'is that she's worried about you.'

'Of course I'm worried about her!' Mum cried. 'I'm worried she's going to throw away a perfectly well-paid and secure job just because she's bored!'

She turned to me, a determined look on her face. 'Well I forbid you to do it, Gracie.'

'Ellen –' Dad started.

'You can't forbid me!' I said, almost laughing. 'I'm twenty-four years old!'

'But you're still my daughter,' Mum said.

'I'm an adult,' I said firmly, 'and I'll do as I like.'

I sounded a lot surer than I felt. In truth, before tonight I hadn't really given much thought to looking for another job. But the fact that my mother didn't want me to do so made me all the more determined to take the idea forward.

'You were never this insolent when you were with David,' Mum said, pouting.

'Yes, well David and I are no longer together,' I reminded her. 'Accept it.'

Mum actually looked upset at this. I wasn't surprised by her reaction – I often got the impression that she'd like to see David and I get back together, despite all that he'd done.

She said nothing further on the subject though and, as I had nothing left to say to her, an uncomfortable silence quickly descended over the dinner table.

Suddenly remembering the fact that we had company, I glanced guiltily across the table to where Amy was sitting.

Amy was looking down at her plate, picking at the remainder of her meal with her fork – clearly trying to remain invisible to avoid getting dragged into the family argument.

Sitting next to her, however, Warren continued eating his dinner as if nothing had happened. I guess it wasn't anything he hadn't seen before, but I thought it a little strange he didn't seem more embarrassed that his new girlfriend had witnessed such an outburst.

Not knowing what to do next, I glanced at my father, sending out a silent plea for help. He didn't look at me, but seemed to hear my cry all the same, as he suddenly coughed, breaking the silence.

'Right then,' Dad said. He looked around the table at each of us in turn, grinning cheerfully. 'Anyone for dessert?'

Trust my father to try and solve a problem with food.

❄ ❄ ❄

Having refused dessert due to the fact that she was 'counting calories', Amy had hurriedly made her excuses to leave. Now, standing in the hallway and saying her goodbyes, she looked like she couldn't get out of the front door quick enough.

I guess I couldn't blame her.

'It was lovely to meet you, Amy,' my father said politely.

'Thanks,' Amy replied, but she barely had time to say even that before my mother scooped her up in a hug.

'Thank you so much for coming,' Mum told her. 'You'll come back and see us again soon, I hope?'

'Of course,' Amy smiled – rather unconvincingly it has to be said – as my mother released her from the hug.

I had a strange feeling that Amy wouldn't be coming back here in a hurry.

'I'll see you to your car,' Warren told Amy.

Trust Warren to find himself a girlfriend with her very own car. Warren didn't have a car of his own and, much to his annoyance, Mum and Dad refused to buy him one on the grounds that he wasn't yet responsible enough to own a vehicle. But I guess now he could get a ride whenever he wanted one.

Warren opened the front door and ushered Amy outside, shutting the door firmly behind him.

Which was when my mother suddenly exclaimed: 'Oh dear, Amy forgot her coat! It's hanging up in the bedroom.' She looked at me, smiling sweetly. 'Gracie, be a dear and go fetch it for her.'

Fetch? What was I – her dog? Still, I knew better than to argue with my mother.

'Fine,' I grumbled and, as my parents disappeared into the kitchen, I made my way upstairs and grabbed Amy's coat from my parents' bedroom.

Taking the coat with me, I hurried downstairs and out the front door after my brother and his girlfriend. Outside, Warren and Amy were standing by Amy's car, talking. I approached them, glad that was all I had caught them doing – which was when I saw Warren hand Amy some money.

'Not interrupting anything, I hope?' I asked, as I stepped up to meet them.

Warren jumped and turned around to glare at me, while

Amy quickly shielded the money from my view. Too late – I had already seen it.

'What are you doing out here?' Warren asked me.

I ignored him and turned to Amy instead.

'You forgot your coat,' I told her, holding the garment out to her. Amy took it from me, all the time avoiding my gaze.

'Thanks,' she said, and then quickly turned to Warren. 'I'd better go,' she told him, opening her car door and climbing inside.

'Okay,' Warren replied. 'See you tomorrow.'

As Amy started her car, Warren made his way back towards the house. Guess he wasn't going to wave her goodbye. I followed after him, stepping into his path and blocking his way as he reached the front door.

'What's going on?' I asked him.

'Get out of my way,' Warren scowled.

'Not until you tell me what's going on,' I smiled at him.

God, I loved to annoy my brother. You would've thought I'd have grown out of it by now – but no, even after all these years it was still fun.

'There's nothing going on,' Warren insisted.

'Then why were you giving Amy money?' I asked him.

'I didn't give her any money,' Warren lied.

'I saw you,' I told him. 'And it's not just the money either. Dinner was a complete disaster and yet you don't seem in the least bit embarrassed. That makes no sense! Shouldn't you be worried that our dysfunctional family has managed to scare Amy away?'

Warren thought for a moment, as if deciding what to

say. I could practically hear his little brain whirring as he mulled over all the possible lies he could tell.

'And I want the truth,' I told him, 'not one of your usual fairy stories.' There was no way he was going to wriggle his way out of this one.

'Okay, fine,' Warren eventually agreed, 'but you have to promise not to tell Mum and Dad.'

'Tell Mum and Dad about what?' I asked him, my curiosity building.

Warren took a deep breath, as if he were about to spill his deepest, darkest secrets.

'I paid Amy to come to dinner tonight,' he admitted.

I stared at him, completely surprised by his admission.

'Why would you do that?'

'Well would *you* come here for free?' Warren asked me.

He had a point – even if it made no sense whatsoever.

'Amy's your girlfriend,' I reminded him. 'It's kind of her duty.'

'Amy's not my girlfriend,' Warren revealed. 'She's just a friend from college. We were pretending – that's all.'

'Let me get this straight,' I said, getting more confused by the minute. 'You paid Amy to pretend to be your girlfriend?'

'Yeah,' Warren nodded.

'That's pretty desperate, Warren,' I frowned, not quite sure if he was telling the truth or not, 'even for you.'

'I needed a girlfriend Mum would approve of,' Warren explained, 'and this was the easiest way to get one.'

'Why did you need a girlfriend?' I asked him, even more confused now.

'Because Mum was planning on setting me up with Rebecca Stewart,' Warren grimaced. 'I heard her talking to Abigail about it on the phone last week.'

'Oh,' I said. Well now I understood his reasons completely.

Abigail Stewart was a friend of my mother's (or at least Mother claimed they were friends – though she actually didn't seem to like Abigail all that much and frequently talked about the woman behind her back) and Rebecca was her completely insufferable sixteen-year-old daughter.

Like her mother, Rebecca had a superiority complex of the highest order. She thought she was better than everyone else and wasn't afraid to say so. She was rude, demanding and spoilt (Rebecca gave new meaning to the words 'high maintenance'). Not exactly great girlfriend material – especially for someone as laid-back as Warren.

'So you figured that if Mum liked Amy she'd forget about Rebecca?' I asked my brother.

'Exactly,' Warren replied.

'And just how long are you planning on keeping up this little charade?' I enquired, interested despite myself.

'As long as possible,' Warren grinned. 'Don't you see? It's a foolproof plan – Amy is the perfect excuse.'

'The perfect excuse for what?'

'Everything,' Warren laughed. 'Dinner parties, family meetings, weddings, funerals – if there's anything I want to get out of, I'll just say I have plans with my girlfriend.'

My mouth practically dropped open in shock at the extent of my brother's deception.

'You'll never get away with it,' I told him. 'Mum will just tell you to bring Amy along with you.'

Warren waved away my concerns.

'It'll work,' he said, grinning cockily now. 'I'm sure of it.'

'Whatever you say,' I sighed, shaking my head.

And with that, I made my way back into the house – doing my very best to pretend I wasn't in the least bit interested in Warren's plan.

Though the truth was, I was cursing myself for not having come up with the idea first.

❄ ❄ ❄

'So she wasn't an escort girl then?' Cleo asked, sounding almost disappointed.

Cleo and I were at work and, as was the norm for us, weren't really getting much in the way of actual work done. In fact, I had just spent the last ten minutes telling Cleo all about my brother's strange behaviour at dinner the night before – including the story of his fake girlfriend.

I figured I wasn't breaking any secret pact. After all, Warren had asked me not to tell Mum and Dad. He hadn't said anything about Cleo.

'You know, that never even occurred to me,' I replied. 'But then I don't think even Warren's that desperate.'

'Don't be so sure,' Cleo said. 'Did Warren happen to say how much she charged him for that little visit?'

'He said he gave her £30.'

'In that case, you're right – definitely not an escort girl. She came too cheap.'

'And how would *you* know?' I asked Cleo.

Cleo just smiled at me wickedly – which got me wondering. Although I'd meant the question as a joke, there were a lot of things about Cleo's past I didn't know. Most probably, there were a lot of things about Cleo's past I didn't *want* to know.

Catching me watching her, Cleo burst out laughing.

'Oh come on, Gracie!' Cleo exclaimed. 'Would I really be working here if I knew I could make a living out of escorting rich guys to fancy parties?'

'I didn't say anything!' I protested. Cleo, however, knew me better than that.

'But you were thinking it,' she said. I must have looked guilty, because she smiled at me and added: 'Don't worry – I'm flattered you think I could earn money that way.'

And the funny thing was, although Cleo had all but denied it, I still wasn't sure. Cleo wasn't a liar, but she did like to tease – and she always took great pleasure in subverting people's expectations. She was my best friend, but in many ways was still a mystery to me – and probably to everyone who knew her. No wonder my mother disliked her so much.

'Incoming,' Cleo suddenly said, breaking into my thoughts.

Cleo turned to face her computer, tapping away at the keyboard and staring at the screen as if engrossed by its contents. Without turning around, I did the same, continuing work on adding a new job vacancy to our database – the very same vacancy that had been up on my screen for the past hour or so.

Cleo's sudden change in behaviour, I knew, could mean

only one thing – that a manager was heading down the office towards us.

The agency I worked for was a large one and, consequently, we had a number of managers in our office – probably more managers than we had regular staff, actually. But despite that, I knew exactly who was making their way towards my desk, as I sat pretending to be doing some actual work.

And so I wasn't at all surprised when Penelope Davenport (or Penny, as she likes to be known) stopped by my side and quietly coughed to get my attention. I looked up at her, meeting her serious hazel eyes as they peered at me from behind gold-rimmed glasses.

'I hope I'm not interrupting your work,' Penny said, a look of concern on her face.

'Not at all,' I smiled back politely – a smile I had perfected through closely watching my mother.

Penny looked relieved. Sometimes I wondered whether Penny really was that stupid, or if it was all an act and she did actually realise what Cleo and I got up to when she wasn't around. Which was, in all honesty, pretty much nothing at all.

'I was wondering if we could have a little chat,' Penny said, smiling.

'Sure,' I smiled back, 'that would be fine.'

But it wasn't fine. It was far from fine. It was yet another of Penny's famous heart-to-heart sessions. I had lost count of the number of times she'd called me away from my desk for 'a little chat' since my split with David. You see, Penny's one of those managers who take the 'I may be your manager, but I'm also your friend' approach to dealing with staff. And she really thought it worked. Poor, deluded cow.

I looked at Cleo as I stood up and caught her mouthing the words 'good luck' at me. Penny, as ever, didn't notice.

I smiled back grimly at Cleo, before following Penny to her office. Once we were inside, Penny quietly shut the door.

'Sit down,' Penny said.

I rolled my eyes, making sure Penny didn't see me do so. Between the instructions issued recently by Penny and my mother, I was getting a little tired of being treated like a trained dog.

However, I did as I was told. The one good thing about Penny's office was that she had some really comfy chairs in there. I had grown accustomed to them lately.

I watched as Penny sat down in the chair opposite mine. But instead of leaning back in her chair and relaxing, as I did, Penny sat forward, leaning towards me, her hands clasped together and resting on her knees. This was Penny's 'tell me what's wrong' pose.

'Gracie,' Penny began, 'is there anything you'd like to talk to me about?'

Aha! A slightly new tactic.

'No,' I said, 'not really.'

Penny looked at me, as if she wasn't expecting this response. I'm not sure why – it was the same response I'd given her at each and every one of our talks.

'You know if there's something wrong you can talk to me about it, don't you?' Penny asked, smiling sympathetically.

'Yes,' I said.

Penny waited, as if hoping I would elaborate. I didn't.

'Gracie, I know what happened between you and David was terrible –' Penny began.

'I'm over it,' I said, interrupting her.

'Are you sure?' Penny asked in a soothing voice, as if talking to me like I was six months old would encourage me to spill my deepest, darkest secrets. 'These kinds of things often take a while to get over. And they can have further reaching effects as well – something you might not notice at first.'

'Are you trying to say I've been damaged psychologically as a result of my split with David?' I asked, trying to hide my amusement.

This got to Penny. I knew it would. She thought she had offended me, and that was a big faux pas in our office.

'No, no,' Penny said quickly, 'nothing like that. I just meant that since the split with David you haven't quite been yourself.'

'In what way?'

'Well, you always used to be so enthusiastic about your work, Gracie,' Penny said, 'but lately you don't seem to be showing any interest at all. Something obviously caused this change, and the only thing I can think of is what happened with David.'

I had to hand it to her – she was right. However, that didn't mean I had to like it. And so I said nothing. By this time, Penny was looking increasingly concerned. 'Gracie, please talk to me,' Penny said. 'If there's something about your employment here that you're unhappy with, I need to know.'

Yes, I thought. I hate you, I hate this job, I hate this office – and I need to get out of here! Of course, that's not what I said.

'I'm fine,' I smiled sweetly. 'I'm not unhappy about anything.'

'Really?' Penny looked almost relieved.

'Really,' I said firmly.

'Well, that's good,' Penny said, smiling, seemingly convinced.

I smiled back. Mission accomplished.

Just a few minutes later, I found myself making my way back to my desk. Cleo looked up as I arrived.

'How did it go?' she asked. 'Still got a job?'

'Unfortunately,' I said, sitting down.

'And Penny still thinks you want to spend the rest of your life in this shit-hole of an office?'

'Some people are so deluded,' I replied.

Deciding that I should probably attempt to appease Penny by doing some work today, I picked up the stack of job vacancies that were sitting on my desk and began flicking through them. They had all been provided by companies who were using our recruitment service exclusively in order to find their staff.

The vacancies were due to be inputted into our database – and from there would be uploaded onto our recruitment website so that some lucky person could apply for them.

I say 'lucky' because most of these jobs looked a whole lot better than the one in which I was currently employed. And my dismay at this revelation must have shown on my face, because Cleo quickly picked up on it.

'Are you okay?' she asked me. 'You look really depressed. What did Penny say to you?'

'It's not Penny,' I said, tossing the job vacancies down onto my desk. 'I just hate having to find people jobs that are better than mine!'

As the pile of papers hit my desktop, one of the sheets came loose and floated to the floor. Sighing, I bent down and picked it up, glancing at it as I did so.

The job vacancy contained on this sheet of paper immediately caught my eye. It read as follows:

Personal Assistant Wanted for
TV/Film Personality.
Must have previous office experience.
To apply, please fax CV and covering letter to Ms
Olivia Hunt on the number below.

It was a small, surprisingly brief advert (the kind I liked, as short adverts could be inputted extremely quickly), but it had certainly caught my attention.

'Perhaps you should apply for one of the vacancies yourself?' Cleo suggested.

She was joking, I knew – but suddenly the idea didn't seem quite so ridiculous to me.

'Maybe I will,' I told her, smiling.

Cleo narrowed her eyes and looked at me suspiciously. 'What have you got there?' she asked me.

I handed the sheet of paper to Cleo. She quickly read its contents before looking back at me.

'You're actually going to apply for this?' Cleo asked.

'Yeah,' I said. 'I think I might.'

Cleo handed the advert back to me. She didn't seem convinced.

'You know, not to sound like your mother here, but do you really think there's any point?' Cleo asked. 'Of course you'd be great at the job, but there'll be hundreds of other applicants. I mean, who doesn't want to work for a TV star? It'll be like entering a lottery just to get an interview.'

'Oh, I don't think there'll be many other applicants,' I said, smiling. 'In fact, I don't think there'll be *any* other applicants.'

'Gracie, once this vacancy appears on the website their fax machine will go mad,' Cleo pointed out.

'Ah,' I said, still smiling, 'but you're assuming the advert is going to make it as far as the website.'

Making sure Cleo was watching, I folded the sheet of paper containing the job advert and placed it in my desk drawer. I looked back at Cleo and smiled mischievously.

'Gracie Parker,' she said, flashing a grin that stretched right across her face. 'I think you've just crossed the line – and I like it.'

'Thanks,' I smiled back, determining there and then to fax my CV to Ms Olivia Hunt and apply for the position.

It was time to take control of my future.

Chapter Three

The house was strangely quiet when I arrived home that evening. Which was unusual, because most of the time the place was a hive of activity.

My mother is one of those people who can't sit still for a minute. She has to feel like she's making the best use of her time and not wasting one precious morsel of it. So as well as working part-time and keeping the house clean and tidy, she volunteers at the local hospital, does gardening for our elderly neighbour, goes to aerobics class (and the gym, of course), and is an active member of the local Women's Institute – which she has recently been trying to get me to join (the fact that this is possibly my worst nightmare apparently having escaped her attention).

But tonight, for some reason, my mother was nowhere in sight.

'Mum?' I called out, hoping against hope that I would get no answer.

I should be so lucky.

'I'm in the kitchen!' Mum called back.

Kicking off my shoes, I wandered into the kitchen – where I found my mother making two cups of tea.

'Thanks Mum,' I smiled at her wearily. 'That's just what I needed.'

I reached for one of the cups, but she swept it away before I could pick it up.

'Sorry, darling – you'll have to get your own.' I watched her, confused, as she picked up the remaining cup. 'This is for my guest.'

'What guest?' I asked, as she headed out of the kitchen. She didn't answer, so I followed her into the living room.

There my question was answered. Sitting on our sofa was a pretty young woman of around the same age as me. She had long, curly, golden-brown hair (which my mother no doubt absolutely adored), blue eyes, and a sweet face adorned with freckles. Her name was Gretchen Wells and, between the ages of four and fifteen, she had been my very best friend in the whole world.

'Hi, Gracie,' Gretchen smiled at me, as she took the cup of tea from my mother. 'I hope you don't mind me popping round?'

'Of course not,' I replied unenthusiastically, sinking into the nearest armchair – directly across the room from where my mother was sharing the sofa with Gretchen.

Gretchen and her family used to live next door to us, so we had pretty much grown up together. We'd been inseparable from the day we'd started nursery to the day that I'd decided to move on to college, while Gretchen had opted to receive her further education at school. I'd made new friends at college; likewise Gretchen had grown closer to others at the school. And after Gretchen's family moved house that very same year, we'd drifted even further apart.

Eight years down the line, we only ever saw each other when our respective families decided to get together (usually as a result of my mother's doing). We had remained sociable, but were nowhere near being close friends again.

That is, until the break-up with David – when I'd suddenly started to see a lot more of Gretchen. Ever the Good Samaritan, Gretchen had done her very best to help me get over the split, but her efforts, always put forward on behalf of my mother it seemed, really weren't what I'd needed.

The only person who'd really understood how I felt was Cleo (having suffered through the cheating exploits of several loser boyfriends in the past), and she had been the one to pull me through with nights out and ice cream. But here Gretchen was, still not giving up on me.

'Gracie, darling, please sit up straight,' Mum said, looking at me in disapproval. Then she turned to Gretchen and smiled affectionately. 'So how are the wedding plans going, Gretchen? No hiccups yet, I hope.'

My mother doted on Gretchen Wells. Ever since we were little, Mum had been comparing us – always wondering why I couldn't be a bit more like Gretchen.

Why couldn't I be the one who came home with a clean dress after going out to play? Why couldn't I be the one who saved my pocket money for a rainy day, rather than wasting it on sweets and magazines? Why couldn't I be the one to find a nice young man who wouldn't cheat on me?

None of this was Gretchen's fault, of course. In fact, I think she was a little embarrassed by it all. But it annoyed me all the same. Plus, Gretchen was getting married this year – something that, three months ago, I still thought I was going to be doing.

'Actually, that's what I came to talk to Gracie about,' Gretchen said, turning her attention towards me. 'I was hoping she would do me a big favour.'

Uh oh. This didn't sound good.

'Well, I'm kind of busy right now,' I mumbled.

'Nonsense!' Mum said immediately. 'You're not at all busy. Your father and I have a better social life than you do at the moment.'

'Thanks Mum,' I grimaced. Trust my mother to make me feel worse than I already did about my sad little life.

Gretchen listened to our exchange before smiling at me uncomfortably.

'Well, Gracie,' she said hopefully, 'I was wondering if you would like to take part in the wedding – as my maid of honour.'

I said nothing, so she added quickly: 'But please don't feel obliged. You don't have to do it if you don't want to.'

'Of course she'll do it!' Mum replied on my behalf. 'What a wonderful thing to ask, Gretchen. How nice of you!' She looked at me. 'You would be honoured to do it, wouldn't you, Gracie?'

Memories from the last time I was bridesmaid at a wedding flooded into my mind. Bad, bad memories. Memories of nearly tripping over the bride's veil as she walked down the aisle. Memories of being paired off with the extremely repulsive best man. Memories of wearing a dress that closely resembled a fluffy pink meringue.

I grimaced. 'Love to,' I finally said, through gritted teeth.

'Good. That's settled then,' Mum said, before I could change my mind. 'Gracie will be the maid of honour.'

I watched as she smiled delightedly at Gretchen. Gretchen smiled back at her sweetly.

I felt like throwing up.

❄ ❄ ❄

'So you're going to be maid of honour?' Cleo asked, a huge smile on her face. 'Well this is something I can't miss. When do I get my invitation?'

'Never,' I replied, shocked, 'the less people that see me at this wedding the better.'

It was Friday night, and I had decided an evening out with Cleo was just what I needed. Just what I needed to keep my sanity, that is.

'So let me get this straight,' Cleo said, absentmindedly stirring her drink with a little cocktail umbrella. 'You agreed to be Gretchen's maid of honour – despite the fact that the whole thing is pretty much your worst nightmare. Why does this sound like your mother's doing to me?'

'She was hell-bent on having me do it,' I said. 'I didn't really have a whole lot of choice in the matter.'

'You could've said no,' Cleo pointed out.

'Right – because *that* would've worked.'

'Gracie, you're twenty-four years old!' Cleo wailed. 'When are you going to start making your own decisions?'

'I do make my own decisions!' I said defensively. 'It's

just that it's sometimes easier not to argue with my mother. You know that.'

'From painful experience,' Cleo agreed. 'Still, you're going to have to learn to stand up to her sooner or later.'

'Make that later,' I replied.

Cleo rolled her eyes and took a sip of her drink.

'You know,' she said, looking as glum as I felt, 'you're not the only one with parental problems. All my mum can talk about lately is Brian. Anyone would think he's some kind of sex god or something.'

'Didn't you tell her he made a pass at you?' I asked her, confused.

'Yep,' Cleo nodded. 'She said he was just trying to be friendly. My mother is so unbelievably deluded.'

Unlike my mum and dad, who would be celebrating their silver wedding anniversary this year, Cleo's parents had split up when she was just five. Cleo no longer saw much of her father – not that this bothered her – but she was constantly having to look out for her mother's best interests. And Brian, Cleo's mother's new boyfriend, was definitely *not* in her best interests.

'What does Trott think about all this?' I asked her.

'You know Trott,' Cleo said. 'She told me to mind my own business. Said Mum's old enough to make her own choices – however bad they might be.'

'Trott's not often wrong,' I pointed out.

'Yeah, but at the moment she's pissed because Mum hasn't been to see her in a while,' Cleo said. 'Not that she'll admit it, of course.'

Trott was Cleo's grandmother, on her mother's side. Her

full name was Rosemary Trotter, but to Cleo she had always been Nanny Trotter, or Trott for short. She was a stubborn, independent and outspoken woman – traits which appeared to have skipped a generation and been passed on to Cleo.

Cleo shared a house with Trott, which allowed her to look after her grandmother, without Trott realising she was being looked after. Trott was also the reason why, after the break-up with David, Cleo and I hadn't been able to move in together. Because as much as Trott often got on Cleo's nerves, Cleo really did love her grandmother.

'And what does she think about your secret liaisons with Jason?' I asked Cleo.

'Are you kidding?!' Cleo spluttered. 'Like I'm really going to tell my grandmother that I have animal sex with my boss in the stationery cupboard at work.'

'Well perhaps not using those exact words,' I agreed, 'but you could tell her about the relationship at least.'

'That *is* the relationship,' Cleo told me. 'Sex in the stationery cupboard. Oh, and once on top of the photocopier.'

'I take it that was after office hours?' I asked, not really expecting an answer. I didn't get one. Cleo downed the rest of her drink in one swift gulp, then looked at me.

'Gracie, do you think I'm really stupid?' she asked sorrowfully.

'Because of the thing with Jason?' I asked her. She nodded. 'Well, what are you getting out of the relationship?'

She thought for a moment.

'Great sex,' she finally answered, with a huge smile on her face.

'Then congratulations,' I said, 'because that's more than I'm getting at the moment.'

'Oh, Gracie, don't be sad,' Cleo said, pouting. 'Here, let me buy you another drink.'

'I haven't finished this one yet!' I protested.

'Excuses, excuses,' Cleo lectured. 'Honestly, Gracie, you can be such a lightweight when it comes to drinking!'

With that, she stood up and made her way towards the bar.

I watched her go, and then turned back to my drink, deciding I should attempt to finish it. I took a large gulp of the drink and, as I did so, realised that someone was sitting down next to me at the table. Someone who looked an awful lot like my ex-fiancé.

'Hi, Gracie,' the new arrival – the one and only David McAllister – said.

Completely surprised by David's sudden appearance, I ended up spitting the drink back out of my mouth. And most of it landed on my lying, cheating, scumbag of an ex-fiancé's expensive-looking suit. What a shame!

I sat there and watched as, pulling a disgusted face, David grabbed a napkin from the table and frantically tried to sponge the mess from his jacket. Finally, he gave up and looked at me instead. 'You could at least apologise,' he said.

'You deserved it,' I threw back in return.

I couldn't believe his cheek. He actually thought I should apologise? After what he'd put me through?

He stared at me for what seemed like ages before he finally spoke again.

'You're right,' he sighed.

'I am?' I asked, surprised he'd been so quick to agree with my judgement of him. I soon recovered. 'Wait, of course I am. You don't deserve an apology. I'm the one who deserves an apology, David – because I never did get one, did I?'

'Do you really think me apologising now will help?' David asked.

'Not really,' I said.

'Then what's the point?'

'I just want to see you grovel, I guess,' I smiled.

'I'm not going to grovel, Gracie.'

'Oh,' I said, faking disappointment, 'I was rather hoping you would.'

'Could we please just discuss this like two adults?' David sighed.

'Well we could,' I said, 'but there's only one adult here – and it sure isn't you.'

David didn't reply to this remark. He just sat there, staring at me like I was part of some sort of freak show. 'What?' I finally asked, annoyed.

'What's happened to you, Gracie?' David asked, still staring.

'What's that supposed to mean?'

'You're not acting like yourself at all. When did you get so bitter?'

'When did I get so bitter?!' I exploded, causing more than a few people in the general area to turn and look in my direction. 'Gee, I don't know, David. Maybe when I caught you cheating on me with another woman?!'

'Gracie, calm down,' David said, looking highly

embarrassed. 'We don't want a repeat of the restaurant situation, now do we?'

'Well *you* obviously do,' a voice behind David said, 'or you wouldn't have come over here.'

I looked up to see Cleo standing behind David, two drinks in her hands. She didn't look happy. 'Gracie, what is he doing here?' she asked, looking at me.

'He was just leaving,' I informed her.

'Good,' she said, glaring at David like she wanted to hack him into little pieces. 'Because he's in my seat.'

The glare obviously worked, because David quickly got up. Cleo took his place at the table, putting down the drinks.

'Gracie,' David said, still not taking his cue to leave, 'we have to discuss this.'

'Are you still with Lorna?' I asked him.

'Yes.'

'Then there's nothing to discuss.'

'I love Lorna,' David said sorrowfully, 'I can't help that –'

'You're right,' Cleo interrupted him, 'you're a man – you can't help being controlled by your dick.'

'But that doesn't mean we have to throw away three years together,' David continued, ignoring Cleo. 'We could still be friends,' he added hopefully.

'I like to be able to trust my friends,' I said, looking at him sadly. 'And I'm sorry to say that I don't trust you anymore, David.'

'Couldn't you at least try?' David asked.

'No,' I said firmly, and then turned away from him, downing the rest of my drink, before reaching for the next glass. As I started on that one, I saw Cleo look at David.

'I think that's your cue to leave,' she told him.

I didn't look up from my drink, but I could feel him standing there, watching me. After what seemed like hours, but was probably only seconds, I heard him move away from the table.

'Is he gone?' I asked Cleo, still not looking up.

'He's gone.'

'Good,' I said, and finally looked up, watching David walking further and further away from the table. Watching him walk out of my life.

And I felt terrible. Despite all that he'd done, all I wanted to do was call him back and ask him if we could start over again.

'I know what you're thinking,' Cleo said. I looked at her. Somehow Cleo always knew what I was thinking. 'But you don't want him back, Gracie. You're past that now – you don't need him anymore.'

'No. I need another drink,' I said, before quickly finishing up the one I had in front of me.

Cleo looked at me, sighed, and then pushed her drink across the table towards me. I picked it up, taking a huge gulp.

'Just make sure you don't see this as a long-term solution,' she said. 'I'm supposed to be the irresponsible one, remember?'

'Then I shall follow your example,' I smiled, 'and drink away my troubles.'

'You'll regret it in the morning,' Cleo chided.

'No, I won't,' I said happily, taking another large swig of my drink. 'Because tomorrow morning I won't remember any of this. I won't remember the huge amounts of alcohol I've consumed. I won't remember embarrassing myself in front of a room full of people – again! And best of all, I won't remember that terrible conversation I just had with my ex-fiancé.'

I smiled at Cleo, waiting for her to confirm this.

'Don't be so sure,' she said.

❄ ❄ ❄

It was a bright and sunny spring day. The sky was blue, the air was warm, and I could hear birds singing as the car I was travelling in pulled up outside the church. And what a beautiful church it was. It looked like it had jumped straight out of a Jane Austen novel (*Emma* had always been my favourite of the 'classics').

The churchyard was covered with lush green grass and flowers were blooming all around. Little girls in pretty dresses were scattering rose petals from the baskets they carried, onto the pathway leading up to the church doors. Others were being playfully chased around the churchyard by boys of the same age, who were dressed in little pageboy outfits. People were standing around talking, all looking happy and glowing.

As I made my way down the pathway, I saw my father standing by the church doors, a look of immense pride on his face. When I reached the church steps, he offered me his arm, which I accepted.

'You look beautiful, Gracie,' he said.

For the first time, I looked down at what I was wearing.

I gasped to see the beautiful white fabric surrounding me, rippling in the soft breeze. I felt like a princess.

And then I was inside the church. Rows and rows of people, stretching as far as the eye could see, all turned around to stare at me as I entered. Suddenly very afraid, I turned to go back the way I had come. But the church doors slammed shut behind me.

I was trapped. I felt my father tugging on my arm, pulling me down the aisle – past all the people who were watching me, whispering to each other.

'I hope she doesn't cause another scene,' I heard a lady in a huge pink hat say loudly to her friend.

Her friend, a rather plump lady wearing a suit that was an awful shade of green, turned to look at me disapprovingly. I quickly looked away.

I found myself getting closer and closer to the church altar. After a while, my father let go of my arm and I walked on alone. But there was someone waiting for me at the altar. I smiled as I realised who it was. David. He turned around and looked at me.

'Glad you could make it, Gracie,' he said, then turned his back on me.

And that was when I realised there was already a bride in the church, standing in front of the altar at David's side. I tried to see her face, but couldn't; it was covered by a thick white veil.

Then the vicar (who for some reason was wearing an 'I Love Paris' T-shirt) spoke. And what he said echoed all around my head:

'If anyone present knows of any reason why these two

should not be joined in matrimony, please speak now, or forever hold your peace.'

The whole church was silent. Except for me.

'Wait!' I said.

Once again, everyone turned to look at me.

'Here we go again,' I heard the pink-hatted lady say to the woman in the awful green suit.

'He can't marry her!' I shouted, ignoring them. 'He's supposed to be marrying me!'

'But I love her, Gracie,' David said, looking at me.

'You don't even know who she is!' I said, looking at the bride, whose face was still obscured by the heavy veil.

'Gracie!' said the bride, as if calling me to her. I ignored her and turned back to David.

'You're actually going to marry her?' I asked him.

'Why not?' he replied.

'Gracie!' said the bride once more.

'WHAT?' I shouted, looking at her.

'Gracie, wake up!' the bride said.

'Huh?' I mumbled, confused. Then I watched, shocked, as the bride removed her veil to reveal who was underneath.

'Mum!' I cried. She gave me a little wave and a smile. 'You're the one marrying David?'

'Gracie, wake up!' she said once again.

'What?' I asked, confused.

'Gracie…'

She was getting further and further away from me. The whole church was moving away from me. Mum, David, the pink-hatted lady, the woman wearing the awful green suit. They were disappearing into darkness.

'Gracie!' I heard again, louder this time.

I opened my eyes. I was in my room, in bed – correction, on top of my bed – and still wearing last night's clothes. Mum was leaning over me, shaking my arm.

'Gracie, wake up!' she said, sounding rather annoyed.

'I'm awake,' I mumbled, 'leave me alone.'

At that, Mum stopped shaking me and stepped away from the bed.

'There's no need to snap,' she said, and made her way over to the window, where she briskly pulled the curtains back, letting bright sunshine enter the room.

'Mum!' I cried, shielding my eyes from the morning sun. 'What time is it?' I groaned.

'Almost two o'clock,' she said.

'In the morning?' I asked hopefully.

'In the afternoon.'

Check. Make that afternoon sun.

'Okay, I'm getting up,' I said. But then I tried to actually move. And the pain in my head was similar to being hit with a sledgehammer. Not that I know what that actually feels like, but you know what I mean.

I immediately flopped back down on the bed. 'Or maybe not,' I said, defeated, trying not to move a muscle.

'You're getting up,' Mum said. 'You have a visitor.'

'I do?' I asked. 'Is it Orlando Bloom?'

'No,' Mum said.

'Then tell them to go away.'

'Gracie! I expect this sort of behaviour from your brother,' Mum said, 'but not from you.'

'Why not from me? Because I'm a girl?'

'Because you're a young lady,' she corrected me. 'Now what on earth did you get up to last night?'

I cringed. Suddenly all the events of last night came flooding back to me – every detail; every word. Apparently the alcohol hadn't done its job. Except on my head, of course.

'Nothing,' I said meekly, hoping she would be convinced. She wasn't.

'Then why did you come home singing at three o'clock in the morning?' she asked.

'Singing?' I asked, confused. She nodded. 'I don't remember singing,' I told her. 'What was I singing?'

'It sounded a bit like "Puff the Magic Dragon",' she said, 'but only a bit.'

'That song's about drugs, you know,' I told her, still not thinking straight.

'Nonsense!' Mum cried. 'Don't be so silly!'

'But it is –' I started, ready to explain my reasoning. But then there was a loud knock at the door (well, it sounded loud to me anyway) and Gretchen poked her head inside the room.

'Is it alright to come in?' she asked cheerily.

Don't you just hate people who are that perky first thing in the morning? Oh, okay – afternoon. Without waiting for an answer, she entered the room anyway. 'Hi, Gracie,' she said.

I didn't answer. I just gave her a little wave of the hand, most of my arm still shielding my eyes from the sun.

'Gretchen asked you to help out with making plans for

the wedding, Gracie,' Mum said, 'but it seems to have slipped your mind.'

Great - trust that to be the only thing I'd forgotten.

'Were we supposed to meet somewhere?' I asked Gretchen.

'At my house,' Gretchen replied, not sounding at all angry, 'but here is just as good.'

'That's nice,' I said, then closed my eyes, hoping the darkness would make my headache go away. After a few moments, I heard Gretchen's voice:

'Um, Gracie?' she said quietly. 'You promised to go and meet the vicar with me to arrange the rehearsal?'

'Today?' I asked, groaning.

'Yes, today,' I heard Mum say chirpily, 'and a promise is a promise!'

I removed the arm that lay across my face and chanced a look at my mother and Gretchen. They both stood smiling down at me.

Wonderful. I had been woken by the Brady Bunch.

I smiled back.

❄ ❄ ❄

As I stepped through the imposing archway that marked the entrance to St James', our local church, it occurred to me that I hadn't actually visited the building for some time now. Well, okay, for a number of years – fourteen to be exact.

A fact I blamed completely on my parents who, despite getting me christened (as was the in thing to do) had never really encouraged church attendance while I was old enough to be forced to go. And it wasn't until I was a young adult, with a mind of her own, that my mother had suddenly discovered religion (at about the same time as she realised joining community church groups was the best way of finding out all the local gossip).

Consequently I, unlike Gretchen, had never gotten into the habit of paying frequent visits to church, and was feeling decidedly out of place.

'So do you think Reverend Winters will remember me?' I asked Gretchen nervously.

I really hoped not. Reverend Winters had always given me the creeps when I was younger. I'd had a friend called Paul, back when I was about six or seven, who'd told me that Reverend Winters had once caught him stealing a bar of chocolate from the local sweet shop. That in itself had scared him. But then, allegedly, the good Reverend had told Paul that he was evil and would go to hell for what he'd done. I'd had nightmares for weeks following that story, and been scared of Reverend Winters for years after.

Paul, incidentally, hadn't gone to hell as a result of stealing the chocolate bar – though he *had* ended up with an illustrious career cleaning floors in a fast food restaurant, so kudos to the Reverend for a pretty close guess.

'Reverend Winters?' Gretchen asked, surprised. She turned to look at me through narrowed eyes. 'Gracie, when was the last time you came to church?'

'Couple of years ago maybe,' I said innocently. 'Why?'

'Because Reverend Winters retired nearly six years ago,'

Gretchen answered, a smile playing at the corners of her mouth.

'Really?' I asked, trying to sound casual. 'Guess I must've missed that one. So who's in charge around here now?'

'That would be me,' a rich, male voice said.

I looked up. Coming down the aisle towards us was a rather handsome and rather youthful (well, he couldn't have been a day over thirty-five), muscle-bound man. The kind of man you might see working out at the gym and fantasise about. Or at least, you might if you ever bothered going to the gym – something I never did, despite my paid-up membership.

And this man was a vicar. Or at least, he was dressed like a vicar. But –

'No way are you a vicar!' I exclaimed, putting my thoughts into words before I could stop myself. I clamped my hand over my mouth as I realised my error.

'Gracie!' Gretchen spluttered, looking at me in amazement. I could feel my cheeks flushing with embarrassment as the vicar came to a stop in front of us.

'It's okay,' the vicar said, laughing. 'I'm used to that sort of reaction.'

'You are?' I asked, removing my hand from my offensive mouth.

'Yes,' the vicar smiled, 'a lot of people are surprised by how young I am when they first meet me.'

'Well, that's not *exactly* what I was thinking,' I said sheepishly.

Gretchen elbowed me in the side to shut me up. The

vicar, however, didn't appear to have heard me, and continued with his explanation.

'I'm not quite sure why,' he said, 'but there seems to be a general consensus that men of the cloth should all be elderly and old-fashioned. And seeing as I'm neither of those things, I think it sometimes unsettles people. When they first meet me, at least.'

He looked at me and smiled. 'I hope I haven't put you off coming here?'

'Not at all,' I smiled back. 'In fact, I was just telling Gretchen how awful I feel about letting my visits to church lapse so greatly. I know I'll make a much bigger effort to attend in future.'

I flashed him my most dazzling smile. 'So, you work here permanently, do you?'

❄ ❄ ❄

'You know, I think it's time I took up religion,' I said, as Gretchen and I made our way out of the churchyard – a place that only half-an-hour ago had made me nervous but now looked full of the joys of springtime.

Suddenly, Gretchen stopped and turned to face me. 'What were you thinking?' she asked.

'What do you mean?' I replied, not really getting the question.

'Gracie, you were flirting with the vicar!' Gretchen exclaimed, her voice steady. If she was angry, she didn't show it. Unlike me, Gretchen had always been able to hold her temper.

'Was not,' I said indignantly.

'You asked him if he was married,' she reminded me.

'I was just being friendly!'

'And when he said no, you asked if he was allowed to have sex.'

'Well, I couldn't remember that 'celibate' word.'

I looked at Gretchen and wondered if she was mad at me yet. She didn't look it. In fact, she looked as calm and serene as she always did. Not a hair out of place – that was typical of Gretchen. No wonder my mother liked her so much.

'Gracie, what's gotten into you lately?' Gretchen sighed. 'You never used to behave like this.'

'Like what?'

'Well, you never used to flirt with men like that for one thing,' she, quite correctly, pointed out.

'No. That's because I used to have a fiancé,' I replied.

'You know how sorry I am about what happened between you and David,' Gretchen said sympathetically, 'but I thought you'd moved on, Gracie. It almost felt like you were ready to put it behind you.'

'Maybe I was,' I smiled thinly at her. 'Until last night anyway, when my ex-fiancé turned up at the exact same place I'd gone to forget my problems.'

'You saw David last night?' Gretchen asked me, surprised.

'Briefly.'

'Well, I guess that explains the state you're in today then,' she said.

Coming from anyone else, that would've sounded harsh. Coming from Gretchen, it sounded like fact. I didn't like it.

'I don't have a hangover,' I insisted.

Gretchen chose to ignore that statement. We both realised she knew the truth, so there wasn't really much point in arguing further.

'Why do you think seeing David again has affected you like this?' she asked me.

'Because he cheated on me with another woman?' I suggested.

'That's what he did,' Gretchen admitted, 'but that's got nothing to do with the way you feel about him.'

'Why do I suddenly feel like I'm in therapy?' I asked her, slightly exasperated.

'I'm just trying to help,' she replied, sounding a little wounded. 'I really think you need to admit your feelings for David before you can move on from them.'

'Fine,' I said, 'if it makes you happy, I'll say it. I'm still in love with him. I'm still in love with David. Even after all he's done.'

I looked at her for her response, expecting a look of shock. I didn't get it.

'I'm not surprised,' she said kindly. 'You and David were together for a long time. I'd be worried if there wasn't some part of you that still loved him.'

'I just want to be over him,' I said miserably.

'I know,' Gretchen said, and smiled at me, 'but don't worry – you'll get there.'

And just for a moment, I believed her.

Chapter Four

Monday morning began as it always did – starting with a loud knock on my bedroom door, which caused me to snap rudely awake.

It was my mother. Without waiting for an answer, she strode into the room.

'Time to get up, Gracie,' she chirped, though it sounded more like a bark to my half-awake ears.

I opened my eyes and watched as she leaned across my bed and tugged on my curtains, pulling them open and letting the early morning sunshine stream into the room. I quickly closed my eyes again as the light hit them.

A moment later, my alarm clock went off. On reflex, I threw out an arm to shut it up. I'm not sure why I even bothered setting the thing. My mother was like a walking, talking alarm clock. Always up at the crack of dawn; always there to wake me in the morning.

'Gracie, you don't want to be late for work, do you?' she asked me.

No. I wouldn't want that…

'I'll be up in a minute,' I told her.

And so she went away. And I went back to sleep.

Then, what felt like ten seconds, but was actually ten minutes later, she was back in my room, shaking me awake. 'I'm getting up!' I snapped at her.

I've never really been a morning person. And by morning, I do mean everything up until noon.

Which is why it was lucky that the impromptu team meeting that had been called at work was taking place after lunch and not before.

I was currently sitting in that meeting, which had apparently been called for no other reason than to make the resident managers feel needed (quite typical for our office really). I vaguely listened as topics changed from the important (should we start using environmentally-friendly cups with our water dispenser?) to the extremely important (should we allow the work experience boy to answer the telephone?).

Then I heard someone using my name.

'What do you think, Gracie?'

I very suddenly snapped back to reality. And then a cold panic swept over me, as I realised I had no idea what had just been discussed. And Jane Marker was looking at me, waiting for an answer to her question.

Uh oh. Jane Marker was the big boss. She was in charge of the whole office. In fact, with the exception of Jason, the agency's regional director (whose visits to the office usually coincided with his and Cleo's sexual urges, rather than with any pressing business needs), Jane was everybody's superior. And didn't she just love reminding us all of that fact?

So I was in big trouble if I didn't come up with an answer, and quick.

'Um, I think it's a great idea,' I said, with a hopeful smile.

'Good,' Jane smiled back at me, 'then it's decided.' And, as I wondered just what horrible thing I might have agreed to, she moved immediately to the next item on her list: morale (or 'moral' as it was often spelt on the agenda sheet, which, as I always pointed out, made it a completely different word) – a very popular topic and one that was discussed at every team meeting.

Basically, Jane would move around the circle of her employees (we always sat in a circle for team meetings – it was kind of like being in group therapy) and ask each person in turn how much they were currently enjoying their job, on a scale of one to ten. And everyone would lie. Everyone except Cleo anyway, who always told the truth. But we were used to that by now.

As expected, Jane was now moving around the circle, murmuring 'good' or 'wonderful' in response to people's sevens and eights out of ten. Then she reached:

'Cleo?'

'Three,' Cleo simply replied. Which wasn't bad for Cleo, who often answered with a one or a two or – on one particularly memorable occasion – a zero.

Jane moved straight on without comment – to me.

'Gracie?'

I was tempted. Very, very tempted. But I didn't. As always, I answered: 'Seven.'

A fairly neutral number. High enough to keep Jane happy, but not so high that it made my answer exceptional. Let's face it; the last thing I wanted was Jane Marker giving me extra work to do because she thought I was enjoying it so much.

Jane accepted this answer without question, as always, and moved on to the next person in the circle – Penny Davenport. Who always overcompensated for everyone else with her:

'Ten!'

Which was always accompanied by an encouraging smile, as if she hoped everyone asked after her might respond in the same manner.

Of course, with morale in this office being what it was, the only way *that* would happen would be if Penny were to hold everyone at gunpoint and force a top score out of them. Although, considering Penny's obvious delusional nature, it was quite possible she was unbalanced enough to do just that.

Looking at Penny's enthusiastic face, I nearly gagged. I needed to get out of this office urgently. It was becoming a matter of life and death. As in, if I didn't escape soon, I was likely to kill someone – most probably Penny.

Still, would going to prison really be that much worse than living at home with my mother? Somehow I doubted there would be any difference.

❄ ❄ ❄

'So you're really going to do this?' Cleo asked me. 'You're actually going to stand up to your mother?'

Pulling my keys from my bag, I moved to unlock the front door of my parents' house. Cleo was standing next to me on the doorstep. I had invited her round after work – despite the ban on her presence that my mother was still rigidly enforcing.

'Yeah, well I live here too,' I replied. 'I should be able to bring home whoever I want.'

'Aren't you worried what she'll say?' Cleo asked, clearly intrigued.

'I don't care,' I insisted. 'If she doesn't like it, then that's just tough.'

Almost as soon as I'd said it, I realised I had gone too far. I was a terrible liar – especially where my mother was concerned – and Cleo knew it.

Narrowing her eyes, Cleo looked at me suspiciously. 'Your mum and dad aren't home, are they?' she asked.

I unlocked the front door and swung it open, before turning to face Cleo.

'I'm pretty sure they're not,' I admitted, smiling guiltily at her.

'Gracie!' Cleo complained. 'You said they were going to be here!'

'No, I didn't,' I reminded her. 'I just never said they *weren't* going to be here.'

'That's the same thing,' Cleo grumbled.

And I suppose she was right. The truth was, despite letting Cleo believe my parents would be home this evening, I'd known all along that they actually had plans elsewhere and therefore wouldn't be around – something which seemed to be confirmed by the fact that my father's car was missing from outside the house.

Still, it never hurt to double-check these things.

'Hello?' I called into the (hopefully empty) house. 'Anyone home?'

There was no answer. Which came as a great relief to me because, despite my brave words, I really wasn't feeling up to a confrontation with my mother this evening.

'Well that's just boring then,' Cleo pouted.

I ushered Cleo into the house, following her inside and shutting the door behind me.

'I thought you'd be glad Mum isn't home?' I asked her, once we were inside. 'You didn't really want to see her, did you?'

'You know me,' Cleo said. 'I love to antagonise your mother.' She frowned at me in mock sorrow. 'Gracie, you've taken away all of my enjoyment!'

I wasn't quite sure if Cleo was being serious or not, though I thought it was likely she was. After all, she did seem to get some sort of perverse pleasure out of taunting my mother.

'Oh come on!' I exclaimed. 'As if I would really bring you home if Mum was going to be here!'

'Mum *is* here,' a voice suddenly said, making both Cleo and me visibly jump.

That voice belonged to Warren, and I turned to glare at him as he emerged from the living room.

'Mum isn't here,' I informed him. 'She and Dad have gone to the theatre this evening. They won't be back for hours.'

Warren shook his head. 'Mum had a migraine, so she stayed behind.'

'Dad's car is gone,' I quickly pointed out.

'Yeah,' Warren agreed. 'That's because Mum told him to go without her.'

'So where is she then?' Cleo asked Warren, clearly not convinced.

'She went upstairs to lie down,' Warren replied.

Warren looked past Cleo and me, motioning up the stairs which stood behind us. And as he did so, his face suddenly took on a look of pure surprise.

'Mum!' he suddenly exclaimed. 'What are you doing up?'

I felt my stomach lurch in dismay and, like Cleo, immediately spun around to look – certain I would see my mother's angry face looming down at me.

The stairs, however, were empty.

I turned back to look at Warren, whose face immediately broke into a huge grin. 'You should've seen your faces!' he laughed.

'You're such a jerk, Warren,' I scowled at him.

'Yeah, nice sense of humour,' Cleo said sarcastically.

Looking between Warren and me, Cleo shook her head. 'You know,' she said, 'I find it so hard to believe you two are related.'

'Well I find it hard to believe you're related to the human race,' Warren told Cleo. He reached out and fingered a lock of her long, blue-black hair, examining it closely. 'What's the look this month?' he asked her, grinning. 'Alien skank?'

Cleo batted his hand away. 'You are so rude!' she told Warren. 'If you were any younger, I'd put you across my knee and spank you!'

'I'd like that,' Warren winked at her. Cleo clipped him

round the ear. 'Hey!' Warren exclaimed, ducking out of her reach.

'Don't do that,' I told Cleo. 'You'll only encourage him.' I glared at Warren, though I was amused to see he was keeping as far away from Cleo as possible. 'He's twisted like that.'

'Speaking of which,' Warren said, rubbing his injured ear. 'What's it worth to you that I keep Cleo's little visit a secret from Mum?'

'Blackmail's a dirty word, Warren,' I replied.

'I know,' he grinned, 'but if you have the ammo, then you should use it.'

'It's lucky I have the ammo then, isn't it?' I asked him.

Warren looked confused. Poor thing – he was a little slow on the uptake. 'Tell me, Warren,' I said, taking great delight in what I was about to say. 'How's Amy? Have you two been out on any dates lately?'

Warren scowled at me.

'I thought we agreed to keep that between us?' he reminded me.

'Oh, I won't tell anyone,' I told him, before exchanging a glance with Cleo. She knew exactly where I was going with this.

'But I might,' Cleo finished, grinning.

Warren sighed and held up his hands in surrender. 'Fine,' he agreed, defeated. 'I didn't see a thing.'

'Good,' I said. 'Just make sure you remember that when Mum gets home.'

I made my way into the kitchen, with Cleo following. Warren trailed behind us.

'I don't suppose I could borrow some money?' Warren asked me.

I turned to look at him in disbelief.

'Are you kidding?' I questioned him. 'After the little stunt you just pulled?'

'I was only playing around,' Warren protested.

'That's all you ever do,' I reminded him. 'If you want some money, perhaps you should try working for once.'

'I do work,' Warren frowned. 'I go to college.'

'I think what Gracie's trying to say is – get a job,' Cleo spelled it out for him.

'Who asked you?' Warren scowled at her.

As Warren turned back to face me though, the scowl disappeared – replaced by an expression of pure innocence.

'So?' he pleaded. 'Can I borrow some money or not?'

'What do you need it for?' I asked him.

I had no intention of lending him any money. However, I was curious as to why he wanted the cash.

'It's a surprise,' Warren said cryptically.

'If you won't tell me, then you can't have the money,' I informed him.

'He probably needs it to buy more dates with,' Cleo grinned.

'No, I don't,' Warren said. 'I need it to buy a birthday present for Amy.'

'Amy your fake girlfriend?' Cleo asked.

'Amy can buy her own birthday present with the money you paid her for coming to dinner,' I told Warren.

Warren opened his mouth to argue, but I stopped him in his tracks. 'End of discussion.'

'Fine,' Warren grumbled. 'Just don't expect me to lend *you* money ever again.'

'You've never lent me money in your entire life,' I reminded him.

'And now I never will,' Warren said, sulking.

Warren flounced away, leaving Cleo and me alone in the kitchen. Cleo watched Warren go, clearly amused.

'He's such a happy soul, isn't he?' she asked me.

'You get used to it after a while,' I told her.

I picked up my post from the kitchen table. There wasn't much of interest – mostly junk mail and loan offers – but one envelope caught my eye. It was large and brown and had my name and address written across the front of it in perfectly neat lettering. I didn't know who it was from, so I immediately moved to open it up, feeling a sense of anticipation as I did so.

It's amazing what I get pleasure from these days.

'That's still sealed?' Cleo asked, watching me. 'I'm surprised your mother hasn't steamed it open already.'

'She's not quite that bad,' I replied.

I decided not to mention that, in the past, Mum had frequently opened my post without permission. In fact, it had been a major issue between us before I'd moved in with David. I could only hope she'd since learnt her lesson for good.

'Of course not,' Cleo said, her voice dripping with sarcasm. It was quite clear she didn't really believe me.

Ignoring Cleo, I opened the envelope and pulled out the letter I found inside, quickly scanning its contents. It was good news, I suppose – though I quickly realised that not everyone would see it that way.

'You okay?' Cleo asked, watching me with concern. I must have looked worried.

'More than okay,' I told her, smiling now. 'I got a job interview!'

'Really?!' Cleo asked, excited. 'Let me see!'

I handed the letter to Cleo, who read the first few lines out loud:

'Dear Miss Parker. Thank you for your recent application for the position of Personal Assistant. I am pleased to inform you that you have been selected to attend an interview for this post...'

Cleo skimmed the rest of the letter silently, her face forming into a frown as she did so. 'That's odd,' she said, as she finished reading the letter.

'What's odd?' I asked her.

'It doesn't say whose assistant you'll be,' Cleo replied.

She handed the letter back to me and I quickly read through it again myself. I hadn't noticed it on my first read, but Cleo was right – there was no mention in the letter of whom I would be working for should I get the job.

'I guess they'll tell me at the interview,' I shrugged.

'Probably,' Cleo agreed. She grinned at me. 'Gracie, how exciting is this? Just think – in a few weeks, you could be working for a celebrity!'

'Yeah,' I replied, smiling back at her. 'Imagine that.'

I wanted to share Cleo's enthusiasm, but it just wasn't happening. The truth was, I was far too busy worrying about what my mother would say.

❄ ❄ ❄

It was Tuesday morning. It was cold. And I wasn't at work.

I had woken up as usual, roused from a lovely dream about Orlando Bloom by my mother (damn her). I had showered, gotten dressed, and eaten my breakfast. And I had set off for work.

But this had all been for my mother's benefit, because once I reached the halfway point between home and work – a peaceful park, which I enjoyed walking through each morning, but hurried to get to the other side of once it was dark and shadows jumped out at me from behind every tree – I went no further.

Instead, I sat down on a park bench, took my mobile phone from my bag, and made the call I'd been dreading. A call to work.

To my surprise, Cleo answered, sounding less-than-enthusiastic.

'Yeah?'

'Cleo?' I asked, though I knew it was her – nobody else in the office would dare answer the telephone in such an unprofessional manner.

'Gracie!' she cooed. 'I can't believe you really did it! I'm so proud of you!'

She was referring, of course, to my going absent-without-leave from work in order to attend my job interview with Ms Olivia Hunt.

'I haven't done it yet,' I warned her. 'I could still change my mind.'

'Don't you dare!' Cleo exclaimed. 'You're going to that

interview, Gracie, if I have to drag you there myself!'

'That won't be necessary,' I told her, smiling. Cleo certainly had a way with words.

'Good,' she said, then: 'I'm assuming you're calling Penny to tell her how ill you are?'

'Yes, I'm very ill,' I smiled. 'So ill I can barely get out of bed – except to throw up, of course. I think it might be one of those twenty-four-hour things. But what's upsetting me most about it is that it's stopping me coming to work.'

'Very good!' Cleo said. 'I especially liked that last little bit at the end. Penny will be so touched by that.'

'Where is Penny?' I asked her.

'Shut in her room doing 'important' managerial work,' Cleo replied. 'She's forwarded her phone to me and said she's not to be disturbed unless absolutely necessary.'

'Well, I guess you'd better put me through,' I sighed.

We had an office policy which stated that all absences needed to be reported directly to a manager. I think it was so they could listen to your voice and work out how ill you actually were. Luckily for me, Penny was easy to fool over such things. She just never thought that anyone would actually lie to her.

'Okay then,' Cleo said. 'I'm putting you through. Good luck, Gracie. Call me when it's over, okay? Love you!'

There was a beep at the end of the line, and a moment while Cleo transferred the call – no doubt telling Penny that poor, sick Gracie was calling. Then Penny came on the line.

'Hello? Gracie?'

'Hi, Penny,' I croaked into the phone, trying to sound sorry for myself. It wasn't hard. I just had to think about where I worked.

'Cleo tells me you're not too well today?'

I could hear the sympathy in Penny's voice. Which should have made me feel guilty. But it didn't.

'Yes,' I confirmed, and launched into the speech I'd earlier practised on Cleo, adding in just a few more details about how terribly sick I was and how awful I felt at letting Penny down.

Penny told me to take as much time off as I needed and to concentrate on getting myself well again. Which should have made me feel guilty. But it didn't.

Feeling strangely pleased with myself, I turned off my phone, stood up, and started towards my job interview.

Before realising that it wasn't for another two hours.

❄ ❄ ❄

After sitting for a bottom-numbing hour-and-a-half on a cold park bench – during which time I'd been accosted by an over-friendly dog; come precariously close to being shitted upon by a none-too-friendly pigeon; and somehow been conned into handing over my breakfast to an old homeless lady – I was relieved to finally reach the address where my interview was to be held.

But far from being the huge, shiny, modern office block of my expectations, the building in question was actually a rather disappointing, old four-storey structure. It was a spectacularly unimpressive place for a TV personality's headquarters to be located, with paint peeling off its greying walls, and bags of rubbish piled up outside.

Clearly, someone wanted to remain incognito.

I pressed the buzzer for the second floor of the building, as instructed in the letter I'd received from Ms Olivia Hunt. The name by the button read 'Ramsden & Hunt.' A lady answered (Ms Hunt, I think) and, after formally announcing myself, I was buzzed in and invited upstairs.

A few minutes later, I finally met Olivia, who looked exactly as I'd pictured her while reading the excessively formal letter she'd sent to me.

In other words, she looked uptight. She even had her hair pulled securely into a bun, with what looked like knitting needles poking out either side. Her hair was a rich, auburn colour, though speckled with grey. At a guess, I would have placed her at around fifty years of age.

'Miss Parker?' she asked, holding out her hand in an unsurprisingly formal gesture. I shook it.

'Pleased to meet you,' I smiled, 'and just Gracie is fine.'

She didn't comment on that. She simply turned around and motioned for me to follow her. 'This way please.'

She led me into a surprisingly small room. I was expecting to find a number of people working there on the TV personality's behalf, but the office was empty.

'Quiet day?' I asked, looking at Olivia.

'What do you mean?' she asked me, her eyebrows arched disapprovingly.

'Where's everybody else?' I clarified, though certain that the meaning of my original question had been quite clear.

'There is nobody else,' Olivia said. 'There's just me – and you, if you get the job.'

She walked over to a desk (one of only two in the room, I now noticed) and sat down behind it, motioning for me to take the chair in front of the desk. I did so.

'So, Miss Parker,' Olivia began, completely ignoring my earlier request for her to call me by my first name, 'I understand you work for the same recruitment agency with which this position was advertised?'

Olivia looked at me expectantly and I felt my heart sink. Did she know what I had done?

'Yes,' I replied, just about managing to squeak the words out, 'that's correct.'

Olivia continued to stare at me and I had to resist the urge to squirm under her gaze. I was almost certain she could see right through me.

'What does your role at the agency entail?' Olivia asked me.

'I'm in charge of the recruitment website on which all of the open competition job vacancies are advertised,' I told her.

I was aware that I was probably digging my own grave, but for some reason I couldn't stop talking. 'I make sure all the job vacancies we receive are uploaded onto the website at least a week before their closing dates, so that potential applicants can view the information and see how to apply.'

'Well, that certainly sounds very impressive,' Olivia commented (though it has to be said that she didn't actually *sound* very impressed). 'But unfortunately, I haven't had the pleasure of viewing your website,' she continued. 'I don't use the Internet – it's full of lies and pornographic material from what I've heard.'

'No more than the daily tabloids,' I attempted to joke. Olivia didn't even crack a smile.

Still, I was feeling a little more confident now. Because if Olivia hadn't seen the website, then she had no way of knowing her job vacancy hadn't appeared there.

'I expect you had a big response to your advert?' I asked her.

'Actually, no,' Olivia said. 'Surprisingly, you were the only applicant.'

I'd known full well what Olivia's answer would be, of course – and my intention in asking the question was to remind her of that very fact. After all, if I was the only applicant, surely she had to give me the job?

'How strange,' I said, presenting Olivia with my most innocent look. 'I added the vacancy to the website myself.'

I don't know if Olivia believed me or not, though she didn't question me any further on the subject.

'Why do you want to leave your current job, Miss Parker?' she asked instead.

Um, because I hate it, I thought. Of course, that's not what I said.

'I'm ready for a new challenge,' I told Olivia. 'I've been in my current job a few years now and I've achieved a lot, but I'd like to try something a little different – expand my horizons.'

There – that sounded good.

'And why did you apply for this job in particular?' Olivia asked me.

I quickly thought through all of my reasons for applying: glamour, excitement, fame, a chance to show my mother (among others) that I'd made something of my life without David. Not one of my reasons was suitable for voicing in front of Olivia.

'I think I could do the job well,' I eventually answered her question. 'I have excellent organisational and interpersonal skills. I'm hard-working and I'm very committed – I always give one hundred percent.' Which wasn't strictly true, but then Olivia didn't need to know that. 'I applied because I was sure I'd make an excellent personal assistant.'

Nodding, Olivia picked up some papers from her desk and scanned them with her eyes. 'Your CV is certainly very impressive,' she told me.

It should be, I thought. Most of it was wildly exaggerated after all.

Oh come on – who doesn't lie on their CV?

'Thank you,' I smiled.

I had faxed Olivia the papers from work. Not exactly an official use of office supplies, but I'd done it while Penny and Jane weren't around, so I figured it didn't really count.

'It says here you have an interest in birdwatching,' Olivia commented.

Birdwatching? Right – and that would be one of the lies on my CV. When writing the damn thing, I'd been at a loss for what to include on my list of hobbies and interests. Watching television and reading sounded boring and antisocial – and going out drinking with Cleo definitely wouldn't have been an appropriate inclusion. Which didn't leave a whole lot else really.

And so I had claimed to enjoy birdwatching. But so what? I occasionally threw out bread for the birds in our garden. And Warren did own a pair of binoculars (though I suspected he used those for looking at a rather different type of bird). So it wasn't *that* much of a stretch.

'Do you have a favourite?' Olivia asked me, breaking into my thoughts.

'What?' I asked her back. I must've looked pretty blank, as she rephrased the question.

'Do you have a favourite type of bird?' she tried again.

'Oh,' I said, 'yes, I do.'

I quickly racked my brains, trying to think of the name of a bird I could give to Olivia. Pigeon? No, nobody liked pigeons, right? Sparrow? No, too small. Robin? Not around enough. I needed something colourful but not too obvious.

And then it came to me.

'I like woodpeckers,' I told Olivia with a smile.

'Do you get woodpeckers in your garden?' Olivia questioned me further.

'Oh, you know – just one or two,' I replied, hoping I sounded convincing.

I mean, really – what were the chances that Olivia would be a birdwatching enthusiast? I just hoped she didn't play chess and do yoga as well. I'd stretched the truth far enough for one day, thank you very much.

Still, my apparent penchant for birdwatching seemed to have warmed Olivia to my case a little. After browsing through my CV one last time, she looked up at me and said:

'How much notice do you need to give your current employer?'

'Three weeks,' I told her.

'Three weeks will be fine,' Olivia said, looking at me. She seemed to be waiting for me to speak.

'So does that mean I've got the job?' I asked her.

'Yes, Miss Parker,' Olivia replied impatiently, 'it does.'

Apparently Olivia had reverted back to her prim and proper manner already, our previous bonding experience now forgotten.

'Okay,' I said, surprised by the speed at which my success had been confirmed (obviously Olivia really wanted another birdwatcher around the office). 'But do you think you could tell me a little more about the position before I accept it?' I asked her, hoping I wasn't pushing my luck. 'I mean, I don't even know who I'll be working for yet.'

'The position offered is that of personal assistant,' Olivia told me, clearly not about to give anything away. She didn't look at all amused by my curiosity.

'Yes, I know,' I said, 'but –'

'This is your contract of employment,' Olivia interrupted me. She passed a document across the desk to me, which I obediently accepted. 'I think you'll find everything is in order,' she added, as I began reading through the contract.

Ignoring her, I continued to read, stopping at the bottom of the document's first page.

'Wait, what's this?' I asked her.

At the foot of the page was a clause marked 'Confidentiality Agreement'.

I quickly scanned the text – it read like the Official Secrets Act. Basically, I wasn't allowed to discuss where I worked, who I worked for, and what kind of work I did.

'That's just to protect your employer,' Olivia said.

'And who might that employer be?' I asked again, my curiosity only growing each time Olivia avoided the question.

Olivia stared at me, as if deciding whether or not I could be trusted with the secret. Then, with a smile of sorts, she picked up a silver photo frame that had been lying face down on her desk and turned it to face me.

'That would be this gentleman,' Olivia said proudly.

I stared at the photograph in the frame – a photograph of Roman Pearson. Roman Pearson, TV/film personality. Roman Pearson of *Hearts & Minds* fame. Roman Pearson: 'Best Actor' at the TV Awards for two years running and 'Most Fanciable Male' for four.

'Now, Miss Parker,' I heard Olivia ask me, 'do you want the job or not?'

'Yes,' I managed to squeak, before grabbing a pen from Olivia's desk and signing the contract in front of me. I handed it back for Olivia to sign.

'Welcome to the team,' Olivia said, sounding less-than-enthusiastic about my appointment.

I just smiled back at her.

❄ ❄ ❄

By the time I left the offices of Ramsden & Hunt, I was in an incredibly positive and upbeat mood. A sense of delight had settled over me (something I hadn't experienced for several months) coupled with a general feeling of success. I'd done it. I'd gone out and secured myself a job as a personal assistant – Roman Pearson's personal assistant, no less. Life was finally beginning to look up for me.

Unfortunately, I was so lost in my thoughts as I made my way down the stairs of the office block, that I didn't notice the young man stepping through the front door of the building until it was too late – and I walked straight into him.

(Much to my horror as, for a fleeting moment, I was totally convinced the man I'd collided with was in fact Roman Pearson himself.)

Even worse, in the midst of my clumsiness, I'd managed to knock the small, white cardboard box the man had been carrying out of his hands. Time seemed to move in slow motion as the box flew through the air, before landing on the hard concrete floor of the building's entrance hall with a loud splat.

That didn't sound good.

'Sorry!' I said immediately, taking a step back.

To my great relief, I quickly realised the man standing in front of me was not Roman Pearson.

However, like Roman, he was handsome. He had short brown hair, with a wispy fringe that threatened to obscure his vision, and his eyes were the colour of melted chocolate. They were eyes you could drown in (as I'm sure Cleo, with her particular addiction, would agree). He looked quite young, though I suspected he was in his late twenties. And as he smiled at me, I could feel myself blushing with embarrassment.

'It's my fault,' he said kindly. 'I wasn't looking where I was going.'

'Same here,' I admitted quickly.

I appreciated the lie, even if it was an obvious one.

'Well, no harm done,' he said cheerily.

'What about your box?' I asked him, nodding towards where it still rested, face down on the floor.

I watched as he bent down and scooped up the box from the floor. Opening the lid, he peeked inside, shaking his head sadly.

Then he tilted the box so I could see what he was looking at.

'I think you killed the doughnut,' he said, with mock solemnity.

Inside the box were the damaged remains of what had apparently once been a cream cake.

'Sorry,' I said guiltily. 'I hope that wasn't your lunch?'

'Not mine,' he told me, 'Olivia's. She works upstairs.'

'Olivia Hunt?' I asked him. 'That's *her* doughnut?'

'That *was* her doughnut,' he corrected me, smiling mischievously.

'It's not funny!' I protested. 'You don't understand. I can't afford to get on Olivia's bad side – not yet anyway.'

'Don't worry,' he laughed. 'I can keep a secret. I'll just tell Olivia that Gus on the third floor did it – she hates him anyway.'

I studied him for a moment, trying to determine if he

was serious or not. With him still smiling like that it was hard to tell, but I eventually decided he was speaking the truth.

'Thanks,' I smiled at him, 'that's really nice of you.' And then I thought about what he'd said. 'Though I'm not sure Gus would agree with you.'

'Gus can take care of himself,' he promised. I nodded in reply. 'So how do you know Olivia?' he asked me.

'I had an interview with her today,' I explained, 'for a personal assistant's job.'

'You must be Gracie then,' he smiled. 'Olivia mentioned you were coming in for an interview.'

'She did?'

'I'm Billy Ramsden,' he introduced himself with a grin.

'Ramsden?' I asked. I recognised the name immediately. 'As in Ramsden & Hunt?'

'That's the one,' he confirmed.

'So do you work for Mr Pearson too?' I asked him.

'You could say that,' Billy smiled. 'What about you though?' he asked, quickly changing the subject. 'How did your interview go?'

'Well, I got the job – so I guess it went okay,' I told him. 'Though I don't think Olivia liked me much.'

'Olivia doesn't like anyone much,' Billy said. 'Don't take it personally, okay?'

'I won't,' I promised him.

'Good,' Billy said.

He looked up the stairs. 'Well, I'd better go,' he told me, 'before Olivia sends out a search party.' He looked back at me and smiled, giving me his full attention. 'I look forward to working with you, Gracie.'

'Yeah,' I smiled back at him, 'me too.'

With one last final smile, Billy took his battered cake box and made his way upstairs. I waited until he'd disappeared before finally leaving the building.

It had been a bizarre day so far, but I knew one thing for sure – I was happy. I only hoped everyone else would be as pleased for me as I was for myself.

Chapter Five

About an hour after my meeting with Billy, I found myself walking back into work. Any sensible person, of course, would have gone straight home and then returned to work the next day – cured of their twenty-four-hour affliction and ready to hand in their notice. But unfortunately, I had never been a sensible person. Or a patient one.

Which probably explained why I was currently walking past the open door of my manager's office with a big grin on my face.

'Hi, Penny,' I called.

'Gracie?' Penny asked, looking up from her work.

I carried on walking, heading down the office towards my desk – feeling a number of inquisitive pairs of eyes on me as I did so.

I was amused, but not surprised, to find Cleo sitting at the desk opposite mine, totally engrossed in something that was quite obviously not work-related. In fact, it looked suspiciously like the latest issue of *Vanity Fair*.

I dropped my bag onto my desk with a loud thump. Startled, Cleo yelped, dropped the magazine, and then pretended to be staring intently at something on her computer screen which – quite tellingly – currently featured nothing but a colourful screensaver.

'Not very convincing,' I commented. Cleo looked up.

'Gracie!' she cried. 'You almost gave me a heart attack!' She lowered her voice. 'What are you doing here? You're supposed to be at your job interview!'

I was about to reply when I heard another voice calling my name.

'Gracie!'

I turned around. It was Penny, who obviously wanted to know just what was going on. 'Gracie, what are you doing here?' she asked. 'I thought you weren't well?'

Penny's voice was ringing with concern, but I noticed a note of suspicion starting to creep in there as well.

'I suddenly felt a lot better,' I told her brightly.

'Well, that's good –' she started.

'And I wanted to give you this,' I interrupted, pulling a folded piece of paper from my bag and handing it to her. It was a letter; something I'd prepared as soon as I'd been offered the job interview. I had simply been biding my time until I could give it to its rightful recipient.

Penny opened up the letter, scanned its contents, and frowned.

'What is this?' she asked.

There was a moment of complete silence following Penny's question, as if the whole office were waiting for my reply (and they probably were). I could practically hear Cleo holding her breath behind me.

'It's my letter of resignation,' I explained. 'I'm handing in my notice.'

Penny just stared at me. I smiled sweetly at her, before sitting down at my desk. Sitting opposite, Cleo was also staring at me in shock.

'What?' I asked her, my smile getting wider.

'You just quit your job!' Cleo spluttered.

'Yes,' I said, 'just like you've been telling me to do for months.'

'Yeah, but I never believed you'd actually do it!' she exclaimed.

'Believe it,' I smiled at her.

And then it suddenly occurred to me just what I'd done. And I panicked.

❄ ❄ ❄

'Here, breathe into this!' Cleo said, shoving a paper bag into my hands.

'Cleo, I'm not hyperventilating!' I cried.

'Not yet,' Cleo said, watching me warily.

We were in the ladies' bathroom, where I'd hurried, thinking I was going to throw up, as the panic had set in. Cleo had followed me, chased some poor woman out of the bathroom, then commandeered it solely for our use by blocking the door with a sanitary disposal bin.

I handed the bag back to Cleo.

'I'm fine,' I told her.

'You don't look fine,' she said. 'You look like a woman on the verge of a nervous breakdown.'

'Thanks,' I said, 'that helps. Can I have the bag back now please?'

Wordlessly, she passed the bag back to me. I took it and held it over my mouth, forcing myself to take long, deep breaths.

And then I stopped because: a) it wasn't actually helping; and b) I probably looked really stupid doing it. I crushed the bag between my hands.

'I'm okay,' I said, trying to sound earnest.

'Gracie, you just quit your job,' Cleo said, as if she still didn't believe it.

'Yes, I did.'

'You just quit your job!' she said again, laughing this time.

'I know!' I said, joining in with her laughter.

'So this is good, right?' Cleo asked me between giggles. 'This means you got the job?'

'You're looking at the new personal assistant to a TV and film personality,' I told her proudly, my panic finally over.

'Gracie!' Cleo squealed, hugging me. 'I'm so proud of you! You're actually getting out of this place!'

Releasing me from the hug, she looked at me excitedly. 'So? Don't keep me in suspense. Who is it?'

'Who's what?'

'The TV personality! Who is it?!'

'Oh. I can't say,' I told her.

'What do you mean, you can't say?' she asked. 'You have to say!'

'I'm not allowed,' I explained. 'It's part of my contract – I'm not supposed to tell anyone.'

'But I'm your best friend!' Cleo wailed. 'You can tell me!'

'You know, I'm pretty sure "don't tell anyone" includes best friends,' I said.

'Gracie!' Cleo cried. 'You have to tell me. If you don't, I'll never speak to you again!'

'That's a little bit drastic, don't you think?' I smiled, knowing full well that she didn't mean it.

'Come on, Gracie,' Cleo tried again. 'I'm your best friend. I won't tell anyone.'

She paused, waiting for my answer. It was no good. I'd never be able to keep it from her.

'Okay,' I said reluctantly, 'I'll tell you. I expect you would've found out eventually anyway.'

'Well go on then – who is it?' she asked. I could practically hear Cleo holding her breath in anticipation.

I waited a few moments for dramatic effect, and then came out with it.

'Roman Pearson,' I said.

Cleo stared at me, as if waiting for me to say more.

'No, really,' she asked, 'who is it?'

'Roman Pearson,' I said again.

'You're joking,' Cleo stated, 'right?'

'I'm not joking,' I said, laughing. 'I'm going to be Roman Pearson's personal assistant.'

'As in Roman Pearson of *Hearts & Minds*?'

'That's the only Roman Pearson I know.'

'Gracie!' Cleo squealed again (she'd done a lot of that today).

'What?' I asked her, trying not to laugh.

'You're going to introduce me, right?' she asked, looking at me hopefully. I couldn't help but smile.

'I'll see what I can do,' I told her.

❄ ❄ ❄

And that was the easy part over and done with. Because despite how uncomfortable it was working in the office over the next few weeks, following my big announcement; and however much it had made me panic to actually take the plunge and quit my nice, safe job; it was nothing compared to the absolute feeling of dread I was experiencing at the thought of telling my parents what I had done.

Crazy, I know. I mean, I'm twenty-four years old. It's not like I need to ask their permission.

And yet there it was. Like a returning feeling from childhood, of knowing I'd done something wrong and would ultimately be punished for it when my parents found out.

So far I'd done a pretty good job of making sure they *didn't* find out. But time was running out. I had only two days left to serve in my current run-of-the-mill job. And on Monday morning, I would be starting my sparkling new career, as personal assistant to Roman Pearson.

So they had to know sooner or later. And I couldn't put it off any longer.

'Mum, Dad,' I said, looking from one to the other, 'there's something I have to tell you.'

'Yes, dear?' Mum asked, before popping another dainty piece of food into her mouth and beginning to chew.

We were sat at the dinner table: me, Mum, Dad, and Warren, who had very uncharacteristically joined us for dinner (when he wasn't bringing fake girlfriends home, he usually spent meal times alone in his room with a packet of cream crackers, or out with his friends at one of the various fast food outlets where they worked) – almost as if he was expecting something exciting to happen.

I just hoped we wouldn't get into an *American Beauty* situation, with Mum's asparagus having to be scraped off the wall.

'Well,' I started, 'I have a surprise for you.' With a flourish, I revealed the holiday brochure that I'd been hiding on my lap under the table.

Hey, nobody said I couldn't use diversionary tactics.

I handed the brochure to my mother, who stared at it, bemused.

'How would you like to go to Amsterdam?' I asked, as my father leaned over to look at the brochure.

'Why would we want to go there?' my mother replied, frowning.

'Why not?' I asked hurriedly. 'It's AMSTERDAM!' I shouted the last part, rather too excitedly.

'Yes,' Mother said, 'and it's full of drug peddlers and prostitutes.'

'That's as good a reason to go as any,' my father chuckled, before being quietened by a look from my mother.

'Great! So when do we leave?' Warren asked (the first time he had spoken all evening, not counting the grunts he'd given to indicate how many potatoes he wanted with his meal).

'*We* are not leaving,' I said, looking at him sharply. 'This holiday's for Mum and Dad.' With a scowl, Warren went back to eating his dinner.

I turned to face my parents. 'I booked it for you,' I explained to them. 'A long weekend in Amsterdam – as an early anniversary present.'

'Gracie, what a lovely thought!' Dad said, smiling. I smiled back, then turned to look at my mother. She wasn't smiling.

'Mum?' I asked her. 'You *are* pleased, aren't you?'

'Well, I would've preferred Paris,' she said, lips pursed.

I stared at her. 'But you're always saying how much you hate the French!' I exclaimed. Things weren't exactly going the way I'd hoped.

'I don't hate the French!' Mother protested. 'Why would you say such a thing, Gracie?'

I sighed. There was no point in arguing with my mother. I couldn't win.

'Sorry,' I said, not quite sure why I was apologising. 'But you'd like to go to Amsterdam, wouldn't you?' I asked hopefully.

'We'd love to,' Dad said, shutting my mother up before she even had a chance to open her mouth.

'Good,' I smiled.

So much for that idea.

I'd thought Mum would've been thrilled with Amsterdam. So thrilled, in fact, that she'd cast aside anything I said following the holiday announcement with a smile and wave of the hand. This, I could tell, was not to be. My distraction tactics had been a complete and utter failure.

Still, there was no point in putting off the inevitable any longer. I had to tell them.

'Mum, Dad,' I said once more, looking from one to the other. 'There's something else I have to tell you.'

I was about to blurt out the truth when my mother suddenly piped up.

'Oh my God, she's pregnant!' Mum exclaimed, looking so shocked it was almost comical.

'What?! Why would you think that?' I spluttered.

'Gracie, tell me it's not true,' Mother said.

'No –' I began.

'No, it's not true?' Mother interrupted.

'Yes –' I began, but was again interrupted by my mother.

'Yes, it is true?'

'NO!' I practically shouted. 'I am *not* pregnant!'

I looked around the now silent table and attempted to quieten my voice a little. 'I have a new job,' I told them, 'that's all.'

During the hush that followed, all I could hear was Warren (rather loudly it seemed) chewing his food. Meanwhile, my mother was staring at me and my father was staring at my mother, as if waiting to see what she would do next. Finally, she spoke.

'What sort of new job?' she asked tightly.

'I'm going to be the personal assistant to a TV personality,' I informed the whole table.

Warren stopped chewing and gave a snort of laughter. My father gave a little shrug, before returning to his dinner. My mother continued to stare at me.

'What?' she asked.

'I'm going to be the personal assistant to a TV personality,' I repeated.

'I heard what you said,' Mum snapped in response. 'What does that mean?'

Huh. Good question.

'Well...' I began, trying to think of something that would impress my extremely hard-to-please mother, 'it means that –'

'It means that she'll be making the tea,' Warren interrupted me.

'No!' I said quickly, desperate not to let my mother get the wrong impression. 'It means that I'll be reading film scripts, and helping with publicity, and attending film premieres.'

'Who with?' Warren quipped. 'One of the rejects from *Big Brother*?'

'No,' I said, completely without thinking, 'with Roman Pearson.'

'Never heard of him,' my mother said haughtily, as if I was making it all up.

'Roman Pearson?' my father mused. 'Is he the one from *Gladiator*?'

'No, Dad,' I said patiently, 'that's Russell Crowe.'

'Oh,' Dad said. 'Is he in *EastEnders*?'

'*Hearts & Minds*,' I told him.

'Oh, yes,' my father nodded, as if he'd known that all along.

'Never heard of it,' my mother said.

'It doesn't matter,' I replied, through clenched teeth. 'The fact is, he's famous and *I'm* going to be his assistant.'

Then I suddenly remembered my contract of employment and the security clause I'd agreed to. And already broken twice. 'Oh, but you can't tell anyone,' I informed them, 'it's supposed to be top secret.'

'Why would I tell anyone?' my mother said disapprovingly. 'The last thing I want is for everyone to know what a mess my daughter's made of her life.'

And with that, she stood up and walked out of the room, all the time ignoring the rest of us.

After a few moments passed and she didn't return, my father sighed loudly, then stood up and made his way after her. I looked over at Warren, who was still contentedly eating his dinner.

'She'll be back,' I said confidently. Warren shrugged, but didn't stop eating to bother with a reply. 'She'll be back,' I said again.

But she didn't come back.

❄ ❄ ❄

After two days of being completely ignored by my mother, I could take no more. You'd think I'd be pleased that I was finally getting some peace and quiet, and a respite from her lectures and scoldings. But no – somehow her silent disapproval of the choice I'd made was even worse than her usual disposition. And it was affecting the whole household.

Even Warren had taken it upon himself to substitute the awkward silence currently invading our home with a conversation topic of his very own.

'I know how you can get back in Mum's good books,' he told me confidently, as we sat together on the garden patio, enjoying the Saturday morning sunshine.

I looked up from the book I was reading – *Wuthering*

Heights. I'd not yet managed to get past the halfway point in the saga of Heathcliff and Catherine (this after three attempts) and was determined to read the book from start to finish on this occasion. Therefore, I didn't particularly appreciate Warren's (most probably pointless) interruption.

'I'm not interested in taking part in any of your schemes, Warren,' I told my brother, before turning my attention back to Catherine's current predicament.

'It's not a scheme,' Warren sighed. 'Look, just hear me out, okay?'

'I don't want to hear you out,' I told him, without looking up. 'I want to read my book.'

'Why?' he asked. 'They probably all just die in the end anyway.'

I ignored him.

'Turn to the back of the book, read the last page, and you're all set,' he stated matter-of-factly. 'Why bother reading four hundred pages when one tells you all you need to know?'

I looked up from my book again, this time openly glaring at him.

'You're not going to shut up until I give in and listen, are you?' I asked, though I already knew the answer. Warren grinned.

'So I was thinking –' Warren started.

'Really?' I interrupted him, not being able to resist the joke, obvious as it was. 'Did it hurt?'

Warren scowled at me in return, but continued. 'I was thinking,' he said, 'of a surprise party.'

'And if you were thinking of Mum's birthday, it was

three months ago,' I informed him. 'I believe you forgot it.'

'Actually, I was thinking of Mum and Dad's anniversary,' he replied. 'You gave me the idea when you booked them that holiday in Amsterdam. And what better way to celebrate twenty-five years of wedded bliss than with a gathering of all their friends and family?'

'And you're doing this out of the goodness of your heart, are you?' I asked him.

'No,' Warren said, 'in case you'd forgotten, it's my eighteenth birthday this year.'

'So?'

'So I need a car,' Warren explained.

'You don't *need* a car,' I told him. 'You *want* a car. There is a difference.'

'Fine, so I *want* a car,' he corrected. 'But what better way to get one than to throw your parents a party?'

'I didn't get a car for *my* eighteenth birthday,' I grumbled. 'So why should I help you get one?'

'This isn't about me,' Warren said slyly. 'This party would benefit you more than it would me. *You're* the one Mum's not speaking to at the moment.'

'And how would organising a party she knows nothing about make her speak to me again?'

Warren considered that for a moment.

'Okay, so maybe it won't have immediate effect,' he admitted, 'but once it's been and gone she'll love you forever.'

I wasn't completely convinced. Who would be? But I had to admit, it was better than any idea I'd come up with.

'Okay,' I told him, 'I'm in. But only if you promise to organise the thing. I imagine I'll be very busy in my new job. I won't have the time to be booking halls, making invitations and what have you. That'll be up to you.'

'Of course,' Warren said, waving my concerns away. 'I wouldn't expect anything less. I just need one thing from you.'

'What's that?' I asked him suspiciously.

'Six hundred pounds ought to cover it,' he smiled at me. 'For now.'

I glared at him. 'Just how much money do you think I have?'

'Are you kidding?' Warren asked. 'You're Roman Pearson's PA – you must be earning loads.'

'I haven't even started working for him yet,' I reminded Warren. 'And besides,' I told him, 'my new salary is actually a little less than my old one.'

It suddenly occurred to me that I probably shouldn't have revealed that fact to Warren. I could only hope the admission would stop him constantly asking me for money.

I didn't consider it a step down to have accepted a job with a lower salary and less employee benefits. Yes, I was taking a risk – but I was sure my new career would end up being very profitable for me, both in terms of salary and personal satisfaction. However, I knew my mother would be horrified if she found out about my drop in earnings (yes, even more horrified than she was now).

'Just don't tell Mum, okay?' I requested of Warren.

'What's it worth to you?' Warren immediately grinned at me.

That was it – Warren had asked me that question *way* too many times. And so in response, I threw my book at his head. The plan was for him to block the book and catch it, but instead Warren ducked. Meanwhile, the book continued flying through the air, landing in our garden pond (no doubt scaring the hell out of my father's fish) with a loud splash.

As I groaned in dismay, Warren just grinned at me. Somehow he always seemed to come out of these situations on top.

'So what do you say?' he asked me.

'Fine,' I sighed, willing to do just about anything to shut him up. 'I'll give you four hundred to spend on the party – but that's all.'

'Great,' Warren grinned.

'But I want a breakdown of costs,' I told him. 'I want to know exactly where my money is being spent.'

'You got it,' Warren agreed, mock-saluting me.

'And you owe me a new book,' I grumbled at him.

So far this party had cost me four hundred pounds and a copy of *Wuthering Heights*. And we hadn't even entered the planning stages yet.

Why did I have a feeling this was all a terrible idea?

❄ ❄ ❄

I was dreaming again. Only this time I knew I was dreaming. Nothing that felt this good could possibly be real.

Cleo and I were stretched out on sun loungers, both looking fabulously thin and tanned in our bikinis. The setting was a tropical paradise: golden sands; beautiful blue ocean; palm trees…

And we were being served cocktails by two extremely hunky waiters. Who were wearing nothing but bow ties and some very flimsy sarongs.

It had to be a dream – and it was. A dream from which I was rudely awoken when my alarm clock went off with a sudden shrill ring.

Half-awake, half still relaxing in my tropical paradise, I reached out a hand and thumped the alarm clock into silence. Then I relaxed once more, closing my eyes and willing myself back to those golden sands.

It was Monday morning, I knew. But I also knew Mum would wake me again in about ten minutes or so.

She always did.

❄ ❄ ❄

I was in the process of asking my hunky, sarong-wearing waiter for another drink, while simultaneously flirting outrageously with him and squeezing his (rather quite impressive) biceps, when I was awoken once more. This time by the sound of a slamming door. This, I knew, was Warren – who couldn't bring himself to leave the house without letting everyone know about it, neighbours included.

It crossed my mind how strange it was that Warren was leaving for college quite so early. He didn't usually emerge from his bedroom until at least eight o'clock. To get up any time before that, he claimed, would be subhuman. And it wasn't until my half-open eyes strayed to the time showing on my alarm clock that I realised how wrong I was.

Warren wasn't running early. He'd left the house at his usual time, quarter-to-nine. I, however, was running nearly two hours late.

Suddenly, I was wide awake – and panicking. I hastily threw back my covers and swung my legs out of bed, slamming my knee into the bedside cabinet as I did so.

'OW!' I yelled, before sparing myself a moment to gingerly feel the affected area, which I knew would very soon be sporting an ugly grey-green bruise. I made a mental note to change my choice of outfit for that day from skirt (above-the-knee) to self-inflicted-injury-hiding trousers.

Standing up, I hurried to the door (careful to avoid any pieces of furniture along the way), threw it open, and ran along the hallway towards the bathroom. I dived inside, shutting the door behind me, and leapt into the shower as if I'd been training for the hundred-metre sprint.

Four minutes later, and following the quickest shower I'd ever taken in my entire life, I hurried out of the bathroom and over to my makeshift wardrobe – a clothes rail situated in the hallway (my room was far too small for a wardrobe and, indeed, for most of my clothes).

I grabbed my pre-chosen outfit from the rail and ran to my bedroom to put it on, before remembering my current need to wear trousers. One time-consuming trip back to the clothes rail later and I'd replaced the incorrect piece of clothing with my revised selection.

I raced downstairs just two minutes later, still buttoning

up my blouse, to find my mother in the kitchen, cleaning the worktops in an apparent attempt to make them sparkle.

'Why didn't you wake me?' I asked her irritably, throwing her an accusing glance as I hurried to the refrigerator.

'I didn't realise that was *my* job,' she replied, equally irritably.

'Mum, you *always* wake me,' I shot back, as I grabbed an apple, a yoghurt, and a bottle of water from the refrigerator, slamming the door shut once I was done pillaging.

'I saved you some breakfast,' Mum said, looking disapprovingly at the hoard of food in my hands. 'I made pancakes.'

'Well, that's lovely,' I said, through clenched teeth, 'but I don't have time for breakfast now, do I?'

'If you want to take responsibility for yourself, darling, then that's fine,' Mum sighed, 'but unfortunately that also means getting yourself out of bed in the morning.'

I was angry at her. It was quite obvious that she'd left me sleeping on purpose, knowing the consequences it would have.

'You could've woken me!' I snapped at her, as I hurried out of the room.

I grabbed my bag from where I'd left it by the front door and threw all that I'd gathered inside it, before swinging it over my shoulder. Without looking back, I hurried out the front door, slamming it behind me.

I was about two minutes down the road when I realised that something wasn't quite right – that my feet felt unusually cold against the hard, concrete pavement. I looked down. And found I was still wearing my slippers. My fluffy, pink slippers.

'Shit!' I swore (which was totally unlike me, but I really was at the end of my tether).

Unfortunately, my outburst was timed to exactly coincide with Mrs Higgins, our grouchy and God-fearing next-door-but-one neighbour, passing me on her way back from her early morning trip to the local greengrocers.

Mrs Higgins shot me a look of pure horror and disapproval, and I knew right there and then that this shameful incident would be recalled a hundred times over to Mrs Higgins' various acquaintances (most certainly including my mother) before the day was out.

Still cursing, but this time under my breath, I made my way back home again.

By the time I finally arrived at my new place of employment, I was nearly a whole hour late.

Not such a great start.

❄ ❄ ❄

Olivia looked up at me, eyebrows raised, as I entered the office. She didn't comment on my late arrival, but her look told me all I needed to know – she wasn't impressed.

'Sorry I'm late,' I said, giving her my most apologetic smile. 'It won't happen again, I promise.'

'That's quite alright, Miss Parker,' Olivia replied stonily, getting up from where she sat at her desk and coming towards me.

As she approached, I felt a sudden urge to take a step

backwards, but managed to hold my ground, even when she came to a stop right in front of me. She looked me up and down – starting with my head, travelling all the way down to my toes, and then back up again – like an army general inspecting his troops.

Seemingly satisfied with what she saw, or accepting it at least, she waved her hand towards a coat rack that was standing by the door. 'You can hang your coat up over there,' she told me.

Eager to gain some breathing room, I moved away from Olivia and hung up my coat as instructed. I turned back to find that she was still watching me. Without saying a word, Olivia walked across the room and came to a stop by a small desk, containing nothing but a computer and a telephone.

'You can sit over here,' she said, then waited – making it clear she expected me to do so right away.

Reluctantly, I made my way over to the desk and sat down behind it. To my great relief, Olivia then moved away; though she returned just a few moments later, dragging a rather heavy-looking grey post sack behind her. With a grunt, she thrust the post sack forward so that it landed by my feet.

I looked down at the post sack, then up at Olivia, awaiting instruction.

'Within that sack is all the letters this office has received in the past three days,' Olivia told me.

'Wow, not all bills, I hope?' I attempted to joke. But Olivia appeared to have had a sense of humour transplant. She didn't even smile.

'No, Miss Parker,' she said. 'Everything in that sack is for Mr Pearson – from his fans.'

'Oh,' I said.

I looked again at the sack, trying to estimate how many letters were inside. My guess was a lot.

'I'd like you to open these letters,' Olivia said, 'and read them on behalf of Mr Pearson.'

'Oh,' I said again, my illusions a little shattered now. 'You mean he doesn't actually read the letters himself?'

I looked up to find Olivia staring at me very strangely indeed. And then I figured out why. 'Not that *I've* written to him,' I quickly added, 'because I haven't.'

Olivia chose to ignore this.

'Mr Pearson would very much like to read all of the letters sent to him by his fans, but unfortunately he just doesn't have the time,' Olivia explained.

'So you just want me to read them?' I asked her.

'For now,' Olivia replied. Then she left my side and made her way back to her own desk, on the other side of the room.

I waited a moment in case Olivia decided to give me any further instructions. However, it soon became clear that I'd been given my task and was now expected to perform it. So, resigned to a morning of reading someone else's mail – I smiled, as it suddenly struck me how much my mother would've enjoyed this task – I opened the post sack and looked inside. There were a *lot* of letters in there – maybe three or four hundred envelopes.

It seemed a strange job to be handed to a personal assistant – and certainly not what I'd expected for my first day. But,

I reminded myself, it *was* only my first day. Olivia was probably just trying to ease me slowly into my new role.

And so I thrust my hand into the post sack and pulled out my first letter of the day (obviously a love letter, as the envelope was decorated with red hearts, carefully drawn on with a felt-tip pen). After opening the envelope, I unfolded the piece of paper that I found inside. The letter was written in scrawled, childish handwriting, on *Forever Friends* notepaper. I began to read:

Dear Roman,

My name is Charlotte and I am 9 years old. I will be ten on my next birthday which is in October. You are my favourite actor. I think you are a very good actor and that you are very handsome. Do you have a girlfriend? If you don't, can I be your girlfriend?

I already have a boyfriend. His name is Sam and he is 9 but I would rather be your girlfriend. If I was your girlfriend we could go to the park together and to the cinema and we could go swimming. We would have lots of fun.

Will you come and visit me? My mummy likes you too so she wouldn't mind. She says you are sexy.

Please write back.

Lots of Love,

Charlotte (Age 9)

x x x x x x x

'Oh, what an adorable letter!' I cooed, after coming to the end.

I looked over at Olivia, but she was paying me no attention at all. Still, I figured even Olivia couldn't fail to be moved by what this little girl had written, and I decided she should hear it.

'Listen to this,' I began, and I started to read: 'Dear Roman. My name is Charlotte and I am nine years old. I will be ten on my next birthday which is in October. You are my favourite actor. I think –'

'You are a very good actor and are very handsome,' Olivia interrupted. 'Do you have a girlfriend? If not, can I be your girlfriend?'

I stared at her, stunned into silence. 'Would you like me to continue?' Olivia asked.

'How did you know what the letter said?' I questioned her, a little intrigued and more than completely spooked. 'You got that practically word for word.'

'Miss Parker, we get hundreds of those letters every month,' Olivia sighed, 'and after the first fifty or so, I guarantee you won't find them nearly so adorable.'

'What do you do with them?' I asked her, my enthusiasm more than a little dampened by Olivia's attitude.

'Send them a signed photograph,' Olivia replied, now concentrating on her own work once more.

'Oh,' I said.

Not quite sure what to do next, I turned back to my desk. Which was when I noticed a pile of photographs stacked on one side of the desktop. I picked up the top photograph to examine more closely. It was a typical publicity head-and-shoulders shot, featuring Roman Pearson and his trademark sexy smile and come-to-bed eyes – and it had been hand-signed at the bottom in blue ink.

I put the photograph with the letter I'd just opened and left them to one side, making a mental note as I did so to slip one of those signed photos into my bag later as a present for Cleo.

Turning back to the bulging post sack, I pulled out another letter. This time the envelope was simple and plain; although as I slit it open, the unmistakable scent of ladies' perfume wafted out.

Sliding out the note from inside the envelope, I began work on my task once more. The letter, written in an elegant, almost classical style, began:

> *My Darling Roman,*
>
> *It seems forever since we last met, though it has only been six weeks. Six weeks? Is that really all it has been? I can still feel the touch of your hand on my skin, of your lips on mine. My body aches while you are away. I feel it throbbing with the anticipation of being with you once more.*
>
> *Oh Roman, when will you be here so we can make love again? I long to feel you inside me, to feel your warm, strong body pressing against mine, to touch your—*

'Okay!' I yelped, folding the letter shut and not daring to read another word, 'I think this one might be a personal letter.'

Grabbing the empty envelope, I quickly stuffed the letter back inside.

'Why? What does it say?' Olivia asked me from across the room, not even bothering to look up.

'Oh, you really don't want to know,' I replied, feeling myself blush at the memory of the words in the letter and their personal and private nature. 'Let's just say that it was obviously for Roman's – sorry, Mr Pearson's – eyes only.'

'Somehow I doubt that,' Olivia commented.

'You didn't read the letter,' I told her.

'It wasn't from Angela by any chance?' Olivia asked.

'I don't know,' I confessed. 'I didn't actually get that far.'

'Well, you might want to check,' Olivia said, still concentrating on what she was doing and not even affording me a glance.

'Okay. I'll check,' I said, still not convinced, and I pulled the letter back out of the envelope to do so.

Hastily, I turned to the very last page of the letter, trying not to let my eyes run over too much of its content as I did so. And signed at the bottom of the letter, with a single kiss underneath, was the name 'Angela'.

I looked back at Olivia. 'Is Angela Mr Pearson's girlfriend?' I asked, thinking how upset Cleo would be when I gave her the news.

'No,' Olivia said, 'Angela is a forty-six-year-old woman who is obsessed with Mr Pearson. Despite what she claims in her letters, she has never met Mr Pearson and has certainly never had sexual relations with him. Her letters are constructed from the fantasies in her head and nothing more.'

'So it isn't a personal letter?' I asked, just to confirm.

'Most certainly not,' Olivia said.

'So Mr Pearson won't mind me reading the rest of it then?' I joked, then immediately wished I hadn't as Olivia fixed me with her steely glare.

My fiancé cheated on me! I wanted to shout at her. *I have no sex life! I am an extremely desperate woman!*

But somehow I refrained from doing so and, with a sigh, I crushed the letter in my hand, tossed it into a nearby wastepaper bin, and reached into the post sack for the day's next piece of thrilling literature.

❄ ❄ ❄

'How was your first day, Gracie?' my father asked me that night.

I thought back over all I had done that day, or rather, all of the letters I'd read and, as it turned out, been expected to answer on behalf of Mr Pearson. I'd certainly read some interesting things and, despite what Olivia had said, I hadn't grown bored of the countless letters from adoring young girls that had fallen out of the post sack.

But still, it definitely hadn't worked out as I'd been expecting. Of course, I couldn't let my parents in on that fact.

'Lovely, thanks,' I replied, acutely aware that my mother, in the next room, was no doubt listening to our conversation. 'I think it's going to be a great move for me.'

And I hoped to God that my second day as Roman Pearson's personal assistant would prove that to be true.

Chapter Six

'When will I get to meet Mr Pearson?' I asked Olivia.

I was by now both curious about, and slightly irritated by, the continued absence of my employer. This was day two of my new, supposedly high-profile career. Lunch break had already been and gone and yet Roman Pearson was nowhere to be seen.

Worse still, I had spent the entire morning in the exact same way as I'd passed the whole of my first day in the job – reading and answering letters from an assorted collection of weirdos and obsessives, with just a few genuine fans thrown in for good measure. Needless to say, I wasn't exactly jumping up and down with enthusiasm anymore.

'Miss Parker, I sincerely hope you didn't take this job for the wrong reasons,' Olivia said, clearly intimating at something.

'What's that supposed to mean?' I threw back at her, desperately trying to mask my annoyance.

'Let's just say I hope you didn't accept this job out of any sort of affection for Mr Pearson,' Olivia said, almost smiling (which, coming from her, was quite a disturbing thing to witness).

'What makes you think that?' I asked her.

'Well,' she said, with her almost-smile, 'you do seem awfully eager to meet Mr Pearson.'

'That's because I was hired to be Mr Pearson's personal assistant,' I reminded her. 'Which is going to be a little difficult if he's never around.'

'He may pop in sometime this week,' Olivia said, 'or he may not. He is, after all, a very busy man.'

And with that, she got up and left the room, effectively ending our discussion. I could do nothing but stare after her, wondering just where I'd gone wrong. At what point had my dream job turned into a nightmare? And, worse still, what would I tell my parents?

Resigned to my fate, I turned to the pile of letters that had quickly built up on my desk, all waiting for a reply. And I was about to start reading again when a loud buzzing noise distracted me from my task. It was the downstairs intercom; someone wanting to be let into the building.

I hurried over to the intercom box, a feeling of intense anticipation building up inside of me. That is until I realised that Roman Pearson, TV personality, would have a key to the building and would therefore have no need to use the intercom.

But I answered the buzzing anyway as, if nothing else, it was driving me crazy – like a ringing telephone waiting to be picked up.

'Yes?' I asked, speaking into the intercom. I didn't really know whether or not to announce my name, or for whom I worked, though I thought it better not to. 'Can I help you?'

'It's Billy,' a man's voice came back. 'Can you buzz me in?'

I thought for a moment. Both the voice and the name sounded familiar – and then I realised why.

'Billy Ramsden?' I asked him.

'Yeah,' Billy replied. 'Is that Gracie? I didn't realise you'd started work already.'

'I started yesterday,' I replied, 'but at this rate, I'm not sure how much longer I'll be here.'

'Olivia getting on your nerves, huh?' Billy laughed.

'How did you guess?' I began, before realising that Olivia had returned to the office and was now standing right behind me.

'Come in, Billy,' Olivia said, sounding not at all amused. She buzzed him in before heading back to her desk.

'She heard that, didn't she?' Billy's voice came back over the intercom.

'Afraid so,' I replied.

Catching Olivia staring at me, I quickly left the intercom and returned to my pile of letters. A few moments later, I heard the office door open and I looked up to see Billy enter the room.

As I watched, he made his way over to Olivia's desk and flashed at her what he obviously thought was his best grin.

'Hi, Olivia,' he said easily. 'How are you?'

'Fine, thank you,' Olivia replied brusquely, obviously still smarting from overhearing Billy's earlier comment.

'I brought those photographs you requested,' Billy told her, handing over a small brown envelope. 'All signed by Roman.'

'How is Roman?' Olivia asked him. 'He hasn't visited for a few weeks now.' Then, as if this comment displayed some kind of weakness in her, she added: 'Miss Parker was wondering when she would get to meet him.' She nodded in my direction.

'Oh, *Miss Parker* was wondering when Roman was coming to visit, was she?' Billy asked Olivia.

Billy turned to look at me, still smiling, obviously amused by what Olivia had said. His smile, although subtle, was infectious and I found myself smiling back. 'I'll be sure to mention that next time I see him,' Billy said, aiming the comment directly at Olivia.

And then, to my great delight, he left Olivia's desk and crossed the office, approaching me.

'Hello again, Miss Parker,' he said, stopping in front of my desk, a little smile playing at the corners of his mouth. He seemed to be enjoying imitating Olivia's formal manner.

'Gracie,' I corrected him, smiling – still amused by the way he'd handled Olivia.

'Gracie,' he repeated, taking a seat on the corner of my desk. 'So how are you enjoying your new job so far?'

'It's been interesting,' I lied.

Well what could I possibly say with Olivia listening in?

'Really?' Billy asked, raising an eyebrow in surprise. He seemed to be all too aware that I wasn't telling the truth.

'Well, it's certainly been an eye-opener,' I admitted.

'I expect it has,' Billy smiled. 'Roman's fan mail has a tendency to be a little bizarre sometimes.'

'You're telling me!' I agreed. 'It seems like every woman in the country is in love with Roman Pearson.'

'Yeah, Roman does tend to have a strange effect on women,' Billy said. 'I've never quite been able to understand it myself.'

I picked up one of the signed photographs of Roman from the pile on my desk and studied it closely.

'Well, he is the quintessential tall, dark and handsome,' I pointed out to Billy.

'And doesn't he know it,' Billy agreed. Then he lowered his voice, obviously not wanting Olivia to overhear what he had to say next. 'You know what happened to Roman's last PA, right?' he asked me.

'No,' I said, 'Olivia didn't mention it. What happened?'

'She quit,' Billy told me, 'right after Roman dumped her.'

'They were having a relationship?' I asked him.

'*She* thought they were,' Billy said. 'But Roman just saw it as a bit of fun. It completely ruined their working relationship. She walked out of here the day Roman broke things off with her and she didn't come back.'

'I guess that explains why Olivia needed help so quickly,' I thought out loud, as I realised the speed of my appointment hadn't been so strange after all.

'Oh yeah, poor Olivia was swamped with work after that,' Billy agreed. 'Still, I'm surprised she took you on though.'

'Why are you surprised?' I asked him.

Truth be told, I felt a little put out by Billy's statement. It sounded like he was questioning my appointment. And I'd had quite enough of that from my mother, thank you very much.

'Roman has a habit of making the same mistakes twice,' Billy explained. 'And you're young, beautiful – you might just prove too tempting for him to resist.'

On another day, Billy's compliments might've made me blush. But right now, they annoyed me more than anything else. I mean, did he seriously think I had no self-control? I wasn't just going to jump into bed with Roman Pearson – with my boss. I wasn't *that* stupid.

'Look, please don't think I'm being rude,' Billy said quickly, 'because I don't mean to be. It's just that I know Roman really well – and I wouldn't want you to end up losing your job because of him.'

So that was it? He was worried about me? I was getting more confused by the second.

'I wouldn't make that mistake,' I told Billy confidently.

Billy smiled back at me.

'Glad to hear it,' he said.

And then the moment was broken by a persistent ringing noise coming from Billy's jacket pocket. 'Excuse me,' Billy said, as he took out his mobile phone and answered the call. 'Hello? Roman?'

I looked up sharply at the sound of Roman's name. Meanwhile, Billy frowned – though whether in response to my gesture or to what the caller had said, I couldn't be sure.

'Where are you?' Billy asked the caller, who I presumed was Roman. 'Yeah, I know it,' he continued. 'Wait there and I'll come pick you up.'

At that point he ended the call and turned back to Olivia. 'I've got to go,' he told her, already making his way towards the door.

'Is everything okay?' Olivia called after him.

'Everything's fine,' Billy called back, before disappearing out the door.

After watching Billy leave, I glanced at Olivia, whose eyes were still fixed on the empty doorway. Catching me staring at her, she quickly turned away, picking up her telephone to make a call. Clearly I wasn't going to get much conversation out of her today.

Feeling incredibly ignored, I finally returned to looking at the pile of letters on my desk. My head was still swimming with thoughts of Billy and the rather confusing conversation we'd just shared, but I picked up the top letter to read anyway. It began:

> Dear Roman,
>
> My name is Holly-Ann. I am 11 years old, nearly 12. I think you are a great actor and I have a question to ask you:
>
> Do you have a girlfriend?

I sighed. This was going to be a long afternoon.

❄ ❄ ❄

'Gracie, I've missed you so much!' Cleo said, hugging me tightly.

'I've missed you too,' I told her, hugging her back. 'I can't believe it's only been four days.'

And it *had* only been four days since I'd last seen Cleo, though what a long four days they had been. I'd waved goodbye to Cleo on Friday, shortly after waving goodbye to my old, boring job. And now it was Tuesday night, and Cleo and I had met up for dinner at our favourite restaurant.

'The office isn't the same without you,' Cleo complained, as we sat down at our table. 'I have nobody to talk to. And Penny seems to think that you leaving will have a negative effect on my work – that I'll get really depressed or something.'

'Oh no,' I cringed, 'she hasn't been having little chats with you, has she?'

'Worse,' Cleo grimaced, 'she's moved to your old desk for the whole of this week, so she can keep an eye on me and make sure I'm okay. Now I actually have to do some work!'

'Well at least it's only for a week,' I said, trying to cheer her up.

'Gracie, it's been so long since I did anything in that office that I can't even remember what I was hired to do in the first place!' she wailed. 'Although,' she added, suddenly perking up a bit, 'I did work rather late last night.'

'Let me guess,' I smiled, 'after office hours?'

'Way after,' Cleo said, getting excited, 'and Gracie, I have never experienced sex like the sex I experienced last night. It was animal – it was fantastic! I really think Jason's been working out.'

A loud cough suddenly interrupted Cleo's vivid reminiscence, and we looked up to see a waiter standing by our table, preparing to hand out menus.

'Thanks,' Cleo said, unabashed, taking one from him.

I, a little more embarrassed, avoided eye contact as he handed the second menu to me. I waited until he'd walked away before turning back to Cleo.

'You know,' I smiled at her, 'I think it's great you're enjoying yourself with Jason. I'm just not sure the whole restaurant wants to know about it.'

'Sorry,' Cleo apologised, 'was I a little loud?'

'A little,' I said, thinking back to a similar experience of my own, 'but you still have nothing on me.'

'So?' Cleo asked, quickly glancing over the contents of her menu. 'Are you trying to keep me in suspense or what? When are you going to tell me all about the delectable Roman Pearson?'

'There's nothing to tell,' I said. 'I haven't even met him yet. I did get you this though,' I told her, producing a signed picture – that I had earlier cunningly swiped – from my bag and handing it to her.

'Gracie! Thank you!' Cleo squealed. 'I'll treasure it forever!' She flashed the picture at me. 'Isn't he gorgeous?' she asked.

'I guess,' I partly agreed, 'but I can't really say how he looks in person, as he hasn't even had the decency to say hello yet.'

'He's probably just really busy,' Cleo said, echoing Olivia's earlier statement.

'Yes, but I'm supposed to be his personal assistant,' I argued. 'How can I do my job if I never see him?'

'Everything will work out,' Cleo told me sympathetically. 'I know it will.'

'I'm not so sure,' I confessed. 'I'm not even sure I made the right decision in taking the job. I mean, all I've done so far is open Roman's fan mail. And I have to work with this really grouchy, old – well, I don't want to say *bitch*, but...'

'Gracie, who cares what the job is?' Cleo grinned, obviously trying to reassure me. 'You're working for Roman Pearson!'

Her enthusiastic efforts didn't work, however.

'I may as well be working for the Invisible Man,' I told her glumly. 'I thought Penny and Jane were bad to work with, but this is worse. Roman's never around; I'm seriously beginning to think Olivia is the offspring of Satan...'

I rolled my eyes. 'Oh, and then there's this guy –'

'There's a guy?' Cleo interrupted me, her attention aroused.

'Billy,' I explained. 'He works for Roman.'

'Does everybody work for Roman but me?' Cleo grumbled. I ignored her.

'He thinks he knows everything,' I complained. 'And he's completely rude. Like today, he practically warned me not to sleep with Roman.'

'But surely that's a perk of the job?' Cleo grinned wickedly.

'Apparently Roman had a relationship with his last PA and she quit her job after he dumped her,' I told Cleo.

'So the moral of the story is – don't get dumped?' Cleo smiled.

'It's not even an issue,' I protested. 'Because I have no intention of sleeping with Roman Pearson – not that it would be any of Billy's business if I did. Besides, just because his last PA slept with him, it doesn't mean *I'm* going to.'

'Right,' Cleo agreed, 'of course you're not going to sleep with Roman Pearson. Why would you?'

'Roman's my boss,' I continued. 'And my job is important to me. I'm not going to jeopardise it just for a bit of fun.'

'Exactly who are you trying to convince here?' Cleo asked me.

'I'm serious,' I told her. 'Nothing is going to happen between Roman and me – not even if he gets down on his knees and begs me to go out with him.'

'Really?' Cleo asked. She looked disappointed. 'Don't forget, this *is* Roman Pearson we're talking about here. And God knows you deserve some fun, Gracie.'

'He's not even that good-looking,' I lied.

'You must have some seriously high standards if you don't think Roman Pearson's good-looking,' Cleo commented. 'Though I wonder if you'll feel the same way once you've seen him in person?'

'If I ever get to see him in person,' I grumbled.

'I'm sure he'll turn up sooner or later,' Cleo said. 'Just be sure to dress your best every day. Oh, and wear lacy underwear. You know, just in case.' She winked at me. 'Don't forget – every office has a stationery cupboard.'

'Thanks,' I told her, rolling my eyes, 'that's really helpful.'

'Glad to be of service,' Cleo said chirpily.

Cleo quietened down as our waiter reappeared. He dropped off the drinks we'd requested at the bar on our arrival, then took our orders as quickly as possible. This time, Cleo managed to keep the details of her sex life to herself.

However, you could always rely on Cleo to liven things up a little.

'Cute butt,' Cleo commented loudly, leaning out into the aisle to watch as our waiter walked away.

Several people sitting at the surrounding tables turned to look at us, their faces a mixture of amusement and disgust. They clearly didn't know what to make of Cleo (which wasn't entirely surprising, as most people didn't know what to make of Cleo).

Meanwhile, our poor waiter came to a stop halfway down the aisle, having obviously overheard Cleo's comment. I could practically see his butt tighten in his trousers in response to what she'd said, as if he was convinced that everyone in the restaurant was watching him. And he was right; they pretty much were (at least, all the ones who weren't looking at Cleo anyway).

'You're such a show-off,' I told Cleo.

'I know,' Cleo replied, smiling. 'I can't help it.'

As the waiter returned to the kitchen, the other diners returned to their meals, and the restaurant returned to normality, it suddenly occurred to me just how much I missed seeing Cleo every day. Working with her had certainly never been dull – even considering the monotony of my job. And now it seemed I had the monotony, but no Cleo. It wasn't exactly an improvement.

'I'm starting to think I made the wrong choice,' I admitted, as much to myself as to Cleo. Cleo looked at me in surprise.

'Deciding not to sleep with Roman?' she asked.

'Deciding to take the job,' I told her.

Cleo shook her head. 'No, you definitely made the right choice,' she reassured me. 'No question about it.'

'But what if it doesn't work out?' I asked, looking at her hopefully. 'Do you think Penny and Jane would take me back?'

'Not a chance,' Cleo said, sniggering. Then she must have caught my worried expression, because she suddenly stopped. 'Sorry.'

'Why not?' I asked her, a little hurt.

'Let's just say you're not exactly their favourite person at the moment,' she said.

'Has this got anything to do with me walking out?' I asked, already knowing the answer.

'You think?' Cleo replied, sniggering again.

Not knowing what else to do, I started laughing with her. Then, remembering my plight, I stopped.

'Seriously though – do you think they'd take me back?' I asked again. Cleo finally stopped laughing.

'Gracie, read my lips,' she said. 'Not. A. Chance.'

And that was that.

❄ ❄ ❄

Now I *had* arranged to meet up with Cleo again on Friday night. But, as ever, my mother had something entirely different in mind for me.

'I've invited Gretchen and her parents over for dinner on Friday,' she informed me. 'I think you should be there.'

'I have plans,' I told her immediately.

'With a man?' she asked, an air of hopefulness in her voice.

'No,' I sighed, 'with Cleo.'

'Oh,' Mum said, as if she had a sudden bad taste in her mouth. 'Her.'

'Look, I know you don't like Cleo,' I said, pretty much stating the obvious, 'but she's my best friend and she always will be, so you'd better just get used to it.'

'I remember when you used to say that Gretchen would always be your best friend,' Mum sniffed.

'Well, things change,' I told her. 'People change.'

'Gretchen hasn't changed,' Mum said proudly. 'She's still a lovely, level-headed young woman. I just don't understand why you couldn't have –'

'Turned out a bit more like her?' I interrupted, which was maybe a little unfair on my mother (who would never have actually voiced such an opinion), but I couldn't help but think that was what she was feeling.

'What I was going to say,' Mum said, scowling at me, 'was that I don't understand why you couldn't have remained friends with Gretchen.'

'We *are* friends,' I protested, although I knew that wasn't strictly true – not anymore. 'I'm going to be her maid of honour, aren't I?'

'Which is one of the reasons why you should be at dinner Friday night,' Mum said, somehow steering the conversation back to its original topic.

'I already told you – I have plans with Cleo,' I insisted.

'Then cancel them,' Mum ordered, in a tone of voice that made it clear she was *not* to be argued with, 'because now you have plans with me.'

❄ ❄ ❄

I did as I was told and cancelled my plans with Cleo – mainly just to keep the peace with my mother if nothing else (she wasn't really someone you wanted mad at you).

Which meant that after three more long days spent opening Roman Pearson's fan mail, without so much as a fleeting appearance by the man himself, I had nothing to look forward to on Friday night other than listening to my mother gush about how wonderful my former best friend was.

And although Gretchen, to her credit, had so far seemed suitably embarrassed by my mother's excessive praise, it really didn't make me feel any better – especially seeing as I'd been practically ignored all evening. I might as well have gone out with Cleo, as planned.

'So remind me, Gretchen,' Mum said, as we all sat around the dinner table – me, Gretchen, Mum, Dad, and Gretchen's parents (Warren supposedly had 'plans' with Amy this evening). 'What does Robert do for a living?'

As if she didn't already know.

'He's a doctor,' Gretchen replied.

'Oh, what kind?' Mum asked.

'He works in paediatrics,' Gretchen smiled, obviously proud of her husband-to-be.

Robert was Gretchen's fiancé. I'd only met him once before, at a party, though he and Gretchen had been dating for nearly two years. He was nearly twenty years older than Gretchen, although nobody seemed to mind this (no doubt if he'd been *my* fiancé, there would've been endless comments about the age gap). He was a doctor – a paediatrician. And in my opinion, he was a little *too* perfect.

(Not that I'm jealous, because he's completely not my type.)

'How lovely,' Mum said, 'a man who cares for children.' I knew exactly what was coming next. 'And should we be expecting the patter of tiny feet a bit closer to home anytime soon?' she asked.

My mother has a serious grandmother complex. And apparently having given up all hope of me ever finding a husband and giving birth, it seemed she'd turned her attentions to Gretchen instead.

'Give them a chance to get married first, Ellen!' my father said, as Gretchen blushed.

My mother gave him a look which quite plainly warned him to be quiet and butt out, before turning back to Gretchen.

'Speaking of marriage, how are the wedding plans going, Gretchen?' Mum asked.

'Great, thank you,' Gretchen replied. 'Although I was going to ask Gracie if she'd help me work out a seating plan for the reception after dinner.'

Gretchen looked at me expectantly, waiting for my response.

'Shouldn't Robert be helping you with that?' I asked, not really over-enthusiastic about the task.

'Well he would, but he's working very long hours at the moment,' Gretchen informed the whole table. 'He's very dedicated to his job.'

As heads around the table nodded in appreciation of

Robert's commitment to his work, I couldn't help but snigger.

'That's what David told me, you know – that he was working late.' I laughed again. 'Well, it turned out *that* was a big fat lie!'

Suddenly everyone was staring at me. I don't know why. I'd only told the truth.

'Honestly, Gracie!' Mum cried. 'I don't know what gets into you sometimes!' She smiled apologetically at Gretchen and her parents. 'I'm so sorry about Gracie's behaviour,' she told them, as if I wasn't even there. 'She just hasn't been herself lately. I might've put it down to a mid-life crisis, but she's far too young for that excuse. Perhaps a mid-twenties crisis though?'

Mum chuckled to herself, obviously very amused by what she'd said, and Gretchen's parents politely joined in with her. 'To be honest, I think Gracie's odd behaviour is all due to the stress of her break-up with David,' Mum continued. 'She was even silly enough to quit a perfectly good job to go and work for some man off the television.'

'Actually, I think it was very brave of Gracie to do that,' Gretchen said, smiling at me.

I didn't ask Gretchen how she'd already heard about my new job – I didn't have to. No doubt my mother had told Gretchen and her parents all about it, most likely wailing down the telephone at them about her irresponsible daughter. She'd probably even asked Gretchen to try and talk some sense into me.

Well it looked like that idea had failed. I couldn't help but smile at the thought of my mother's disappointment.

'Yes, how *is* your new job, Gracie?' Gretchen's mother asked me. 'Is it terribly glamorous?'

Well, what could I say? I couldn't very well tell them the truth now, could I? Not with my mother sitting there, waiting to say 'I told you so'.

'Yes,' I said, 'I suppose it is quite glamorous. After all, I'm working side by side with one of the biggest stars on television.'

'What's Roman like?' Gretchen asked, seemingly genuinely interested.

'He's very nice,' I told the whole table, blatantly lying through my teeth. 'He's extremely down-to-earth – not at all showbizzy. Although he does have lots of famous friends,' I added, hoping I wasn't contradicting myself.

'Really?' Gretchen's father asked. 'Have you met any of them?'

'Yes, quite a few already,' I replied, aware that my lies were in danger of spiralling dangerously out of control. 'Though I'm not really supposed to discuss what went on.'

'Of course,' Gretchen's father said, as he and his wife nodded their agreement. 'Well, it does sound very exciting.'

'It is,' I said, looking at my mother triumphantly. 'It really is.'

❄ ❄ ❄

'You're so lucky, Gracie,' Gretchen said to me later, after we'd gone up to my room to work on the wedding reception seating plan in relative peace and quiet.

'What makes you say that?' I asked, genuinely intrigued as to why Gretchen would think me lucky. After all, *I* was the one who'd caught my fiancé cheating on me in a restaurant bathroom.

'Because even after all that's happened to you, you've managed to fight back,' Gretchen told me. 'You've gone out into the world and done exactly what you wanted to do. Not many people would be able to do that.'

'Well, I wouldn't say it's *exactly* what I wanted to do,' I replied cagily.

Gretchen looked at me, not at all suspicious. 'Do you remember when we were kids?' she asked me. 'I always wanted to play at being nurses or teachers.'

I remembered it well. Unlike me, Gretchen had always been very focused on her interests, and had decided on her choice of career quite early in life. And so, just as she'd always planned, Gretchen now worked as a nursery school teacher. And as far as I knew, she loved every minute of it. Gretchen had discovered what had eluded me for so long – job satisfaction.

'But you were different, Gracie,' Gretchen continued. 'You wanted to play at being celebrities. You'd pretend we were at film premieres and parties and that lots of famous people were there. We used to dress up in your Mum's clothes and put on her make-up – we thought we looked really glamorous.'

I remembered that too. Those had been some of the happiest times of my life. You know, before crappy jobs, crappy men and that pesky little thing called adulthood had come along.

'But now you have a chance to do that for real,' Gretchen told me. 'And that's why you're so lucky – because you're doing what you always wanted to do.'

I looked at Gretchen's enthusiastic face. She really believed in all the lies I'd told at the dinner table. Which made me feel awful. Of course, those lies had been for my mother's benefit, not Gretchen's.

But as much as I wanted to tell Gretchen the truth, I didn't. I knew that if I confessed to her, then sooner or later the truth of the situation would get back to my mother. And I couldn't have that.

And so I kept quiet, and decided to let Gretchen believe my stories. After all, how much harm could a few little white lies do?

❄ ❄ ❄

Saturday morning, I awoke fairly late (my mother by now having completely washed her hands of the responsibility of getting me out of bed).

I'd been sleeping in at weekends quite frequently lately. I had no reason to get up, after all – my bed was warm and comfortable and, as I'd discovered over the past few months, the one advantage of sleeping alone was that there was nobody around to steal the covers.

In fact, I probably would've been content to stay in bed all morning, had I not heard an unusual rustling sound emanating from outside my bedroom door.

Climbing out of bed, I padded over to the door (a lengthy distance of at least three steps) – just as a folded piece of paper bearing my name suddenly shot into the room from underneath it. Resisting the temptation to immediately pick up the note and read it, I instead swung open the bedroom door.

Standing directly outside the door was Warren. I could see that I'd startled him, but he quickly recovered – Warren always did.

'It's the Creature from the Black Lagoon,' Warren quipped, pulling a face as he looked me up and down.

'What are you up to?' I scowled at him, while simultaneously trying to tidy my hair a little.

'Nothing,' Warren said immediately – a sure sign that he was definitely up to something. Probably something I wouldn't like.

'What's this?' I asked him, looking down at the note on the floor.

'That? Oh, that's nothing,' Warren said.

'Right,' I said, not convinced. 'So it's just a blank piece of paper, is it?'

'It's a little note,' Warren said, 'an update really.'

'An update on what?'

'On Mum and Dad's party,' he explained. 'I just thought I'd let you know where I am with the planning – so you don't worry.'

'Why would I worry?' I asked him suspiciously. 'You have it all in hand, right?'

'Of course I have,' Warren said. 'It's all under control.'

I didn't know whether to believe him or not. Warren was an accomplished liar – a fact he was immensely proud of, even if his so-called 'skill' didn't impress anyone else.

'So why the note?' I asked him. 'Why not tell me in person?'

'I didn't want to wake you up,' Warren said.

Warren being considerate? That'll be the day. Something suspicious was definitely going on.

'I wouldn't have been in bed all day,' I pointed out to him.

'Yeah, but I'm going out now,' Warren said. 'I'm going away for the weekend.'

Here we go – major excuse coming up.

'Dare I ask?'

'Rock festival,' Warren explained. 'I'm going with some of the guys from college.'

'Is there some sort of family gathering this weekend that I know nothing about?' I asked him.

'No,' Warren said. 'I really am going to the festival. It's not a lie.'

'Makes a change,' I muttered.

'You know,' Warren said, 'it hurts that you think so little of me – your own brother.'

'I have good reason to,' I reminded him.

Warren didn't have time to defend himself, however, as the peaceful quiet of the morning was suddenly interrupted by a blast of loud rock music and squealing of tyres. I was about to look out of the bedroom window, to see who was making such a commotion, when Warren answered that question for me.

'That's my ride!'

I turned around to look at Warren, but he'd already left my bedroom doorway and was heading for the stairs. It was too early in the morning to chase after him, so I let him go. He'd left me some information about the party, after all.

Picking up Warren's note from the floor, I began to read:

Gracie,
Remember that rock festival I was trying to get tickets for? Well, I got some. Will be away all weekend – back on Monday. While I'm gone, do you think you could take charge of the party organising? We still need to book a hall, a DJ, and the caterers. And we need a guest list.
Have fun!
Warren

With a very loud, exasperated cry, I crushed the note in my fist. This was Warren's idea of having things under control?!

I hurried to the window and threw it open. Outside, rock music blasted from the speakers of a battered old car, into which Warren was currently climbing.

'Warren!' I yelled out the window. 'Get back here now!'

Seeing me, Warren grinned and gave me a little wave. 'Thanks, Sis!' he yelled back at me. 'I'm sure I'll have a great time.'

And then he disappeared into the car, closing the door behind him.

As I watched in dismay, the car roared off down the road, tyres squealing in protest – taking Warren with it.

Feeling completely frustrated, I slammed my bedroom window shut. That was just typical of Warren – leaving me with all the responsibility! I really should've seen it coming. And after he'd promised me to my face that he'd do all the planning for the party!

This, no doubt, had been Warren's plan all along though.

You see, Warren knew my conscience wouldn't allow me to leave such things undone. Even when we'd been younger and Warren had consistently forgotten to do his chores, I'd always finished them for him – mainly because I realised these things needed to be done, and that if I didn't do them, nobody would. And I was getting the same feeling about the preparations for Mum and Dad's party.

But no, this time would be different!

This time I would make myself promise *not* to do the work for Warren. It was his responsibility and that's the way it would stay.

I wasn't going to make one phone call on behalf of my brother.

❄ ❄ ❄

'Yes, I'd like to make a booking for an anniversary party, please,' I told the woman on the other end of the line.

I was sitting on the kitchen floor – phone in one hand, *Yellow Pages* resting on my lap – silently cursing myself for breaking the promise I'd made just hours earlier.

'How many people will be attending?' the woman asked me.

'How many?' I echoed.

'Yes,' the woman replied, somewhat impatiently I thought. 'In order to give you a cost estimate, I need to know roughly the numbers you'll be expecting.'

'Oh,' I said. I had absolutely no idea how many people would be attending my parents' party. Suddenly, I felt extremely stupid indeed.

'I'll call you back,' I told the woman, then hung up the phone before she had a chance to argue.

Guess I should have drawn up the guest list first.

Chapter Seven

After an entire weekend spent planning a party that wasn't even my idea in the first place, I actually found myself quite relieved to be back at work on Monday morning.

That is, until I realised nothing had changed. One week after starting my 'exciting' new career and it still consisted of replying to Roman Pearson's fan mail which, by now, was getting to be a very repetitive task. Even the countless letters from Roman's adoring younger fans were proving to be more tedious than endearing. And as for the letters from Angela, Roman's not-so-secret admirer, well, they were just plain disturbing.

But with Olivia still ignoring me, and the mysterious Mr Pearson a continual no-show, I had nothing to do but read.

Selecting another envelope from the TARDIS-like post sack, I opened it up and pulled out the note I found inside; waiting for the same familiar words to jump off the page at me. This letter, however, was different. It read:

Dear Mr Pearson,

I realise what a busy man you must be, and how many letters like this you must receive each day, but please read this letter and give some consideration to what I ask before throwing it away or passing it on to your secretary to reply to on your behalf.

My daughter, Jade, is fourteen years old and is perhaps your biggest fan in the whole world. She has every episode of Hearts & Minds on tape and her bedroom is covered in pictures of you. She buys every magazine you appear in and has scrapbooks full of articles about you. She even sent you a birthday card last year, with a poem she had written for you, although she received no reply to this.

The reason I am writing to you is this: Jade was walking home from school last Friday when she was attacked from behind by a group of girls who punched her and pushed her to the ground. They then wrenched Jade's watch (which was a birthday present from her father) from her wrist and stole it, along with Jade's mobile phone, before running off and leaving Jade hurt.

Thankfully, Jade has recovered from her physical injuries, but ever since the attack, she has been frightened to leave the house. She refuses to go to school and thinks the only place she is safe is in her bedroom. Jade's friends have brought schoolwork home for her to do, but she has barely touched it, and she's hardly eaten a thing in the past week.

As you can imagine, I'm very worried about Jade, and I don't seem to be able to do anything to help. She wants to see her father, but he works abroad and cannot spare the time to visit at the moment. This is why I was hoping that you might be able to help me. If you could spare the time for a quick visit to Jade, or even a telephone call, however short, I'm sure it would help her enormously. I know this is a lot to ask, but Jade really is one of your biggest fans and I'm sure you could make all the difference.

My address and contact numbers are below. I would be happy to hear from you at any time.

Please consider this request. Thank you.

Yours Sincerely,

Ms Laurel Cooper

'Olivia, I think you should read this letter,' I said. Striding purposefully over to Olivia's desk, I held the handwritten note out to her.

'I thought you were past this stage, Miss Parker,' Olivia said, staring at me with disapproval. 'Obviously I was mistaken.'

'This is different,' I insisted, thrusting the letter towards her face. 'Read it and you'll see.'

'Very well,' Olivia sighed, taking the letter from me.

After a quick scan of its contents, however, she held the letter back out to me. 'Send them a signed photograph,' she said, apparently not moved in any way by the sad story told within.

'Did you actually read the letter?' I asked her incredulously.

'Yes,' Olivia said, 'and a signed photograph is the correct response.'

'This girl was beaten up and mugged!' I cried. 'Don't you think she deserves a little bit more than that?'

'Miss Parker, you may not have worked here long enough to realise this, but some people will say anything to meet Mr Pearson,' Olivia said. 'In fact, I wouldn't be surprised if it's the mother that's a fan, and not her daughter, as she claims.'

'You don't have a lot of faith in people, do you?' I asked, staring at her.

She didn't reply, instead going back to her work, the letter remaining in her outstretched hand.

Realising I was getting nowhere, I snatched the letter from her and stormed back to my desk. But once there, I didn't know what to do. How could I reply to a letter like that with a lousy signed photograph? If I were Jade's mother, I would've been insulted to receive such a thing, so why should Laurel Cooper be any different?

Then, just as I was despairing of ever finding a solution to this problem, the office door opened. And in walked Roman Pearson.

I blinked, not believing my own eyes. Yet there he was. Roman Pearson – TV personality, heart-throb extraordinaire. And it had to be said, he looked even better in reality than he did on television.

'Hi, Olivia,' Roman said, making his way over to her desk, while smiling his best smile.

'Roman!' she cried affectionately, and shot up out of her seat to greet him. I'd never seen her move so fast. 'What a nice surprise!'

She leaned forwards, clearly expecting a kiss in greeting. Roman obliged her with a peck on the cheek. 'How are you?' she asked him, with a somewhat mothering tone that I'd never heard her use before.

'I'm doing okay, thanks,' Roman said. 'How about you?'

'Very busy,' Olivia smiled at him. 'Your fans love you more than ever, of course, and we've had lots of correspondence in the past week.'

'We?' Roman asked, picking up on Olivia's choice of words.

Clearly he hadn't noticed my presence yet. Which was a little insulting, but I decided to seize my opportunity all the same.

'Excuse me, Mr Pearson?' I said, doing my best to appear confident and businesslike as I stood up and made my way towards him. 'I'd like to introduce myself.'

Upon hearing his name spoken, Roman Pearson turned around to look at me. Cleo, I quickly decided, had been right all along – he *was* gorgeous, if in an obvious way.

As in his photograph, Roman had dark-brown eyes, though his dark, curly hair was a little longer than it had been in the picture. And one thing I did notice was that Roman looked older in person – probably around thirty-two or so (which meant that his publicity shot was actually a good few years old). But it was the disarming smile which crossed Roman's face, reaching his twinkling eyes as they locked on mine, that stopped me in my tracks.

'Please do,' Roman said, still smiling at me intently.

His presence really was quite unsettling – but in a good way. I took one step forward and held out my hand for him to shake.

'I'm Gracie Parker,' I said, keeping eye contact with him. 'Your new PA.'

'Is that so?' he asked, shaking my hand. He seemed to be smiling and frowning all at the same time. 'I wasn't aware I'd hired a new PA.'

'That's the job I applied for,' I told him, slightly annoyed (he might've been famous, but that didn't mean he could treat me like I was stupid). 'Although all I've done since I started working here is reply to your fan mail.'

'Well, we'll have to see what we can do about that, won't we?' he smiled.

I snatched my hand back, determined not to be taken in by his charm.

'Yes,' I said boldly, 'we will.'

Roman laughed and turned to look at a person standing just inside the office doors. It was Billy Ramsden. I hadn't even seen him come in.

'You didn't tell me I had a new PA,' Roman scolded Billy.

'It must've slipped my mind,' Billy replied, rather unconvincingly.

Billy was staring at me. I just stared back at him – he and I both knew why he hadn't mentioned me to Roman.

'I find that hard to believe,' Roman said to Billy. He turned back to look at me. 'How could you forget about someone as pretty as this?'

I could feel myself blushing – something which Roman seemed to take great enjoyment in, as he grinned at me.

Looking down at the floor in order to avoid Roman's gaze, I suddenly realised that I still held Laurel Cooper's letter in my hand. To hide my embarrassment, I thrust it towards Roman.

'Here,' I said. 'I think you should read this.'

Roman took the letter from me and frowned. 'What's this?'

'A letter,' I told him. 'From the mother of one of your biggest fans.'

'Miss Parker,' Olivia began, 'I've already told you how to respond to that letter. Mr Pearson doesn't have the time –'

'I have the time,' Roman interrupted her, as he stood reading the letter. 'And if Miss Parker thinks this letter is important, then it obviously is.'

Olivia's mouth clamped tightly shut in an instant, and I couldn't help but smile to see her sit back down, silently fuming.

Once he'd finished reading the letter, Roman passed it to Billy to read. And as Billy scanned its contents, Roman turned back to me. 'What do you think I should do about this, Miss Parker?' Roman asked, looking directly at me.

'Well,' I said, desperately trying not to blush again under his intense gaze, 'I think you should go and visit Jade. After all,' I told him, 'she doesn't live much more than forty-five minutes drive from this office.'

Roman stared at me for a moment, as if contemplating this suggestion. Then he shrugged.

'Then that's what I'll do,' he said.

'You will?' I asked him, completely taken aback. I hadn't been expecting a positive response to my suggestion.

'Why not?' he smiled. 'As long as you come with me, of course. After all, you are my PA, are you not?'

'Yes,' I smiled back at him. 'I am.'

'Good,' he said. 'Then let's go.'

Roman started towards the door, only to find Billy – who by now had finished reading the letter – standing in his way.

'Roman, I don't think this is such a good idea,' Billy said. 'You can't just turn up on the woman's doorstep like that.'

'I can and I will,' Roman said. He took another step forwards, but Billy put out a hand to stop him.

'Why don't you call the girl instead?' Billy suggested. 'I'm sure that would mean just as much to her.'

Roman paused and, for a moment, I thought he was going to agree to Billy's suggestion. But then he turned to look at me.

'What do *you* think I should do, Miss Parker?' Roman asked me, for the second time that day.

I didn't know what to say, but I had to say something. Both Roman and Billy were waiting for my answer. Roman appeared confident that I would agree with him, while Billy seemed to be silently pleading with me to take his side.

'It's your decision,' I finally told Roman, trying my best to be diplomatic, 'you should do what you feel is right.'

'Did you hear that?' Roman asked, looking at Billy. 'It's *my* decision.'

Billy opened his mouth to speak, but Roman held up a hand to stop him. 'And I've decided that we should go and visit Jade,' he announced.

Roman started forward again. This time, Billy moved out of his way, letting him leave. Once Roman had gone, Billy turned to look at me.

'Are you ready to go?' he asked.

Clearly Billy was far from happy with Roman's plan, though it seemed he was willing to go along with it.

'Sure,' I told him. I grabbed my bag from underneath my desk and moved to join Billy by the office door. Meanwhile, Olivia sat behind her desk, glaring at me. I got the distinct impression that she wanted to be the one accompanying Roman on this little field trip.

'Don't take too long, Miss Parker,' Olivia warned me, 'there's still plenty to do here.'

'I'll try not to,' I agreed, though I was secretly hoping that the excursion to Laurel Cooper's house would take most of the rest of the day.

I followed Billy out of the office door and down the stairs of the building. Roman was nowhere in sight – apparently he was already way ahead of us.

'Why don't you want Roman to visit Jade?' I asked Billy, as we descended.

I'd found Billy's attitude towards Laurel's letter to be a little uncharitable, to say the least.

'It's not Jade that's the problem,' Billy replied, 'it's Roman.'

'What do you mean?' I asked him.

For a moment, Billy looked as if he was going to reveal

something important, but then he appeared to change his mind. He frowned instead – an expression that, on him, was quite endearing. Or at least it would've been if he hadn't obviously been hiding something from me.

'Just trust me,' Billy said. 'I've known Roman long enough to realise that these things never end well.'

'I'm sure it'll go fine,' I reassured him, as we reached the front doors of the building.

Opening the doors, Billy ushered me outside with a grim smile.

'Let's just wait and see,' he said, clearly not convinced.

❄ ❄ ❄

I was sitting in a car with Roman Pearson. Which, on a scale of one-to-ten – with one being normal and ten being absolutely unbelievable – was pretty much a ten. I had the sudden urge to call Cleo and scream down the phone at her that I, Gracie Parker, was in a car with Roman Pearson. But I managed to resist – just.

And then I realised that Roman was talking to me.

'Gracie?' he asked.

'Yes?' I answered, hastily snapping out of my daydreams.

'Can I call you Gracie?' he continued.

'Yes, of course,' I replied, regaining my senses.

Luckily, Roman, who was sitting in the front passenger seat of the car, wasn't actually looking back at me while we talked. Billy, however, kept checking his rear-view mirror – though I thought it a bit presumptuous to assume he was looking at me (he was driving, after all).

'Good,' Roman said. 'And you should call me Roman. No more of this Mr Pearson crap, okay?'

'Okay,' I agreed, not quite sure what to make of his tone of voice.

'Why did you want to be my PA?' Roman asked. 'Are you a fan?'

'Um, well…' I began, not quite sure how to answer for the best.

If I said no, Roman might be offended. But then if I said yes, he might think that was the only reason I'd taken the job in the first place. Thankfully, Billy saved me from having to make the choice.

'Don't answer that, Gracie,' he told me. 'You're not here just to boost his ego.'

Although I appreciated Billy's intervention, I wasn't so sure Roman would. When I chanced a glance at him, however, I found that Roman looked surprisingly unaffected by Billy's comment.

'Do you watch *Hearts & Minds*?' Roman asked, turning to look at me this time.

'Sometimes,' I admitted.

Roman smiled. 'I like that you're honest.'

'Thanks,' I smiled back.

'Are you single?'

'What?' I asked, surprised by the suddenness of the question.

'Are you single?' Roman asked again. 'Or do you have a significant other?'

'Roman,' Billy chided, 'that's not really any of your business.'

'Enquiring minds want to know,' Roman replied. He smiled at me with seemingly effortless charm, waiting for an answer.

'I'm single,' I confirmed.

'Really?' Roman asked, apparently surprised by my answer. 'I find that hard to believe.'

'Well, I *was* supposed to be getting married this year,' I told him, before I could stop myself.

'What happened?' Roman asked. 'You get cold feet?'

'Not me,' I admitted. 'My fiancé. He was cheating on me.'

'How'd you know?' Billy asked, obviously listening to my story, despite himself.

'I saw them together,' I said. 'That is, after I heard them together.'

'Ouch,' Billy said sympathetically. 'Sorry I asked.'

'That's okay,' I said. 'I'd rather know. Besides, I'm better off without him, right?'

'Exactly,' Roman said. 'And you're over him now?'

'Yes,' I said firmly. 'I'm over him.'

I didn't know if that was strictly true, but it felt really good to say.

'That's good,' Roman said, as the car rolled to a stop.

'This is it,' Billy said, as he turned off the engine. 'This is the address on the letter.'

Billy handed the letter back to Roman, who slipped it into his jacket pocket.

'Then let's go make a little girl very happy,' Roman said.

As if hit by a sudden burst of energy, Roman opened

his door, jumped out of the car, and started making his way towards the front door of the Coopers' house; all before I'd even unclipped my seat belt.

'Is he always like this?' I asked Billy, staring after Roman.

'This is one of his better days,' Billy replied, turning to look at me. I noticed he wasn't smiling.

'Oh,' I said.

'We should go after him,' Billy said, and climbed out of the car before I could ask another question. I couldn't do anything but follow.

The door to the house was already opening as Billy and I made our way up the garden path. A blonde lady in her late thirties looked out.

'Can I help you?' she smiled.

And then, as her eyes locked on Roman, her smile promptly disappeared – replaced with an expression of pure shock.

'You must be Laurel?' Roman asked the woman, flashing his endearing, friendly smile at her. 'I'm Roman Pearson. I got your letter about your daughter, Jade.'

Roman took the letter from his jacket pocket, unfolded it, and handed it to Laurel Cooper. This seemed to jog her memory, as she finally spoke.

'You've come to see her?' she asked, obviously not believing her eyes.

'Yes, I have,' Roman confirmed. 'I've heard she's a big fan.'

'Very big,' Laurel agreed. 'She just adores you, Mr Pearson.'

'Roman, please,' Roman said, smiling at Laurel.

That seemed to put Laurel at ease, as she smiled back. 'Won't you come in?' Laurel asked, opening the door a little wider.

Was it my imagination, or was Laurel flirting with Roman? Or was it the other way around?

Laurel stepped back to let Roman enter the house, something he did without hesitation. I looked at Billy, who motioned for me to follow Roman. So I did, with Billy bringing up the rear. Once we were all inside the house, Laurel shut the door behind us.

'Jade's in her room,' Laurel explained. 'I'll just go fetch her.'

'That's okay,' Roman said, 'I'll go to her – lead the way.'

Laurel, however, didn't seem so keen on that idea.

'No,' she insisted. 'You stay here and I'll get Jade. I'm sure she'd be embarrassed if you were to see her bedroom – it's covered in posters of you.'

Before Roman could argue, Laurel hurried upstairs, leaving Roman, Billy and me in the open-plan living room adjacent to the front door.

Billy looked after Laurel, frowning. 'Did that strike anyone else as odd?' he asked.

'Not really,' I shrugged. 'I know I wouldn't want Roman seeing *my* bedroom.'

'Why? Do you have posters of me too?' Roman grinned.

I didn't answer Roman's question. Instead, I picked up a framed photograph of a teenage girl and showed it to Billy.

'At least you know Jade really exists,' I smiled at him.

'Of course she really exists,' Roman said. He looked at Billy, obviously amused. 'What, did you think Laurel made her up just so she could meet me?'

Despite Roman's light tone, I was worried I'd gotten Billy into trouble, so I quickly answered for him.

'Olivia seemed to think so,' I told Roman, putting the photo back in its place. I didn't really care about getting Olivia into trouble.

'That's because Olivia's paranoid,' Roman replied, smiling fondly. 'Or at least, she is where I'm concerned. It's quite touching really.'

Laurel suddenly reappeared, making her way back downstairs. She was, however, alone – Jade was nowhere in sight.

'Jade is just getting dressed,' Laurel explained. 'She wants to look her best for you,' she added, smiling at Roman.

'I'm sure she's quite pretty enough already,' Roman replied with a smile. 'Just like her mother.'

I cringed, though Laurel beamed at Roman, delighted with the compliment. I wonder if Roman even realised he was shamelessly flirting? Who knows, perhaps he just did it with everyone he met. Well, every woman that is. In any case, it suddenly made me feel just a little bit less special in his eyes.

'Would anyone like some tea while we wait?' Laurel asked.

'That sounds lovely,' Roman answered for all three of us. 'Why don't I help you make it?'

With a smile, Laurel disappeared into the kitchen, Roman following after her.

'I'm sure she's perfectly capable of making tea,' Billy called after Roman, but to no avail.

Billy and I were left alone in the living room. Not knowing what else to do, I took a seat on the sofa. Meanwhile, Billy busied himself with studying the various pictures and photographs displayed around the room.

'Do you do this often?' I asked Billy. 'Visit Roman's fans, I mean?'

'No, this is a first,' Billy said, turning to look at me. 'Olivia usually keeps a pretty tight rein on Roman's fan mail. If it hadn't been for you, Roman wouldn't even have seen Laurel's letter.'

'Well, I'm glad he *did* see it,' I told Billy. 'At least he had a chance to make up his own mind about what to do.'

'Yeah, but you see, Roman's not so good at making decisions,' Billy told me, with a smile. 'You'll come to realise that once you get to know him a little better.'

Or in other words - I know Roman better than you do.

'How long have you worked for Roman?' I asked him, genuinely curious.

'Long enough,' Billy replied, although his comment was accompanied by an amiable grin.

'And how about the ever-cheerful Olivia?' I asked him. 'She certainly seems to be very fond of Roman.'

'Yes, Olivia loves Roman,' Billy agreed. 'Olivia would like to be permanently attached to Roman if that were possible. In fact, I'd say that she pretty much worships the ground he walks on.'

'Isn't she a little old for him?' I asked, more than a

little disturbed by the image of Olivia and Roman together.

'I think it's more of a motherly love,' Billy said. 'She's been with Roman since the beginning, watched his career blossom.' He grimaced. 'At least, I *hope* that's all it is.'

'I don't think she likes me very much,' I admitted.

Apparently tired of pacing the floor, Billy came over to join me on the sofa.

'She's just got to get used to you,' Billy said, sitting down on the seat at the other end of the sofa. 'She's really quite nice once you get to know her.'

'I'll take your word on that,' I smiled at him, still not convinced.

'So why *did* you want to be Roman's PA?' Billy asked me, quite obviously trying to conceal his interest in the answer.

'Okay, first of all,' I smiled, 'I didn't *know* I was applying to be Roman's PA. Olivia didn't even mention his name until the end of the interview. It's not like I'm a crazed stalker or anything.'

'That's good to know,' Billy grinned at me.

Sitting so close to Billy, I couldn't help but notice the dimples that formed in his cheeks when he smiled. And the way his hair fell forward so that it nearly covered his eyes. It was completely annoying, of course – I just wanted to reach out and tuck it behind his ears.

And then, just as I was contemplating sitting on my hands to stop me doing just that, Roman and Laurel returned to the living room. Roman was carrying a tray, upon which sat four cups of tea and a sugar pot. He looked like such a perfect little house husband that I couldn't help but smile – all that was missing was the apron.

Roman put the tray down on the small coffee table that sat in the middle of the room, picked up one of the cups of tea, and then nestled down into the middle seat of the sofa, between Billy and me.

'Please, help yourselves,' Laurel said, as she sat down in the armchair across from the sofa.

Billy and I both took a cup of tea from the tray – Billy adding a teaspoon of sugar to his drink, I noticed. Meanwhile, Laurel took the remaining cup and sipped from it slowly, keeping her gaze fixed firmly on Roman as she did so.

Roman didn't seem to mind the attention though. In fact, he practically revelled in it.

'I was so sorry to hear about what happened to Jade,' Roman told Laurel. 'It must have been a dreadful experience for her.'

'It was terrible,' Laurel confirmed. 'She wasn't badly injured, thank God, but the attack really frightened her. It completely shook her confidence.'

Laurel smiled sadly. 'Not to mention mine,' she added. 'I mean, what sort of world do we live in when a fourteen-year-old girl can't walk home from school by herself in broad daylight?'

'Did they catch the girls who did it?' I asked Laurel.

'No,' Laurel replied, shaking her head. 'Jade couldn't identify her attackers and no witnesses came forward. I called Jade's phone in case anyone answered, but all I got was the voicemail. The police are keeping an eye out for her watch though; they think the girls might try and sell it.' Laurel sighed. 'Jade loved that watch – it was a present from her father.'

'She must have been distraught at losing it?' Roman asked sympathetically.

'She was,' Laurel confirmed, 'but when her father came home –'

Laurel stopped abruptly. 'When her father *comes* home,' she tried again, 'he's promised to buy her a new watch.' Laurel smiled at us, before suddenly putting down her cup of tea and standing up. 'I'll just go check on Jade,' she said. 'I can't imagine what's taking her so long.'

Before we could argue, Laurel swiftly made her way upstairs, disappearing from sight. Billy looked after her in bemusement.

'Something strange is going on here,' Billy said, turning to Roman. 'Shouldn't Jade have raced down the stairs to meet you by now?'

'You heard Laurel,' Roman reminded him, not at all suspicious, 'Jade wants to look her best for me.'

'And when you're a fourteen-year-old girl, that can take a while,' I pointed out.

Roman laughed and turned to look at me. I was sitting closer to him than I had been to Billy and could see practically every line on his face. He had stubble covering his jaw and chin that was just the right length to be deemed sexy, and his eyes danced when he smiled. It was extremely distracting.

'Gracie, I want to thank you for bringing Laurel's letter to my attention,' Roman said. 'I wouldn't have even known about Jade if it wasn't for you.'

'That's kind of my job,' I said, trying not to blush under his gaze.

'I'd like you to come out with me tomorrow night,' Roman said, smiling at me. 'I've been invited to attend a party, a charity event, and I can't think of anyone else I'd rather have accompany me.'

'I thought you weren't going to that party?' Billy asked Roman. Which was lucky for me, as I didn't have a clue how to respond to Roman's invitation.

'I changed my mind,' Roman said.

'Are you sure that's such a good idea?' Billy asked, looking at Roman pointedly. A silent look seemed to pass between the two of them.

'Yes, I think it'll be the perfect opportunity for me to get to know my new PA,' Roman said firmly, then looked at me expectantly. 'Gracie?'

What could I say? He was offering to make my new job everything I'd hoped it would be – glamorous, high-profile and exciting. I couldn't very well turn him down now, could I? Besides which, Cleo would kill me if she ever found out I'd rejected Roman Pearson.

'I'd love to come,' I said, smiling at him.

'Perfect,' he said, smiling back.

Billy, however, didn't look so happy – though he didn't get a chance to comment further, as Laurel came back downstairs. She was still alone.

'Jade will be down soon,' she reassured us. Laurel looked at each of us in turn, seemingly at a loss as to what to do next. After wringing her hands together nervously for a moment, she smiled.

'Would anyone like some biscuits with their tea?' she asked quickly. Not waiting for a reply, Laurel disappeared into the kitchen.

'Something strange is *definitely* going on here,' Billy commented.

Which was when the front door suddenly opened and a man in his late thirties entered the house. The man was followed inside by a blonde teenage girl, whose face I recognised from her photograph. It was Jade.

'We're back!' the man called out.

He came to a sudden stop as he saw the three of us sitting on the sofa. Coming up behind the man, Jade nearly bumped into him.

'Dad!' she complained.

But Jade's annoyance at her father's clumsiness was soon forgotten, as she saw Roman sitting on the sofa. The girl's open jaw practically dropped to the floor.

'Hey! Aren't you supposed to be in your room?' Roman asked Jade suspiciously.

'Who are you?' Jade's father asked us, frowning.

'Dad,' Jade said, her voice an awed whisper, 'that's Roman Pearson.'

Meanwhile, a flustered-looking Laurel reappeared from the kitchen. 'I can explain everything!' Laurel cried, addressing the whole room.

Billy had been right all along – something strange *was* going on here. And I had dropped us right in the middle of it.

I guess that was the end of my date with Roman.

❄ ❄ ❄

It had been a quiet ride back to the office so far. I had a horrible feeling that Roman blamed me for the whole Jade debacle, though he hadn't yet mentioned what had taken place at the Coopers' house. And it had certainly been a memorable visit, if nothing else.

After begging Roman's forgiveness, Laurel had explained that while her letter had been genuine at the time of posting, the desperateness of Jade's situation had decreased slightly since then. You see, in the time since Laurel had written to Roman, Jade's father had answered his daughter's plea to return home, and had managed to get the girl out of the house and back on her feet again.

So it seemed Roman's visit had come a little too late (hey, was it *my* fault we had a huge backlog of letters to get through at the office?).

However, concerned that if she told the truth, Roman would leave, and Jade, who'd gone out for the morning with her father, would miss him, Laurel had lied to us. Apparently, Jade would never have forgiven her mother if she'd let Roman get away. And so Laurel had set out to keep us entertained in the hope that her daughter would arrive home in time to see her heart-throb. Something I guess she'd achieved.

We hadn't stayed for much longer after Jade's return though. Roman had been nice and polite to the teenager, posing for pictures and signing autographs. But he'd seemed eager to get away and, as if sensing this, Billy had ushered us out of the house as quickly as possible.

So as it turned out, Billy had known all along that dropping in unannounced at the Coopers' house wasn't such a great idea. Maybe I should have listened to him.

'Now, don't forget about tomorrow night,' Roman said, breaking into my thoughts.

I suddenly realised that the car had slowed to a stop – we had arrived back at the office.

'Tomorrow night?' I asked him.

'The party,' Roman reminded me. 'I'll pick you up at half-seven.'

'You still want me to go? I asked him, completely surprised.

'Of course I still want you to go,' Roman said. 'Why wouldn't I?'

'Aren't you mad?' I asked him. 'After what happened today…'

'That was hardly *your* fault,' Roman pointed out. 'I'm just sorry I couldn't get there in time to be more help to Jade.'

'I think just seeing you helped her,' I told him.

There's nothing like sucking up to the boss, is there? Although I did actually mean what I'd said to Roman. I was sure his visit would've helped Jade immensely.

'We'd better go,' Billy said suddenly, interrupting our conversation.

Billy had been as quiet as Roman all through the journey back. Every attempt I'd made to start a conversation with him had been met with either silence or a simple one-word answer, which had killed the topic off.

I'd obviously done something to upset him, though I had no idea what that something was.

'Yeah, I suppose I'd better get back to work,' I agreed, opening the car door.

'See you tomorrow,' Roman grinned at me, as I climbed out of the car. Billy said nothing.

Leaving the car behind, I headed towards the entrance of the building in which I now worked. I was about to press the intercom and ask Olivia to buzz me in, when I heard footsteps behind me and a voice calling my name.

'Gracie!'

I turned around to find that Billy had followed me out of the car. Wondering what he was doing there, I thought for a brief moment that he was going to explain why he seemed so upset with me. But instead, he said: 'Roman needs your address – for tomorrow night.'

'Oh!' I said. 'I didn't think of that.'

I rummaged around in my bag and found a pen and an old receipt, onto the back of which I hastily scribbled my address. I handed the piece of paper to Billy, smiling as I did so.

Billy didn't smile back. Instead, he immediately turned around to leave.

'Is everything okay?' I asked him, before he could walk away.

'Everything's fine,' Billy said, stopping to look at me. 'Why wouldn't it be?'

'I don't know,' I said truthfully. 'You just seem a little on edge.'

'I'm fine,' Billy said, without much enthusiasm.

I suddenly felt incredibly annoyed with him. 'Okay,' I agreed, 'whatever you say.' If he didn't want to tell me, that was fine – I didn't care anyway.

Stepping up to the intercom again, I prepared to press the button for Ramsden & Hunt. Finally, Billy spoke.

'Gracie, wait,' he said.

I turned back to face him, expecting an apology. I didn't get one. 'I don't think you should go to the party with Roman tomorrow,' he told me.

'What?' I asked him, annoyed. 'Why not?'

'It's just not a good idea,' Billy said. 'Roman's your boss – do you really think you should be seeing him outside of work as well?'

'As well as what?' I asked him. 'The only person I see at work all day is Miss High-and-Mighty Olivia. Besides, I'm supposed to be Roman's PA – it's my job to attend parties and things with him.'

'That's a little naive, don't you think?' Billy asked.

'I don't know what you're talking about,' I replied, genuinely perplexed by his attitude.

'Oh come on, Gracie!' he laughed. 'You don't honestly think Roman wants you there as his PA, do you?'

'Yes,' I said, 'I do.'

Annoyed, I pressed the button on the intercom, hoping Olivia would answer quickly. Ever efficient, she did just that. 'Ramsden & Hunt,' Olivia's voice sounded over the system.

'Olivia, it's Gracie,' I said. 'Please let me in.'

After a brief pause, there was a buzz, and then the door to the building unlocked. I immediately pushed it open.

'You won't fit in there,' Billy said, watching me. 'Why even bother going?'

'Because I deserve to,' I told him.

Without looking back at Billy, I quickly made my way into the building and up the stairs to the office.

Roman Pearson had invited me to a party, and I was going to go. No matter what Billy Ramsden said.

Or, as it turned out, my mother.

Chapter Eight

'Mum, I'm going out tonight,' I said firmly. 'I've told you that. I've already cancelled my plans for you once in the past week and I'm not going to do it again.'

'But the Stewarts are coming to dinner tonight, darling,' my mother said.

'You don't even like Abigail Stewart,' I reminded her. 'So why on earth have you invited her to dinner?'

There had to be an ulterior motive involved here; there always was where my mother was concerned. And I suspected that, despite Warren's supposed relationship with Amy, there might still be a dose of matchmaking going on between Mother and Abigail. I briefly wondered if I should warn Warren, though I eventually decided not to – he wouldn't have done the same for me.

'Gracie, why would you say such a thing?!' Mum protested. 'That's complete nonsense! I have nothing against Abigail Stewart!'

'Whatever you say.'

Leaving my bedroom, I made my way to the clothes rack in the hallway. I was attempting to get ready for my big night out, though my mother seemed determined to stop me. Which she proved by following me out of the bedroom.

'Surely whatever you're doing tonight can't be that important,' she said. It should've been a question, but she stated it more as a fact. Which it most definitely wasn't.

'I've been invited to a party by Roman Pearson,' I reminded her, as I searched through the clothes on the rack. 'I am *not* going to cancel on Roman Pearson.'

I found the dress I was looking for and carefully pulled it out. It was beautiful; and unworn. David had bought it for me back when we were still together (and I was still deluded). I had protested because of the price and the certainty that I would never actually wear it, but David had promised to find time in his busy schedule to take me to the opera, the ballet, or somewhere equally sophisticated, so that I could show off my new dress. Of course, that had never happened.

Still, I was going to have the opportunity to wear the dress tonight – and at David's expense too. I couldn't help but smile at the thought.

'I still don't know who this 'Roman Pearson' is,' Mum sniffed. 'I can't believe he's as famous as you make him out to be.'

'Believe whatever you want,' I sighed.

Quickly, I made my way back into my bedroom, shutting the door behind me. I expected my mother to intrude into the room again. But, to my surprise, she didn't.

I guess that meant I'd won the argument.

❄ ❄ ❄

Nearly an hour later, I finally emerged from my bedroom. I was ready. My dress was still a perfect fit and (in my opinion anyway) looked quite stunning. I had pinned my hair up in an elegant chignon, with just a few strands framing my face for effect. My make-up, though more noticeable than I usually preferred, was flawless (I'd somehow managed to avoid the typical misfortune of a noticeably large spot erupting on my face just in time to spoil my evening). My shoes were stylish, although surprisingly easy to walk in. And I'd topped the look off with just a subtle spray of my favourite perfume.

Brimming with self-confidence, I made my way downstairs. My father was the very first person I saw.

'Gracie, you look lovely,' he said, smiling at me.

'Thanks Dad,' I smiled gratefully in return.

'Bit overdressed for dinner though, aren't you?' he asked, then disappeared into the dining room.

'What?' I asked, confused.

I followed him into the dining room to find my mother setting the table.

'Oh, Gracie,' she said. 'I've put you over here, between your father and Martin Stewart.' She indicated a place setting at the table.

'What?' I asked again, not quite believing my ears.

'Well, you can sit elsewhere if you'd like,' Mum said. 'I'll put you next to Abigail.'

She smiled at me calmly, as if everything was fine and she hadn't just totally undermined my wishes. I tried my very best not to get angry (after all, I didn't want my face to look all red and flushed when Roman arrived), but I couldn't help myself.

'I already told you,' I said, trying to keep my voice steady. 'I'm not staying for dinner.'

'Don't be silly, dear,' my mother said. 'I've cooked extra just for you.'

'Well you shouldn't have,' I said, repeating myself, 'because I'm *not* staying for dinner!'

'Gracie –' Dad began, attempting to defuse the argument brewing between his wife and daughter. His efforts were interrupted by the sound of the doorbell.

'That'll be the Stewarts,' Mum said, making her way into the hall.

This time, I followed *her*.

'No,' I said, 'that'll be Roman.'

Mum opened the door. Abigail and Martin Stewart were standing outside. Mum looked at me triumphantly.

'Ellen!' Abigail cried, in a rather obvious false show of affection. 'How nice to see you again!'

'I hope you don't mind, but we've brought a little something along,' Martin said, handing my mother a bottle of (what looked like very expensive) wine.

'Oh, how lovely!' Mum said, her tone of voice matching Abigail's perfectly.

'Gracie?' Martin asked, looking me up and down. 'Well, don't you look delightful tonight?'

I cringed. Martin Stewart had always given me the creeps. 'You'll be joining us for dinner, I hope?' he added, leering at me.

'Yes,' Mum said, 'she will.'

I would've corrected my mother right then, but at that point my attention was focused elsewhere. On the long, black limousine that had pulled up outside our house, to be exact.

'Actually, I'm going out tonight,' I told them, as I watched the limousine. 'I have a date. With Roman Pearson – the TV star? And he's just arrived to pick me up.'

I nodded towards the limousine. Abigail and Martin turned to look, as did my mother (though she made a greater effort to hide her interest). After a few moments of stunned silence, Abigail turned back to look at me in disbelief.

'You have a date with Roman Pearson?' she asked incredulously.

Well, it never hurt to stretch the truth a little.

'Yes,' I smiled at her. 'Now, if you'll excuse me – I wouldn't want to keep Roman waiting.'

I grabbed my coat from where it was hanging by the door, folded it over one arm, then stepped outside. Abigail and Martin parted to allow me passage, watching my departure with barely-contained jealousy. This seemed to please Mother no end.

'Of course, Gracie has a very glamorous job now,' I heard her announce, as I made my way to the car, 'and we're all so very proud of her.'

I couldn't help but smile at my mother's outrageous lie, as the chauffeur who was waiting for me by the limousine opened the car's back door. I climbed inside to find Roman sitting alone on the back seat.

Now, for the past twenty-four hours or so, I'd been

spending an awful lot of time imagining just what this precise moment would be like. I'd imagined Roman, smartly dressed in his designer suit, handing me a single red rose, before pouring us both a glass of celebratory champagne.

What actually happened was quite different – and not nearly so romantic.

'Gracie!' Roman said, leaning rather uncomfortably close to me. 'You look beautiful.'

His breath, it had to be said, absolutely stank of alcohol. I tried to remember if it had smelled the same way the last time we'd met. But then it occurred to me that I'd never been *quite* this close to Roman Pearson before.

'Thank you,' I smiled in response, studying his face.

He looked as charming and attractive as ever, of course. Only there were bags under his eyes now and the beginnings of a beard covering his lower face, which he'd obviously still not gotten around to shaving.

It certainly wasn't how I was used to seeing him on television.

'Drink?' he asked.

But it wasn't a bottle of champagne he offered me. Instead, he pulled a half-empty (or half-full, I guess, if you're an optimist) bottle of Scotch from his designer jacket pocket and waved it in my face.

'No, thank you,' I said.

Roman shrugged and took a swig himself instead. If the amount he swallowed could be called a swig.

'Gracie,' he said, wiping his mouth with the back of his hand, 'we're going to have fun tonight. I can feel it.'

'Yes,' I smiled at him. 'I'm sure we will.'

So why didn't I feel convinced?

❄ ❄ ❄

'You're gonna love this,' Roman said, as the limousine pulled to a stop.

'Love what?' I asked. But even as I did so, Roman was already on the move, opening the car door.

As Roman stepped out of the limousine, the world outside suddenly exploded with blinding flashes of light. I shielded my eyes from the glare and it was a moment before I realised that Roman was leaning back in the car, holding his hand out to me.

'Well come on,' he said, with mock impatience. 'Our adoring public are waiting.'

Hesitantly, I took Roman's outstretched hand and let him help me out of the car. I didn't even have time to survey my surroundings before the lights exploded once more and I found myself squinting into the brightness. Soon my eyes adjusted though, and I could see where the lights were coming from – the flashbulbs of the waiting press photographers' cameras.

Although completely bewildered by the situation I found myself in, I had the irrepressible urge to smile, just as I always did when faced with a camera. And then I realised that I was grinning from ear to ear. I must have looked moronic.

I glanced at Roman for his reaction, but he was wearing a grin similar to mine, apparently totally at ease with the attention he was receiving. A few moments later, I realised

Roman had his arm around my waist, though by then he was already ushering me into the building outside which the limousine had stopped.

'The trick is to keep them interested by not giving too much away,' Roman explained. 'It'll keep them busy figuring out who you are.'

'Oh,' I said, not sure that was an entirely good thing, 'great.'

Once inside, I suddenly found myself being fussed over by numerous hands, as people in smart clothing greeted us and took away our coats. I somehow managed to hang onto my bag though, which I was quite pleased about.

Roman, looking completely unperturbed by all of this intense attention, took my arm and led me into another room, which turned out to be both deceptively large and full of people – many of whom turned to stare at us as we entered.

Just a moment later though, the attentions of those same people wandered elsewhere. Apparently our arrival wasn't that exciting to them after all.

I finally got my champagne when a waiter approached with a tray of drinks, offering them to Roman and me. We each took a glass – but while I was content to just hold mine, Roman made a start on his straight away.

As I stared at him, he polished off the drink in one go, placed the empty glass back on the waiter's tray, then took another full glass of champagne from it.

'Thanks,' he smiled charmingly at the waiter. The waiter raised an eyebrow, but said nothing and moved away.

Roman must've caught me staring at him, as he laughed

out loud and said: 'Don't worry. It's all free, you know!' before taking a sip of his fresh champagne.

'I thought this was a charity event?' I asked, confused.

'It is,' Roman said, laughing.

As I wondered just how giving away champagne to people who could afford to pay for it could possibly benefit any charity, Roman put his arm around my waist again. 'Let's mingle,' he said.

And he led me into the crowds of people.

❄ ❄ ❄

Two hours later, and after making roughly ten sweeps of the room, I found myself standing on the fringes of a group of people that anywhere else would have caused quite a commotion, but here were just commonplace.

Along with Roman, I was in the company of a children's TV presenter; an ex-reality TV star, who'd just released a book telling all about his co-stars; two members of a new girl band who were currently doing the rounds on *Top of the Pops*; a radio DJ; a football player and his glamour model girlfriend; and a soap actor, whose real name I didn't know.

I shifted from foot to foot as one of the girl band members (I had no idea which was which) launched into what seemed a blatant attempt at promoting her band's new single.

My feet really hurt. I mean, don't get me wrong, my shoes were great. In that they matched my outfit. But they weren't the most comfortable things in the world. And I'd been standing all night, as had everyone else. Hadn't these people ever heard of sitting down? I guess chairs weren't sophisticated enough for them.

'Roman?' a female voice asked from behind us.

Roman and I both turned to look, as did most of the rest of the group, although the girl band bimbo (I'm sorry, but she was) continued talking, totally oblivious.

'I didn't know you were going to be here tonight,' the (admittedly quite attractive) new arrival said.

I recognised her as one of Roman's co-stars. I think she played Jill, the next-door neighbour of Roman's character, Simon.

'Hi, Layla,' Roman said, without much enthusiasm. 'Nice to see you.'

Roman turned back to the group, who immediately all switched their attention back to the girl band bimbo, pretending to be listening attentively. Well, all except for the reality TV star anyway, who kept his eye fixed firmly on Layla.

I didn't know what to do, so I smiled with embarrassment at Layla and shifted my weight from my right foot to my left foot once more.

'Aren't you going to introduce us?' Layla asked Roman.

She took a step towards me, placing herself between me and Roman.

Roman turned to look at Layla and, after a slight pause, apparently decided to appease her. 'This is Gracie Parker. *My date*,' he said, particularly emphasising those last two words. He nodded at me. 'Gracie, this is Layla Morgan. She plays Jill on the show.'

'Nice to meet you,' I smiled at Layla. She didn't return the smile. Instead, she looked at Roman.

'What happened to that other girl?' she asked him, a sly smile playing at the corners of her mouth. Roman didn't answer her, so she prompted him again. 'What was her name? Jenna, was it?' Roman ignored her again. 'I liked her.'

'I don't remember anyone called Jenna,' Roman finally replied.

'No,' Layla said, smiling sweetly. 'You probably don't remember much of anything, do you?'

As I wondered just what point Layla was trying to make, the soap star (who I was referring to as 'Scott', as that was his character's name) sidled up next to me.

'Roman and Layla used to date,' he stated, as if that explained everything. 'Roman dumped Layla.'

'Oh,' I said, not knowing how to respond. 'What a shame.'

I looked back at Roman to find that he and Layla had been joined by another of their co-stars – a rather thin and gangly man in his early thirties, who played Eric, the requisite joker of the group.

'Roman! I thought you weren't coming tonight?' 'Eric' asked, looking a little uneasy at the prospect of a Roman-Layla reunion.

'I changed my mind,' Roman said bluntly, but without a hint of the rudeness he'd displayed towards Layla's queries.

'And he brought a date,' Layla said, tilting her head towards me.

I felt myself blushing, knowing I was under scrutiny. 'I'm not exactly –' I began to say, but 'Eric' had already crossed the gap between us and was right now shaking my hand.

'Nice to meet you,' he smiled reassuringly at me, apparently relieved there was someone available to talk to other than Roman and Layla. 'I'm Declan. I work with Roman.'

'Hi, Declan,' I said, just about managing not to call him by his character's name. 'I'm Gracie. I work *for* Roman.'

Declan laughed. 'Poor you,' he said.

'So did you hear about Patrick?' I heard Layla ask Roman.

Declan shot a wary look at the two of them, like an animal sensing danger. I did the same.

'What about him?' Roman asked with disinterest.

'He's been given a permanent contract,' Layla said, grinning. 'He made such an impression with his guest appearances this year that he's been asked to come back next series. Rick and Martha are planning on marketing him as the show's new heart-throb.'

Layla stared at Roman, waiting for his reaction, but his expression remained unchanged. 'Nothing to say, Roman?' she asked him finally.

Roman looked at her and I saw anger flicker in his eyes.

'You know, Layla,' Roman said sharply – and a little too loudly. 'The only reason you're even still on that show is because you're sleeping with the producer. Once he gets bored of you, it's over.'

With that, Roman stormed off, knocking Layla out of the way in the process.

'Hey!' she called after him, but he ignored her. 'Jerk,'

she muttered finally, though there was no way Roman could have heard her.

'Nice one, Layla,' Declan said, shooting her a look of disapproval.

'Oh, stop trying to play the diplomat, Declan,' Layla snapped back. 'It really doesn't suit you.'

And then she realised that the rest of the group had stopped their conversation and were staring at her instead.

'I'm not sleeping with the producer!' Layla insisted angrily.

Nobody argued with her.

I looked around for Roman and spotted him sitting down alone on the other side of the room. Ah, so they did have chairs then.

'Um, I should probably go and...' I started, before realising that I'd become invisible to these people as soon as my 'date' had walked away.

Seeing as the group were no longer paying me any attention, I made my way across the room towards Roman. Reaching his side, I realised he'd picked up where he'd left off with the bottle of Scotch in his pocket. He was almost at the bottom of the bottle and seemed content to continue drinking until it had all disappeared.

'Are you okay?' I asked him, though it was obvious that he wasn't.

Roman downed the rest of the Scotch, wiped his mouth with the back of his hand, and tossed the empty bottle onto the table that stood on one side of his chair, narrowly missing a flower arrangement that was serving as the table's centrepiece.

He looked up at me. 'Gracie, do you know what it's like to go from being everything to nothing at all?' he asked. 'One day you have everything you've ever wanted, the next day it's gone.'

'Yes,' I said, thinking of how happy I'd been with David, until that feeling had been cruelly snatched away, 'I do.'

There was another chair standing next to Roman's, and at that point I sat down on it – although more to ease my own pain than to comfort Roman. After all, he was a good-looking, successful, wealthy actor. How bad could his pain be? My feet, on the other hand, hurt like hell. I decided to use the opportunity to remove my shoes – just for a little bit.

'Do you want to talk about what's bothering you?' I asked Roman.

I slid my shoes off and attempted to massage my sore feet. It struck me how odd it was that I was doing this in front of Roman Pearson, though he did look pretty drunk, so I figured he wouldn't remember it anyway.

'Patrick Maguire,' he said, practically spitting out the name.

'Who's that?' I asked.

But when I looked up for Roman's answer, I realised he was no longer sitting next to me. He'd left his seat and was striding across the room to where a small group of people had just entered – fashionably late apparently. This didn't look good.

I grabbed my shoes up from the floor, and was about to squeeze them back onto my feet when I heard Roman's voice, raised above all others in the room, and knew I didn't have time for even that.

And so, shoes in hand, I got up from my resting place and made my way towards Roman.

After all, I was his PA, right? I was supposed to keep him out of trouble. Although it was looking a little too late for that.

'What are you doing here?' I heard Roman ask, as I reached the edge of the expanding group of people. I managed to elbow my way to the front of the crowd, which presented me with a good view of Roman.

He was standing extremely close to another man – a tall, dark and handsome specimen (Patrick Maguire, I presumed) – and was staring him straight in the face.

'Come to replace me, have you?' Roman asked him, then laughed and looked around the group, addressing everyone. 'My replacement has come to replace me. How ironic.'

'You're drunk,' Patrick informed Roman. 'I think it's about time you left anyway.'

'Oh, you'd like that, wouldn't you?' Roman said, turning back to Patrick. 'Then you really *would* be the big star around here. Well, it's not gonna happen.'

'You're just embarrassing yourself, Roman,' Patrick said.

And I had to agree with him. Roman was sounding pretty ridiculous right now.

'No,' Roman said. 'I'm telling the truth. You just don't want to hear it.'

'The *truth* is that you're a drunken, washed-up, has-been who's gonna be doing cheesy commercials, karaoke shows, and pantomimes for the rest of his career,' Patrick threw back at Roman.

Ouch. Bitchfest. A collective gasp went up around the group following Patrick's comment.

Roman didn't say anything to Patrick in return. Instead, he pulled back his arm, threw his fist forward, and aimed a punch at Patrick's perfect face. And that punch probably would've landed right on target too – had Patrick not managed to dodge Roman's fist.

The momentum from the swing continued carrying Roman forward though, and he lost his balance, toppled over, and ended up flat on his face on the floor.

Patrick said nothing more to Roman. He simply walked away. And one by one, the rest of the group that had gathered to watch the showdown followed him.

I was left standing there alone, barefoot, my shoes in my hands and my 'date' on the floor. The evening definitely wasn't turning out as I'd expected.

❄ ❄ ❄

'I feel terrible,' Roman said, without much enthusiasm. I half expected him to attempt an apology then, but he didn't. 'I think I've had too much to drink.'

'You don't say,' I shot back, trying not to sound too sarcastic but failing miserably.

Roman didn't seem to notice my tone of voice though. He was off in his own little world, smiling despite all that had taken place.

'But did you see the look on Patrick's face when I hit

him?' he asked with delight. 'He didn't even know it was coming.'

'You missed him,' I reminded Roman.

'What?'

'You missed him,' I said again. 'You swung and you missed and you ended up on the floor.'

'I didn't even get him a little bit?'

'No,' I said, starting to feel very agitated.

And I had good reason to feel that way. Roman and I were still at the party, but we'd been exiled to the cloakroom. We were currently sitting on the cloakroom floor, our backs against the wall, surrounded by coats of the rich and famous.

At any other time, I might've been playing a game of match the coat to its celebrity owner (in addition to snooping through the pockets for any potentially interesting discoveries), but right now I was too exhausted. All I could do was sit.

However, Roman, it seemed, had other ideas.

'Let's go,' Roman said, getting unsteadily to his feet. 'This party sucks.'

I was about to grab Roman by the arm and drag him back down again but, as it turned out, I didn't need to bother. A clearly-drunk Roman fell back down of his own accord.

'And I suppose you're going to drive?' I asked him.

'We could take the limo,' Roman suggested.

'Good idea,' I said. 'We'll just walk out the front door past all those press photographers. I'm sure they'd love that.'

'Publicity is good,' Roman said, as if the fact had been drummed into him.

'Not that kind of publicity,' I replied. 'Besides, Billy said to stay here. Let's do what he says.'

'I'm always doing what Billy says,' Roman grumbled, though he kept quiet after that.

Not knowing what to do after the incident with Patrick (except, that is, keep Roman away from the photographers lurking outside the building), I'd managed to convince my 'date' to accompany me to the cloakroom (though he hadn't had much of a choice – it was either that or get thrown out).

There I'd found Billy's number on Roman's mobile phone and had called him for advice. Billy had immediately volunteered to come down in person to sort out the problem – for which I was very grateful, as I wasn't sure I could handle Roman alone. Roman hadn't been too much trouble so far, but I continued to wait in anticipation for Billy's arrival.

Luckily, I didn't have to wait too much longer, as just a few minutes later, the door opened and Billy poked his head inside, looking around.

'Roman?' he whispered. 'Gracie?'

'We're down here,' I said wearily, directing his attention from eye to floor level.

Spotting us, Billy made his way over and crouched down beside me. He shot a concerned look in Roman's direction. I looked too. Roman appeared to be half-asleep. Which explained why he'd suddenly grown so quiet.

'What happened?' Billy asked.

'I think he had a *little* too much to drink,' I replied, suppressing the sudden urge I had to giggle at the absurdity of the situation.

'I can see that,' Billy snapped back. 'What did he do?'

'Tried to hit Patrick Maguire,' I replied, slightly offended by Billy's tone of voice. 'He missed.'

'Has anyone gotten a photo of him like this?'

'No!' I said, openly annoyed now. 'I told you I'd keep him away from the photographers, didn't I?'

'We need to get him out of here,' Billy said, standing up and making his way over to Roman's other side. 'You'll have to help me move him though.'

'I don't remember that being in my job description,' I shot back at him.

'I warned you not to come tonight,' Billy said. I watched as he crouched down and draped one of Roman's arms around his neck. 'I'm not trying to say I told you so, but –'

'But you told me so?' I interrupted. 'Or rather, you gave me some lame excuse why I shouldn't go out with Roman. Though it's funny – I don't remember the words "lousy drunk" being mentioned.'

I was really quite angry now – my evening had already been ruined and now Billy was making it even worse. 'You know, I think I should just leave,' I told Billy, getting to my feet. 'I can catch a taxi home.'

I waited for Billy to say something – to try and stop me leaving – but he kept quiet, his attention on Roman. So instead I rifled through the coats in the cloakroom until I found mine (not a particularly difficult search, considering it was the only one present not created by a top fashion designer), slipped the garment on, then made my way towards the cloakroom door.

'You won't get very far without your shoes,' I heard Billy say behind me.

I stopped and turned around. My shoes (which I hadn't put back on my feet, due to the fact that they wouldn't actually go back on) were still sitting on the floor where I'd left them. 'Why did you need to take your shoes off anyway?' Billy asked.

'Because they're not Jimmy Choo,' I said sarcastically, as I walked over and snatched the offending items up from the floor.

I had turned my back and was making my way towards the door once again, when Billy had a sudden change of heart.

'Gracie, wait,' he said, so imploringly that I couldn't help but stop to hear him out. 'I'm sorry,' he continued. 'I shouldn't have snapped at you. If it weren't for you, we'd be in even more of a mess than we are now.'

'We?' I asked, turning to look at him. 'And this concerns me because?'

'Because I can't get Roman out of here discreetly without your help – and I know you'll help me because you're a good person and you always do what's right.'

'How do *you* know that?'

'It's like a sixth sense I have,' Billy grinned. 'I can read you like a book.'

'Don't be so sure,' I replied, my desire to walk away shaken by Billy's engaging smile. 'I might just be mean and leave you here.'

'But you won't,' Billy said assuredly. I could feel my resolve slipping away. 'And if you won't do it for me, at least do it for Roman.'

'Do you have any idea how infuriating you are?' I asked him.

He grinned again. 'It has been mentioned.'

I sighed. It looked like my evening was far from over. 'Okay,' I said, 'I'll help. Just tell me what to do.'

Chapter Nine

'Nearly there,' Billy said, sounding as breathless as I felt. Which was understandable, seeing as we'd just dragged Roman all the way from the cloakroom to the back of the building.

'Roman doesn't look this heavy on TV,' I complained.

'You get used to it,' Billy grumbled back.

'Have you had to do this before?' I asked him, surprised by what his comment had implied.

Billy didn't answer. Instead, he stopped shuffling forwards. Out of necessity, I also came to a halt.

'Can you get the door if I support Roman?' he asked.

I looked up, and was surprised to discover that we'd already reached our destination – a fire exit at the back of the building.

'I think so,' I said, and carefully ducked out from under Roman's arm, which had been resting across my shoulders.

I reached for the bar which would open the door, but then, struck by a sudden thought, I stopped. 'Wait,' I said, 'are you sure there won't be any photographers out there? I mean, won't they be covering all the entrances in case someone tries to sneak in and out?'

'Gracie, did you actually meet any of the people at this party?' Billy asked me, though he didn't stop to wait for an answer. 'They're publicity seekers, every one of them – they love the attention. The main reason they attend these events is to get their picture taken, so the press know they're not going to catch them sneaking out the back door. And besides, this was only a B-list event. Most of the photographers would've headed home by now.'

'That was B-list?' I asked, forgetting everything else Billy had said. 'But Roman was there.'

'My point exactly,' Billy said. 'Now do you think you could get that door open, because Roman's getting kind of heavy.'

As if to illustrate his point, Billy made a considerable effort to shift Roman's weight – but only ended up bearing more of the burden.

'Sorry,' I cringed, realising this probably wasn't Billy's ideal way of spending an evening either. 'I'll get it now.'

I pushed down the bar on the door, managing to get the fire exit open. Though of course, it wouldn't stay open. So while I held open our escape route with one hand, Billy brought Roman closer, until I could slip his arm around my neck again. (Roman had, by this time, fallen into a complete state of unconscious stupor.)

Together, Billy and I managed to carry Roman outside, where I found Billy's car waiting for us. Though thankfully, as Billy had predicted, there were no members of the paparazzi on the prowl.

After much fumbling, we managed to get Roman propped up and strapped in, in the back seat of the car. I chose to ride next to Billy in the front, though wondered if I'd made the right choice.

'Will Roman be okay by himself back there?' I asked Billy, as he started up the car.

Billy looked at me, then glanced into the back at Roman. 'He'll be fine,' he said. 'Just let him sleep it off.'

As Billy steered the car along the narrow back streets behind the building, eventually taking us out onto the main road, I considered his response. It was not unlike one he'd given me earlier that evening.

'You never answered my question,' I blurted out, sounding, even to my own ears, quite bold.

'I told you,' Billy said, glancing at me. 'Roman will be fine. Don't worry.'

He sounded a little uncomfortable, which I found surprising, but I carried on with my enquiries regardless.

'Not that question,' I said. 'Just before we came outside, I asked you if you'd had to do this before. You never answered me.'

Billy remained silent, apparently concentrating on his driving. It was as if I hadn't even spoken.

'And you're not going to answer me now, are you?' I asked him, not really expecting an answer.

I looked at Billy, waiting for a response. Any response. But Billy just stared straight ahead. Giving up, I turned instead to look out of my window, literally giving Billy the cold shoulder. 'Fine,' I muttered. 'Ignore me then.'

'Gracie, you don't want to get involved in this,' Billy said finally. 'Trust me.'

'I already *am* involved in this,' I said, turning back to

look at Billy. 'So why don't you tell me exactly *what* I'm involved in?'

'Why do you care so much?' Billy asked me. 'You barely even know Roman.'

'This isn't about Roman,' I replied. 'It's about you. You obviously don't trust me.'

'I do trust you,' Billy insisted. 'But for Roman's sake, the less people that know about this, the better.'

'I'm supposed to be his PA!' I said. 'Surely on a need-to-know basis, I need to know?'

'Olivia should never have hired you,' Billy said quietly. 'It wasn't fair of her to dump all this on you.'

'Why don't you let me be the judge of that?' I prompted him gently.

Billy fell silent for a moment, as if considering this. I decided to let him do so, rather than press him further for an answer. It turned out to be the right decision.

'Roman has problems,' Billy said. 'Big problems.'

'Go on,' I encouraged him, resisting the urge to throw out a sarcastic response.

'Roman likes to drink,' Billy finally explained. 'A lot. And as much as he tries to deny it, he has a major alcohol problem. Which isn't the best problem to have when you're in the public eye. You saw yourself how it affected him tonight. If the press had gotten a photo of him in that state, it would've been splashed all over tomorrow's front pages.'

Billy turned to look at me. 'Which is why I'm glad you were there with him.'

'After you told me not to go out with him?' I asked.

'I only said that for your own good,' Billy replied. 'I didn't mean to upset you.'

'I know that now,' I said pointedly, 'but it would've been a lot easier if you'd told me the truth in the first place.'

'Sorry about that,' Billy grinned. 'I was going for the moody and mysterious angle.'

'Well, you pretty much got it down,' I smiled back. 'You must've been taking tips from Roman.'

Billy considered that for a moment. 'You like him, don't you?' he asked me. 'Roman, I mean?'

'I like him better when he's sober,' I replied, glancing into the back of the car at the still-unconscious Roman.

He looked nothing like Roman Pearson, TV star, at that moment. In fact, he was bordering more along the lines of Roman Pearson, drunken tramp – and yet he was strangely still very attractive.

'Has Roman been getting any help for his problem?' I asked, choosing my words carefully so as not to offend.

'He's had a couple of sessions in rehab,' Billy confided. 'They seemed to do the trick for a while, but the past few months he's been getting bad again.'

'Any idea why?' I asked, trying not to sound like I was prying. Because I wasn't. *Well, maybe a little.*

'He's scared,' Billy said. 'He's frightened that one day soon he'll wake up and he won't be Roman Pearson, TV star, anymore – he'll be Roman Pearson, washed-up and out-of-work actor.'

'I don't understand,' I said, genuinely confused. 'Roman's a star. Everyone loves him. I have to plough through his fan mail every day, so I should know. Why would that happen to him?'

'In five weeks' time, Roman's contract with *Hearts & Minds* runs out,' Billy explained, 'and the producers have already told him that it won't be renewed.'

'You mean he's been sacked?' I asked, shocked. 'But he's the show's main heart-throb – he's been in *Hearts & Minds* since it began!'

'And now the producers are looking for fresh blood,' Billy chipped in, before I could continue further. 'They've already got Roman's replacement lined up.'

Suddenly, the reasons behind Roman's actions earlier in the evening became clear to me.

'Patrick Maguire,' I stated.

'Yep,' Billy grimaced. '*Hearts & Minds*, the next generation. Which pretty much leaves Roman out in the cold.'

'But he's Roman Pearson!' I exclaimed, my heart suddenly going out in sympathy to Roman. 'Surely he can get work elsewhere?'

'If he had an agent, maybe he'd already have something lined up,' Billy said. 'But unfortunately, he doesn't have an agent anymore. They had a little disagreement after Roman got the bad news from *Hearts & Minds*. It definitely wasn't one of Roman's better days. He lost his job, and his lifeline to new ones, in one fell swoop.'

'Wow. That explains a lot,' I said, as the pieces of the puzzle began to fall into place.

'Like why Roman's business is managed from one floor of a run-down old office block?' Billy asked.

'Now that you mention it,' I replied, cursing myself for

not having asked questions before. I had really gotten myself in deep this time.

'The office was originally used as Roman's fan club premises,' Billy told me. 'Olivia – she's been in charge of Roman's fan club from the very beginning – ran the place and Roman barely dropped by. Now all of Roman's business takes place there. Which I guess makes Olivia happy at least, as she gets to see a lot more of Roman.'

'So Olivia's acting as Roman's agent?'

'More or less. She's trying to hunt down some new roles for him, but I'm not sure how far she's getting. The trouble is, Roman's always played the young, single, heart-throb – and he's getting too old to secure those types of roles now.'

'That's ridiculous!' I exclaimed. 'Roman's not old! He can't be more than thirty-two!'

'Try a little higher,' Billy said, with a wry grin.

'Thirty-three then,' I conceded. Then a thought struck me. 'No, wait. I'm sure I read somewhere that Roman's thirty-two.'

'He *is* thirty-two,' Billy said, 'as far as the public are concerned anyway. But if you want his real age, you'll have to add six years onto that.'

'Thirty-eight?' I frowned, after doing my maths. 'Are you sure?'

'Well, if anyone would know, it would be me, right?' Billy asked, laughing. I wasn't quite sure what he meant by that, but I decided to let it slide – I had too many other questions to ask.

'Why would Roman lie about his age?' I asked.

'Like I said, there are a lot of roles that Roman's considered too old for now – even at his fake age,' Billy said. 'I guess it's just Roman's way of trying to roll back the years. But everyone involved in the business does it – and a lot of others as well probably. You've just got to remember the golden rule.'

'What's that?' I asked him, intrigued.

'The six-year rule,' Billy explained. 'To get a person's true age, always add six years onto the age they claim to be. Works every time.'

'Interesting,' I murmured, making a mental note to remember Billy's rule. I looked at Billy. 'So how old are you?' I asked him.

'I'm twenty-eight,' Billy replied with a smile.

I thought about that for a moment. Billy really didn't look that old, but I just knew he was playing with me.

'Okay,' I said, smiling back. 'So in reality, that means you're actually thirty-four then?'

'No,' Billy said, laughing. 'I *am* twenty-eight. I'm not one of those people who lie about their age.'

'Oh,' I said, feeling the smile drop off my face. 'Sorry.'

'That's okay,' Billy said. 'As long as you don't think I *look* thirty-four?'

'I don't,' I said quickly. 'You look twenty-eight. Definitely.'

'Well thank God for that,' Billy said, grinning at me. 'For a minute there, I thought I was gonna have to book myself in for a facelift.'

'Oh, your face is fine as it is,' I said, pretty much without thinking.

Billy smiled, apparently pleased with my comment. 'I

like it well enough,' he said. 'After all, not everyone wants to look like Roman Pearson. Especially not at the moment.'

I glanced at Roman, still asleep in the back of the car.

'So what happens next?' I asked Billy. 'Will he go back for more rehab?'

'If he can be persuaded,' Billy said. 'He's usually pretty stubborn about it, but after tonight I don't see he'll have much choice.'

Suddenly, I realised the car was slowing to a stop.

'Home safe and sound,' Billy said. I looked out of my window and realised he was right – I was home. And I was just thinking how it would have been nice for the journey to take a little bit longer, when Billy chipped in with an apology. 'Sorry you didn't travel both ways in the limo.'

'That's okay,' I said, looking at Billy. 'It's not your fault. Besides, I enjoyed the ride back more than I did the ride there.'

Billy smiled and unclipped his seat belt. 'Let me see you to your door.'

'Actually, I'm not sure that would be such a good idea,' I said quickly. 'I have a feeling my mother will be waiting up for me and, trust me, you really don't want to deal with her tonight. I think I upset her earlier, and she doesn't forget these things in a hurry.'

'You know what they say,' Billy smiled. 'Mother knows best.'

'Yes, well that just shows you've never met *my* mother,' I replied, while getting out of the car.

'I'm sure she's not that bad,' Billy laughed.

'Oh no, she's not *that* bad,' I said, looking back in the car at Billy. 'Compared to Hannibal Lecter anyway.' Smiling at Billy, I went to shut the car door. 'Thanks for the lift.'

'Gracie, about Roman,' Billy suddenly said. I stopped and listened to him. 'If any of this stuff about Roman's problems was to leak out, it would ruin his career for good. I mean, I know you won't say anything, but –'

'I'll keep it to myself,' I interrupted, as Billy seemed to be struggling for the right words. 'Cross my heart.'

'Thank you,' Billy said, smiling at me.

'No, thank *you*,' I replied. 'For trusting me. That means a lot.'

'No problem,' Billy smiled, obviously relieved.

'Goodnight,' I said, finally shutting the car door.

'Night, Gracie,' I heard Billy say in return, before the door closed.

And with that, I made my way towards the house, wondering just what lay in wait for me behind the confines of its walls.

I was in for a surprise.

❄ ❄ ❄

As I turned my key in the lock of the front door, I half expected my mother to wrench the thing open at any moment, intent on lecturing me on my earlier behaviour as soon as possible. But it didn't happen.

I cautiously stepped inside the house, certain that my mother would be lurking in the hallway somewhere, ready to pounce the moment I got home. But even through the darkness, I could see no one was there.

It was strange – very strange indeed. And it left me with a terrible feeling of foreboding. It seemed Mum had already gone to bed, without taking the opportunity to scold me for missing her dinner party. Something about this just wasn't quite right.

The only light in the hallway was coming from under the living room door, and I could tell the television was on in there. I decided it must be Warren watching TV, as my parents never stayed up this late.

I hadn't seen Warren since his disappearing act Saturday morning. Although he'd arrived home yesterday (as evidenced by the pile of muddy clothes he'd brought back from the festival with him), he'd quite conveniently gone to stay at a friend's house before I'd returned home from work. So I hadn't yet had the chance to tackle my wayward brother about his abandonment of the party preparations.

Quickly realising this would be the ideal opportunity for me to do just that – not to mention question Warren over what he'd done with the four hundred pounds I'd given him to pay for the party – I decided to pop my head around the door and say hello.

Big mistake. Because it wasn't Warren sitting in the living room at all. It was my mother.

I cringed at my error, and was just about to splutter out some excuse as to why I had to immediately depart for my room, when I realised Mum hadn't even noticed I was there. She was busy watching something on television, her eyes transfixed on the screen.

I glanced at the television myself, suddenly realising that I recognised one of the voices coming from it. On the screen was Roman Pearson, acting opposite Layla Morgan. My mother was watching *Hearts & Minds*!

'Mum?' I asked (against my better judgement), turning to look at her.

For a few moments, she didn't reply. And I noticed it wasn't until Roman was temporarily off-screen that she chanced a glance at me.

'Hello, Gracie,' she said pleasantly. 'Did you enjoy your evening?'

She turned immediately back to the television, while I gaped at her in amazement. It took me a few moments to recover.

'Mum?' I asked finally. 'Why are you watching *Hearts & Minds*? What's going on?'

I watched as my mother picked up a remote control and used it to pause the DVD she was watching, freezing Roman's features up on the screen. She looked at me and smiled, barely able to contain her excitement.

'Gracie, after you left earlier, Abigail Stewart told me how impressed she was that you were travelling in a limousine,' Mum began.

'Of course,' I interjected. 'And obviously I was only doing it to impress Abigail Stewart.'

Mother ignored me. 'Abigail wanted to know everything about your new job,' she continued. 'She was very interested in the whole thing.'

'I'm sure she was,' I said snidely, but was ignored again.

'I told Abigail I had reservations about you working

for an actor,' Mum went on, 'but she was very excited about it – and she explained to me exactly who Roman Pearson is.'

'You told Abigail Stewart who I was working for?!' I exclaimed, thoroughly dismayed. 'I told you that was supposed to be a secret!'

'It was just Abigail,' Mum said, waving away my protests as if Abigail wasn't the second-biggest gossip in town (my mother was the biggest, of course). 'Anyway,' she continued, 'Abigail told me all about *Hearts & Minds* and she made it sound so wonderful I just had to see it for myself. So Abigail offered to lend me her collection of *Hearts & Minds* DVDs, and I started watching them straight away.'

'How long have you been sitting here?' I asked, totally disorientated by my mother's strange behaviour.

'Nearly four hours,' Mum said, glancing at her watch.

'Then don't you think you should go to bed now?' I asked her, somewhat patronisingly.

She didn't comment on my tone of voice, however (which was just about unheard of where my mother was concerned). Instead, she picked up the remote control again.

'I want to watch the rest of this episode first,' she pouted. 'It's getting very exciting. Simon was about to tell Jill that he loved her when Jill got a telephone call saying her boyfriend, Mark, had been seriously injured in a car accident. Simon drove Jill to the hospital, but then Jill told Simon that she loved Mark and was going to stick by him – even though Mark slept with her sister, Megan.'

'Fascinating,' I said, though I thought it was anything

but. My mother, however, appeared to be enthralled by the whole thing.

'Personally,' she continued, 'I think Jill should have dumped Mark and gotten together with Simon. Simon's much nicer. He's very good, isn't he?'

'Who?'

'Your Roman Pearson,' Mum said. 'He's a bit of a stud really, isn't he?'

'Mum!' I cried. 'Are you trying to creep me out?!'

'He's got very strong-looking arms,' my mother continued, staring dreamily at the picture of Roman that was frozen on the screen.

That was it. I could take no more.

'I'm going to bed,' I announced.

Mum didn't even glance at me. 'Okay, dear,' she said, and pointed the remote control at the screen, letting the *Hearts & Minds* episode continue playing. She stared at the television, completely engrossed. It was as if I wasn't even there.

I wasn't sure what was going on with my mother but, deciding not to take it for granted that it would last, I quietly slipped out of the living room while I could.

No doubt she would be back to her old self by morning.

❄ ❄ ❄

I woke the next day to the sound of my alarm clock, which had rapidly become my best friend (not to mention my worst enemy) since my mother had relinquished her duty of waking me each morning.

So I didn't think it at all strange that I didn't see my mother during the thirty minutes that elapsed between my getting out of bed and making my way downstairs for breakfast. And when I found the kitchen deserted, I just assumed she was already seated at the dining table, enjoying drinking her tea while reading the morning paper.

However, after pouring myself a glass of orange juice and making my way into the dining room, I was surprised to find not my mother, but my father, sitting at the table.

I frowned at this peculiarity. 'Where's Mum?' I asked, before taking a sip of my orange juice.

'Your mother's having a lie-in,' my father said, looking up at me.

I almost spat out the orange juice I had in my mouth in shock. As it was, I just managed to swallow it in one huge gulp.

'She's what?' I asked, not quite believing my ears.

'She's having a lie-in,' my father repeated patiently.

'But she never lies-in,' I said, confused. 'She thinks it's a sin to sleep past seven in the morning. Is she ill or something?'

'I think the fact that she didn't come to bed until three o'clock in the morning might have something to do with it,' my father said.

'She was watching *Hearts & Minds* until three o'clock?' I asked, joining my father at the table.

'Oh yes,' my father said. 'She's a big fan now. And she woke me up to tell me all about it. *At three o'clock in the morning.* Personally, I don't know what all the fuss is about though,' he continued. 'I watched one of Abigail's DVDs with your mother last night, and I didn't think it was that good.'

'Actually,' I said, chuckling, 'it's not that good. It's pretty much a soap opera masquerading as serious drama.'

My father nodded his agreement.

'But your chap was quite good,' he conceded. 'Robin, is it?'

'Roman,' I corrected him. 'And he's not *my* chap,' I added. 'I work for him – that's all.'

My father nodded again, accepting my explanation. Unlike my mother, he wasn't one to pry into other people's business – even his own daughter's.

'Gretchen called last night,' he said, changing the subject.

'Great,' I grumbled, knowing that could only mean I was in demand again. 'What did she want?'

'She was wondering if you could pop over her house tonight and go through some more of the wedding arrangements with her,' my father replied, not picking up on my negativity. 'And your mother already said you would go.'

'She did what?!' I exclaimed, not quite believing the level of my mother's interference.

'Gretchen said to get there about seven,' my father said, before picking up his empty coffee mug and leaving the table; apparently sensing he might be in dangerous territory.

And he was right – I was fuming. But there was nobody around to take my annoyance out on.

So I just sulked and drank my orange juice.

❄ ❄ ❄

I arrived at work in a somewhat foul mood, following both my father's revelation and a sudden downpour of rain, which caught me unawares and out in the open without an umbrella.

My hair was soaking wet and would no doubt dry into a frizzy mess, my best shoes were making a squelching sound as I walked, and I had dirty splash marks all over my tan tights as a result of stepping in a rather muddy puddle.

However, I was immediately cheered up by the sight of a beautiful bouquet of flowers resting on my desk.

'When did these arrive?' I asked Olivia who, as usual, had declined to greet me on my arrival.

'About ten minutes ago,' she replied in a clipped tone, purposefully, it seemed, avoiding looking at me. I decided to have a little fun with her.

'Who are they from?' I asked her, trying not to smile.

She looked at me then, and I couldn't help but notice that she seemed a little flustered.

'I don't know,' she answered primly. 'I didn't read the card.'

'I'm sure you didn't,' I said, under my breath, as I turned back to my desk.

I picked up the bouquet and pulled out the card to read, finding I was both surprised and pleased by what was written on it:

Gracie,
Thank you for all your help last night. I'm sure Roman will be very grateful too once he wakes up! Hope you like these.
Billy.

I found myself smiling for the first time that morning. I certainly did like the flowers. And it was a lovely gesture on Billy's part. But I didn't have time to ponder over my gift any longer, as the telephone on my desk suddenly rang.

After carefully putting the bouquet of flowers back onto my desk, I sat down and picked up the phone.

'Ramsden & Hunt. Can I help you?'

Although I still hadn't received any official instructions as to how to announce my place of employment when answering the telephone, I'd picked up on Olivia's use of the name Ramsden & Hunt and had put it to use myself. Though not often, it had to be said, as the phones in the office were never exactly ringing off the hook.

And this call soon proved to be less than business-related.

'Gracie?' I heard a voice say. It was Cleo. I was about to greet her when she carried on regardless. 'Gracie, what were you thinking?'

'What was I thinking when?' I asked, genuinely confused.

'I called your house last night,' Cleo stated, somewhat accusingly. I waited for her to expand on that statement, but she chose not to.

'I wasn't home,' I finally said.

'I know you weren't home,' Cleo said impatiently. 'I spoke

to your dad. He told me you were out with the man you worked for.'

Thinking Cleo was finished, I prepared to jump in with an explanation. But she continued. 'He said the man's name was Ronan. Gracie, did he mean Roman? Were you out with Roman Pearson last night?'

'Only in the literal sense,' I replied, a little put out by her interrogation.

'And how exactly did you forget to tell me this?' Cleo demanded. 'I mean, I assume he just turned up on your doorstep and whisked you away without warning – leaving you no time to call and tell me what was going on. Right?'

'Um, not exactly,' I admitted.

'Gracie!' Cleo cried. 'You had a date with Roman Pearson and you forgot to tell *me* – your best friend!'

'Okay, first of all, it wasn't a date,' I told her.

Catching Olivia staring at me from across the room, eyebrows raised in clear disapproval, I quickly turned my back on her and lowered my voice. 'I'm Roman's PA,' I continued into the phone. 'Or, at least, I'm supposed to be. And we went to a charity event together – it was part of my work.'

'Bull!' Cleo cried. 'You went on a date with Roman Pearson!'

'I did not!' I protested.

'Did so,' Cleo retorted.

'This is stupid,' I said, trying to act like an adult for once. 'It wasn't a date. Honestly.'

'And I suppose you didn't even enjoy it?' Cleo asked mockingly.

'Actually, now that you mention it, it *was* pretty awful,' I said.

'Oh yeah,' Cleo said. 'I can imagine spending the evening with one of the most fancied men on television must have been pretty awful.'

'You have no idea,' I said, not picking up on her use of irony for a moment. Finally, I fell in. 'Oh,' I said, 'you meant that sarcastically.'

'No,' Cleo replied, her voice still dripping with sarcasm. 'I was serious. Now are you going to tell me everything that happened or not?'

I was about to answer her, when Cleo kicked in again. 'And I want all the gory details. I want to know where you went, who was there, what you did. I want to know what aftershave Roman Pearson wears!'

'Cleo, I can't tell you everything,' I said, trying to keep my voice down so Olivia wouldn't hear. 'Certain things happened last night that I promised to keep a secret.'

'Oh my God, you slept with him, didn't you?' Cleo yelled excitedly.

'What? No!' I replied, caught off guard. 'I didn't sleep with him!'

'What then?' Cleo asked me, still pumping for information.

'Cleo, I really don't think now is the best time to discuss this,' I said, practically feeling Olivia's eyes burning into the back of my head.

'Okay, so let's meet up,' Cleo said, her enthusiasm unabashed. 'We'll get together for drinks tonight and you can tell me all about it.'

'Yes,' I agreed quickly. 'Good idea. I'll come meet you after work – around six-thirty?'

That, at least, would give me some time to get my story straight. Cleo was my best friend, true. But I'd given Billy my word that I wouldn't say anything to anyone about Roman's drunken escapade. And I intended to stick to that promise.

'Great,' Cleo said. 'I'll see you then.'

'Okay,' I replied. But then I was struck by a memory from that morning – of something my mother had promised I would do. 'No, wait,' I jumped in, before Cleo could hang up. 'I can't meet you tonight. I'm sorry.'

'Why not?' Cleo asked, sounding a little hurt for a moment. Then she bounced back to her usual jovial self. 'Do you have another date with Roman?'

'No,' I admitted. 'I have to go to Gretchen's house after work tonight.'

'Gretchen's house?' I could practically hear the distaste in Cleo's voice. 'Why would you want to go there?'

'Gretchen wants my help organising some more wedding stuff,' I explained. There was a sudden silence at the other end of the line, so I added quickly: 'Believe me, I'd much rather be out with you, but I don't have a choice. I *am* supposed to be her maid of honour.'

'That's okay,' Cleo said, after a moment. 'I understand.'

But she obviously *didn't* understand. Which made me feel incredibly guilty.

'Maybe we could meet up at the weekend?' I suggested. 'We could spend a day together then?'

'I can't,' Cleo sniffed. 'I'm going away for the weekend.'

'Oh,' I said, feeling really bad now, 'anywhere nice?'

'Jason's taking me to a country hotel,' Cleo said.

'Well, that'll be...romantic,' I managed to say, though knowing full well that what Cleo and Jason were planning to spend the weekend doing would be less romantic, and more...frantic.

'Yeah, it'll be nice,' Cleo said. 'So I'll speak to you next week then, Gracie?'

'Okay,' I said. 'I'll call you on Monday.'

'Yeah,' Cleo said, 'whenever you can find the time.'

I was about to say goodbye, but Cleo hung up before I had the chance.

I knew I'd upset her – Cleo never hangs up the phone first. I toyed with the idea of calling her straight back and apologising but, with Olivia still watching me – no doubt waiting for me to get down to some actual work – I thought it better to let Cleo get our little disagreement out of her system first.

Which a weekend away with Jason should take care of nicely.

❄ ❄ ❄

So much had changed since the last time I'd seen Gretchen. As she opened the door of her parents' home (Gretchen and Robert had decided to take the traditional step of not living together until they'd been properly married), I wondered how long it would be before Gretchen asked me to spill all the details of my night out with Roman.

After all, Gretchen had thought my job was glamorous

and exciting back when I was spending all day, every day, opening Roman's fan mail.

However, it seemed I'd underestimated Gretchen. Patient as ever, she didn't raise the subject until nearly an hour after my arrival.

'So how is your job going, Gracie?' she asked me, clearly attempting the subtle touch.

'It's good,' I replied, wondering how much I could elaborate without breaking my promise to Billy (the confidentiality agreement I'd signed when starting work had long since been given up on).

'When I called your house last night, your Mum told me you were out with Roman Pearson,' Gretchen informed me.

'You know, I think you should go with the smoked salmon,' I told Gretchen, deliberately changing the subject.

'Do you think so?' Gretchen asked.

Gretchen and I were currently sitting at the kitchen table, going over options for the menu at her wedding reception. But so far, the only thing we'd decided upon was a rather tasty-sounding strawberry sorbet as one of the dessert options.

'It's *your* wedding,' I reminded Gretchen, 'you should go with what you like best.'

'But what if what I like best isn't what my guests like best?'

'So?' I asked, not at all bothered by that concept. 'They're getting a free meal – they can't really complain about what's dished up.'

Sometimes Gretchen was far too nice for her own good. Besides, I really liked smoked salmon.

'Okay,' she finally conceded. 'Smoked salmon it is.'

Gretchen made a note of her selection on the page in front of her. Typically for Gretchen, she was so organised that she actually had a notebook (quite cleverly titled 'The Wedding Book') containing all the information pertaining to her big day: contact numbers, guest list, menu choices...

Proof if anything that Gretchen was meant to be getting married, while I wasn't really cut out for the whole wedding thing.

'So did you have fun with Roman last night?' Gretchen asked, returning to her earlier line of questioning. Clearly, she wasn't about to give up anytime soon.

'Yes,' I smiled, 'it was certainly an interesting evening.'

'I bet you had the full five-star treatment?' she asked.

'We rode in a limousine,' I admitted.

'How exciting!' Gretchen exclaimed.

'Yes, I suppose it was,' I agreed, caught up in Gretchen's enthusiasm.

'And did you and Roman...you know?' Gretchen asked.

'No,' I said, laughing. 'I don't know.'

'Did he kiss you?' Gretchen asked, elaborating this time.

'No!' I said. 'There's nothing going on between me and Roman. We work together, that's all.'

I'd already stretched the truth far enough where Gretchen was concerned. I wasn't about to lie to her any further. 'You know, you're starting to sound like Cleo,' I told her.

'Oh,' Gretchen said, clearly distressed by this comparison (as I knew she would be).

Gretchen had never met Cleo, but I knew she'd formed a less-than-glowing opinion of her, based on information passed on by my mother. 'How is Cleo?' she asked, attempting politeness towards my absent friend.

'She's a little mad at me at the moment,' I confided. 'She wanted to meet with me tonight, but I told her I had to come over here to help you with the wedding plans. She wasn't too happy about that.'

'Gracie, you should've said something,' Gretchen said, sympathetic as always. 'We could have rescheduled tonight.'

'No, it's okay,' I told her. 'I offered to meet up with Cleo this weekend, but she already had plans. She's going to be off at some hotel having fun, while I'll be stuck indoors by myself – so don't feel too sorry for her.'

'Oh,' Gretchen said, 'okay.' A moment later, her face lit up. 'I have a fantastic idea,' she told me excitedly. 'If you don't have plans for this weekend, why don't you come over here on Saturday and stay the night? We can have a proper slumber party – just like old times!'

'Aren't we a little old for that?' I asked her, finding the thought a little scary.

'No!' Gretchen cried. 'You're never too old for a slumber party! It'll be fun – we can rent some videos and eat ice cream and give each other makeovers. Just like when we were younger.'

I must have looked extremely unconvinced, as Gretchen quickly moved onto another tactic. 'Please say yes, Gracie. Once I'm an old married woman, I won't be able to do these things anymore!'

'Okay,' I said, laughing at the thought of 'old married woman' Gretchen. 'I'll stay over this weekend. Just like old times.'

'Wonderful!' Gretchen said. 'It'll be so much fun, Gracie. Just wait and see.'

Gretchen was so full of enthusiasm for this slumber party idea that I wished I could believe her.

Unfortunately, I didn't.

Chapter Ten

Okay, I admit it. When Gretchen said we'd have fun, I should have believed her.

Saturday night, I found myself sitting on Gretchen's bed in my favourite non-sexy, but very cute, pyjamas. And I was having fun. It really was just like old times. At Gretchen's request, we'd banned all talk of her wedding. And at my request, we'd banned all talk of my job and Roman Pearson.

So we were just Gracie and Gretchen. For one night only, we could pretend we were still at a point in our lives where nothing else mattered but whether the cute boy at school that we had a crush on would ask us to the dance; whether we would be able to save up enough money to buy the expensive jacket that was the must-have look of the season; or whether our parents would allow us to stay out past curfew so we could go to that concert with our friends.

We'd started the evening by watching a film that was a staple of almost every sleepover we'd ever had during our teenage years. That film was *Grease* – which, of course, had prompted a number of instances during its running time where Gretchen and I had grabbed our hairbrushes and sung along to the songs we still knew word-for-word. (I won't mention the dance routines, but needless to say they were heavily improvised.)

And after watching the slumber party scene in *Grease*, Gretchen and I had been inspired to go for the full sleepover treatment. And so we'd busied ourselves with painting our toenails and slapping pore-cleansing beauty masks on our faces.

As a result of which, we were now both sitting on Gretchen's bed; our faces covered in what looked like green mud; hair pinned up messily in rollers that we'd commandeered from Gretchen's mother's dressing table; and with cotton wool pieces stuffed between our toes to allow the sparkling silver nail varnish we'd applied to dry successfully.

Oh, and we were eating ice cream – as promised by Gretchen. Meanwhile, I'd put one of those 'girl power' compilation discs in the CD player, and we were singing along to 'It's Raining Men' between mouthfuls of our tasty chocolate-chip-flavoured desserts.

At the same time, we were flicking through the pages of one of those celebrity gossip magazines (also borrowed from Gretchen's mother), reading the latest showbiz news together and envying the lifestyles of the rich and famous.

'I really like this dress,' Gretchen said, pointing to a picture in the magazine.

She was admiring a celebrity-sported outfit; one which neither of us would ever have the money to buy. 'I wish I could afford a dress like that.'

'Oh, I don't know,' I said, trying to make light of the

fact that we were just poor, ordinary, human beings. 'I think it makes her look kind of fat.'

Gretchen giggled, as did I.

She pointed to another picture, where an equally beautiful dress was being displayed on the figure of an equally beautiful actress.

'What about this one?'

'Hideous,' I said, though the dress was far from it. 'Absolutely hideous!'

As I scooped the last of the ice cream from my tub, Gretchen laughed and turned the page.

'This is nice,' I heard her say, but then she stopped. I could see her finger was frozen in mid-air, hovering over the picture in question. 'Oh my God!' she exclaimed.

'What?' I asked, leaning in closer to get a better look.

'Gracie, this is you!' Gretchen said, pushing the magazine towards me so I could see.

'Don't be stupid –' I started to say.

Until, that is, I got a closer look at the photograph. Gretchen was right. It *was* me. 'Oh my God,' I said, echoing Gretchen's earlier comment.

It was a photo of me with Roman, taken before we'd entered the charity event on Tuesday night. I looked stunned – like a startled rabbit, caught in the headlights of a speeding car. Meanwhile, Roman was smiling with ease, his arm around my waist.

'I don't believe this,' I said, still shocked. 'How did they get that photo so quickly?'

Gretchen took the magazine from me and flicked its front cover over so she could see the date of publication.

'It was only published today,' she shrugged, 'they must've added it in at the last minute.'

She turned back to the page on which the offending photograph appeared. 'I guess where Roman Pearson's involved, anything's possible.' She studied the page again, then smiled, and passed the magazine back to me. 'Gracie, have you read the caption yet?'

I took the magazine from her, glancing at the caption that accompanied the photograph. It read: *Hearts & Minds' Roman Pearson and mystery new girlfriend.*

'Is there something you're not telling me?' Gretchen asked, amused.

'What?!' I exclaimed, even more shocked. 'I'm not Roman's girlfriend! Why would they say that?!'

'Well, the picture's certainly very incriminating,' Gretchen smiled. 'I mean, just look where Roman's hand is!'

I studied the picture more closely, wondering what Gretchen had noticed that I hadn't. Roman's arm was around my waist, but his hand was hidden behind my back.

'You can't *see* where Roman's hand is,' I told her, confused.

'Exactly,' Gretchen said, still smiling.

Finally realising what Gretchen meant, I looked at her and rolled my eyes.

'This is just great,' I said sarcastically. 'Now everyone's going to think I'm dating Roman.'

'But the question is, are you?' Gretchen asked me. 'Are you dating Roman Pearson or not, Gracie?'

I was saved from having to answer Gretchen's obviously ridiculous question by the sound of a telephone ringing.

Gretchen sighed, then climbed off the bed, and stepped out into the hallway to answer the call from the upstairs extension. From my position on the bed, I heard mumbled talking. Then Gretchen returned, looking less-than-pleased. 'It's for you,' she said, sitting back down on the bed.

I wondered just who could be calling me at Gretchen's house. 'Oh no,' I said, fearing the worst, 'it's not my mother, is it?'

'No,' Gretchen said, 'it's Cleo.'

'Cleo?' I asked, confused. 'How did she get your number?'

'She said your dad gave it to her when she called your house,' Gretchen told me, but I was already on my way off the bed and into the hallway by this time.

Out in the hallway, I picked up the phone. 'Cleo?' I asked, not quite believing she was calling me at that particular moment.

'Gracie!' Cleo cried. 'Gracie, I need your help!' She sounded upset.

'Okay,' I said, in my best soothing voice. 'Just calm down and tell me what's wrong.'

'I need you to come pick me up,' she said quickly.

'Pick you up?' I asked. 'What, now?'

'Yes,' Cleo said. 'Please come. I don't have anyone else to ask.'

'What happened to Jason?' I asked, growing more concerned by the minute. 'Why can't he drive you home? Cleo, what's going on?'

'Jason and I had a fight,' she said.

'Cleo, did he hit you?' I asked her, not really sure I wanted to know the answer.

'No!' Cleo said. 'I was upset because Jason said he had to go home and he said I should go with him and I didn't want to – and he drove off and left me here!'

'Okay, okay,' I said, trying to decipher what Cleo had just babbled down the telephone at me. 'Don't worry, I'll come and get you. Just tell me where you are.'

After getting the necessary information from Cleo, and promising to be there to pick her up as soon as humanly possible, I hung up the phone and went back into the bedroom. Gretchen turned to look at me expectantly.

'I have to go,' I told her. 'Cleo needs me to pick her up.'

I felt Gretchen watching me as I gathered up my clothes and pulled them on over my pyjamas.

'Why do you always run when Cleo calls?' Gretchen asked finally.

'Because she's my friend,' I replied, not wanting to get into an argument with Gretchen about it.

As quickly as I could, I removed the pieces of cotton wool from between my toes and, hoping that the varnish on my toenails was now dry, pulled on my favourite pair of black boots.

I was in the process of shoving the rest of my things into a bag when Gretchen spoke up again.

'Gracie?'

'Yes?' I asked, looking at her. I noticed she was staring at me.

'Nothing,' she finally said, with a little smile.

I wasn't quite sure what had amused Gretchen so greatly, but I didn't really have the time to worry about it. Besides, it was encouraging that Gretchen was in a good mood. Because there was something I needed to ask her.

'Gretchen,' I said, putting on my best grovelling voice. 'I need a favour.'

'What?' Gretchen asked me, her eyes narrowing suspiciously.

'I need to borrow your car,' I smiled at her.

❄ ❄ ❄

It wasn't until I was nearly half-an-hour away from Gretchen's house that I finally realised what had amused Gretchen so greatly back in her room. I was still wearing my face pack – my *green* face pack (oh, but aren't they always?).

I adjusted the rear-view mirror and looked at my reflection in horror. It was worse than I'd first thought. Not only was I still wearing the face pack, but my hair was still pinned up in Gretchen's mother's rollers.

'Oh no,' I groaned, to no one in particular.

With my eyes just about on the road, and one hand on the wheel (I dread to think what my mother would say if she ever caught me driving so irresponsibly), I applied my free hand to my head, in a desperate attempt to disentangle some of the rollers from my hair. But it was an impossible task – and all it seemed to result in was a lot of pain on my behalf.

I decided to change tactics and try to remove some of the gunk from my face instead. But a quick search of the dashboard, glove compartment and front of the car showed there were no tissues – or anything else that would provide similar cleaning properties – in the general vicinity. And I couldn't very well use my hands to remove the green goo, lest it end up spread all over the interior of Gretchen's car as a result.

Gretchen! How could she let me leave the house like this? And she called herself my friend! It was the sort of mean joke that Cleo or I would play on someone – but not Gretchen. She was supposed to be above that sort of thing!

I thought about telling my mother what her precious Gretchen had done, but quickly realised that Mum would only tell me it was all my fault and that I must've deserved it. Still, Mum had been acting very strangely lately. Some people might even say 'nice' (but not me, I knew better – my mother was incapable of 'nice'). So who knows what her reaction might have been?

In any case, I looked a complete mess, and I had no way to rectify the situation before meeting Cleo. Cleo, of course, wasn't the problem. I knew she wouldn't mind my dishevelled appearance (though she would doubtless find it amusing for some time to come). The *problem* was that I'd arranged to meet Cleo in the bar of the hotel in which she'd been staying. Which, at this time of night, would probably be a bar full of people.

In terms of nightmare situations, this was right up there with the best of them.

❄ ❄ ❄

Nearly thirty minutes later, I steered Gretchen's car to a stop in the grounds of Cleo's hotel. I had seen just one rest stop along the way which, despite its title, hadn't really seemed like a place where anyone would actually get any rest (they would definitely get something there, but that something, I promise you, would *not* be rest).

So I had declined the chance to stop there and, as a consequence of turning down my one and only opportunity of correcting the disaster that was my face, I'd arrived at the hotel still looking like the Creature from the Black Lagoon (oh, how Warren would've loved to have seen me now).

Of course, this meant that my actually getting out of the car was going to be completely out of the question. No, what I had to do was find some way of getting Cleo to come out to me.

Grabbing my mobile phone from where it lay on the front seat of Gretchen's car, I punched in Cleo's number.

To my relief, Cleo's voice answered almost immediately. 'Hello?'

'Cleo, it's me,' I began.

'Hello?' Cleo asked again. 'I can't hear you – please speak up.'

'Cleo, it's Gracie!' I said, more loudly this time. 'Listen, I'm waiting for you outside the hotel. I need you to come out –'

'Just kidding!' Cleo's voice laughed, interrupting me. 'I'm not here right now – so leave a message, okay?'

There was a beep and then Cleo's voicemail kicked in.

I swore down the phone at Cleo's answering machine. There – that would make a nice message for Cleo to find later.

I knew all about Cleo's teasing voicemail message of course, and I wasn't usually fooled by it. But tonight I was in a hurry and, distracted by my urgent need to let Cleo know I was outside, I'd forgotten the whole thing was a trick. I'd actually thought I was speaking to Cleo.

I should have known it wouldn't be that easy.

And so, with Cleo's phone out of the equation, I did the only thing left I could think of doing – I hit the horn of Gretchen's car.

It was loud; so loud I cringed at the sound. But I kept on going regardless, hitting the horn and building up a steady rhythm. It suddenly occurred to me that knowing Morse code would've come in really handy at this point. Of course, that would only be true if Cleo also knew Morse code – which she didn't.

But that didn't matter, because I was certain Cleo would realise I was the one outside making all of this noise.

I looked out of the car window to see if I'd drawn anyone's attention yet, and noticed someone striding purposefully towards the car. Unfortunately, that someone wasn't Cleo. It was a smartly-dressed, angry-looking man.

Uh oh, I thought – management.

I immediately removed my hands from the horn and placed them in my lap, trying my best to look innocent – just as I'd done back when I was a child and had been caught doing something naughty (which had happened quite frequently).

However, it seemed the damage had already been done – as attested to by a sudden impertinent knocking on my window. Reluctantly, I rolled the window down – and heard the ranting of the man outside (who I could only assume was the hotel's manager) before I actually saw him.

'What the hell do you think you're doing?' he asked angrily. 'There are people inside trying to sleep!'

He started to bend down so he could look in the car window, and I prepared to show him my most apologetic face (which wasn't easy, as my face pack had started to harden, making cracking any kind of smile rather problematic).

'Do you want me to call the –' he began, but didn't finish.

Instead, he just stared into the car at me, mouth gaping open in shock. I could only assume it was my 'interesting' appearance that had caused him to come to a spluttering halt. But whatever it was, I was grateful for it. He was kind of tetchy.

'Call the what?' I asked innocently, though I knew he'd been about to threaten me with arrest. Apparently now he wasn't so sure.

'Never mind,' he said quickly, and stood back up.

'Are you okay?' I asked, leaning my head out of the window to look at him.

He immediately began to back away. I was actually scaring him. I didn't know whether to laugh or cry about that.

'Fine,' he said, never taking his eyes off me. 'Carry on.'

And with that, he made a quick spin on his heels and

took off back towards the hotel – moving noticeably faster than he had on the way out.

'Hey, wait!' I yelled after him.

It had suddenly occurred to me that I could've asked him to go and find Cleo for me. But it was too late for that now – he wasn't stopping for anyone.

He probably thought I was some sort of crazed, murderous escapee from a mental institution or something, and that he was going to become my latest victim; skewered on the end of the hook I had in place of a hand. Somebody had obviously seen one too many horror movies.

But the thing was, he'd left me with no options. I now had no choice but to go into the hotel and get Cleo myself.

Groaning inwardly, I opened the car door and stepped outside.

Let the fun begin.

❄ ❄ ❄

Cleo, of course, wasn't waiting at the door for me. Oh no – that would've been too easy. So that meant I actually had to go further into the hotel.

Luckily, I spotted the hotel bar straight away and made a beeline towards it, keeping my head down and avoiding eye contact with everyone around. I'd already decided that I should make my visit a quick one, before the manager returned (with back-up, no doubt).

But Cleo wasn't waiting at the bar, where she'd promised to be. I stood at the bar, scanning the row of faces that currently populated it. No, definitely no Cleo. But lots of other people who'd all taken a sudden interest in me, their whispering and giggling beginning in earnest.

I turned my back on the people at the bar and instead scanned each table in the lounge area, frantically searching for Cleo's face. But she wasn't there.

Suddenly, I heard someone behind me clearing their throat. 'Can I help you?' a man's voice asked.

I turned around and found myself looking into the face of a rather handsome bartender. He waited for my answer, a questioning look on his model-like face. He was beautiful – there was just no other word for it. He looked like he belonged on a catwalk rather than behind a bar.

'Can I get you something?' he prompted me.

I blinked, and realised I'd spent the last minute just staring (actually, make that gawping) at him.

God, how embarrassing.

I felt my cheeks begin to flush, then realised this didn't matter, as he couldn't see my cheeks in any case. At least the face pack had one advantage then.

'I'm looking for my friend,' I finally told him, racing to get the words out. 'Her name's Cleo and –'

'Gracie?' a voice interrupted me.

I whipped around to find Cleo standing beside me. As soon as she saw my face, she burst out laughing.

'Gracie, is that you?' she asked, between fits of giggles.

'I thought you were in trouble!' I frowned, watching her with disapproval. 'You were practically crying down the phone at me earlier! So what happened?'

'You just cheered me up,' Cleo said, wiping tears of laughter from her eyes. 'That's what happened.'

'It's not funny!' I protested, hands on hips. Cleo was too busy laughing to answer, so somebody else did it for her.

'Actually, it *is* pretty funny,' the bartender said.

'Nobody asked you,' I glared at him, before turning back to Cleo. 'Where were you?' I asked her. 'You said you'd meet me at the bar!'

'I was in the bathroom!' Cleo replied, composing herself. 'Nature called – you know how it is.' Then she started to laugh again.

'What now?' I asked, still annoyed.

'I'm sorry,' Cleo said, through her laughter. 'I just can't believe you actually came in here looking like that!'

'I didn't have much choice, did I?' I replied. 'I tried to get your attention from outside, but apparently you were having too good a time to notice a car horn blaring.'

'That was you?' Cleo asked incredulously, still amused by my antics.

'No,' I said sarcastically, 'that was the *other* crazy person in the face pack and hair rollers.'

'Excuse me,' an American accented voice said politely.

Cleo and I both turned around. Standing there, grinning at me, was a rather large man in his early forties. He had sandy-blond hair and perfect teeth – and was holding a camera.

'Hi,' he said in greeting. 'My name's Randy and I'm visiting from Memphis, Tennessee. And I was just wondering if I could take your picture?'

He held up his camera, as if indicating what he meant. 'I have a nephew at home who'd love to see it!'

I gaped at him, mouth open, not quite believing what I'd just heard. It took me a moment to gather my thoughts.

'WHAT?' I yelled at him.

Randy jumped so high in the air it was as if I'd given him an electric shock. Now *there* was an amusing sight.

'I'm sorry,' he stuttered, backing away.

Meanwhile, Cleo grabbed my arm and began to pull me away from Randy. 'Okay, Gracie,' she said. 'Time to go now, I think.'

'Oh, *now* you want to go?' I asked, but I let her lead me away anyway.

As we made our way out of the bar, I chanced a glance back at the gorgeous bartender. He was staring after us, a look of great relief on his face. 'I think I scared the bartender,' I confessed to Cleo, as we exited the hotel.

'Never mind the bartender!' Cleo smiled. 'What about poor Randy? I don't think he'll be coming back here in a hurry!'

At the thought of Randy's horrified face, I had to laugh. Cleo joined in. 'At least you're seeing the funny side,' she added.

'There's a funny side?' I asked.

'One day,' Cleo smiled, 'you'll be telling your grandchildren all about this.'

'Don't bet on it,' I grumbled. 'If I can't get this face pack off, I won't have any grandchildren to tell!'

Cleo stopped walking and looked at me, inspecting my appearance. 'On the bright side,' she said, 'your hair's gonna look great later.'

'Thanks,' I said, half-smiling. 'Can we go now?'

'Yeah,' she smiled back, 'let's go.' She looked around for a moment, and then glanced back at me, confused. 'Where's your dad's car?'

'I didn't bring Dad's car,' I told her. 'I was at Gretchen's house when you called, remember?'

'So whose car did you bring?' Cleo asked.

'I brought Gretchen's car,' I told her, leading the way towards it.

'Gretchen's?' Cleo repeated, obviously surprised. 'Gretchen lent you her car so you could come and pick me up?'

'After a little persuasion,' I informed her.

'Oh no,' Cleo grumbled. 'Does this mean I owe Gretchen a favour?'

'No,' I glared at her, as we climbed into the car. 'It means *I* owe Gretchen a favour.'

❄ ❄ ❄

'So are you going to tell me what happened?' I asked Cleo. We'd been driving for some time, but talking little, and Cleo had yet to reveal what had happened between her and Jason.

'What happened?' Cleo asked. 'You mean with me and Jason?'

'You know full well what I mean,' I replied, growing impatient.

'Okay, okay,' Cleo said, responding to my tone. 'I'll tell you. It's just that I think I might've made a bigger deal out of it than I needed to.'

'Cleo, just tell me,' I said, sighing.

'Well, Friday night was great,' Cleo breathed. Then a knowing smile appeared on her lips. 'Actually, Saturday morning was great too. If you know what I mean.'

'I think I can imagine,' I grumbled, desperately trying *not* to do just that.

'But it was getting to Saturday afternoon,' Cleo continued, 'and all we'd done with our weekend away was stay in bed which – don't get me wrong – was great. But I thought it was about time we did something else together and so I told Jason that.'

'Let me guess,' I sighed. 'Jason wasn't interested?'

'He was at first,' Cleo recalled, 'but that was only because he'd misinterpreted my meaning. When I suggested we get out of bed and go out somewhere, he was all for it. So we went for a walk along a nature trail near the hotel grounds.' Cleo shook her head. 'Silly me, I thought we'd be looking at birds and squirrels and stuff. I even took my camera. But Jason had other ideas. He pulled me behind a tree and started undressing us both. And when I asked him what he was doing, he said he was thrilled I was up for sex, alfresco.'

'He wanted sex on the nature trail?' I asked, disbelieving. 'God, it's not as if he wasn't getting it elsewhere!'

'Exactly,' Cleo said.

'You know, I think Jason might have some sort of problem,' I told her.

'Yeah, but it's a good problem to have,' Cleo grinned wickedly.

'Oh,' I said, disappointed. 'So you gave him what he wanted?'

'No!' Cleo said. 'I didn't. I mean, I wanted to. I really wanted to. But it's the principle of the thing. I mean, the whole point of us going out there was to spend time together like other couples do – you know, getting to know each other?'

'Did you tell Jason that?' I asked.

'Yes – and he said that's not what our relationship's about,' Cleo said glumly. 'He said he thought I understood we were only together for a bit of fun and weren't an actual couple.'

'You used to be okay with that,' I pointed out to her. 'It used to be enough for you.'

'Well, now I guess I want more,' Cleo sighed. 'It's all your fault, Gracie.'

'My fault?' I spluttered. 'How is this my fault?'

'You're the one always questioning my relationship with Jason,' Cleo replied. 'And you're always going on about love and romance – well, you did while you were with David anyway – and I guess I got to thinking that I didn't have that with Jason. And I wanted it.'

'I had it,' I reminded her, 'and look where it got me.'

'Well so far *not* having it hasn't gotten me anywhere,' Cleo replied, obviously feeling sorry for herself.

'So you told Jason you want more?' I prompted her.

'Yes,' Cleo said. 'I told him I want a proper relationship with proper dates – that I want to go out to dinner and to the theatre. I said I wanted him to admit to his friends that he has a girlfriend and –' she stopped suddenly.

'And?' I encouraged her.

'And I said that I thought we should meet each other's parents,' Cleo quickly spat out.

'Oh,' I said, not quite sure how to tell Cleo that she'd just made the biggest mistake of her life. 'And what did he say?'

'He said we'd talk about it later and that he was going back to the hotel room.'

'Tell me you didn't follow him?' I asked.

'No, I was too angry,' Cleo said. 'So I decided to walk along the nature trail by myself. But when I got back to the hotel room, I found Jason packing his things. He said he'd had a call from work and needed to go back immediately.'

'Oh sure,' I said, remembering all the times David had used that very same excuse, 'that old chestnut.'

'That's what *I* said!' Cleo cried. 'I accused Jason of running away because of what I'd told him. But he said I was paranoid and that he had to go back to work. He said I should stay at the hotel and enjoy the rest of the weekend, but I said I didn't want to stay there alone. So he said I should go with him, but I said I didn't want to go anywhere with him, so he said "fine". And then he left – without me.'

Cleo took a deep breath. She was obviously upset, though doing her very best to hide it. I let Cleo calm herself a little before questioning her further.

'And then you called me?' I asked her.

'I didn't have anyone else to call,' Cleo admitted. 'I'm sorry if I ruined your weekend with Gretchen. I guess you two are best friends again, huh?'

'I wouldn't exactly say that,' I replied.

Especially after tonight, I thought, but didn't voice that opinion.

'But you two were doing the whole sleepover thing!' Cleo protested. 'You were doing face packs and hair rollers – and I bet you had ice cream!'

'There was some ice cream involved,' I admitted.

'And I bet you were having loads of fun until I called. I really wrecked your evening, didn't I?' Cleo asked glumly. 'You should've just hung up on me.'

'And miss the humiliation I suffered in that hotel?' I joked, trying to cheer her up. 'Never!'

'I'm serious,' Cleo said. 'You shouldn't have come.'

'Cleo!' I exclaimed. 'What's wrong with you? Yes, I was having fun with Gretchen, but there's no way I was going to ignore your call. You were upset and you needed my help. And God knows you've been there enough times for me in the past!'

'But you don't need me anymore!' Cleo pouted.

'What are you talking about?' I asked her, trying not to laugh.

Cleo could be such a drama queen sometimes. She had more in common with my mother than she'd ever care to admit.

'Well, you have your new job now,' Cleo said. 'You work for Roman Pearson and you go to big celebrity parties. And you have sleepovers with Gretchen, who was your best friend for, like, ever. And I can't compete with that.'

'There's nothing to compete with!' I exclaimed, not quite sure how the conversation had taken this turn.

'I feel like we're drifting apart,' Cleo said. 'Like we're not best friends anymore.'

'Cleo, I'm here, aren't I?' I replied. 'Who else but your

best friend would drive out into the country in the middle of the night – *looking like this* – just to pick you up? That's something only a best friend would do.'

Cleo thought about that for a moment, then smiled.

'No,' she said. 'That's something only the very best of best friends would do.'

'Exactly,' I smiled back. 'And one day, I expect you to do the same for me.'

'No problem,' Cleo agreed quickly. 'But just without the face pack, okay?'

'Oh no,' I said, 'face pack included.'

Cleo laughed, apparently relieved of her fears.

'Okay,' she said. 'It's a deal.'

❄ ❄ ❄

After dropping Cleo home, and assuring her that we would get together very soon, I decided to return home myself. It was late, Gretchen was undoubtedly asleep and, in any case, I didn't want to get into an argument with her about either myself or Cleo's irresponsible actions while the incident was still so fresh in her mind.

I could drop Gretchen's car back tomorrow, first thing in the morning. She wouldn't mind. Or at least, if she did, she wouldn't say so.

Gretchen was like that.

❄ ❄ ❄

'Gracie, I can't believe you!' Gretchen exclaimed, as she

opened the front door of her house to me. I hadn't even had a chance to utter a word of greeting yet. 'First you take my car without telling me where you're going to be driving it to, and then you don't bring it back for nearly twenty-four hours!'

'I had a late night,' I mumbled in excuse. 'I slept in this morning.'

It was true. By the time I'd gotten home last night (or rather, this morning), not to mention battled for nearly an hour in the bathroom to remove the gunk that covered my face and the rollers which seemed to be permanently attached to my hair, I hadn't had the energy to do anything but fall into bed.

And I'd stayed there until nearly one o'clock this afternoon, when my mother had entered the room and shrieked in shock at finding me asleep in my own bed and not at Gretchen's house, as I was supposed to be.

Needless to say, there had been some explaining to do. And, as expected, I hadn't given my mother any semblance of the truth.

'Did you even bother replacing the petrol you used?' Gretchen continued.

Uh oh – she was starting to nag. This didn't look good.

'Um, no,' I said. 'But I'll pay you back, I promise.'

'That's not the point,' Gretchen said.

'So what *is* the point?' I sighed, wishing Gretchen would just say whatever it was she was trying to say, so I could go home and get back to bed.

'It isn't like you to be so irresponsible, Gracie,' Gretchen said.

'Irresponsible?' I asked her, confused. 'I was helping out a friend in trouble. I'd hardly call that irresponsible. Besides, how would *you* know if it was like me or not?'

'Gracie, I know we're not best friends anymore,' Gretchen said sadly. 'We've both changed too much for that. And I realise now that we can't turn back the clock to how things used to be.' She took a deep breath. 'But I really hope we can stay friends. And not just because our parents want us to, but because *we* want to.'

She stopped then and looked at me, waiting for my answer. It wasn't fair. Why did Gretchen always have to be the sensible and mature one? And why did she always have to be right?

'I'd like us to stay friends,' I eventually smiled in reply. 'After all, I am your maid of honour, am I not?'

'Yes,' Gretchen smiled back, 'you are.'

'So. A truce then?' I asked her.

'A truce,' Gretchen agreed.

'Okay,' I grinned. 'But if you ever let me go out again looking like I did last night, then the truce is over.'

'Last night?' Gretchen asked, with wide, innocent eyes. 'Gracie, I don't know what you're talking about.'

'Oh, sure you don't,' I smiled at her. 'Because you're far too nice to ever do a thing like that, right?'

'You know me,' Gretchen smiled back wickedly.

And at that moment, I realised I'd assumed far too much about Gretchen Wells. I wasn't the only one who'd changed since our childhood days. Gretchen was different too. And that was a good thing.

'Yes,' I replied with a smile. 'I think I do.'

Chapter Eleven

I arrived at work on Monday morning and, as usual, pressed the intercom button to request entry to the building. However, today when I pressed the button, something strange happened – nobody answered.

After waiting a few more moments, I tried again. But still there was no reply – and I didn't hear the familiar sound of the front door unlocking.

Now this was unusual. So far, on each and every day of my employment with Ramsden & Hunt, Olivia had let me into the building. Without fail, she was always the first to arrive at the office in the morning and the last to leave it at night. In fact, her presence was so constant I'd briefly wondered if she actually went home at all – although I'd eventually figured out that she must pop home, at least for a few hours, as she was always wearing a change of clothes the next day.

Still, just the fact that I'd wondered said it all – talk about dedicated to your work. But today, for some reason, Olivia wasn't around.

Luckily, Olivia had given me a key to the building, which she'd instructed me to use only 'in emergencies' (guess she didn't like the idea of me sneaking up on her). Deciding this could be classed as an emergency, I rummaged around in my bag and found the key, then used it to open the door, making my way up to the second floor.

The office was dark, empty and silent when I arrived, which wasn't something I was used to seeing at this time of day. Though I only just had the chance to take off my coat and switch on the lights before the quiet was rudely interrupted by the sound of a ringing telephone.

I hurried over to Olivia's desk and picked up the receiver of her phone.

'Ramsden & Hunt,' I said politely.

'Miss Parker?' a female voice asked.

'Yes. Who's this?' I asked.

'It's Olivia,' came the impatient reply.

Apparently Olivia was annoyed I hadn't recognised her voice. But who could blame me? She sounded like she had a heavy cold.

'Oh! Hi, Olivia,' I said pleasantly, making a special effort to keep my voice sweet and friendly. It was easy really – I just copied my mother's telephone manner.

'I'm afraid I won't be coming into the office today,' Olivia told me briskly. 'I'm not feeling too well.'

'No – you don't sound too good,' I replied sympathetically.

Although, truth be told, my new-found kindness towards Olivia was more to do with the fact that I was thrilled to have the office to myself than to any real sense of sympathy I felt for her.

'I don't often get sick,' Olivia said defensively, as if taking a day off was something to be ashamed of.

'I expect you don't,' I told her, trying not to laugh. 'Well, you take as long as you need,' I reassured her. 'Don't come back until you feel better.'

'I'll be back tomorrow,' Olivia said.

'Why don't you take a few days off?' I quickly suggested. 'Rest up. I've got things under control here.'

'I'll be back tomorrow,' Olivia repeated firmly.

Wow. She really didn't trust me with her precious Roman. Though after the events of last week, who could blame her?

'Okay,' I conceded. 'I'll see you then.'

Olivia hung up the phone without saying goodbye. But I didn't care. All that mattered to me was that I was free of her for one whole day.

Replacing the receiver of Olivia's phone, it slowly dawned on me that today I could do whatever I wanted.

And I wanted to have some fun.

❄ ❄ ❄

Well as it turns out, making paper aeroplanes will only keep a person entertained for so long – about half-an-hour or so to be exact. After that, the novelty kind of wears off. And so, with no magazines to browse through, no Internet access, and no Cleo to keep me entertained, there was little else I could do but get back to work.

There were always letters to be read, after all. They continued to pour into the office each week – a never-ending river of adoration for Roman Pearson.

If only they knew.

I'd spent the past few hours dipping in and out of the post sack, and was just beginning to read my tenth letter of the day when the office door suddenly opened – and Billy walked in.

His unexpected arrival caused me to jump. Billy must've noticed this, as he smiled apologetically.

'I remembered my key today,' he said, by way of explanation.

'Luckily, so did I,' I smiled at him.

I briefly wondered if Olivia had sent Billy to check up on me and suddenly felt glad that I was hard at work. Nobody needed to know about the paper aeroplanes.

'What can I do for you?' I asked him.

'I was wondering if I could buy you lunch?' Billy asked, approaching my desk. 'As a thank you for helping me out with Roman last week.'

'You already sent me flowers,' I reminded him. 'And thank you for those, by the way,' I smiled at him, 'they were lovely.'

Billy smiled back at me. 'You're welcome.'

'You don't have to buy me lunch as well,' I told him.

'But I want to,' Billy insisted. 'I promise I'll take you somewhere nice.' He made the sign of a cross over his heart and gave me his most genuine smile, his big brown eyes pleading with me from behind his hair.

Talk about a convincing argument.

'I can't come out,' I told him, shaking my head in disappointment. 'Olivia's off sick and I'm the only one here in the office.'

'Olivia's off sick?' Billy asked, shooting a glance at my

co-worker's empty desk. 'But Olivia's never off sick! Are you sure she isn't faking it?'

'I don't think Olivia's the type to take a sickie,' I pointed out to him.

But Billy, it seemed, wasn't interested in Olivia anymore.

'You can still come out,' Billy grinned at me mischievously. 'It doesn't matter if you leave the office empty for a while.'

'You are *such* a bad influence!' I scolded him.

'I know,' Billy smiled. 'I can't help it.'

And I couldn't help smiling back, though I'd already made my decision.

'I can't leave,' I told him. 'I have too much to do here. We've got a huge backlog of mail as it is.'

'More letters from Roman's adoring fans?' Billy sighed.

'They just keep on coming,' I confirmed. 'It's amazing how popular he is.'

'I can't argue with that,' Billy shrugged. Then he grinned again. 'Well, if you can't go out to lunch,' he said, 'then I'll just have to bring lunch to you.'

He started for the door.

'Wait! Where are you going?' I asked him.

'I'm going to buy you lunch,' Billy said. 'Be back soon!'

And before I could utter a word of protest, Billy had disappeared out of the door.

❄ ❄ ❄

A little under half-an-hour later, Billy returned – carrying two bags of shopping.

'I wasn't sure what you liked,' Billy said, 'so I bought a selection.'

'A selection of what?' I asked him.

'I said I was going to buy you lunch,' Billy reminded me. 'And I did.'

After clearing some space on my desk, Billy emptied out the contents of his carrier bags. His purchases spilled out, and I could see that, as Billy had promised, there was an impressive selection of food available – including sandwiches; various pieces of fruit; crisps; biscuits and salads. He'd even bought a few little cartons of fruit juice and some mineral water.

I made a mental note to let Billy shop for me again.

'Take your pick,' Billy said, motioning to the food in front of us. 'I think you'll find my choices constitute a healthy, balanced diet.' He winked at me. 'Well, some of them anyway.'

'Wow. I definitely approve of your shopping habits,' I told him.

Feeling hungry, I took a BLT sandwich, a red apple and a biscuit bar from Billy's selection of goodies. Meanwhile, Billy brought over Olivia's chair and sat down across the desk from me, before choosing his own food from the pile.

We were basically using my desk as a picnic table, which was fine with me. I couldn't think of a better use for it.

'So how's Roman?' I asked Billy, after taking a bite of my sandwich. 'Has he recovered from his big night out yet?'

'He's recovering,' Billy said. I frowned at him, not quite sure what he meant. 'Roman's back in rehab,' he explained.

'Oh,' I said, nodding. Guess I wouldn't be seeing Roman for a while then. 'I suppose that's the best place for him.'

'Roman doesn't think so,' Billy said. 'He probably won't stay long – he never does. He'll claim to be cured after a few days and check himself out.'

I couldn't help but notice just how concerned Billy sounded. He seemed to be genuinely worried about Roman's welfare. Billy's loyalty to Roman was endearing really, and I briefly wondered if he'd be as loyal while in a relationship. My bet was he would be. After all, not all men were like David McAllister.

'Just so you know, I haven't told anyone about what happened last week,' I reassured Billy. 'And I won't – I'll keep Roman's secret.'

'I appreciate that,' Billy smiled at me. 'And I'm sure Roman will too.'

'I'm not doing it for Roman,' I told him, the words tumbling out of my mouth before I could stop them.

Damn. I really need to learn to think before I speak.

There was a moment of silence, and then Billy looked at me seriously. 'Then why *are* you doing it?' he asked me.

I couldn't meet Billy's gaze. I had to look away or I knew I'd end up blushing furiously.

I'm doing it for you. That's what I wanted to say. However, this time my inner monologue proved effective, and I didn't blurt the words out loud.

Instead, I said: 'Because it's my job.'

'A lot of people wouldn't see it that way,' Billy pointed out.

'Yeah, well I do,' I told him.

Better for Billy to think I was dedicated to my job than to think…what? That I was in love with him?

I didn't love Billy – I barely even knew him. But I did like him a lot. And the truth of the matter was that my loyalty to Roman had mostly been inspired by Billy.

'I realise it must be hard for you not being able to talk about this with anyone,' Billy said. 'And I don't want to put you in the position of having to keep secrets from people –'

'It's not a big deal,' I told him quickly.

'I think it is,' Billy said. 'What about your family? Your friends? It must be difficult keeping things from them?'

'Well, not telling Cleo has been tricky,' I confessed, glad for the slight change of subject, 'because I pretty much tell Cleo everything.' Billy looked confused, and I suddenly realised I'd never mentioned Cleo to him before. 'Cleo's my best friend,' I explained.

'Oh,' Billy nodded.

'But not telling my family?' I said. 'That's not so hard. I keep most things from them anyway – especially my mother. It's a necessary evil.'

'So do you and your mum not get along?' Billy asked me.

He sounded genuinely interested, though there was really no reason for him to be. There was no great story behind the crumbling of my relationship with my mother. It had happened over a number of years, as I'd grown up and we'd grown further and further apart.

Though I couldn't remember a time when my mother hadn't been critical of me. And she'd always been controlling – that's just the way she was.

'Now there's an understatement,' I told Billy. 'I mean, don't get me wrong – she's my mum and I love her. It's just that she's impossible to live with sometimes.'

'Then why did you move back in with her?' Billy asked.

It was a fair enough question, I suppose.

'I didn't have much choice,' I told him.

'There's always a choice,' Billy replied.

'That's easy for you to say,' I quickly defended myself.

But I realised Billy was right. If I'd really, really wanted to, I could've found somewhere else to live. So what did that say about me? Had I secretly wanted to go home? Was I trying to get back my childhood? The thought was more than a little disturbing.

'The truth is,' I eventually admitted, 'after everything that happened with David, I just wanted something familiar to hold onto.'

I couldn't believe I was telling Billy all of this – stuff about my family, about my past. But I just felt so comfortable around him. He was incredibly easy to talk to and he actually listened, which made a nice change. Even when we'd been together, I'd often got the impression that David's thoughts were elsewhere during some of our more intense conversations. I'd always assumed he'd been thinking about work, but now I knew better. He'd had his mind on other people – on Lorna, to be exact.

'David was your fiancé?' Billy asked.

'No,' I told him. 'David was the biggest mistake of my life.'

'I like the way you think,' Billy smiled at me.

'Yeah, well it took me a long time to get around to thinking that way,' I admitted to him.

'Would you ever make the same mistake twice?' Billy asked me.

He didn't look at me for my answer, almost as if he didn't want to know what it would be. But there was only one reply I could give to that question.

Would I ever get back together with David?

'I wouldn't be that stupid,' I told him.

Besides, it wasn't even an issue – David was with Lorna now. We were through.

'Listen,' Billy said, breaking into my thoughts. 'If you ever *do* want to talk to anyone – about anything – you know you can talk to me, right?'

But at least I had something to thank David for. Because if it hadn't been for David, I would never have met Billy.

'I know,' I smiled at him.

And I had the feeling Billy and I were going to become very good friends indeed.

❄ ❄ ❄

That evening, I finally caught up with my brother again. Despite us living in the same house, I hadn't seen Warren for more than a few moments for over a week now. Ever since he'd done his disappearing act in running off to that rock festival and leaving me to make the arrangements for our parents' party in fact.

Warren, it seemed, had been deliberately avoiding me. But now his luck had run out. Mum and Dad had gone out to dinner at my aunt and uncle's house – which meant Warren had been left at my mercy.

'Warren!' I called, hearing my brother come downstairs.

Nothing. He just ignored me. I heard him stomping into the kitchen (Warren never did anything quietly).

Sighing, I got up from my seat at the dining table. I'd been sitting there for over an hour now, handwriting a batch of invitations to Mum and Dad's surprise party, and was feeling a little cranky. I made my way into the kitchen, just in time to see Warren open a carton of milk and drink straight from it.

'Warren!' I cried. 'That's disgusting!'

Warren finished his drink and looked at me.

'What?' he asked, as if he didn't already know.

'Other people have to use that milk, you know,' I told him, as I snatched the carton from his hand and put it back in the fridge (making a mental note as I did so *not* to use that milk).

I turned back to Warren, giving him my best annoyed look. 'I need to talk to you,' I told him.

'Whatever it was, I didn't do it,' he replied quickly. A typical Warren answer.

'No,' I agreed, 'you didn't. You didn't do anything – even though you promised you would.'

'Huh?' Warren asked, faking confusion.

'Mum and Dad's party?' I prompted him. 'Remember that? That bright idea of yours?'

'Oh yeah,' Warren said nonchalantly. 'How's that coming along?'

'Fine,' I replied. 'No thanks to you.'

'I've been busy!' Warren protested.

'Busy doing what?' I asked him. 'Playing computer games with your loser friends?'

'Parties are girl things,' Warren said, not answering my question.

'Then you can be a girl for the evening,' I told him, 'because I need you to write some invitations.'

'Can't,' Warren simply replied.

'Why not?!' I asked, annoyed that Warren was still shirking any form of responsibility.

'Have to set up for the gig,' Warren told me.

'What gig?'

'The band's gig. It's tonight.'

'What band?' I asked him, having absolutely no clue as to what he was talking about.

'My band,' he replied with a smile.

'You're not in a band,' I reminded him suspiciously.

'Yes, I am,' he insisted.

'No, you're not,' I replied. Though I was starting to wonder if I'd missed a huge chunk of my brother's life.

'Yes, I am,' he said again.

I studied Warren's face. Like I said before, my brother is a fantastic liar. You can never quite tell if he's speaking the truth or not.

And this time was no different.

'Okay, fine,' I sighed, deciding to give Warren the benefit of the doubt. 'I'll write the invitations.'

'Great,' Warren said, before heading towards the front door.

'Wait a minute,' I said, following him into the hallway.

'I gave you four hundred pounds to spend on this party. What's happened to it?'

'Four hundred?' Warren asked innocently. 'Are you sure it wasn't more like two hundred?'

'It was four hundred,' I insisted, not amused.

'Okay, don't sweat it,' Warren said. 'It's right here.'

Warren reached into his jacket pocket and pulled out a wad of notes which he thrust into my hands. Just a quick glance told me the full amount wasn't there.

'Gotta go,' Warren said quickly, as he opened the front door.

'Wait!' I commanded, sticking out an arm in front of Warren in order to block off his escape route.

I quickly flicked through the money in my hand, counting it. 'There's only two hundred here,' I informed Warren (who no doubt already knew this, hence his eagerness to leave). 'What happened to the other two?'

'Repairs to the van,' Warren said.

'What van?' I asked him, lost again.

'The band's van,' he replied. 'We need it to get to gigs.'

'You're not in a band!' I told him once more – sure he was spinning me a web of lies.

'I'll pay you back,' Warren said. Then, before I knew what was happening, he very cunningly slipped under my outstretched arm and out the front door. As he left, I heard him add: 'When I'm rich and famous!'

'Warren!' I called after him. But he'd already disappeared into the night.

With a heavy sigh, I shut the front door with a slam my brother would've been proud of.

Well that was two hundred pounds I'd never see again.

❄ ❄ ❄

Aside from Monday's very welcome visit by Billy, it had been a quiet week at work so far. And in truth, following the hectic events of the past fortnight, I was actually quite grateful for that.

Olivia had returned to the office on Tuesday, as promised, having recovered from the worst of her cold. Meanwhile, getting back into the routine of opening Roman's fan mail had proved extremely therapeutic for me; allowing me the chance to relax and my life to return to some semblance of normality.

But all that changed on Thursday morning, when Olivia's telephone rang.

I didn't pay much attention at first. Olivia answered the call as she did any other, in her prim and proper manner. Then my interest was suddenly piqued, as I heard her mention my name.

'Miss Parker?' she asked the caller. 'But –'

The person on the other end of the line obviously interrupted Olivia there, and I could tell she didn't like what they were saying, as her lips tightened into a thin line. 'Just a moment,' she finally told the caller sharply.

Sensing that Olivia was about to look my way, I shifted my weight on my chair, so that my attention wasn't quite so obviously focused on her conversation. 'Miss Parker!' I heard Olivia bark.

I waited a moment, trying to create an air of disinterest, before glancing at Olivia.

'Yes?' I asked innocently.

'It's for you,' Olivia said, holding up her telephone receiver. She didn't look pleased.

I put down the letter I'd been reading, got up from my chair, and made my way over to Olivia's desk.

'Thanks,' I began, reaching out a hand to take the phone from Olivia.

She practically threw the thing at me. Luckily, I managed to get a grip on the receiver and lifted it to my ear. 'Hello?' I asked into the phone, acutely aware that Olivia was staring at me, making no attempt to hide the fact that she was listening to my conversation.

Hey, at least I'd *tried* to pretend otherwise.

So I turned my back on her. Well, as much as I could, considering the telephone was still resting on Olivia's desk.

'Gracie!' a man's voice said enthusiastically. 'It's Roman!'

'Roman?' I asked, dumbfounded.

No wonder Olivia had looked so annoyed.

'I hope you don't mind me calling,' he continued, 'but I wanted to apologise for that whole incident at the party last week.'

'Oh, that's okay,' I said, not quite sure how else to respond. 'It's forgotten.' Which was a lie. That was one night I'd never forget. 'Are you okay?' I asked him.

'I'm fine!' Roman replied. 'Feeling better than ever, in fact. I paid a visit to that clinic I seem to give most of my money to nowadays and they sorted me out.'

'That was quick,' I said, not really convinced Roman's problems could have been sorted out in the space of eight days.

'Well I can't stand being stuck in that place for too long,' Roman confided. 'It's full of crazy people.' Then he laughed. 'And most of them used to be famous, you know. I guess that explains a lot?'

'I suppose so,' I replied, though it didn't really explain much at all.

'Listen, Gracie, I really want to make it up to you for spoiling your evening,' Roman continued. 'Although, to be honest, I can't recall everything I did. But Billy told me I behaved like a total idiot, so –'

'He said that?' I interrupted, a little shocked.

'Oh, he said worse than that,' Roman replied. 'But he also said that if it weren't for you, I'd have been in big trouble. So I guess I owe you a big thank you.'

'Oh, that's not necessary,' I spluttered, embarrassed by Roman's attentions.

'Yes, it is,' Roman said. 'And I promise that this time I'll get you back home in the limo.'

'This time?' I echoed.

'A friend of mine's having a party,' Roman explained. 'And this is a strictly private affair. No big celebrities – well, okay, maybe a few – but definitely no press photographers. And nothing like the place I took you to before. So what do you say? Will you go with me?'

'That depends,' I said, trying to skirt around the issue. 'Will Patrick Maguire be there?'

Roman obviously thought I was joking, as he chuckled good-naturedly.

'No,' he said, 'Patrick Maguire will most definitely *not* be there. Don't worry about it, Gracie,' he continued, 'it'll be fun. I'll pick you up at eight tomorrow night, okay? Okay, bye.'

And with that, he was gone, and I was left listening to the dial tone before I'd even had a chance to protest. A little stunned, I turned around to replace the receiver, to find that Olivia was still staring at me. I smiled at her nervously and put the phone down quickly, before scurrying back to my desk.

Picking up the letter I'd been reading, I pretended to be engrossed in my work once more. A successful tactic as, after a few minutes, I sensed Olivia's burning gaze was no longer directed towards me. I glanced over at her, and was relieved to find that she'd indeed grown tired of trying to cause my spontaneous combustion with her stare and had returned to her computer.

With Olivia no longer paying me any attention, it allowed me a little time to reflect on the telephone call I'd just taken. The telephone call from Roman Pearson.

I was going out with Roman Pearson. Again.

Which meant it was time to call Cleo.

❄ ❄ ❄

'Gracie, you must be the luckiest person alive!' Cleo exclaimed down the telephone.

I'd waited until Olivia had gone out to buy herself some lunch before picking up the telephone and calling Cleo. But the way we were going, it didn't look like our conversation would be finished before my co-worker returned. Cleo wanted to know every detail of my conversation with Roman, every word spoken. It was like reporting back to my mother – and I had told Cleo just that.

Cleo, predictably, really hadn't been too pleased with that analogy. But still, she had carried on with her questioning regardless. 'So do you think he likes you?' she asked now.

'He's Roman Pearson,' I reminded her. 'He gets sackfuls of love letters every week. He could have any woman he wants –'

'And he wants you!' Cleo interrupted excitedly. 'So what are you going to do about it?'

'Nothing,' I replied.

'Nothing?!' Cleo practically yelled. 'Are you insane? He's Roman Pearson!'

'Cleo, it's complicated,' I told her, trying to come up with an explanation that wouldn't reveal the secret Billy had entrusted me with. 'I mean, I work for him. You know how complicated office romances can get. Just look at you and Jason – it must be really hard seeing him around the office now you're not together anymore.'

'Um, well actually,' Cleo admitted, 'Jason and I made up. We're still very much together.'

'Now who's forgetting to tell me things?!' I exclaimed indignantly.

'I'm sorry!' Cleo cried. 'I meant to let you know. I was just a little busy with the making up side of things – if you know what I mean.'

I knew exactly what she meant. I *always* knew what she meant.

'So did you two make any decisions about your relationship before getting around to making up?' I asked, pretty sure I already had some idea of what Cleo's answer would be.

'Yes,' Cleo said happily. 'We decided to have sex again – a lot!'

'Cleo!' I complained, a little disappointed, although not at all surprised. 'I thought you wanted love and romance – not just sex?'

'Hey, when the sex is that good, you don't need anything else!' Cleo replied.

'I thought you wanted him to buy you flowers?' I reminded her.

'I have hay fever,' Cleo said quickly. 'Flowers aren't good for me.'

'You said you wanted him to take you on a proper date – out to dinner.'

'Why pay good money for overpriced food, when you can have a pizza delivered right to your door?'

'What about him meeting your parents?' I asked.

'An old-fashioned and outdated concept,' Cleo replied.

I sighed. This was getting us nowhere. Cleo had obviously already made up her mind as far as Jason was concerned.

'As long as you're happy,' I told her.

'I am,' Cleo said firmly. 'Now please stop trying to change the subject. Do you really expect me to believe there's nothing going on between you and Roman Pearson?'

'Yes,' I told her, 'I do. Because it's the truth, Cleo. I promise you, there's nothing going on between me and Roman. We're friends – that's all.'

'You are now,' Cleo agreed. 'But I bet you've changed your tune by Saturday morning!'

'Goodbye, Cleo,' I said in a sing-song voice, having no intention of replying to her last comment.

'You can tell me all about it on Saturday!' I heard Cleo call, as I put the phone down.

Cleo had made me promise to meet up with her on Saturday afternoon, to give her all the sordid details (her words, not mine) of my evening with Roman. She was clearly under the impression that something big was going to happen on Friday night between Roman and me.

And so, as it turned out, was Roman.

Chapter Twelve

We were on our way to Roman's friend's party, travelling in style – in a limousine, of course – when Roman gave me the first indication that his plans for the evening didn't quite coincide with mine.

'Toby has a really great house,' Roman enthused.

Roman had been telling me about the finer points of his friend Toby's house for the last ten minutes. I was starting to think he was trying to sell me the place. But then he dropped in the punchline.

'Oh, and he has a spare bedroom,' Roman added casually. 'He said there's no problem if we need to use it tonight.'

Although Roman's rather presumptuous meaning was perfectly clear, I couldn't help but smile.

'Why would we need to use it?' I asked him. 'Unless you're planning on getting drunk again and passing out on the bed, that is?'

Roman didn't answer. So, a little worried I might've caused offence, I glanced at him. He was watching me, smiling to himself. 'What?' I asked him, uncomfortable being under his scrutiny.

'Do you know why I like you so much, Gracie?' he asked.

'Why?' I asked back, starting to fidget in my seat.

'Because you're not like other women,' he replied.

'Is that a good thing?' I asked, not sure if I should feel flattered or insulted.

'Other women are so desperate for me to like them,' Roman explained. 'They only say the things they think I want to hear. And they throw themselves at me –'

'That must be so hard for you!' I interrupted, the statement coming out with a little more sarcasm than I'd intended. Roman didn't appear to notice, and he laughed.

'Not really,' he said. Then he looked at me. 'I guess there's not much chance of you throwing yourself at me?' he asked.

'Not really,' I said, echoing his earlier reply.

Once again, I found myself caught between the two extremes of being insulted and flattered. Roman certainly had a strange effect on my emotions, if nothing else.

'Didn't think so,' Roman said, sounding not at all dejected. 'Still, that's you, isn't it?'

'What's me?' I asked back, a little exasperated by Roman's vagueness.

'You're not impressed by this whole celebrity thing,' Roman said. 'You're not impressed by me. I like that.'

'You like that I'm not impressed by you?' I asked, repeating Roman's words back to him slowly, as if reminding him of what he'd said.

'I find it refreshing,' Roman said. 'But then, I guess there's a pretty good explanation behind it.'

'And what would that be?' I asked him, a little baffled by the whole conversation.

'You've seen me at my worst,' Roman said, as if that explained everything. 'I guess that took a bit of gloss off the whole celebrity thing.'

'Maybe a little –' I started.

'But you're still here,' Roman interrupted. 'Despite what happened last time, you've come out with me again. Which must mean you're just a tiny bit interested in me.'

'Or that I'm your PA and I'm trying to do my job,' I threw back at him, deliberately trying to stick a pin in his over-inflated ego.

It didn't work. Roman seemed to have an invisible force field protecting him from all of my excuses and denials – in fact, from everything he didn't want to hear.

'You're going to have such a great time tonight,' Roman said enthusiastically. 'I'll make sure of it.'

It was only then I realised the limousine had come to a stop. We had arrived. As our chauffeur opened my door for me, Roman smiled, adding: 'And you're going to love Toby's house!'

❄ ❄ ❄

Toby, as it turned out, was no ordinary Toby. He was Toby Swann, an actor probably better known throughout the country than even Roman. Although Toby was known more for the quality of his work than for his looks, in direct contrast to how Roman's fame had grown.

And Roman was right – Toby did have a fantastic house.

It wasn't huge and overbearing as I'd expected, but was actually quite compact. And insanely beautiful. The decor inside was fantastic.

Unfortunately, it was so fantastic that I was terrified of spoiling any part of it with my presence. Which resulted in me spending the first half of the party standing awkwardly in the middle of each room I entered; not wanting to sit on Toby's plush sofa for fear of tearing the material; or lean against the wall and chance marking the surface; or get close to any of the exotic-looking ornaments and artefacts circling the perimeter of each room in case I proved clumsy enough to knock one over, causing its breakage.

It was bad enough I was putting dents in the carpets and rugs which covered the floor of Toby's home by daring to walk on them with my big, heavy feet (I had actually found myself unconsciously standing on tiptoes several times already).

Roman, however, had displayed no such concerns, and had already taken great delight in showing me every inch of the house (including Toby's spare bedroom) on my very own private tour earlier in the evening. Needless to say, I hadn't made a long stop in the spare room, although it had certainly had a very cosy atmosphere about it. And Roman, thankfully, hadn't made any comments about the room being vacant, as I'd expected he would.

Roman had actually been on his best behaviour all evening, both with me and with others at the party. He'd even taken the time to introduce me to nearly everyone at the party, in a rather exhausting mingling exercise – though I could only remember a handful of the names that had been thrown at me, and they were mostly those of the few well-known celebrities in attendance.

Best of all though, Roman had managed to remain sober all evening, joining me in drinking orange juice. *Yes, orange juice. I couldn't very well go setting him a bad example now, could I?*

I liked to think it was my influence over Roman that had encouraged this good behaviour. However, if my influence *was* the cause, it now seemed to be waning in its effects.

'Roman!' I heard a voice say. 'Join me for a drink?'

That voice belonged to Toby Swann, I discovered as I turned around. He had two open bottles of beer in his hand, one of which he offered to Roman. Roman took the beer without hesitation, raising the bottle to his lips.

He was obviously completely unaware that I was watching him, apparently thinking I was still busily engaged in conversation with Wanda – a make-up artist who'd pulled me aside for further inspection because, according to her expertise, I had 'great cheekbones'.

Unfortunately for Roman, Wanda's conversation was not that stimulating. And as Roman went to take a swig from the bottle, I stepped up next to him and snatched the offending object from his hand.

'Hey!' he yelled, startled. Then he saw exactly who'd stolen his drink, and started looking very guilty indeed.

'Hey yourself,' I said, annoyed. 'What do you think you're doing?'

'Um, is everything okay?' Toby asked.

I rounded on him instead, equally annoyed with the

man who'd supplied the temptation. It didn't matter to me how famous he was.

'And you,' I said, glaring at Toby. 'What do you think you're doing?'

'You know, Roman,' Toby said, chuckling and looking at his friend. 'Your date's very nice and all, but I think she may be a little, oh, I don't know…wacko?'

'Oh, and you're such a good friend, are you?' I asked Toby, heaping on the sarcasm. 'Because handing Roman a beer is such a responsible thing to do.'

Toby seemed unfazed by my accusations. He just laughed again, apparently amused by me.

'It was just a beer!' he protested.

'Gracie, it was just *one* beer,' Roman said, backing up his friend.

I looked at Roman. And in seeing his worried expression, the truth finally hit me. Toby had no idea that Roman had a drinking problem. And Roman really, really wanted to keep it that way. I'd just screwed up as badly as Roman had been about to. Which meant that I needed to remedy the situation.

I thought quickly. Which, as ever, didn't produce the most sensible of results.

'Yes!' I cried, in answer to Roman's protest. 'But you promised me you wouldn't drink tonight, remember?'

I took a step closer to Roman, placed my hand on his chest, then switched into my best seductive mode (which, to be honest, was still pretty lame). 'If we're going to last *all* night, you'll need to be on top form,' I whispered to Roman – just loud enough so that Toby could hear.

While Roman gaped at me – in what I could only assume was a mixture of shock and pleasure – Toby cleared his throat. 'Well, like I said, Roman – the spare room's all yours if you want it.' And with that, Toby beat a hasty retreat.

Roman watched him go, then turned back to me and flashed a wicked smile. 'You heard the man,' Roman said, grinning.

'What is wrong with you?' I asked him, now thoroughly exasperated.

'Hey,' Roman said, still smiling, 'you offered!'

'I was trying to do you a favour!' I cried, slapping him on the arm. 'A pretty big favour considering Toby Swann now thinks I'm a complete slut because of it!'

'Toby doesn't think you're a slut,' Roman said. 'Trust me. The girls he hangs out with are a lot worse than *that*.'

'I feel so much better now,' I glared at him.

'You started it,' Roman said. 'You didn't have to grab my beer like that!' He looked hungrily at the bottle of beer I still held in my hand.

Deciding it would be best to get rid of the drink as soon as possible, I shoved it into the hands of a passing reveller.

'Here. Have a beer,' I told the man in question, who looked at me in confusion before shrugging, and walking off with the bottle.

It wasn't until I'd turned back to Roman that I realised I knew that party guest. He was an actor who'd appeared opposite Toby Swann in a movie about British spies – *Codebreaker*, I think it had been called. And now he also thought I was a complete lunatic. Great. Just great.

I looked at Roman. 'Roman, what was the first thing you told me after picking me up tonight?' I asked him.

'Um...you look great?' Roman suggested, obviously attempting to charm his way out of the situation.

'No,' I said, unmoved by his flattery. 'You told me that you weren't going to drink tonight. Not one drink you told me.'

'It was just one beer!' Roman protested.

'Roman –' I began.

'Okay!' Roman interrupted. 'I'm sorry. I won't do it again. Am I forgiven?'

'I'll think about it,' I muttered, annoyed that Roman was always able to talk his way out of trouble and clearly thought he could do the same with me.

And even more annoyed that he was probably right.

❄ ❄ ❄

Roman, it had to be said, had been on his completely best behaviour throughout the rest of the party. Not a beer in sight. Which probably had something to do with the fact that I hadn't taken my eyes off him since that incident with Toby Swann.

He'd also been on a serious charm offensive though, and was still continuing trying to win me over as the limousine pulled up outside my house at the end of our 'date'.

'Roman, what are you doing?' I asked him, as I stepped out of the limo and realised he was following me.

'I'm walking you to your door,' Roman said, climbing out of the limousine himself.

I looked at the ridiculously short distance between the limousine and my front door, then glanced back at Roman.

'I don't think that's really necessary,' I told him.

'Yes it is,' Roman said, taking my arm and leading me towards the house. 'I should've done this last time, but that was pretty much a complete disaster – so I'm going to make up for it now.'

'Fine,' I sighed in agreement, though I didn't really seem to have much choice in the matter. But hey, having Roman Pearson walk me to my door was okay with me. Or at least it was, until I saw the front door thrown wide open as we approached – and my mother appear in the doorway.

'Gracie!' she cried affectionately. 'It is you! I thought I heard a car.' Although she was talking to me, my mother's gaze was fixed firmly on Roman.

I groaned inwardly. How had my mother found out about my night out with Roman? I'd gone to great lengths to keep this evening a secret from her in order to avoid scenes such as this. (Of course, my coming home in a limo had probably tipped her off that something was going on.)

'This must be Roman,' Mum said. 'Gracie's told us so much about you,' she smiled at Roman.

Uh oh. Trust my mother to put her foot in it.

My first thought was that Roman would assume I'd been giving away his secrets. However, that panic soon proved to be unfounded. I watched in shock as Roman let go of my arm, stepped forward, took my mother's hand, and kissed it.

'Pleased to meet you,' Roman told her, turning on the charm once more. 'You must be Gracie's...sister?'

I watched in embarrassment as my mother giggled. Yes, giggled.

'No!' she told him, while blushing and fluttering her eyelashes in what was a quite blatant (not to mention disturbing) display of flirting. 'I'm Ellen. I'm Gracie's mother.'

'Really?' Roman asked, in what could only be described as feigned shock. 'Are you sure?'

Oh God, I thought. *Don't encourage her, please!*

'Quite sure,' my mother told him, with a grateful smile.

'Well I can see where Gracie gets her dazzling beauty from now,' Roman said, aiming the comment at my mother, but glancing at me to see if the line had impressed.

It hadn't. Once upon a time, I would've been blushing furiously after hearing such a thing. But words like that, I'd discovered, popped out of Roman's mouth on a regular basis. My mother, however, was thrilled.

'Why thank you,' she told Roman. 'That's very kind of you.' Then she moved into full hostess mode. 'Would you like to come in?'

'I'd love –' Roman began.

'He can't,' I said firmly, determined to stop this disgusting display of false affection right where it stood. 'Roman has to get home,' I added quickly – both for my mother's benefit and as a quite obvious hint to Roman himself.

Before Roman could move, I manoeuvred my way in front of him, taking up position in the doorway and placing myself between my boss and my mother.

'That's a shame,' my mother said, apparently believing what I'd said. 'Well, you're welcome anytime,' she told Roman.

'Thank you, Ellen,' Roman said in reply.

It was definitely a cue for my mother to leave and, to my great surprise, she took it, disappearing into the house. 'Your mother seems very nice,' Roman told me politely once she'd gone.

'You don't have to live with her,' I threw back.

'Is she a fan of mine?' Roman asked.

I laughed, despite myself. 'You think everyone's a fan of yours,' I reminded him.

'True,' Roman admitted, 'but that's because they usually are.'

'Can you say egomaniac?' I asked him, smiling.

Roman was a complete egomaniac, it was true. But somehow he also managed to be charming at the same time.

'Can you say "Kiss me, Roman"?' he asked back.

Okay, scrap that last observation. All charm had apparently left the building that was Roman Pearson.

'No,' I told him, 'I can't. But I can say "Goodnight, Roman".'

'Gracie, wait,' Roman said. 'Think about this.'

Then he leaned forward, making a move to kiss me.

'Goodnight, Roman,' I told him, and smiled at him as I shut the front door in his face.

The expression of utter shock and surprise Roman sported as I did so was just fantastic. And it amused me for all of five seconds.

Until I realised I could lose my job because of it.

❄ ❄ ❄

'Roman wouldn't sack you because you didn't kiss him,' Cleo assured me the next day.

Cleo and I had met up for lunch at *Annabelle's* – a little pavement café which was a favourite haunt of ours for lunchtime gossiping sessions. I'd described to her every little detail of my evening with Roman (minus any references to *that* incident, of course) and she'd listened eagerly, waiting until I was finished before offering her counsel. Which, although quite reassuring at first, soon became anything but.

'If anything, he'd sack you for being rude to him and shutting the door in his face,' she told me.

'Thanks, Cleo,' I sighed. 'That makes me feel so much better.'

'I just don't understand what you were thinking!' Cleo cried. 'Why *didn't* you kiss him?'

'It's complicated,' I told her.

'What? Does he have bad breath?' Cleo asked, though it was obvious she didn't believe a word of what she was suggesting.

'No,' I told her. 'He's just…not my type.'

'Handsome, rich and charming isn't your type?' Cleo asked, aghast.

I had to laugh at her completely shocked and baffled expression. 'I didn't kiss him,' I told her. 'Get over it. It's not the end of the world!'

'You're the one worried you might lose your job over it,' Cleo reminded me.

'Again – that makes me feel so much better,' I said.

'Sorry,' Cleo smiled guiltily, finally realising her input

hadn't been too helpful. 'How about we change the subject before I drive you completely over the edge?'

'Good idea,' I agreed quickly. 'So what's been going on between you and Jason? Have you had the flowers and romance yet?'

'No. No romance,' Cleo replied with a wicked grin. 'Just the usual.'

'And you're okay with that?' I decided to check once more.

'Never been happier,' Cleo replied. 'Oh, and I have more good news. Penny is leaving the office to take a job elsewhere.'

'What?!' I cried.

'Yep,' Cleo smiled, 'no more of her little chats.'

'That's just typical!' I grumbled. 'I put up with her all that time and then she leaves the office right after I do!'

'It's good for me though,' Cleo pointed out.

'You're right,' I said, happy for her. 'Hopefully your new manager will be a lot more bearable.'

'Hopefully my new manager will be me,' Cleo replied with a grin.

'Okay,' I frowned, unsure of Cleo's meaning, 'I'm confused.'

'I'm going to apply for promotion,' Cleo clarified. 'For Penny's job.'

'Why?' I spluttered, in a complete state of shock. 'I mean, okay, more money. But you hate that place! And if you get Penny's job, you'll actually have to do some work. So why go for promotion?'

'Why didn't you kiss Roman Pearson?' Cleo shrugged.

'I guess it's just one of those things there's no logical explanation for.'

'You're applying for a promotion and you don't know why?' I asked her, even more confused now – not to mention a little worried about Cleo's state of mind. 'Has this got anything to do with Jason?'

'Nothing to do with Jason,' Cleo said, shaking her head. 'It's just me. I want to do this. I'm not sure why, but I do. Of all people, Gracie, you should understand what that feels like.'

I thought back over all of the sudden and seemingly insane choices I'd made myself in the past few months – beginning with my decision to throw away all that I knew in the search for something better.

And I found that I did understand. Better than anyone ever could.

'I know exactly what you mean,' I smiled at Cleo.

❄ ❄ ❄

I went into work with some trepidation on Monday morning, half expecting Olivia to hand me my P45, in response to my rebuffing of Roman's advances.

But Olivia was her usual grumpy self, and my date with Roman wasn't even mentioned. I actually wondered if she even knew about it, but then it occurred to me that Olivia had been listening intently to my telephone conversation with Roman the other day, and had probably picked up enough details to work it out for herself. Olivia was many things, but stupid was not one of them.

So, with Olivia behaving as per normal, I assumed I was safe and wouldn't be receiving the boot from my impossibly glamorous job today. Or at least, I did – until Billy walked through the office door.

He aimed a brief greeting at Olivia, and then made his way over to my desk.

'Billy, hi!' I said, not quite sure what he was doing there. Then, to my horror, I found myself putting that thought into words. 'What are you doing here?'

So much for that inner monologue.

I cringed at my unintended bluntness, but Billy didn't seem to notice. 'I came to see you,' he smiled at me, sitting down on the edge of my desk.

'Me?' I asked. 'Why?'

Again with the blunt questioning. What was wrong with me today?

'Roman told me what happened Friday night,' Billy said.

'He did?' I asked. 'What did he say?'

As if I didn't already know.

'He said he went to kiss you goodnight,' Billy recalled, 'and you shut the door in his face.'

Oh no. This was it. I *was* to be sacked after all. And Roman had sent Billy to do his dirty work for him.

'Not right in his face,' I said, attempting to defend myself. 'I mean, I didn't hit him with it or anything, right? There wasn't any actual squashing involved?'

'No,' Billy chuckled. 'Roman's fine. The only thing bruised is his ego!'

'It's not funny!' I retorted, shocked that Billy was amused

by this. 'I can't believe you came here to fire me and you're laughing about it!'

'Fire you?' Billy asked, looking extremely confused. 'Why would I do a thing like that?'

'Because I didn't kiss Roman?'

Suddenly, Billy began laughing. I watched him in surprise, a sudden feeling of relief washing over me. 'You're not here to fire me?' I asked him.

'No!' Billy said. 'Don't be silly! I mean, Roman was upset you didn't want to kiss him, yeah. But he'll get over it. And besides,' he added, winking conspiratorially, 'it'll do him good to have a woman reject him for once. It just might bring him back down to earth.'

'Oh,' I smiled back, my confidence returning in Billy's presence, 'in that case, I'm glad I could help.'

'I'm glad you could too,' Billy said, smiling.

'So if you're not here to fire me, then why are you here?' I asked him, hoping I wasn't being too direct. Billy didn't seem to think so.

'Well,' Billy said, taking two slips of paper from his jacket pocket, 'it just so happens I have two tickets to the premiere of the new Orlando Bloom film tomorrow night. And I was hoping you'd like to go with me.'

'You're kidding?!' I exclaimed, taking the tickets from him for a better look. 'I love Orlando Bloom! Where did you get these?'

'From Roman,' Billy confided. 'He didn't want to go, so he said I could have them. So what do you say?' he asked. 'You want to go with me?'

'I'd love to!' I smiled at him. 'Thank you for asking me.'

‘That’s okay,’ he grinned. Then he leaned towards me and whispered: ‘I was tossing up between you and Olivia, but you won out in the end!’

‘Well that’s a relief!’ I laughed.

‘I’ll pick you up around six-thirty, if that’s okay,’ Billy said, taking the tickets as I gave them back to him. ‘Just a regular car though, I’m afraid,’ he added. ‘I don’t get handed limos for free like Roman does.’

‘That’s fine with me,’ I smiled at him. ‘To tell you the truth, I’m getting a little sick of limos now anyway.’

‘Already?’ Billy grinned. ‘I guess we’ll never make an international movie star out of you then?’

‘Not likely,’ I admitted.

I watched as Billy stood up and started making his way towards the door.

‘Bye, Olivia!’ he called to my co-worker. She barely glanced up from her work, apparently attempting to pretend she hadn’t heard him.

Billy looked back at me with a knowing smile. ‘I’ll see you tomorrow,’ he said to me, before disappearing out the door.

‘See you tomorrow,’ I echoed, though I knew he could no longer hear me.

And I had a feeling it was going to be a long and tedious wait until I could see Billy again. But still, I was certain the wait would be worth it.

❄ ❄ ❄

And so far, the wait had definitely been worth it. Everything about the evening I'd spent with Billy had been enjoyable – and so completely different to my two nights out with Roman.

First of all, as advised by Billy, there had been no limousine to whisk me away from home. Instead, Billy had turned up in his own car which, I had since discovered, reflected his personality amazingly well. The car was comfortable, familiar and relaxed. All qualities I'd come to associate with Billy himself.

The drive to the premiere had been similarly themed – conversation flowing freely about various topics (topics that thankfully didn't include homes of the rich and famous). And when we'd arrived at the cinema, there'd been no red carpet treatment for us. Well, the red carpet was there – but as simple 'ordinary' folk, Billy and I had been blissfully ignored by all of the waiting photographers, who were no doubt counting down the time until the actual celebrity guests appeared. (Thankfully, nobody seemed to recognise me from my one and only magazine appearance.)

As a result, we'd been free to enjoy ourselves without worrying about the consequences of being spotted having a good time. And enjoy ourselves we had. Despite the disappointment of not actually bumping into Orlando Bloom himself while at the premiere, I'd had lots of fun – and was pleased that Billy had also found the film to his liking. It made a nice change for a man to express favour towards any film that I'd enjoyed.

And, as if that wasn't enough, Billy had surprised me by announcing he'd booked us a table at one of the best restaurants in town. Which was where we were heading right now.

'So you're not going to tell me the name of this restaurant?' I asked Billy again, desperately trying to pump him for information. Billy, however, held firm.

'No!' he said. 'It'll spoil the surprise if I tell you!'

'I hate surprises,' I grumbled. 'Are we nearly there?' Billy had suggested we walk from the cinema to the restaurant as, he'd claimed, it was only a short distance. But apparently Billy's idea of 'short' didn't coincide with mine.

'Yes,' he laughed. 'It's just around the corner. Did anyone ever tell you how impatient you are?'

'No,' I replied warmly. 'Did anyone ever tell you how infuriating you are?'

'Actually, yes,' he smiled. 'You did.'

'Well, I was right!' I smiled back.

Caught up in my bantering with Billy, I failed to notice we'd already turned the corner of which he had spoken. Suddenly, Billy came to a stop.

'We're here,' he told me, then looked up. 'This is it.'

I followed his gaze to find we were standing outside a restaurant. A restaurant that was very familiar to me.

For it was the very same restaurant in which I'd caught my fiancé cheating on me with Lorna Spence.

'Lovely,' I managed to choke out for Billy's benefit. 'My favourite.'

❄ ❄ ❄

I half expected the same young (not to mention unfortunate) man that had attempted to eject me from the restaurant all those months ago to be waiting to greet us at the door, in what would've been an unconsciously mocking gesture on the restaurant's part. But no, yet another smartly-dressed and rather youthful employee welcomed me on this occasion.

He led me and Billy to our table which, thankfully, wasn't the same one as I'd seen David and Lorna share.

No, that would've been far too cruel.

After we were seated, the young man handed us a menu each.

'Your waiter will be with you shortly,' he told us, before disappearing.

I quickly buried my head in my menu, not wanting to see any more of the restaurant than I had to. Billy, however, with no idea of my plight, was more than happy to study his surroundings.

'This is a great place,' he said enthusiastically. 'It's supposed to be the best restaurant in town.' Then he looked at me. 'Have you been here before?' he asked.

'No,' I lied, not looking up. But when Billy didn't answer, I risked a peep at him over the top of my menu. He was frowning, clearly confused.

'But outside –' he began, then paused to recall before continuing. 'You said it was your favourite.'

I was saved from having to answer Billy's query by the arrival of our waiter. However, my relief was short-lived, as I looked up into the face of the very young man I hadn't wanted to see. The young man I'd probably scared half to death when he'd tried to get me to make a dignified exit on my last visit here. Apparently he'd switched roles to waiting tables now. Typical.

'Are you ready to –' he began to ask, and then stopped suddenly as his eyes locked on me.

Now it might've been my imagination, but I could've sworn that he turned white as a sheet just then. Though what he definitely did do was take a sudden step away from the table – and me. 'It's okay,' he stammered. 'I'll come back later.'

And with that, he was off, racing back towards the safety of the kitchen. Billy watched him go, then looked at me, clearly confused.

I shrugged, as if I had no idea of what had just happened.

I couldn't believe he would still remember me after all this time! I must've scared him pretty bad. Which was weird, because I didn't really think of myself as being a particularly scary person.

'Gracie? Are you okay?' Billy asked. Typical Billy – he'd sensed something was wrong just from the changes in my behaviour. And also, probably, because I'd been staring into space thinking about *that* incident for the past few moments.

'No,' I admitted, closing my menu and putting it down on the table. 'I'm not okay. Could we please leave?'

Billy, to my great delight, didn't question me on this. He didn't even ask me why. He just copied my movements with his menu and stood up.

'Okay,' he said gently. 'Let's go.'

This time there was no big scene. I stood up and Billy quietly motioned me in front of him with a reassuring smile, allowing us to exit the restaurant without causing any kind of commotion. Even when we reached the door, and the young host went to say something, Billy hushed him with a discreet explanation: 'We have to leave now. It's an emergency.'

Once we were outside, and the cool night air hit me, I found myself breathing deeply. It suddenly occurred to me how suffocating the restaurant had seemed.

Billy, caring as ever, gently took my arm and led me away from the road – which, in my relief at escaping the restaurant, I had wandered dangerously close to. 'Are you okay?' he asked again.

Billy's questioning could have come over like an interrogation, and I wouldn't have blamed him if it had – after all, he had a right to know why I'd just dragged him out of the best restaurant in town.

But there was nothing interrogative about Billy's question, and I found myself not only calming down, but also wanting to tell Billy everything.

'I'm fine,' I reassured him. 'But that restaurant…'

Instead of interrupting, Billy waited for me to continue. 'I *have* been there before,' I admitted.

I looked at Billy, to see if he was upset that I'd lied to him, but he seemed to be unaffected – as well as unsurprised – by the revelation. 'Do you remember I told you about David, my fiancé?' I asked him finally.

'Is this the one who was cheating on you, or are there other fiancés I don't know about?' Billy joked, obviously trying to get a smile out of me.

And it worked. If a cynical and wry smile was what he was looking for.

'That's the one,' I confirmed. Again, he waited for me

to continue. 'The last time I came to this restaurant was back in February,' I told him. 'Valentine's Day.'

'Bad memories?' he asked, clearly assuming David had taken me to the restaurant.

'You could say that,' I smiled at him, though I was finding that the memories weren't quite as painful as I'd imagined they'd be. 'I was supposed to be spending Valentine's Day with David,' I recalled. 'Only he couldn't get the night off work. Or so he claimed.' I gave Billy a knowing smile. 'So, instead of a romantic evening in with my fiancé, I ended up playing gooseberry on my parents' evening out – at that restaurant.'

I gestured to the restaurant we'd just exited. Billy gave me perhaps the most sympathetic (though not patronising) look I'd ever seen. Then, apparently not being able to hold it in any longer, he laughed.

'That sounds horrific!' he exclaimed, obviously identifying with my complete despair at being a third wheel on my parents' date. I could do nothing but laugh with him at what was a truly horrible memory.

'It gets worse,' I told him, through my laughter. I found myself glad that Billy wasn't over-sympathising with me about my experience. It made recalling the horrible details of the story so much easier.

'I was in the ladies' bathroom, fixing my make-up,' I explained, suddenly sobering up a little, 'when I heard noises coming from one of the cubicles. And – stupid me – I didn't realise what was going on. Until I saw this shoe shoot out from under the cubicle door. And I remember thinking...*great shoe*.'

I looked at Billy and smiled. He smiled back.

'Jimmy Choo?' he asked.

'Just a poor imitation,' I replied, amused he'd remembered my reference to the totally-out-of-my-price-range designer. 'Anyway,' I continued, 'then I saw this little black dress on the cubicle floor, and I realised what was going on. And I got the hell out of there as quickly as I could.'

'I bet you did,' Billy chipped in.

Despite the awfulness of the story, I couldn't help but smile again. And I was thankful that Billy allowed me to do this without comment or judgement.

'So I thought nothing of it for a while, apart from obviously *get a room*,' I told Billy. 'Until, that is, I spotted David having dinner on the other side of the restaurant – with another woman.'

'Did you know her?' Billy asked, as I paused in my recollections. 'Not that it makes any difference,' he added quickly.

'I knew her,' I told him. 'Lorna Spence. She worked with David. Her father's David's business partner.' Narrowing my eyes, I added: 'And she'd been after David for ages.'

'The black widow,' Billy commented.

'You can say that again,' I nodded. 'So there I was, asking David why he was out having dinner with Lorna – when he couldn't spare the time to spend the evening with me – when I noticed Lorna's shoes…'

'I can guess the rest,' Billy said kindly. 'Poor imitation Jimmy Choos?'

'Market stall poor,' I said bitchily.

'So he begged forgiveness and you refused to take him back?' Billy asked.

'Not even close,' I smiled sadly. 'Not that I would've taken him back if he had. But no – no begging. He told me that he loved her.'

'Oh,' Billy said, seemingly lost for comforting words now.

'Yeah,' I said. 'Except my reaction was a little less charitable.'

'I can imagine,' Billy replied. 'But you're okay, right? I mean, you've moved on? You're over him – like you told Roman in the car?'

'You remember that?' I asked him, genuinely surprised. I was also surprised that Billy looked a little embarrassed by this question. I didn't know Billy Ramsden could be embarrassed.

'I remember,' he replied.

When I realised he wasn't about to add anything else to that answer, I nodded.

'I'm over him,' I told Billy. 'Big time. And I'm better off without him – I'm certain of that.'

'Then that, at least, calls for a celebration,' Billy smiled at me.

'Um, yeah,' I said, suddenly feeling quite guilty. 'Sorry I ruined your dinner plans.'

'No problem,' Billy said, laughing. 'If we can't go to the best restaurant in town, then we'll go to the second best.'

'What's the second best?' I asked him, intrigued.

I followed Billy's gaze, as he nodded to a shop across the street.

'*Ben's Fish & Chips*,' he explained. 'Service with a smile and free chip forks to boot.'

'Sounds good to me,' I laughed.

And we headed towards *Ben's Fish & Chips* together.

❄ ❄ ❄

By the time Billy and I had polished off our fish and chip dinners from *Ben's* (which was definitely, if not the best, then the second best restaurant in town) and made our way back to my house, I'd forgotten all about David McAllister, Lorna Spence, and the events of Valentine's Day.

I guess that meant I really was over it. And Billy had played a big part in that.

'I had a really great time tonight,' I told Billy truthfully, as he stopped his car outside my house.

'So did I,' Billy smiled. 'I think I'll have to start stealing Roman's invitations more often!'

'I think you should,' I replied with a smile.

Then I did something that surprised even me. I leaned over and kissed Billy on the cheek. If asked why I did it, I couldn't have explained – except to say that I really, really wanted to. 'Thanks, Billy,' I said, then got out of the car while Billy was still sitting there, stunned. 'Goodnight,' I added, as I went to shut the car door.

'Night, Gracie,' I heard Billy say as I did so.

I thought back to the last time Billy and I had been in this position and spoken those exact words. And I realised that now they meant so much more.

With a smile on my face, I headed towards my home – the comforting sound of Billy's car chugging into the distance keeping me company.

I was definitely, finally, over David McAllister.

Chapter Thirteen

'What about this one?' Gretchen asked.

'No,' I replied, 'not that one.'

'This one?' Gretchen asked. She pulled a hideous, pink, frilly dress from the rack in front of her. I screwed up my face in response.

'That,' I said, 'has to be the ugliest dress I have ever seen.'

Gretchen studied the dress she was holding and, after her closer inspection, laughed and hurriedly put it back on the rack.

'You know,' she said, 'I think you might be right about that.'

Gretchen and I were in a bridal boutique, searching for a bridesmaid (sorry, maid of honour) dress for me. And it wasn't proving to be an easy task.

Gretchen, ever enthusiastic, had already thrown a number of options at me. I'd disliked them all. It wasn't that I was a fussy shopper – it was just that I didn't want to end up looking like a huge, overblown meringue on Gretchen's big day. (Which was a fair enough point, I thought.)

It seemed Gretchen was getting a little impatient with

my constant critiquing though. 'This one?' she asked, pulling another dress from the rack.

I gave her choice a quick glance, already certain it wouldn't be right for me.

'No,' I said, wrinkling my nose in distaste. 'The sleeves are too puffy.'

Gretchen sighed loudly and put the dress back.

'I found *my* dress quicker than this,' she grumbled, 'and I'm the one getting married!'

I could see Gretchen's point. This was our third boutique. We'd already come up empty-handed twice and Gretchen obviously didn't want that to happen again.

I decided to make a considerable effort to find a suitable outfit from what was available here. Which was when I spotted a rack of dresses so unlike the others in the shop. No frills. No puffy sleeves. No pink. I made a beeline towards them.

'Ooh, this is nice!' I heard Gretchen exclaim from behind me. 'What about this one, Gracie?'

Reluctantly, I turned to look. The dress, to be fair, wasn't bad. However...

'It's purple!' I cried in dismay.

'Grape, actually,' Gretchen corrected me.

'I don't *do* purple!' I told Gretchen. 'Especially at weddings!'

Before Gretchen could argue, I turned back to my chosen rack of dresses. I was sure I'd find what I was looking for here. And I was right.

The dress caught my eye immediately due to its colour – blue (my favourite). And when I pulled it from the rack,

I was delighted to discover that it was devoid of any of the garishness so often associated with bridesmaid dresses.

The dress was a perfect shade of blue, in a simple, long, flowing, halterneck style, that flared in all of the right places. The material was silky to the touch. It was exactly what I'd been looking for.

'This is it!' I told Gretchen happily. 'This is the one!'

'Finally!' I heard Gretchen sigh, as she came up behind me. I turned around to show Gretchen the dress.

'What do you think?' I asked her.

'Well,' Gretchen said, studying the dress, 'it's a little plain, don't you think?'

Exactly, I thought. *That's the point.*

'Not for me,' I told her. 'I don't go for the "no frills, no thrills" rule.'

'As long as you like it, it's okay by me,' Gretchen said, clearly relieved that I'd finally decided upon something. 'Why don't you go try it on?'

'Okay,' I said, 'back in a minute.'

I made my way to one of the boutique's two changing rooms, then pulled the curtain across and began to undress. It was while I was doing so that I heard the bell above the boutique door jangle as somebody entered the shop.

A moment later, I heard a woman talking to the boutique's manager. I didn't hear their whole conversation, but gathered the woman had popped in to pick up her wedding dress.

'Do you mind if I try it on again?' I heard the woman ask.

The manager agreed to this, and I soon heard the curtain being pulled back on the changing room next to mine.

It occurred to me, as I pulled on my chosen dress, that the woman's voice had sounded familiar. However, I couldn't quite place where I'd heard it before. But once I looked in the mirror at my reflection, all thoughts of the other woman disappeared. The dress I had picked out looked great – even better on than off.

As I congratulated myself on managing to find a flattering maid of honour outfit, I pulled back my changing room curtain to show Gretchen the dress.

'Gretchen!' I called to her. 'What do you think?'

Gretchen came towards me for a closer inspection – but she was smiling, which was a good sign.

'That looks great,' Gretchen said. 'It's very you, Gracie.'

'I thought so,' I smiled back at her.

Just then, the curtain on the changing room next to mine was pulled back.

'I thought I recognised that voice,' a voice behind me said.

I turned around, only to find myself faced with a vision in white. 'Gracie Parker,' the voice said, sounding amused.

I looked up into the face of the speaker, and almost immediately wished I hadn't. Standing there, smiling cruelly at me, was Lorna Spence.

And she was wearing a beautiful, white, wedding dress.

'Lorna?' I asked stupidly.

'That's Lorna?' Gretchen asked, but neither I nor my nemesis acknowledged her question.

'So you remember me then?' Lorna asked me. 'But then, I suppose you would, wouldn't you?'

'What – what are you doing here?' I managed to get out.

'What does it look like?' Lorna asked, motioning down to her dress. I must have been gawping at her, as she looked me up and down and grinned. 'Always the bridesmaid, never the bride, huh, Gracie?' she commented.

I felt myself blushing furiously.

'Gracie's my maid of honour, actually,' Gretchen said, trying to step in on my behalf.

But as much as I appreciated Gretchen's efforts, they didn't have any effect on Lorna, who just smiled nastily.

Besides, this was a battle I had to fight for myself.

'And who exactly are you marrying?' I asked Lorna, trying my best to sound nonchalant, despite the fact that I knew her answer was going to tear me up inside.

'David, of course,' Lorna smiled.

I felt like I had been hit by a sledgehammer. It wasn't that I still loved David – because I didn't. I was over him. But the thought of the man I was supposed to marry getting married to Lorna instead? That really hurt – bad.

'Do you love him?' I asked Lorna, trying to keep my composure.

'What's love got to do with it?' Lorna asked back.

'Love has everything to do with it!'

I wanted to scream at her.

'I don't *love* him,' Lorna finally answered. 'Not in the traditional sense anyway.'

'What other sense is there?' Gretchen asked, clearly shocked by Lorna's admission.

'David will make a great husband,' Lorna shrugged. 'He's

hard-working, he earns enough money that I needn't work again…'

She started to count off the points she was making on her fingers. 'He's loyal, so I know he won't go cheating on me –'

'How do *you* know?' I interrupted. 'He cheated on me. Who says he won't do the same to you?'

'Because,' Lorna said, smiling nastily (did she ever smile any other way?), 'I give David what he needs.'

Beyond anger after that last comment, I lunged for Lorna.

But she took a step back – and it was only the quick actions of Gretchen, who grabbed me to try and prevent the oncoming assault, that stopped me from falling flat on my face (in what would've been a pretty good Roman Pearson imitation).

Lorna laughed as she watched this and I would've lunged for her again – damn the consequences – except Gretchen had quite strategically placed herself between me and Lorna, and was currently holding me back, presumably lest I do more damage to myself than I did to my enemy.

'But you know what the best thing about David is?' Lorna continued. I didn't answer her. I just glared. 'The best thing about David,' she said, 'is that he spends so much time at work, he'd have no idea if *I* was cheating on *him*. Or at least, that's the pattern I've noticed so far.'

She grinned at me then, as if she was aware there was nothing I could do. And then, with a flourish, she disappeared back into her changing room.

I felt humiliated – and completely and utterly helpless. Until I realised that I wasn't helpless. There *was* something I could do to stop Lorna.

I could warn David.

❄ ❄ ❄

I hadn't set eyes on Lorna again that day following her disappearance back into the changing room. Which had a lot to do with Gretchen hurrying me out of the bridal boutique so quickly I didn't even have time to change back into my normal clothes. Gretchen had handed some money to the boutique owner in payment for the dress, and then we'd left with me still wearing it, my regular clothes clutched against my chest.

We'd garnered a lot of strange looks while heading back to Gretchen's car, though Gretchen had claimed it was worth it in order to avoid another confrontation with Lorna, which could've gotten us both black eyes.

I'd disagreed, but had done as I was told.

Because at the same time as Gretchen and I had been making our great escape, I'd been formulating a plan in my head. I had to warn David about Lorna's betrayal. It was the right thing to do.

So, once I'd gotten home, and out of earshot of Gretchen's sympathising, I'd picked up the phone and called my ex-fiancé, asking him to meet me for lunch. After all, I figured finding out your partner was cheating on you was something that should be done face-to-face. And I should know.

David, despite expressing reservations about the mystery meeting, had agreed to the rendezvous. And that was the easy part. Now all I needed to do was cancel my plans with Cleo in order to have lunch with David.

'Gracie, why are you calling me now?' Cleo asked. 'We're meeting for lunch in half-an-hour, remember? Can't whatever it is wait until then?'

It was Friday morning, and I was calling Cleo from work. Unfortunately, I knew she wasn't going to like what I was about to tell her.

'That's the thing,' I replied. 'I have to cancel lunch. I can't meet you today after all – something important's come up.' Sensing a need to placate her, I added: 'I'm really sorry. I hope you don't mind.'

'That depends,' Cleo sighed. 'Because if you're meeting Roman Pearson for lunch then I can just about forgive you for ditching me. But anything else? No, sorry.'

'I'm not meeting Roman for lunch,' I told her.

'But you are meeting someone?' Cleo prompted, quite correctly. 'Come on, Gracie! If you're not lunching with me, I need to know who you *are* lunching with!'

I took a deep breath. 'I'm having lunch with David,' I blurted out, as quickly as I could.

'David?' Cleo repeated. 'Did you say David?'

'Yes,' I said again. 'David.'

'David who?' Cleo asked. 'David Beckham? David Hewlett? Because I know you can't mean –'

'You know exactly who I mean,' I interrupted her.

'Gracie, I have just one question for you,' Cleo said. 'WHY?'

'Because there are things he needs to know,' I told her. 'About Lorna.'

'Lorna the bitch he ditched you for?' Cleo asked. 'What about her?'

'She doesn't love him,' I told Cleo.

'And you know this because...?'

'She told me.'

'Oh. Okay,' Cleo said. 'But Gracie, that doesn't mean –'

'I have to tell him, Cleo,' I said. 'Maybe if he knows then –'

'He'll drop her and come back to you?' Cleo suggested, trying to fill in the blanks. 'Gracie, is that what you really want?'

'No!' I protested. 'I don't want him back. It's just –'

'You don't want her to have him,' Cleo interrupted.

'She doesn't deserve him.'

'Oh, I'd say they pretty much deserve each other,' Cleo replied. 'Now can I give you some advice, Gracie? And bear in mind, I'm gonna give it to you whether you want it or not, so you may as well say yes.'

I had to smile. 'Go on,' I told her.

'Stay out of it,' Cleo said bluntly. 'It doesn't concern you anymore.'

I thought about that for a moment before replying.

'I can't,' I finally told Cleo.

'Gracie –' Cleo began.

'I've got to go,' I said, before hanging up the phone.

I would call Cleo later and apologise for my abruptness. But right now, I just couldn't have her trying to dissuade me from what I knew I had to do.

Suddenly, the phone on my desk rang. It was Cleo – it had to be. Rather than answer the call, I picked up the receiver, then put it down again, cutting off the call. Then I took the receiver and placed it on my desk, leaving the phone off the hook.

'Don't let Olivia see you doing that,' I heard a voice say.

I looked up to find Billy standing in front of my desk. 'Just walked in,' he explained with a smile.

'Olivia's at lunch,' I told him.

He smiled and took his regular seat on the edge of my desk. 'Well, I didn't come to see Olivia,' he confided. 'I came to see you. Would you like to have lunch with me today?'

'I'd love to,' I told him truthfully, 'but I can't.'

'Olivia keeping you chained to the desk?' Billy joked, looking under my desk for the supposed chains.

'No. But I have to meet someone,' I told him. Billy looked at me, giving me his full attention. 'I have to meet David,' I told him.

'David?' Billy asked, clearly trying to remember how he knew this person.

'My ex-fiancé,' I clarified.

'Oh,' Billy said, looking a little crestfallen. 'Why are you meeting him?' He attempted a joke. 'Still need to give the ring back?'

'Actually, yes,' I admitted, smiling at the thought. 'But that's not why.'

'Then why?'

'I bumped into Lorna Spence yesterday,' I told Billy. 'She's the one David ditched me for,' I added, somewhat bitterly. I looked at Billy in order to gauge his reaction to my next statement. 'She was trying on a wedding dress.'

'They're getting married?' Billy asked.

'Yes!' I cried. 'Can you believe it? But the worst thing about it is that she doesn't even love him. And she's been cheating on him – she told me so herself.'

'And now you're going to tell him?' Billy asked, putting the pieces together.

'I think he deserves to know.'

'Why?' Billy asked. 'Why does he deserve to know? He didn't think you deserved to know that he was sleeping with Lorna behind your back!'

'That's beside the point,' I snapped. 'Oh, and thanks for bringing that up by the way. I really needed a visual reminder.'

'I'm sorry,' Billy said, softening. 'I just think you're making a big mistake.'

'I've already heard this from Cleo,' I told him. 'I don't need to hear it from you as well.'

'Cleo's your best friend,' Billy reminded me. 'Maybe you should listen to her.'

At that moment, the door to the office opened and Olivia walked in. She saw Billy, but even that failed to raise a smile from her.

'Hello, Billy,' she said politely.

'Hi, Olivia,' Billy replied.

While Billy was distracted by Olivia's return, I grabbed my jacket from where I'd thrown it over the back of my chair, and stood up.

'I have to go now,' I told Billy.

'Okay,' Billy said, seemingly accepting my decision. He stood up. 'Then I'm going with you.'

'Billy –' I began.

'No arguments,' Billy interrupted. 'You either do this with me or not at all.'

'Fine,' I muttered. 'If you insist.'

I made my way out of the office, with Billy following right behind me. To be honest, I was incredibly nervous about what this meeting with David would throw up, and quite liked the idea of having Billy there for moral support.

But of course, I wasn't about to let Billy know that.

❄ ❄ ❄

David was already waiting for me when Billy and I arrived at *Annabelle's* – the café so regularly favoured by Cleo and me. And he was sitting at an outside table, which I was grateful for. It was a little cramped inside, and the last thing I wanted was to end up sharing this conversation with all of the other diners.

'Gracie, hi,' David said warmly.

Well, it *seemed* as if he was pleased to see me. Of course, he hadn't heard what I had to say yet.

David stood up to greet me, but seemed unsure whether I was planning on a hug or a kiss in greeting. I did neither. It was an awkward moment, and I was glad I had Billy with me to provide a distraction.

'This is Billy,' I told David, motioning to my companion. 'Billy, this is David.'

David held out his hand for Billy to shake.

'Pleased to meet you,' he told Billy politely.

'Wish I could say likewise,' Billy replied, ignoring David's gesture.

Uh oh. So much for Billy's presence dispelling any awkward moments.

Clearly a little insulted, David coughed to cover up his embarrassment and sat back down. I followed his lead, taking the chair across from him, and Billy reluctantly sat down next to me.

'Gracie, if you thought bringing me here to meet your new boyfriend would make me jealous, then you were very wrong,' David blurted out.

As I stared at David, shocked by his abrupt accusation, Billy laughed.

'Wow,' he said to me. 'Did you hear that? I think he might have an even bigger ego than Roman!' Then he turned to David, adding: 'And that's a pretty big achievement by the way.'

'Billy!' I chastised him. 'You're not helping!' Billy glared at David, but said nothing further. Grateful for his silence, I turned to David.

'I brought you here to talk about Lorna,' I told him.

'Lorna?' David asked, confused. 'What about Lorna?'

'She's cheating on you,' I told him bluntly.

He stared at me for a moment. I assumed he was in shock at finding out the truth, but apparently my statement had meant nothing to him.

'And how do you know that?' he asked, not smiling.

'She told me,' I replied.

'Oh, Lorna *told* you,' David said, with a mocking smile. 'Do you really expect me to believe that?'

'I saw her yesterday,' I recalled, 'when she was trying on her wedding dress.' The last two words almost stuck in my throat, but I managed to get them out. 'I asked her if she loved you and she said no. And she told me that she'd been cheating on you – and that she'd continue cheating on you once you were married.'

'Really?' David asked. 'She told you all that?'

'You should listen to her,' Billy said, sounding incredibly annoyed. 'She's trying to do you a favour.'

'By telling me a pack of lies?'

'It's the truth,' I insisted.

'It's not the truth,' David replied. 'It's some twisted little fantasy you've created because you can't handle the fact that I'm marrying Lorna.'

I was lost for words. Billy, however, wasn't.

'Why *are* you marrying her?' he asked David.

'What?' David asked, though he'd clearly heard Billy's original question.

'Why are you marrying her?' Billy asked again. 'Do you love her?'

'Yes,' David replied. 'I do. Not that it's any of your –'

'And she claims she loves *you*,' Billy interrupted. 'And so you assume that she's telling the truth. And that because she says she loves you, it obviously means she's faithful to you –'

'Yes,' David interrupted, but Billy wasn't finished yet.

'But you told Gracie that you loved her once, didn't you?' Billy asked. 'And yet you were cheating on her?'

'This is different,' David protested.

'Yeah,' Billy said, leaning back in his chair – his point having been made. 'Whatever you say.'

'I knew I shouldn't have come here,' David said, standing up. 'This was a big mistake.'

'No,' I said, looking up at him. 'The only mistake was mine. I asked you here because I thought you deserved to know the truth. Obviously I was wrong.'

David had no reply for that. Instead, he stepped away from the table, prepared to make a quick exit.

'Goodbye, Gracie,' he said, and then walked away.

Billy and I were left at the table alone. I looked at Billy, but he seemed to be avoiding my gaze.

'Thank you for sticking up for me,' I told him.

After a moment, he turned to look at me.

'Why did you come here?' he asked me.

'I told you,' I replied, confused as to why he was questioning me over this again. 'I wanted to warn David.'

'After what he did to you, why would you even care?' Billy asked.

'Because,' I said, not really knowing how to answer that – how to put my thoughts into words. 'Because –'

'Because you still care about him,' Billy supplied.

'No!' I said. 'I don't!'

'Are you sure?' Billy asked. Without waiting for me to reply, he stood up. 'You deserve better, Gracie,' he told me. 'Better than him.' And before I'd had a chance to answer him, Billy was already walking away.

I might have gone after him except, at that exact moment, Cleo appeared.

'Gracie!' she cried. 'Are you okay?'

'Cleo?' I asked, looking up. 'What are you doing here?'

'I came to try and stop you doing anything stupid,' she told me, 'but I guess I was a little too late for that.'

'How did you know I'd be here?' I asked her, as she sat down next to me at the table.

'Are you kidding?' she replied. 'Where else would you be?' She gestured to the café we were sitting outside. 'Gracie, you're a creature of habit. Face it.'

'Did you see any of that?' I asked her, referring to my confrontation with David. And, come to think of it, with Billy.

'Every little bit,' Cleo admitted. 'I didn't want to interrupt, but when David started being mean to you, I was going to jump in and defend you – only that other guy did it for me. And by the way, who was that guy? Because he was hot!'

'That was Billy,' I told her. 'He works for Roman too.'

'Yeah, I know who Billy is,' Cleo told me. 'You've mentioned him often enough.'

'I have?' I asked, not aware that I'd done so.

'Oh yeah,' she replied. 'And has he got it bad for you!'

'What?' I asked, trying not to laugh. 'What are you talking about?!'

'Billy,' Cleo said. 'He likes you – it's obvious.'

'No, he doesn't!' I protested. 'We're just friends.'

'Oh sure,' Cleo said. 'Whatever you say.'

'Cleo,' I told her again. 'We're just friends.'

'I believe you!' Cleo said.

Then she grabbed a menu from the table and flicked

through it. 'Now, are we going to have lunch or what? Because I'm starving!'

'Okay,' I agreed, if only to stop her interrogation of me. 'Let's have lunch.' I picked up another menu and started to look through it. But I couldn't concentrate on the dishes available. I couldn't think about food.

All I could think about was Billy.

❄ ❄ ❄

That Saturday afternoon, I went out shopping with my father. Yes, that's right – just me and my dad.

I couldn't remember the last time my father and I had been out alone together. Mother usually accompanied him everywhere he went – or rather, dragged him along to whatever social function she was currently attending. But this afternoon, Mum was helping out at the church hall jumble sale, and my father wasn't needed. Which meant we were both blissfully free of her for a good few hours at least.

With Mum's prior engagement in mind, our little shopping expedition had been arranged Friday night, when my father had stealthily requested my help while Mum was busy in the kitchen.

'I need to buy an anniversary present for your mother,' he'd told me. 'Preferably something expensive, or I'll never hear the end of it.'

'It's your anniversary?' I'd asked him, feigning ignorance. 'Really?'

I wasn't about to let him suspect I was planning a surprise party. That just wouldn't do.

'Twenty-five years,' he'd told me with a smile. 'You get less than that if you murder someone.'

I think he was kidding, but it was hard to tell.

'So would you be able to help me choose something?' he'd asked.

'I don't know,' I'd said, not at all keen on the idea. 'I'm not sure I'm the best judge of what Mum likes.'

'I'm sure you know her better than you think,' Dad had assured me. 'Besides, you're the only woman I have to ask. Well, aside from Abigail Stewart, of course. But I just know she'd run straight to your mother and tell her what I'd bought.'

'What about Aunt Celia?' I'd asked, eager to help him find a different solution to his dilemma. 'She's Mum's sister. I'm sure she'll be able to help.'

'I don't think my nerves could stand a day out shopping with your Aunt Celia,' Dad had told me.

Which kind of made me wonder how he'd put up with Mum all these years.

'Okay,' I'd finally agreed. 'I'll help you. But I take no responsibility whatsoever if she doesn't like the gift.'

Because, let's face it – whatever I picked, it would be wrong.

'Done,' Dad had agreed.

Which brings us to the present.

My father and I were currently standing in a jewellery store, browsing the contents of a tray of rings. After much deliberation and traipsing around the various shops, Dad had come to the conclusion that he wanted to buy my mother an eternity ring as an anniversary present. Now it was just a matter of choosing a ring. Which I had a feeling was *not* going to be as simple a task as it had originally sounded.

'What about this one?' I asked my father, pointing at a ring set with diamonds and sapphires. 'This is nice.'

'No,' Dad said, shaking his head in disagreement, 'that's no good.'

'I think it's pretty,' I told him. I would've been delighted to have received such a ring as a gift.

'What about this one?' It was my father's turn to ask the question.

I followed the direction of my father's pointed finger, searching out the ring in question. His selection was a very attractive piece of jewellery, set with diamonds and rubies. The only problem was – it was gold.

'Shouldn't you get her something silver?' I asked him. 'What with it being your silver wedding anniversary and all?'

'No!' Dad said, apparently shocked. 'Your mother *hates* silver jewellery.'

'She does?' I asked him, filled with a sudden sense of dread.

I'd bought my mother a silver bracelet as a birthday gift this year. Guess that had been a huge mistake.

'Yes,' Dad confirmed. 'She only ever wears gold jewellery.'

I tried to remember if I'd yet seen my mother wearing the bracelet I'd given her, but I couldn't recall ever seeing it on her wrist. Which I supposed answered my question. Although in truth, I was surprised that she hadn't simply asked me to take the gift back. Tact had never been one of my mother's strong points, after all.

Or at least, it wasn't where I was concerned.

So I guess I must've caught her on a good day. Well, either that or she'd donated the bracelet to today's jumble sale. Yeah, that was probably more likely.

'What's the point of an eternity ring anyway?' I grumbled to my father. 'You're already married. How much more of a commitment do you need?'

'Commitment's not about marriage,' Dad explained. 'When it comes down to it, marriage is just a piece of paper. Commitment is about loving and trusting a person and working hard to maintain that love and trust.'

I just stared at him.

'Who made you the relationship guru?' I asked him.

'I've been married twenty-five years,' Dad smiled at me. 'You don't seriously think I've lived with your mother for that long without learning something, do you?'

'I honestly don't know *how* you've lived with Mum for that long,' I grinned at him.

Dad shook his head sadly. 'You don't see her like I do,' he replied. 'When I look at your mother, I see a loving, caring, generous woman. Someone who's always willing to help others. Someone who wants the best for her family.'

'Some people might call that interfering,' I commented.

'Well they'd be wrong,' Dad insisted. 'You know, your mother gave up a lot for you and Warren.'

'Like what?' I asked him.

'Like her dreams of stardom,' Dad revealed. 'You don't know this, but when your mother was younger, she wanted to act more than anything else in the world.'

'She did?' I asked him, surprised.

Well this was news to me. 'How come I've never heard about this before?' I frowned at him. 'As far as I knew, Mum worked as a secretary before you two met.'

'That's true,' Dad confirmed, 'but she was also heavily involved in the theatre – and that was her first love. Your mother adored the limelight,' he told me, 'and she wanted more of it, even when we were first together. It was really only when she got pregnant with you that she decided to settle down.'

'Great! So Mum blames me for ending her fledgling acting career?' I asked him. 'No wonder she hates me so much!'

'Don't be ridiculous!' Dad said. 'She doesn't hate you; she loves you. Ellen knew she couldn't be a good mother if she was off chasing fame and fortune. And more than anything, she wanted to be a good mother. So she made her choice – she chose you.'

My head was spinning. My mother an actress? What a bizarre concept. If it had been Warren telling me this, I would've been convinced that the whole thing was nothing more than an elaborate story. But my father? He was as straight as they came – he didn't play mind games.

Although, come to think of it, the whole thing *did* make sense. Mother had always been a drama queen, after all.

'You're not making this up, are you?' I asked my father, though I already knew he was speaking the truth.

'Since you started working for this Roman Pearson chap, your mother's interest in the entertainment world has been reawakened,' Dad told me. 'All the glitter, glamour and fame – that was always her dream.'

He smiled. 'However much she tries to hide it, I know she still craves it.'

'Well, I guess that explains why she likes Roman so much,' I mused, more to myself than to my father.

'You can't really blame her for trying to live vicariously through you,' Dad said, almost sternly.

'Oh, I really don't think that's what she's trying to do,' I told him.

'Trust me,' Dad insisted. 'I know your mother. When she "interferes" in your life, it's firstly because she loves you, and secondly because she envies you.'

Talk about laying a guilt trip on me.

'Speaking of which,' Dad said, 'your mother told me about what happened at the bridal store.'

'What? How did she find out about that?' I asked him.

'Gretchen told her,' Dad said. I opened my mouth to protest, but he held up a hand, silencing me. 'And before you say anything, Gretchen only did it because she was worried about you.'

'Well, there's no need for her to be worried about me,' I told him. 'I'm fine. I couldn't care less that David's marrying Lorna.'

'Really?' Dad asked. He obviously wasn't convinced.

'Really,' I told him firmly. 'I've even met someone else. His name's Billy and he works for Roman too.'

'Is this where I do my fatherly act of disapproval?' Dad smiled.

'No need,' I sighed. 'I'm not sure if Billy's even speaking to me now anyway.'

'Why ever not?' Dad asked.

I didn't answer him straight away. I was too busy debating whether to tell him the truth or not. But I figured that both my mother and father would hear all about my latest encounter with David sooner or later, such was the nature of the local grapevine.

Better that they get my side of the story straight away.

'Because I met up with David the other day,' I revealed. My father raised an eyebrow in surprise, but didn't comment. 'I was trying to convince him not to marry Lorna,' I confessed quickly. 'Billy wasn't too thrilled about it though – he thought I should let David get on with it.'

'Then I like him already,' Dad smiled. 'And I agree with him. David has to realise for himself that he's made a mistake. You can't do that for him.'

'And what if he *does* realise he's made a mistake?'

'Then it's up to you to do what you think is right,' Dad said.

'But how will I know what's right?' I pressed him further.

'Just do what makes you happy,' Dad sighed. 'Oh, and try to be a little kinder to your mother in future, okay?'

I watched as my father pointed at the gold, diamond and ruby ring which was nestling in the tray in front of us, then motioned to the assistant behind the jewellery counter, who immediately joined us.

'I'll take that one,' he said decisively.

At least one of us knew what we wanted.

Chapter Fourteen

'Warren!' I yelled, before banging on my brother's bedroom door once more.

However, just like the first time I'd knocked on Warren's door, I got no reply. Still, I doubted Warren could even hear my calls over the noise of the pulsating rock music blaring out from his stereo. I decided to try again.

'Warren!' I shouted, not even bothering to knock this time. 'I'm coming in! You'd better not be up to anything in there!'

That got his attention (though I decided it was best not to think about exactly what Warren might be up to) and the bedroom door suddenly swung open. Standing in the doorway was my scowling little brother.

'What?' he demanded.

'Warren,' I said, treating him to my sweetest smile. 'I need your assistance.'

'I'm busy,' Warren said.

'Yeah, you're always busy,' I reminded him, determined not to let him fob me off again. 'But this time I really don't care. I want you to help me deliver some party invitations.'

'I can't,' Warren insisted. 'I have company.'

'No, you don't,' I said firmly.

'Yes,' Warren said with a smile, 'I do.'

'I don't believe you,' I told him.

'It's true,' Warren said, shrugging. 'See for yourself.'

Warren opened his bedroom door a little wider, so I could see further into the room. Sitting on Warren's bed, surrounded by CDs and music magazines, was Amy. She smiled and gave a little wave when she saw me.

'Hi, Gracie,' Amy said shyly.

'Hi, Amy,' I replied, before turning back to face Warren. 'Do Mum and Dad know she's here?' I asked him.

'What they don't know won't hurt them,' Warren smiled slyly.

It was Sunday morning and my parents were at church. They'd left quite early, though I had no idea how long Amy had been here. I certainly hadn't heard her arrive this morning. Knowing Warren though, he'd convinced her to climb a ladder up to his bedroom window or something.

'I thought Amy wasn't really your girlfriend?' I asked Warren.

After casting a furtive glance back at Amy, Warren stepped outside his room, pulling the door closed behind him.

'She's not,' he insisted.

'Then what are you two doing in there?' I asked him suspiciously.

'We're just listening to some music,' Warren said. 'I told you before – Amy's a friend.'

I studied Warren for a moment. Despite all of his best

efforts to hide it, I could tell there was something more there.

'You know, if you like Amy, you should tell her,' I advised Warren.

Yeah, like I was really qualified to be handing out romantic advice.

'We're just friends,' Warren claimed. 'Our relationship is purely a business arrangement.'

'Oh, so you're paying her to be here today?' I asked him.

'No,' Warren said immediately.

I could tell Warren was beginning to get agitated. He didn't like talking about Amy – which could mean only one thing. That he really, really liked her.

'You should invite Amy to Mum and Dad's party,' I told him.

Warren scowled at me again.

'Maybe I will, maybe I won't,' he said.

'Maybe you and Amy could discuss it while delivering some invitations?' I suggested.

'Yeah, maybe not,' Warren said.

And before I could stop him, Warren ducked back inside his room. I threw out an arm to stop him closing the door completely.

'Warren!' I cried. 'This isn't fair! So far you've given me zero help with this party. All I want is for you to deliver some invitations.'

'But Amy's here,' Warren said, looking at me sadly through the crack in the open door. 'You wouldn't want to stand in the way of true love, would you?'

Oh, so now he loved her? It was amazing how Warren twisted these things to suit his own agenda.

'The only person you love is yourself,' I told him.

'Well, who wouldn't love me?' Warren replied with a grin, before quickly closing the rest of the door in my face.

I sighed, defeated. I could have barged in there of course, and demanded that Warren help me out. But there really was little point. Once Warren had set his mind on not doing something, not even a semi-naked Angelina Jolie could get him to do it.

Well, maybe a semi-naked Angelina Jolie. But that wasn't exactly a resource at my disposal.

Which meant that I now had a fun afternoon of playing postwoman ahead of me. Not exactly how I'd planned on spending my Sunday.

❄ ❄ ❄

After a quick trip to the nearest postbox to send off all the long-distance invitations, I began going house-to-house, popping invites through letter boxes. And there were an awful lot of invitations to deliver. It seemed Mum and Dad (well, Mum mostly) knew almost everyone who lived down our road. No great surprise, seeing as Mum made it her business to know everyone.

However, it also meant that, by inviting everyone they knew to the party (so as not to offend anyone by leaving them out) I'd created an awful lot of work for myself. Still, I'd been going at a steady pace so far, getting the majority of invitations posted. Until, that is, I came to Mabel and Fred Hoffman's house.

I was just about to pop an invitation through the Hoffmans' letter box, when their front door suddenly opened, causing me to jump in surprise.

Mabel Hoffman, standing inside, smiled at me. 'Gracie Parker!' she cried. 'What a nice surprise!'

I noticed Mabel had her shoes and coat on, and a shopping bag over one arm. Which was good – that meant she wouldn't want to talk for long.

'Hello, Mrs Hoffman,' I said warmly. 'I didn't mean to keep you,' I added, gesturing to her shopping bag, 'I just wanted to give you this.'

I held the invitation out to her, but she didn't take it. Instead, she took a step back into the hallway of her home.

'How lovely!' she said. 'Won't you come in for a nice cup of tea?'

I should have known. Mabel Hoffman always invited everyone inside for a 'nice cup of tea'. She was renowned for it. Whoever knocked on her door, whether postman, double glazing salesman, or even Jehovah's Witnesses – all were offered the same thing. A nice cup of tea.

'Weren't you going out?' I asked Mabel, nodding at her shopping bag again in the hope she would take the hint.

'Oh, I was just going to pop up the shops,' Mabel said. Then, to my dismay, I watched as she put down her bag and started to take off her coat. 'But that can wait,' she added. 'Do come in.'

With a reluctant smile, I stepped inside.

'Thanks,' I told her, not meaning it at all.

I mean, don't get me wrong, Mabel and Fred Hoffman were nice enough. In fact, they were a lovely, sweet, retired couple. But I hadn't exactly pictured myself spending my Sunday afternoon drinking tea with Mabel Hoffman.

This was all Warren's fault. If he'd been delivering the invitations, I would've been safe from this. And he would've been the one drinking tea.

Mabel led me into the kitchen, where she immediately put the kettle on to boil. 'Where's Mr Hoffman?' I asked her.

'Oh, he's where he always is,' she smiled at me. 'In the garden.'

I looked out of the kitchen window and soon spotted Fred Hoffman tending to his vegetable patch. Fred Hoffman was a keen gardener – he'd told me once it helped keep him fit for other activities. I had stopped him before he'd had a chance to go into detail about just what those activities were. The picture that had formed in my head had been icky enough.

After the kettle had boiled, Mabel poured us both a 'nice cup of tea' before leading the way into the living room. There she sat down in an armchair, indicating that I should take a seat on the sofa. I did so.

'So what have you brought me?' Mabel asked excitedly.

I put my nice cup of tea down on the coffee table in front of the sofa, and handed Mabel the envelope I was holding.

'It's an invitation,' I told her, as she opened the envelope and looked inside, 'to an anniversary party for my parents. It's a surprise party,' I added.

'How lovely!' Mabel said, reading the invitation. 'Did you plan all of this yourself?'

'Yes,' I said, deciding that Warren didn't deserve any credit at all, 'all by myself.'

'Well aren't you a wonderful daughter?!' Mabel exclaimed. 'I wish I had children who would do such a thing for me!'

I thought it better not to tell Mabel that both Warren and I had ulterior motives for planning the party. 'And you're such a busy girl at the moment, aren't you?' Mabel continued.

'I am?' I asked, wondering just what Mabel was referring to.

'Well, yes,' Mabel said. 'Your mother told me all about your new job. It sounds very exciting.'

So much for that being a secret.

'Yes,' I agreed with a smile. 'It is.'

'And I'm so glad you've found someone special after all that horrible business with your fiancé,' Mabel said.

'Yes,' I said, automatically agreeing with Mabel. Then I realised what she'd said. 'What?' I asked.

'It's okay, dear,' Mabel said. 'Your mother told me. And I know you want to keep it all under wraps, so I won't tell anyone else.'

'Tell anyone else what?' I asked.

'Well, about you and Roman Pearson of course,' Mabel said. 'That you're...you know.'

'No,' I said, 'I don't know.'

'There's no need to be coy, dear,' Mabel said. 'You should be proud that a handsome man is courting you.'

It didn't take me long to translate Mabel's meaning.

'And Mum told you this?' I asked her.

'Yes,' Mabel said. 'Oh, and she showed me a lovely picture of you two together. I have a copy somewhere – let me find it.'

Mabel rummaged through a pile of magazines on the coffee table and pulled one out, flicking through it until she found what she was looking for.

'Here,' she said, handing the magazine to me. 'Don't you two make a handsome couple?'

It was the same magazine I'd read at Gretchen's house – the one containing the photograph of me and Roman. The incriminating photograph.

I basically had two choices. I could deny the existence of a romance between myself and Roman – which Mabel probably wouldn't believe anyway. Or I could go along with what Mabel was saying.

'Yes,' I said, opting for the latter. 'We do, don't we?'

'You're going to look lovely at the wedding together,' Mabel commented.

'Wedding?' I asked her, my mouth practically dropping open.

That was it. The charade had gone much too far. 'We're not getting married,' I told her.

'No,' Mabel said. 'I know that. I meant your friend Gretchen's wedding. Fred and I are going, you know.'

I must've looked confused, as she added: 'You *are* bringing Roman as your guest, aren't you?'

'Guest?' I asked her, genuinely shocked. 'Since when do I need a guest?'

❄ ❄ ❄

'Why didn't you tell me I needed to bring a guest?' I asked Gretchen over the phone later that day.

After managing to escape from Mabel Hoffman (by promising her that Roman would be at the wedding), I'd run straight home and immediately called the bride-to-be for confirmation of Mabel's theory.

'I thought you knew,' Gretchen said.

'And I thought I was going to be paired up with the best man!' I told her. 'Isn't that traditional?'

'Well, yes, normally it is,' Gretchen admitted. 'But the best man is Robert's brother, Michael. And unfortunately Michael's girlfriend is rather possessive – and she's going to be at the wedding too.'

'So I'm left without a partner!' I cried. 'Gretchen, the wedding's on Saturday!'

'Yes, Gracie, I know that,' Gretchen replied. 'I'm the one getting married, remember? You're supposed to be calming *me* down about things, not the other way around.'

'Sorry,' I apologised, though it didn't make me feel any better.

'That's okay,' Gretchen sighed. 'Look, Gracie, it's not compulsory, you know. You don't *have* to bring someone to the wedding with you. I'm sure Robert and I can find someone to partner you.'

She paused for a moment to think. 'My options are that great, huh?' I asked, when she didn't come up with an answer.

'Sorry,' Gretchen said. 'I can't think. I just have so much to do this week, Gracie.'

'I understand,' I told her. 'And I'm sorry – I shouldn't be bothering you with this right now.'

'I'm sure you'll think of someone to bring,' Gretchen told me.

'Yes,' I said. 'I'm sure I will.'

Unfortunately, it seemed that my choice of wedding guest had already been decided for me.

❄ ❄ ❄

'You have to take Roman!' my mother said. 'Everyone expects you to!'

'Only because you told them we were dating!' I protested.

While bearing in mind my father's earlier advice that I should try and be nicer to my mother, I'd really had no choice but to confront her about the things she'd been telling people. So far, however, I'd gotten nowhere.

'Well you *are* dating!' Mum exclaimed.

'I never told you that!' I cried.

'You didn't have to,' Mum said, with a smile. 'I could see it for myself. It's obvious how fond you are of each other. Plus, there was that photograph –'

'Yes,' I interrupted, 'and how many people did you show that to?'

'Just a few close friends,' Mum said. 'And some of the neighbours. Oh, and I left a copy of the magazine at the hairdressers for people to read.'

'Mum!' I cried.

'I know you wanted it to be a secret, sweetheart,' Mum said, 'but this sort of thing can't be kept quiet for long.

You should be proud you and Roman are together. You're dating the most eligible man in the country, Gracie. You should be shouting it from the rooftops.'

'I don't need to,' I said, looking at her pointedly. 'I have you to do that for me.'

'Can't a mother be proud of her daughter?' Mum sniffed.

'I don't recall you ever being proud of me before,' I reminded her.

'That was different,' Mum said. 'You're dating Roman Pearson now. You've made a success of your life. You need to show people that.'

'And just how am I supposed to do that?' I asked, though I already knew what my mother was about to say.

'Bring Roman to the wedding,' she said, with a convincing smile. 'After all, everyone expects you to.'

❄ ❄ ❄

'I don't really see your dilemma,' Cleo sighed. 'So your mother wants you to take Roman Pearson to the wedding? Big deal! It's Roman Pearson – it's not like she's asking you to take Freddy Krueger as your date!'

It was Monday morning and I'd called Cleo from work in order to ask her advice about the wedding situation. But so far she hadn't been much help.

Of course, I hadn't yet explained all of the circumstances of my dilemma.

'The last time I saw Roman, I shut a door in his face,' I reminded her. 'Who says he'll even want to go out with me again?'

'You won't know until you ask,' Cleo pointed out.

'But what if he doesn't want to go?' I asked her. 'Now everyone's expecting me to bring Roman to the wedding. And if I take him, it'll prove to them I'm not a failure. It'll show them I'm a success and I can get a successful man to go out with me. But if I don't take him, they're all going to think I'm a total failure. And a liar.'

'So you know what you have to do then?' Cleo asked.

'What?' I replied, eager for an easy solution. 'What do I do?'

'You have to make sure Roman goes with you to the wedding,' Cleo replied. 'Get down on your knees and beg him to go. Pay him if you have to. Just make sure you get him there.'

It was a solution of sorts. There was just one problem.

'But –' I began.

'But what?' Cleo immediately interrupted, as if she'd been expecting it.

'But I don't want to go with Roman!' I blurted out.

'Really,' Cleo said. 'What a surprise.'

'You don't sound surprised,' I told her.

'Gracie, you're so predictable,' Cleo said.

'I am?'

'Yes,' Cleo sighed. 'You have a million reasons to ask Roman to go with you and just one reason not to.'

'I want to go with somebody else,' I filled in.

'Exactly,' Cleo said. 'So why don't you just ask Billy and get it over with?'

'How did you know –' I began.

'It was Billy you wanted to go with?' Cleo finished.

'Because I'm your best friend, that's how. Also, that look you gave him when he walked away from you on Saturday was just plain needy.'

'It was?' I asked. I thought she must be exaggerating just a little.

'Oh yeah,' Cleo confirmed. 'Looks like he's not the only one who's got it bad.'

'You think I should ask Billy?' I questioned her.

I looked at my formal invitation to Gretchen's wedding, which I held in my hands. It had, in fact, said 'Gracie & Guest' all along. Which just went to show how totally unobservant I could be sometimes.

'Definitely,' Cleo replied.

And, speak of the devil, who should walk into the office at that very moment but Billy – and Roman.

As the two men greeted Olivia, I attempted to get rid of Cleo.

'They just walked in,' I told her.

'Who?' she asked.

'Billy and Roman,' I replied. 'I'll call you back.'

'Don't you dare!' Cleo protested. 'I want to hear this! Keep me on the line!'

'Okay,' I muttered, and rested the phone receiver on my desk, with Cleo still listening in. Meanwhile, Roman made his way over to my desk. Billy, it seemed, had gotten stuck talking to Olivia.

'Gracie Parker,' Roman said with a grin. 'My favourite PA.'

'Hi, Roman,' I smiled, not sure whether or not he was still smarting over that door-in-the-face incident.

'Did you enjoy Toby's party?' he asked, though he continued before I had a chance to answer. 'Hasn't he got a fabulous house?'

'Yes,' I said. 'Very nice. Listen, Roman,' I added, deciding that I should probably apologise after all, 'I'm sorry about –'

'Your mother's a lovely woman,' Roman continued. He seemed to be in a very good mood today. I wondered if he might've been drinking, but then realised Billy would have been keeping an eye on him – so probably not.

'Yes,' I said, not meaning it. 'Lovely.'

I looked across the room to see what Billy was doing and was pleased to see him making his way towards Roman and me. But while I was distracted by Billy's approach, Roman picked up something from my desk. It was my wedding invitation.

'I love weddings,' he told me, with a smile. Then he asked me the dreaded question. 'Who are you taking as your guest?'

I looked at Roman, who was smiling at me, clearly expecting an invitation himself. I glanced at Billy, who'd just joined me and Roman. He too seemed to be waiting with bated breath for my reply. And I so wanted to ask him.

But when I looked back at Roman, the conversation I'd had with my mother came flooding back to me. Everyone expected me to take Roman. If I didn't, they'd think me a liar. I had a million reasons to ask Roman, and just one reason not to.

'You,' I blurted out to Roman, before I could stop myself.

'I'd like you to go with me. That is, if you don't already have plans – which you probably do.'

'No,' Roman said quickly. 'No plans.'

'Oh,' I said, before deciding that I may as well formally invite him. 'In that case, would you like to go with me?'

'I'd love to,' Roman smiled. I smiled back, and then glanced over at Billy – only to find he was no longer standing next to Roman. Instead, he was making his way towards the door.

Roman followed my gaze, then turned back to me. 'Guess that's my cue to leave,' he said.

'Okay,' I said, a sense of panic already setting in that I had made the wrong choice. 'Well, this is the address for Saturday,' I said, scribbling Gretchen's address down on a Post-it note. 'I'm the maid of honour, so we'll be leaving from the bride's house.' I handed Roman the Post-it.

'Looking forward to it,' Roman said, tucking the address into his jacket pocket. 'And I promise,' he smiled, 'no alcohol.' I couldn't help but smile back, because he sounded so sincere.

With a little wave, Roman made his way out of the office. Billy was already gone. After a moment, I realised a voice was calling me from the telephone receiver that lay on my desk.

'Gracie?' the voice asked. 'Gracie, are you there?'

'Cleo?' I asked, remembering myself and picking up the receiver. 'I'm here.' She didn't say anything else, so I continued. 'I'm taking Roman,' I told her.

'I know,' she said. 'I heard.'

'Did I make the right decision?' I asked her.

'I can't answer that,' Cleo told me. 'Only you can answer that.'

And she was right. Except, at that particular moment, that was one question I really couldn't answer.

❄ ❄ ❄

The rest of the week passed by in a blur of wedding preparations, which thankfully left me little time to consider the consequences of my choice.

As Gretchen's maid of honour, I was right in the middle of everything. And yet I had little to do, as Gretchen, quite typically, was so very well organised. Then, on Thursday night, it suddenly occurred to me that the one thing I probably should have organised – a hen party for the bride – hadn't taken place.

However, noticing my distress at this terrible oversight, Gretchen assured me that she and Robert had already decided against the traditions of hen parties and stag nights, and that neither hen nor stag would be taking place. Which I thought was an extremely boring choice but, still, it had gotten me off the hook.

Then, before I realised what was happening, Saturday morning – and the day of the wedding – arrived, and I made my way over to Gretchen's house for the final preparations. I was accompanied by my parents who – no doubt due to my mother's insistence – had somehow wormed their way into the wedding party.

And that's where we were now – in Gretchen's room,

helping the bride get ready for her wedding. I was already dressed and ready, and feeling quite proud of myself for being so organised. But then, I hadn't had to contend with my mother's interference. She was too busy fussing over Gretchen.

'How about we weave a little blue flower in here?' I heard Mum ask.

She was hovering over Gretchen, who was currently having her hair styled by her own mother – a part-time hairdresser. Gretchen's mother didn't look best pleased with my mother's input.

'I don't think so,' she told my mother, obviously trying to remain polite.

It was funny. At the start of the morning, they'd been the best of friends, but now I think my mother's presence was beginning to grate a bit. And I could see why.

'But she needs something blue!' Mum protested. 'Something old, something new, something borrowed, something blue.'

My mother – ever the traditionalist.

'I have something blue,' Gretchen said, turning to smile at me in my very blue dress. 'I have Gracie.'

Gretchen's mother grabbed her daughter's head and swivelled it back to face forwards. 'Keep still,' she scolded Gretchen.

I had to feel sorry for Gretchen. She had not one, but two mothers fussing over her. She'd managed to remain extremely calm throughout it all though. I wasn't sure I would've been so patient and understanding.

Suddenly, Gretchen's bedroom door opened and

Gretchen's father poked his head inside. 'Gracie!' he called. 'Your date's arrived.'

'Oh!' I said, suddenly starting to panic. After all, arranging for my mother to be in the same house as Roman Pearson might not have been the best decision I had ever made. 'Okay, I'm coming down,' I added.

'Who did you invite, Gracie?' Gretchen asked, turning to look at me again.

I hadn't told Gretchen who my choice of guest was yet. And, for some reason, I felt like I really didn't want her to find out.

'Keep still!' Gretchen's mother scolded, twisting Gretchen's head around again. I was frightened she'd end up twisting it right off soon, but Gretchen didn't seem to mind.

In any case, the intervention had saved me from having to answer Gretchen's question. And thankfully my mother was still too engrossed in 'assisting' the bride to have noted the arrival of my date. Otherwise I expect she would've been thundering down the stairs before me to greet Roman.

While no one was paying me any attention, I slipped out of Gretchen's room and made my way downstairs. But what I saw as I descended the stairs surprised me. Because it wasn't Roman waiting for me in the hallway, as I had expected, but Billy. And he was talking to my father.

They both looked up as I made my way down.

I reached the bottom step, and was just about to open my mouth and question Billy on what he was doing here, when my father jumped in between us. 'Stop right there!' he ordered me, before gesturing to the Polaroid camera he held in his hands. 'I want a picture of my beautiful daughter!'

Then he took a few steps back, before lifting the camera and pointing it at me.

'Dad…' I began to protest, but it was no good.

'Smile!' he said.

I smiled, and was then temporarily blinded by the camera's flash. 'Lovely,' Dad said, and moved out of my way so I could step off the staircase.

While my father grabbed the photo that popped out of the camera and stood to one side, waiting for it to develop, I went to talk to Billy. He smiled as I approached.

'You look great,' he told me.

'Thanks,' I said, blushing, while looking down at my outfit.

'I guess you're wondering what I'm doing here?' Billy asked.

'A little,' I admitted.

'Roman's running late,' Billy explained. 'He's going to go straight to the church and meet you there.'

'Oh,' I said, 'okay.' Then there was a pause between the two of us. A horrible, uncomfortable pause that seemed to go on forever but, in reality, probably only lasted for a few seconds. This was really awkward – I just didn't know what to say. 'Thanks for letting me know,' I finally added.

'No problem,' Billy said.

Another awkward silence. But this time I was saved by a shout from upstairs. 'Gracie! Where are you? You're needed!' It was my mother calling.

'I'd better go,' Billy said, opening the front door to leave.

Which was when I suddenly realised that I didn't want him to go.

'Wait,' I told him quickly. 'Do you want to hang around? Come to the wedding, I mean?'

Billy smiled, but shook his head all the same. 'I can't,' he replied. 'I have plans.'

'Oh,' I said. 'Well, the reception's not until later. Perhaps you could make that?' I added hopefully.

'Yeah,' Billy said, with a smile. 'Perhaps.'

'Gracie!' my mother's voice screeched from upstairs. I looked up the stairs, then back at Billy.

'I have to go,' I told him reluctantly.

'You go upstairs, Gracie – before your mother has an aneurysm,' my father said, stepping between me and Billy once more. 'I'll see your friend out.'

'Okay,' I agreed, smiling at my father, 'thanks.' Then I smiled at Billy again. 'Thanks for coming,' I told him, before making my way back up the stairs.

It wasn't until I was near the top of the staircase, and about to disappear from sight, that I heard anything more from downstairs.

'You know, it's strange,' I heard my father say, 'that you came all this way just to pass on a message, when you could easily have called.'

I paused where I was, waiting for Billy's reply. But Billy kept quiet. And so I made my way back up the remaining stairs and into the inner sanctum of Gretchen's bedroom – where the bride, I discovered, was finally ready to go.

'Doesn't she look beautiful?' my mother asked me as I

walked in, waving her hands around Gretchen as if she were trying to sell an item at auction.

'Yes,' I agreed, smiling at my friend, the bride. 'She really does.'

❄ ❄ ❄

'Are you okay?' I asked Gretchen. 'Do you need anything? Are you okay?' I was aware that I was babbling, yet somehow I couldn't stop myself.

'I'm fine!' Gretchen reassured me with a smile. 'Would you please stop asking me that?'

I could see Gretchen's point. We were in the bridal car, on our way to the church. And the closer we came to our destination, the more fidgety I was getting.

'Sorry,' I said. 'I'm a terrible maid of honour, aren't I?'

'No, you're not,' Gretchen insisted. 'You're the best maid of honour anyone could've asked for.'

'Really?' I asked.

I had the sudden urge to hug Gretchen and instinctively moved to do so, but stopped myself, and Gretchen, at the last moment. 'Better not hug,' I told her. 'If I ruin your hair or something, Mum will go mental.'

'My mother or yours?' Gretchen asked, laughing.

'Whoever survives the journey,' I replied with a smile.

'Do you think it was mean of me not to let them in the car?' Gretchen asked.

Due to our mothers' constant fussing, Gretchen had exiled both sets of parents to a second car. Gretchen and I had the bridal car all to ourselves.

'No,' I said. 'It's *your* wedding day. You can do what you like.'

Gretchen thought about that for a moment, before speaking. 'In that case,' she said, 'can I turn the car around and go back? I've changed my mind – I don't want to marry Robert.'

'What?!' I yelled, looking at her in shock.

Uh oh. This wasn't good. Not good at all. I had to think quickly. 'Gretchen, are you insane?' I asked her. 'Don't do this! You want to marry Robert – you do!' Somehow I had to convince her. She just had cold feet, that's all. And it was my job to help her over them. 'You love Robert –' I began, before realising I'd already run out of convincing arguments.

Then, to my surprise, Gretchen started to laugh. I guess that meant she really *was* cracking up.

'Gretchen!' I cried. 'You have to get married today! If you don't, I'll get the blame for it – I know I will!'

'Gracie, stop!' Gretchen said, through her laughter. 'I was just kidding! I just wanted to see what you'd do.'

'What?' I asked her, confused. 'You mean you don't have cold feet?'

'No!' Gretchen said, smiling at me. 'I'm fine. Honest.'

'Well thank God for that!' I said, slowly recovering from the shock. 'That wasn't a very nice thing to do, you know,' I told Gretchen.

'I'm sorry!' Gretchen giggled. 'But you should've seen your face – it was priceless!'

'Yeah, I'm sure it was hilarious,' I replied sarcastically. 'You know you're only getting away with this because it's your wedding day, don't you?'

'Yes!' Gretchen breathed. 'It's my wedding day. And, Gracie, I'm so happy. This is going to be the best day of my life!'

I just smiled at her and hoped she was right.

But, in her favour, Gretchen was one step ahead of me – she'd actually made it to her wedding day.

Which always helped.

Chapter Fifteen

I was back in the courtyard of St James' Church, only this time I felt no fear. For there was no Reverend Winters to worry about anymore – just his rather-too-good-looking successor waiting inside the church. And I was looking forward to seeing him again.

Gretchen must've read my thoughts, as she suddenly said: 'You're not going to flirt with the vicar again, are you, Gracie?'

For a moment I thought she was genuinely worried, but when I looked at Gretchen I realised she was smiling.

'No,' I smiled back. 'No flirting with the vicar. Absolutely not.' Then I grinned and added: 'Unless he starts it, of course.'

I would never have conceived of saying such a thing had my mother been present, of course. But both of my parents had already made their way inside the church to take their seats. There was just Gretchen and me, as well as Gretchen's parents, left outside the church. Waiting inside was Gretchen's husband-to-be.

So everything was as it should be. Everything was going to run smoothly. Everything was going to be fine.

Of course, they say that you should never speak too soon.

'Mum, do you want to go inside and tell them we're ready to come in?' Gretchen asked her mother.

However, Gretchen's mother's attention was elsewhere. 'Oh my God,' she said, staring over our shoulders. 'That's Roman Pearson!'

We all turned to look. Sure enough, Roman had just jumped out of a taxi outside the churchyard and was making his way towards us.

'Did you invite Roman Pearson to your wedding?' Gretchen's mother asked her daughter.

'No,' Gretchen said, looking at me questioningly. '*I* didn't invite him.'

'Didn't I mention it?' I asked sheepishly, perfectly aware that I hadn't. 'Roman's my guest for the wedding.'

'He's late,' Gretchen's father commented.

'Yes, well he's probably got a very busy schedule,' his wife said in Roman's defence, just loud enough so Roman would hear her as he approached.

'Hello, Gracie,' Roman greeted me with a grin. 'You look stunning.'

'Thanks,' I said, finding myself blushing for the second time that day.

'And this must be the beautiful bride?' Roman asked, stepping towards Gretchen.

'Yes,' I told him, moving forwards to make introductions. 'Roman, this is Gretchen. Gretchen, Roman.'

'Pleased to meet you, Gretchen,' Roman said, with a wink. Apparently he'd decided that kissing the hand of a woman about to get married would be just a little too inappropriate.

'Likewise,' Gretchen said, before shooting a look of amusement at me.

Meanwhile, Roman moved on to Gretchen's mother, taking her hand and kissing it. 'And this must be the bride's sister?' he asked.

As Gretchen's mother stared at him in absolute entrancement, I rolled my eyes at Gretchen. Gretchen seemed shocked, but I was used to this kind of behaviour from Roman. Roman then moved on to Gretchen's father.

'And this must be the bride's…?'

'Father,' Gretchen's dad filled in, without smiling.

Apparently, Roman's charm didn't work quite so well on men. But then, I could've told him that. 'Okay then,' Roman said, stepping away from Gretchen's father, a sense of self-preservation finally kicking in.

'Mum?' Gretchen asked her mother, determined to get things moving again. 'Do you think you could go in now and tell them we're ready? And take Roman in with you?'

'Of course, darling,' Gretchen's mother agreed, her face breaking into a smile. At the mention of Roman's name, she'd seemed to snap out of her trance. She looked at Roman, and held out her arm for him to take. 'Shall we?' she asked him.

'We certainly shall,' Roman said, with a charming grin. He took Gretchen's mother's arm and let her lead him into the church. 'See you inside, Gracie,' he called back to me.

Once they were gone, I turned back to Gretchen. 'Sorry about that,' I told her. 'Are you okay? Are you ready?'

'As I'll ever be,' Gretchen smiled. And for the first time, I noticed a sign of true nervousness in her.

'You'll be fine,' I told her, with an encouraging smile, as I helped her pull down her veil so that it covered her face.

Gretchen smiled at me, and then went to take her father's arm. And before I knew what was happening, the 'Wedding March' had begun playing.

Gathering my posy of flowers to my chest, I followed Gretchen as she swept into the church on her father's arm.

The first thing I noticed as I entered the church was how different it looked to the last time I'd been inside. Before, despite the presence of the far-too-fit-for-his-profession vicar (okay, I admit it, I couldn't actually remember his name), the place had looked rather bare, cold and unfriendly. But now the church looked warm and inviting, the aisles decked out with brightly-coloured flowers and ribbons. And the pews, of course, were full of guests.

Which was the second thing I noticed after entering the church.

There were a lot of guests seated in the pews. However, they weren't behaving as wedding guests were usually expected to. In other words, not every pair of eyes in that church were fixed on the blushing bride, as they should've been. In fact, around seventy-five percent of the people in the church weren't looking down the aisle at our approach at all. Their attention, it seemed, had been diverted elsewhere.

Which was good, in that it gave me less in the way of performance anxiety (the thought of tripping up and falling flat on my face wasn't quite so terrifying if nobody was watching me). However, it was also a very, very bad thing if Gretchen noticed it was happening.

Don't look over there, I thought – sending that thought out as a subliminal message to all those congregated in the church. *Look at Gretchen*, I silently urged them. *Look at the bride*. But apparently my powers of suggestion weren't working very well today, as the guests continued to stare at something near the front of the church. Or at someone.

Who are they looking at? I thought, though I should've known even before catching sight of the object of their attention. They were looking at Roman. I could see him myself now. He was sitting in the second pew from the front on the bride's side of the church, right next to the aisle. And he seemed totally oblivious to all the commotion he was causing.

Gretchen, however, was no longer oblivious. She'd clearly realised there was someone in the church infinitely more interesting to her wedding guests than herself. Thankfully, she'd almost reached the altar and her husband-to-be who – to his credit – hadn't taken his eyes off Gretchen since the moment she'd stepped through the church doors. At least someone was paying her attention.

I prayed that Gretchen would focus on Robert and forget about the rest of the room. And it looked like my prayers had been answered when Gretchen's father left her in Robert's capable hands at the front of the church. However, as I made my way past the couple to take up my position to the side of the altar, I saw Gretchen glancing back to see who'd entranced her guests so completely.

And when she spotted Roman sitting in the pews, Gretchen immediately looked over at me.

I shot her my most apologetic look, mouthing 'sorry' for extra emphasis. But I couldn't tell whether Gretchen was angry or not, as her expression remained the same. Plus, of course, her face was still hidden beneath her veil. However, I think she smiled as she turned back to look at Robert.

In any case, the ceremony began, and I breathed a huge sigh of relief.

'Dearly beloved,' the yummy vicar began, 'we are gathered here today, in the presence of God, to witness the joining of this man, and this woman, in Holy Matrimony.'

There was a rustling throughout the church as the vicar began speaking, and I panicked for a moment, wondering just what the guests were up to now. However, it seemed that, safe in the knowledge that Roman wasn't going anywhere for a while, they'd all simply shifted position in order to watch the marriage ceremony instead of the heart-throb actor.

And for that I was eternally grateful.

Everything would be okay now. I was sure of it.

❄ ❄ ❄

'I now pronounce you husband and wife,' the vicar said proudly. Then he smiled at the newlyweds. 'You may kiss the bride,' he told Robert.

Smiling, Robert lifted the veil from Gretchen's face and kissed her gently. No tongues though. Not in church. Not that it would've mattered because, as soon as the sealing words had been spoken by the vicar, the majority of the wedding guests had turned their attention back to Roman, as if afraid he might slip out while they weren't watching. So nobody would've noticed anyway – tongues or no tongues. Still, you had to remain respectful while in the presence of God, right?

There was a rippling of applause throughout the church following Gretchen and Robert's kiss, but the cheer wasn't as loud as it could've been, and I cringed in embarrassment for the couple.

Robert and Gretchen made their way back down the aisle, arm-in-arm, and I followed behind them. However, I couldn't help but notice that Gretchen still wasn't getting the attention she deserved. And so I did the only thing I could think of. As I walked past Roman's pew, I grabbed his arm, pulled him up and dragged him down the aisle with me. Roman seemed surprised, but also pleased by my actions, and he soon took my arm, escorting me out of the church.

Now all of the guests were looking towards the aisle. Mission accomplished. Except that they were looking more at Roman and me than at Gretchen and Robert. There was just one thing for it. I had to keep Roman as close to Gretchen as possible.

I picked up the pace, bringing us nearer to the happy couple. That was better. The difference didn't seem so obvious now. Then an idea struck me: a way to focus attention back on Gretchen and Robert. Apart from getting rid of Roman, of course.

'Do you have any confetti with you?' I whispered to Roman.

'Sure,' Roman replied, not bothering to keep his voice down. 'What sort of idiot comes to a wedding without bringing confetti?'

'Well once we're outside, I want you to start throwing it over Gretchen and Robert,' I told him. 'And whatever you do, make sure everyone joins in with you.'

'Shouldn't be a problem,' Roman grinned.

We followed Gretchen and Robert outside into the courtyard and, once the newlyweds were a safe distance away from the church doors, and the other guests began to pour outside, I gave Roman a little prompting shove.

Roman obediently let go of my arm and opened the box of confetti he'd been storing in his jacket pocket (made a change from bottles of Scotch, I suppose). Then he made his way towards Gretchen and Robert and, with a quick glance to check that everyone was watching him, threw a handful of confetti their way.

Barely a few seconds later, Roman and – I was glad to note – Gretchen and Robert were literally surrounded by guests. Gretchen and Robert smiled as confetti and congratulations were thrown their way – everyone wanting to follow Roman's example. Gretchen was finally the centre of attention. And she was happy.

Or at least she was, until Roman threw out the last of his confetti and started making his way back to me.

'What are you doing?!' I asked him frantically, as I moved

to intercept him. 'Get back over there!'

'I'm out of confetti!' Roman protested.

'Then steal some from somebody else!' I told him.

But it was too late. The mass exodus had already begun. The guests who'd been surrounding Gretchen and Robert were now converging on Roman. I quickly moved out of the way, not wanting to be trampled by the mob.

Roman didn't seem to mind though. He smiled obligingly and signed every scrap of paper that was thrust in front of him.

And then things got worse – the photographs began. But rather than taking snaps of the happy couple, the wedding guests were queuing (if you could use that word to describe their unruly behaviour) to get pictures of Roman.

I looked over at Gretchen and Robert, to find they were standing all alone, looking completely stunned. As they stared in horror at the scene in front of them, Gretchen burst into tears. Robert tried his best to comfort her, but she pushed him away. And then she stormed towards me, like a charging bull.

'How could you do this to me?!' Gretchen cried, as she skidded to a halt in front of me. 'How could you bring Roman Pearson to my wedding?!'

'Gretchen, I'm so sorry,' I began. 'I didn't realise –'

'You're not sorry!' Gretchen interrupted, still crying. 'You did it on purpose – to steal my thunder!'

'Gretchen, I didn't, I swear,' I said, reaching for her.

Gretchen pulled out of my grasp. 'Leave me alone!' she cried, before running away – heading back towards the church.

'Gretchen, wait!' I heard a bewildered Robert call, as he chased after his new wife. I could do nothing but stand and watch. Going after Gretchen right now would only make things worse. Or make her homicidal – which, considering she seemed to blame me for everything, I didn't want either, obviously.

'Gracie, really. What were you thinking?!' a voice scolded. It was my mother. I turned to face her. 'Look what you've done to poor Gretchen!' she continued. 'How could you bring Roman here – on her wedding day!'

'I didn't realise –' I began.

'Well, I hope you're pleased with yourself!' Mum sniffed. And then I watched in amazement as she quickly made her way over to the throng of people congregating around Roman, and pushed her way to the front, elbows flailing. 'Roman!' she cooed. 'Roman, it's me! Ellen!'

My mother is such a hypocrite! a voice inside me said.

But then another voice spoke up. *Better to be a hypocrite than a destroyer of wedding days – like you, Gracie Parker!*

And that was the voice I listened to.

❄ ❄ ❄

Well, thankfully Gretchen's wedding day hadn't been a complete disaster. I mean, sure, the ceremony itself might've been a bit of a damp squib. And, true, when the time came for the official wedding photographs to be taken, the photographer had experienced a little trouble in rounding up the guests for a shot with the bride and groom (seeing as the guests were much more interested in obtaining a professional portrait of themselves with Roman Pearson).

And, okay, the bride had been so upset that she'd locked herself in the ladies' bathroom for half-an-hour.

But there had been some bright spots too. For instance, the reception dinner – as meticulously planned by Gretchen – had been a big success. By this time, I think, the novelty of Roman's presence had worn off a little, and the wedding guests were happy to tuck into their meals and toast to the bride and groom's future happiness.

However, I gathered that Gretchen hadn't yet forgiven me for my one mistake of bringing Roman to the wedding, as she'd snubbed every attempt I'd made to speak to her since she'd emerged from the bathroom. We were in the middle of the wedding reception now and Gretchen hadn't spoken one word to me – so far tactfully avoiding all contact with her so-called maid of honour.

I watched Gretchen dancing with Robert, her husband. She looked happy to be married, at least. And she was dancing. I hadn't danced all evening. Roman had asked me, of course, and had even tried to drag me out onto the dance floor on one occasion. But somehow I felt stepping onto the dance floor with Roman – in front of everyone – would just end up angering Gretchen. And I wouldn't want her to think I was trying to 'steal her thunder' again.

Which was in no way true, as I'd actually tried to get rid of Roman following the debacle outside the church. But convincing Roman to walk away from his adoring public had proved to be an impossible task. He was, he had told me, enjoying himself far too much to leave. And he seemed to be blissfully unaware of all the trouble he'd caused.

I, on the other hand, was all too acutely aware of what I'd done. And guilt had been gnawing away at me for hours, leaving me with a rather sick feeling in the pit of my stomach. Roman had experienced no such problems though, and no lack of offers for dance partners either. He'd already danced with a string of women (including, on numerous occasions, my mother) and was out there right now with another admirer.

But as I watched Roman enjoying himself, I noticed that Gretchen and Robert were no longer on the dance floor. I looked around for the bride and groom, spotting them leaving the reception room. Realising this might be my last chance to apologise to Gretchen, I impulsively ran to intercept them.

'Gretchen!' I called. 'Gretchen, wait!'

Gretchen and Robert turned around. I was certain that once they saw who was chasing them, Gretchen would insist they continued on their way. But to my surprise, and great relief, Gretchen hesitated, before motioning for Robert to go on without her. Then she turned to look at me stonily as I approached.

'Gretchen, I am so sorry,' I told her. 'I would never have invited Roman if I'd thought –'

'That he would completely ruin the wedding?' Gretchen interrupted.

'I'm sorry!' I said again. I felt like I'd be spending the rest of my life trying to apologise to Gretchen over this. 'I just didn't think.'

'No,' Gretchen agreed. 'You didn't think. Not about anyone but yourself anyway!'

'That's unfair!' I protested.

'Is it?' Gretchen asked.

'Yes!' I cried. 'I never meant for this to happen. I didn't even *want* to bring Roman to the wedding!'

'So why did you?!' Gretchen asked.

'My mother said –' I began.

'Oh no,' Gretchen said. 'Don't go blaming your mother! *You* chose to bring Roman, not her. It was your decision.'

'Yes,' I agreed, 'and it was a terrible decision. Gretchen, I'm so sorry! I know right now you probably hate me, but –'

'I don't hate you,' Gretchen said. 'I'm just really disappointed in you.' With that, Gretchen moved to leave the reception. I moved to try and stop her. She hadn't forgiven me yet – and I needed her to forgive me.

'Gretchen, wait!' I said again.

'Gracie, I have to go,' Gretchen insisted, shaking me off. 'I have to get ready for my honeymoon.' She looked at me pointedly. 'Which will hopefully be better than my wedding day.'

Before I could protest again, Gretchen swept away. And I was left standing there alone, feeling worse than ever.

❄ ❄ ❄

'Don't forget to throw your bouquet!' somebody shouted, as Gretchen and Robert moved to get into the car that was to take them to the airport.

Most of the wedding guests were gathered outside the function rooms where the reception was being held, waiting to see the newlyweds off on their honeymoon. And I was among that crowd, though I hadn't taken the opportunity to kiss the bride goodbye as a number of others had. Somehow, I didn't think my goodbye would've been particularly welcome.

Still, at least Roman wasn't standing out here as a reminder of what I'd done. He'd opted to stay inside, as had a number of female guests, who apparently saw this distraction as a good opportunity to get to know Roman Pearson better. But they were going to miss the traditional bouquet-throwing as a result of their infatuation.

I watched as Gretchen raised her bouquet in the air, preparing to throw it. As she did so, she caught my eye. And for one crazy, insane moment, I actually thought she was going to throw the bouquet directly to me.

But when Gretchen threw the bouquet, she aimed it as far away from me as possible, and it went sailing off to the right of me – caught by Gretchen's recently-divorced aunt, who seemed to be very excited by the whole thing.

By the time I turned back to look at Gretchen, she and Robert had disappeared into the car. I watched with the other wedding guests as the car drove away. But while everyone around me started waving wildly after the vehicle, I just stood there, numb – thinking to myself over and over what a truly terrible maid of honour I'd turned out to be.

And I must've been standing there for quite a few minutes because, before I'd realised what was happening, the other guests had all made their way back inside, and I was left alone, still staring out into the road. Which was when a very familiar vehicle turned into the parking lot where I was standing.

My heart leapt. It was Billy's car! I stood and watched as Billy got out of the car and made his way towards me.

'Gracie?' he asked. 'What are you doing out here?'

'Seeing off the newlyweds,' I told him, without much enthusiasm. Although I was pleased to see Billy, I was finding it difficult to be happy following the wedding disaster. 'So you decided to come after all?' I asked him.

'Yes,' he said, then studied me more closely, apparently sensing something was wrong. 'Gracie, are you okay? You look a little –'

'Guilty?' I asked, interrupting him.

'Well, I was gonna go with sad actually,' Billy told me. 'But while we're on the subject, what have you got to feel guilty about?'

'Roman,' I told him. 'I should never have brought Roman to the wedding. It's all my fault!'

Upset, I flopped down right where I was, on the edge of the pavement outside the reception hall. I was sitting in the gutter. My dress was probably going to get dirty and ruined. But right at that moment, I didn't really care. It wasn't as if I was going to wear it ever again. I mean, who in their right mind would ask me to be their maid of honour after this disaster?

'What did Roman do?' Billy asked me urgently, obviously thinking the worst.

'No, Roman didn't do anything,' I told him. 'It was me – all me. The wedding was a complete disaster!'

'What happened?' Billy asked, looking down at me.

'Everything happened!' I cried. 'When Gretchen was walking down the aisle, nobody was watching her. They were all watching Roman. And when Roman ran out of confetti, everyone else got bored of throwing it too!'

I was aware that I probably wasn't making much sense to Billy but, for some reason, I couldn't stop myself from babbling. 'And when the photographer wanted to take wedding pictures,' I continued, 'nobody wanted to be in them. They all wanted their pictures taken with Roman instead. And it was a complete disaster – and it was all my fault. And now Gretchen hates me!'

I looked up at Billy for his reaction and, hopefully, for some comforting words. But to my surprise, I found Billy wasn't looking very sympathetic at all.

'What did you expect?' he asked me. 'You know how people react to Roman. You should've known better than to bring him in the first place.'

'I didn't know this would happen!' I cried, a little taken aback by Billy's scolding.

'Why *did* you ask Roman to the wedding?' Billy asked, ignoring my protest.

'Because –' I replied.

I was about to claim that I'd wanted to ask Roman. Which would've been a big fat lie. But Billy seemed to sense what was coming and interrupted me.

'Because?' he prompted, clearly looking for the truth.

I sighed, resigned to tell him everything. 'Because,' I

told him, 'my mother thinks that Roman and I are dating –'

'So you brought him to the wedding to please your mother?' Billy interrupted.

'And my mother told everyone else that Roman and I are dating,' I continued. 'And there was this stupid picture of us together in this stupid gossip magazine – and so everybody believed her.'

'Let me guess,' Billy said. 'You didn't correct them? You just played along with it?'

'I thought that would be easier,' I admitted.

'And you didn't think the truth would come out eventually?' Billy asked me. 'Or did you figure they all thought you were dating Roman, so you might as well just do so?'

'No!' I protested, standing up to reach eye level with Billy. I'd been getting a stiff neck looking up at him. 'I don't even like Roman in that way!'

'Well you have a funny way of showing it!' Billy retorted. And he was right, of course. I should never have invited Roman to Gretchen's wedding. It had been a huge mistake all round. 'I think it's about time you started telling the truth, Gracie,' Billy continued. 'Why can't you stop pretending you're something you're not? Why can't you just be yourself?'

'I am myself!' I protested. 'I've never pretended –'

'What do you think you're doing now?' Billy interrupted. 'Letting everyone believe you're dating Roman?'

And he was right again. I should have told the truth way before now. But the truth is a hard thing to tell and, besides, I was getting sick of Billy being right all the time.

'You're not helping!' I snapped at Billy. 'Don't you think I feel bad enough already?!'

'Maybe you *should* feel bad?' Billy suggested, before heading away into the reception hall.

'Where are you going?' I called after him.

'I'm going to get Roman,' Billy replied. 'And then I'm leaving.'

Billy disappeared into the reception hall and I was left standing outside, alone again.

There were a number of thoughts running through my mind at that moment, though the only one that stood out clearly was that I didn't want to still be here when Billy and Roman came back outside.

And so, in light of the situation, I decided to follow Gretchen's example. I ran away and locked myself in the bathroom.

❄ ❄ ❄

I didn't see Billy again that night. Or Roman. In fact, I didn't see many other people at all that evening, on account of the fact I spent the majority of it locked away in the ladies' bathroom, hiding in shame. And in fear. Fear that I'd lost, not only Gretchen's friendship, but Billy's as well. And all over one stupid mistake.

But not knowing what I could do to correct that mistake, I simply carried on with my life – going to work as per usual and fighting my way through the banality of each day. Oh, and hoping and praying that the telephone would ring, and that it would be Billy calling, giving me a chance to apologise.

Well, it was now Wednesday, and the telephone had not yet rung. But I'd just been in the kitchen making myself a cup of coffee, so there was always the possibility that Billy had called while I was away from my desk.

'Has Billy called?' I asked Olivia, as I walked back into the office with my cup of coffee. I looked at Olivia hopefully, waiting for her reply.

'No,' Olivia sighed, looking up at me. 'Billy hasn't called. Just like he hadn't called on the last three occasions on which you asked.'

'Okay,' I said meekly, having obviously upset Olivia. 'Sorry to bother you.'

I was heading back to my desk when Olivia spoke again.

'Why are you pursuing Billy Ramsden?' she asked me suspiciously. I turned to look at her, confused by the question. 'Do you think it will help you get closer to Mr Pearson?'

And now I was even more confused. What did Roman have to do with this?

'Roman has nothing to do with this,' I informed Olivia, thinking aloud. 'Why would he? This is between me and Billy.'

'What happened between you and Billy?' Olivia asked me, a lot less suspicion evident in her voice now.

'We had an argument,' I reluctantly informed her. 'It was my fault. I made a big mistake.'

'Then why are you waiting for Billy to call *you*?' Olivia asked. 'Why don't you call him?'

'Because I don't have his number!' I snapped. It sounded like a lame excuse, even to me.

Olivia studied me for a moment, then took a pen from her desk and scribbled something down on a Post-it note. Once finished, she held the Post-it out to me.

'Here,' Olivia said, gesturing for me to take it. After a moment's hesitation, I approached her and took the piece of paper she offered. 'Now you have his number,' she said. Then she smiled at me. Yes, *smiled*. I know – I was shocked too.

'Thanks,' I stammered, a little wary of this sudden change in personality from my usually rude and abrupt co-worker.

'Don't thank me,' Olivia said, regressing back to her brusque tone of voice. 'Just make sure you call him.'

'I'll do that,' I told Olivia, with a smile.

The change in Olivia may have only been temporary, but at least it proved she wasn't made of stone. There was a heart in there somewhere. And I was pleased about that.

'I'll call him right away,' I confirmed again.

And call him I did.

❄ ❄ ❄

A feeling of déjà vu came over me as I waited for Billy at a table outside *Annabelle's*. Billy had actually suggested our meeting place – though there had been no way I was going to argue with him about it. After all, it had taken enough persuading to get him to meet me in the first place.

Now all I had to worry about was that he didn't stand me up.

While I waited for Billy to appear, I puzzled over Olivia's recent behaviour. I'd seen a brand new side to Olivia this morning. Not only had she been thoughtful enough to give me Billy's telephone number (and to encourage me to call him) but she'd also given me the afternoon off, so Billy and I could 'talk things through'.

It was certainly unlike the Olivia I knew. But then, perhaps I didn't know Olivia as well as I'd thought.

'Hi, Gracie,' a voice said, breaking into my daydreams. I looked up to find Billy standing over my table.

'Billy, hi!' I greeted him.

With a nervous smile, Billy sat down opposite me at the table, immediately launching into a sudden and unexpected apology.

'Look, Gracie, I'm really sorry about the other night,' he began.

'What do *you* have to be sorry about?' I interrupted him.

'Those things I said to you,' Billy explained. 'I shouldn't have said them. They were rude. It was wrong of me.'

'No, it was right of you,' I told him. '*You* were right. Everything you said was right.' I was determined to get my own apology out – whether Billy wanted to hear it or not. And if I didn't say this quickly, I wasn't going to say it at all.

'I haven't been honest with people,' I went on. 'I let them believe that Roman and I were dating and I shouldn't have done. I should have told them the truth – but I didn't. Because I wanted them to think I was successful, and that somebody who was successful wanted to be with me. And I *have* been pretending I'm someone I'm not – you were right. And I'm sorry for that. But I want you to know that when I'm with you, I never pretend. When I'm with you, I'm just me – I'm just Gracie. I've never pretended with you.'

'I know,' Billy said.

But I wasn't quite finished yet. 'And I should never have invited Roman to the wedding,' I continued. 'And not just because of what happened – but because I didn't even want to go with Roman in the first place. I should've invited the person *I* wanted to go with.'

I looked at Billy, aware that I hadn't explained myself terribly well. 'That's you, by the way,' I told him, just to make things perfectly clear.

'Well, that's good to know,' Billy nodded. I waited for him to say something more, but he fell silent, apparently contemplating my words.

'You look a little stunned,' I ventured.

'I am,' Billy said, smiling almost shyly. 'The truth is, I'd just about managed to convince myself that the only reason you were spending time with me was to get closer to Roman.'

'That's exactly what Olivia said!' I told him. 'But I don't understand. Why does everybody think that?'

'Why do you think they think that?' Billy laughed.

'I don't know!' I exclaimed.

(To be honest, I was beginning to get a little frustrated with the way everyone kept assuming I knew what they were talking about. It made me feel kind of dumb.)

'Well, what better way to get close to Roman than to befriend his brother?' Billy asked, as if it were obvious.

'But I don't *know* Roman's brother,' I said, even more confused now.

'Of course you do,' Billy said.

'No,' I told him firmly, 'I don't.'

'You really have no idea what I'm talking about, do you?' Billy asked finally. 'I honestly thought you knew.'

'Knew what?' I asked him.

'*I'm* Roman's brother,' Billy said. 'I thought you knew that.'

'You're not Roman's brother,' I told him, totally confused now. 'You're Billy. Billy Ramsden. You don't even have the same last name as Roman.'

Then a thought struck me – one that really did make me feel kind of dumb. 'Unless,' I asked him, 'Roman changed his name?'

'He's an actor,' Billy grinned. 'Of course he changed his name.'

'Roman's real name is Roman Ramsden?' I asked him.

'No,' Billy grinned. 'Roman's real name is Albert Ramsden.' He laughed. 'Not quite so glamorous, is it?'

'I can see why he changed it,' I agreed.

I studied Billy, still absorbing this new information. 'So?' I asked him. 'You're Roman's brother?'

'Guilty as charged,' Billy smiled. 'Why else do you think I'd put up with him?'

'Actually, that explains a lot,' I smiled.

And it did explain a lot. Why Billy and Roman were always hanging out together. Why Billy was always there to help when Roman was in trouble. Why Roman allowed Billy to talk to him so bluntly. Why Roman always (well, almost always) did what Billy told him to. Oh yeah, that explained an awful lot.

'But you know, there's more to me than Roman,' Billy said quickly. 'I mean, God knows taking care of him is a full-time job in itself, but that's not what I plan on doing for the rest of my life.'

'So what *do* you plan on doing?' I asked him.

Billy grinned at me.

'Let me show you,' he said.

❄ ❄ ❄

'This,' Billy said, making a sweeping gesture as we entered his living room, 'is what I plan on doing for the rest of my life.'

I was standing in the middle of Billy's apartment, which Billy had insisted we visit so he could demonstrate what he hoped to do for a living. And now I saw exactly what that was.

Billy's living room was cluttered with a number of easels and stands, each of which held large sheets of paper filled with paintings and drawings depicting various images. There were sketchbooks strewn all over the sofa and floor, along with boxes of paints and pencils.

'You're an artist!' I declared, looking at Billy for confirmation.

'Nicely observed,' Billy smiled at me. 'Nothing gets past you, does it?'

'Only the obvious,' I smiled back at him. I looked around the room at Billy's work. 'This stuff is really good,' I told him. 'I mean, I'm no expert or anything but I really like it.'

'So do a few other people,' Billy grinned. 'I've been offered some space at an exhibition next month.'

'That's great!' I told him excitedly.

Billy nodded proudly. 'It's my first big break.'

'How long have you been doing this for?' I asked him, wanting to find out as much about this new side of Billy Ramsden as I could.

'About ten years,' Billy replied. 'But it's only now that everything's started coming together.' He looked at me and smiled. 'You must be my lucky charm.'

'Oh, I don't know about that,' I laughed. 'I've never brought myself much luck.'

'Well, perhaps your magic only works on others,' Billy said. 'In any case, since you showed up, things have been going great for me. I've got the exhibition space, I've been producing better work than ever, and I'm now a newly-qualified teacher.'

'I didn't know you were training to be a teacher!' I exclaimed.

'Yeah, that's probably because you're always seeing me chasing around after Roman,' Billy reminded me. 'But like I said, I do have a life away from my brother, believe it or not. And I've always wanted to be a teacher – it just took me longer than expected to get there.'

'So will you be teaching art?' I asked him.

'That's the plan,' Billy said. 'I'll be looking for work in secondary schools and colleges – older kids really.'

'You know, you should talk to Gretchen,' I told him.

'She could probably give you some advice on teaching.'

I thought about that for a moment. Would Gretchen really want to help out a friend of mine after all I'd done? Probably not.

'Just don't mention *I* sent you,' I added. 'Gretchen's not too thrilled with me at the moment – though I can't say I blame her after what happened at the wedding.'

It suddenly struck me that reminding Billy of the disaster that was Gretchen's wedding day might not have been such a good idea. Bad memories and all that. Billy didn't seem bothered by the reference though. His thoughts were clearly elsewhere.

'Speaking of the wedding,' Billy said, 'there's something I have to show you.' Billy crossed the room, stopping next to an easel. This one had a sheet draped over it, hiding whatever masterpiece was underneath. 'This,' Billy explained proudly, 'is my latest work. I hope you like it.'

He removed the sheet covering the easel, revealing the drawing beneath – a beautiful, three-colour sketch of me, Gracie Parker, in my maid of honour outfit.

'Oh my God!' I exclaimed, shocked, as well as absurdly pleased. 'How did you do this?'

'Remember when I visited Gretchen's house on the morning of the wedding?' Billy asked. I nodded. 'Well, your dad slipped me the photo he'd taken of you on the stairs,' Billy explained. 'I used that as my template.'

He looked back at the drawing. 'Do you like it?'

'Like it?' I asked incredulously. 'It's wonderful!'

'Well, I had a good subject to work from,' Billy said, as he came to stand beside me.

'Nobody's ever drawn me a picture before,' I smiled at Billy.

'I'm glad you like it,' Billy smiled back at me. 'So does this mean we're friends again?'

'Is that what you want?' I asked him, deciding that Billy deserved one last chance to back off from me if he wanted.

'No,' Billy said.

'Oh,' I replied. Perhaps I shouldn't have given him that chance after all.

'I want to be more than friends,' Billy smiled at me.

'Oh,' I said, a little lost for words again. But it didn't take me long to recover. 'Well good,' I told him with a smile, 'because so do I.'

Billy smiled at me – happy that we were finally in agreement.

And then he kissed me.

Chapter Sixteen

'Well?' Cleo asked me. 'What happened next?'

'I kissed him back,' I told her. 'Obviously.'

'No!' she said. 'After that. What happened after that?'

I was back at *Annabelle's* again (I think I must have been their very best customer ever), this time with Cleo, to whom I was recounting the events of the previous day.

'Not much,' I told her, in reply to her question.

'You didn't...' Cleo began.

'No, we didn't,' I interrupted, before Cleo could go on. I knew what she'd been about to say in any case.

'Why not?' Cleo asked mournfully.

'Because,' I explained, 'we're taking things slowly. Billy and I are good friends now – and I don't want to risk that by rushing in head first.'

'You're so sensible,' Cleo grumbled.

'No,' I corrected her. 'I'm just learning from my past mistakes.'

'Like taking Roman to the wedding instead of Billy?' Cleo asked.

'Exactly,' I replied.

'Or like wasting three years of your life on that lying,

cheating, scumbag, David?'

'Yeah, that too.'

'Or like believing your brother when he said he'd do all the planning for your mum and dad's party?'

'Okay!' I told her. 'I think we've had enough examples now!'

'Sorry,' Cleo smiled, realising she'd put her foot in it. 'So,' she said brightly, apparently attempting to change the subject, 'I have some good news.'

'This isn't in any way related to Jason, is it?' I asked her.

For some reason, Cleo still seemed to think I had a hidden desire to hear all about her rampant sex life – which I definitely didn't.

'No,' she said. 'Well, not directly anyway.'

'So what is it?' I asked her, curious now.

'I have an interview lined up with the promotion board at work,' Cleo announced, clapping her hands together excitedly.

'Oh,' I said, admittedly with more surprise than interest. 'Congratulations. That's great.'

'Don't try and sound *too* enthusiastic about it, will you?' Cleo grumbled.

'I'm sorry,' I told her honestly. 'I'm just still having trouble wrapping my head around the idea of you taking over from Penny.'

'I don't know why,' Cleo said. 'You of all people know how bossy I can be. I'm sure I'll make a great manager!'

'I think there's more to it than that,' I told her.

'I know, I know,' Cleo said. 'But I'll learn as I go along. And Jason thinks it's a great idea too.'

'Will he be part of the promotion board?' I asked her, with a smile.

'No,' Cleo replied, shaking her head firmly. 'I've told Jason to steer well clear. I don't need his help. I want to do this on my own.'

'Good for you,' I told her.

'Although,' she added, smiling guiltily, 'he *is* coaching me for the interview. Giving me tips on what questions they might ask and how to answer. It's sort of like inside information, I suppose. Do you think that's wrong?'

'Not really,' I replied. 'And it sounds like a step forward in your relationship too. Something other than what you two usually get up to.'

'Oh no, you misunderstand me,' Cleo said, grinning wickedly. 'Jason's been coaching me *while* we do what we usually get up to.'

'How does it always come back to this?' I asked her, shaking my head in disbelief.

'That's my life,' Cleo shrugged. 'I wouldn't want to change it, even if I could.' Cleo picked up her cup of coffee, downing what was left of the drink in one gulp. 'What about you?' she asked me, once she was done. 'Has Gretchen forgiven you yet for ruining the wedding?'

'No,' I said glumly. 'She's still on honeymoon.'

'When's she back?'

'Sunday,' I told Cleo. 'And I'm hoping she's had a good time, because that should make apologising to her a little easier.'

'Where did she go on honeymoon?' Cleo asked me.

'Barbados,' I told her.

'Shouldn't be a problem then,' Cleo grinned.

I just hoped she was right.

❄ ❄ ❄

It was Tuesday evening before I gathered up enough courage to pay the newly-married Gretchen a visit. And even then I went to the wrong house – ringing the doorbell of her parents' home, before being told that Gretchen, quite obviously, was now living with her husband.

Just how stupid did I feel at that moment? The only excuse I could summon up was that, subconsciously, I'd been so nervous about the impending confrontation with Gretchen that I'd deliberately made my way to the wrong house.

But, nervous or not, I was determined to get this apology over and done with. And so, after collecting Gretchen's new address from her parents, I made my way to the suburban home that my former best friend now shared with her other half.

I was standing outside the house right now, examining it closely. It was quite the family home – I could just picture Gretchen becoming the 'old married woman' she'd described within it. Well, hopefully that 'old married woman' would believe in forgiving and forgetting.

Not wanting to hesitate any longer (just in case I ended up changing my mind and running for the hills instead), I pressed the doorbell. I waited on the doorstep and, after a moment, heard footsteps padding towards the front door.

Then the door was opened. By Gretchen.

'Hi, Gretchen,' I said nervously, waiting for her reaction. To my surprise, and great relief, Gretchen smiled.

'Gracie, hi!' she said, before opening the door wider in an invitation to me. 'Come in.'

'Um, okay,' I said, and stepped inside the house.

Gretchen shut the front door behind me with an ominous click, and I found myself wondering if I'd made a huge mistake (yes, another one) in coming here so soon. Was Gretchen suddenly going to fly into a rage at me, once again accusing me of 'stealing her thunder'?

'How are you?' Gretchen asked me with a smile.

'I'm okay,' I replied.

Was that the right answer? Was I supposed to be okay after what I'd done?

'Good,' Gretchen said, before ushering me into the living room of her brand new home. I looked around. It was a lovely, cosy room, but it was missing one thing – Gretchen's husband.

'Where's Robert?' I asked Gretchen.

'He's working nights at the hospital,' Gretchen explained. 'He wanted to get some more time off following the wedding, but they're short-staffed over there and they just couldn't spare him.'

'Oh,' I said. 'That's dedicated of him.'

Gretchen sat down in an armchair and motioned for me to do the same. So I perched on the edge of her sofa, ready to make a quick getaway if need be. 'Listen, Gretchen,' I said, wanting to get everything out in the open, 'the reason I came over was to apologise for that whole thing at the wedding. I realise having Roman there ruined your big day, but if I'd known that was going to happen, there was no way I would've brought him. And I wasn't trying to steal your thunder, I swear –'

'Gracie, relax,' Gretchen interrupted me. 'It's fine. Really it is.'

'It is?' I asked, shocked. 'But – how can it be fine? I ruined your wedding. I'm a terrible maid of honour! I'm a terrible person!'

'You're not a terrible person!' Gretchen reassured me. 'You made a mistake, that's all. And we all make mistakes.'

'Some of us more than others,' I commented. 'Gretchen, I really am so sorry.'

'You're forgiven!' Gretchen chuckled. 'It's not a big deal, honestly. For one thing, I totally overreacted. But now I've had a lovely honeymoon with Robert and I've had time to think it over and I'm much calmer about it all.'

'Barbados,' I smiled knowingly, making a mental note that if I ever upset my mother again, Barbados – and not Amsterdam – was the place to go for.

'Barbados was lovely,' Gretchen sighed, clearly wishing she was back there.

'I'm glad you had a good holiday,' I told her.

'It was fantastic,' Gretchen agreed. 'But it's so nice to be back here and to be married and living with Robert. It's like a whole new chapter in my life.'

'That's great,' I said, really pleased that Gretchen was happy.

I may have been a destroyer of wedding days, but at least I wasn't a destroyer of lives. Gretchen had still had her happy-ever-after ending.

'But what about you?' Gretchen asked me excitedly. 'You've started a whole new chapter in your life as well!'

'I have?' I asked. I thought immediately of Billy, before realising there was no way Gretchen could've known about us.

'Yes!' Gretchen exclaimed. 'You and Roman Pearson! Gracie, you're dating a superstar!'

'Yes,' I said. 'Well, actually...'

I faltered. I'd almost fallen back into my old habit of letting people believe their extremely untrue assumptions about me and my life. And after I'd promised Billy that I'd start telling the truth!

There was only one thing for it. I had to tell Gretchen everything. 'I'm not dating Roman,' I finally said.

'You're not?' Gretchen asked, surprised.

'No,' I confirmed. 'Roman and I aren't romantically involved. I've been out with him twice – well, three times if you count the wedding – but they weren't even proper dates. I'm not in love with Roman. I never was.'

'So you really are just his PA then?' Gretchen asked.

'If you can call it that,' I smiled. 'Gretchen, you somehow got the impression that my job is incredibly glamorous – and I let you believe that. But I shouldn't have done. Because the truth is, what I pretty much do at work every day is open Roman's fan mail. It's not glamorous at all. It's boring and routine, and I should never have let you believe otherwise.'

'I can understand why you did,' Gretchen said sympathetically. 'Oh, Gracie, why didn't you tell me you were so unhappy?'

'I'm not,' I told her. 'I'm not unhappy.'

'But you just said –'

'I know,' I interrupted. 'And it's true, my new job *is* boring. But I still prefer it to my old job. And, best of all, it allowed me to meet Billy.'

'Billy?' Gretchen asked, trying to recall the name. 'You told me about him. He works for Roman, doesn't he?'

'Not exactly,' I replied. 'I didn't find this out until last week, but Billy is actually Roman's brother.'

'And what does Billy have to do with this?' Gretchen asked, getting a little confused now.

'Billy's the one I'm in love with,' I told her. 'Or at least, I think I could fall in love with him.' I stopped, attempting to explain myself a little better. 'He's been such a good friend,' I told Gretchen, 'and it took me a while to see it, but –'

'He makes you happy?' Gretchen asked.

'Yes,' I agreed. 'He does. Although I'm not sure Mum will approve when she finds out. I think she had her heart set on me and Roman becoming a couple.'

'You have to stop worrying about what other people think, Gracie,' Gretchen advised. 'Especially your mother. Start doing what you want, and not what everyone else expects you to.'

'It's funny,' I said, smiling. 'Billy said something very similar to me.'

Gretchen grinned. 'Then I like him already,' she said.

'Well that's good,' I told her, 'because you'll be getting a chance to meet him very soon.'

'Really?' Gretchen asked. 'I'd like that.'

'It's Mum and Dad's surprise party on Saturday night,' I explained. 'Billy's going to be there, helping me get everything set up.'

'Wait a minute,' Gretchen said. 'Wasn't this party Warren's idea? Shouldn't *he* be the one doing all the work?'

'Probably,' I agreed. 'But he's informed me that someone needs to escort Mum and Dad to the party, to make sure they arrive at the right time.'

'And that someone is Warren?' Gretchen guessed correctly.

'Which leaves me with the setting up,' I nodded. 'But the thing is, I'm not sure I'll be able to handle it all alone. I've already roped in Billy and Cleo to help out but – and I realise this is a lot to ask, considering I pretty much wrecked your wedding day and all – I was hoping you'd like to give me a hand as well?'

'I'd love to,' Gretchen said, laughing. 'I'll even bring Robert along as an extra pair of hands. On one condition though.'

'What's that?' I asked, willing to grant her just about anything at that moment.

'That Roman Pearson doesn't put in an appearance,' Gretchen grinned.

'I think that can be arranged,' I grinned back.

❄ ❄ ❄

'Roman's not coming, right?' I asked Billy. 'I mean, he's not suddenly going to pop his head round the door, smile that dazzling smile of his, and lead all my party guests away like he's the Pied Piper or something?'

'Don't worry,' Billy assured me. 'I can guarantee you that Roman will *not* be putting in an appearance tonight.' Then he started to laugh.

'What?' I asked him.

'Sorry,' he smiled. 'I was just picturing Roman as the Pied Piper. You know, with the tights and the little cap and everything?'

'I can see how that would be disturbing,' I agreed, laughing with him.

Billy and I were standing by the buffet table, in the function hall I'd hired for my parents' party. The caterers had done a wonderful job and, not for the first time, I congratulated myself on the decision I'd made to hire them, rather than attempting to prepare the party food myself. Sometimes a little extra expense was more than worth it.

The party was already in full swing. Most of the guests had arrived and were either standing around chatting in groups, or showing off their rhythmic 'talents' on the dance floor. Bizarrely, the dancing had so far been led by Gretchen and Cleo – who'd apparently discovered an affinity for shaking their booty, and were even now clicking their heels on the dance floor to the classic sounds of The B-52s' 'Love Shack'.

'I'm surprised how well Cleo and Gretchen have gotten along,' I told Billy. 'They've been hanging out together all evening. It's really weird – they hated each other before they met.'

'They didn't know each other before they met,' Billy reminded me. 'I guess they found out they'd judged each other too soon.'

I smiled at Billy. 'Have you always been this wise?' I asked him.

'Oh yeah,' he replied, smiling back. 'Always.'

It was so great having Billy there by my side. I'd had a couple of stressful moments during the party set up when I'd felt like I wouldn't make it through the evening. But Billy had always been there with a helping hand.

And I was pleased we'd decided to take our relationship slowly. Billy and I were friends, and that was what really mattered. We hadn't even kissed again since that time in Billy's apartment. But I was sure we'd get back to that very soon.

The only real problem I'd encountered so far was when the party guests had started to arrive – many of whom had taken their chance to ask after my 'boyfriend' Roman Pearson. And I'd wanted to tell them all the truth, I really had. But with so many people asking the same question in such a short space of time, I hadn't been able to explain myself properly. And so the myth of Roman and Gracie still prevailed.

I'd caught Billy's eye a couple of times earlier this evening, after he'd heard me being questioned about Roman, and he'd looked terribly disappointed in me for not owning up to the truth. But he'd said nothing about it, and so I'd left the matter there – where hopefully it would stay for the rest of the evening.

'Hi, Gracie,' a voice said, breaking into my thoughts. I turned around to look at the speaker – a young, rather lost-looking redhead.

'Amy!' I exclaimed, smiling at her. 'It's nice to see you again.'

'Thanks,' Amy smiled back. 'I hope you don't mind me coming over. It's just that I don't really know anyone else here but you.'

'Of course I don't mind,' I told her. 'And I'm glad Warren decided to take my advice and invite you to the party after all.'

'Oh, he didn't just invite *me*,' Amy blushed. 'Warren invited a whole group of people from college.'

'He did?' I asked her, looking around the room nervously. That was all I needed – Warren's friends arriving and totally trashing the function hall.

'I haven't seen any of them though,' Amy said. 'Actually, I don't recognise anyone here from college.'

Warren's friends missing a party? The only way that would happen is if they didn't *know* about the party. Which meant that Warren had lied to Amy, no doubt to get her here alone. Great start to any future relationship.

'Well, don't worry,' I reassured her. 'Warren will be here soon.'

Amy smiled at that and seemed to relax a little. Despite Warren's insistence that he and Amy were just friends, I got the distinct impression they both liked each other a lot. It was sweet really – though why anyone would be stupid enough to fall for my brother, I don't know.

Checking my watch for what must've been the tenth time in ten minutes, I wondered when Warren was going to arrive at the party with Mum and Dad. And then, as if on cue, I heard a faint beeping noise coming from my mobile phone. The noise was barely audible over the thumping beat of the music being played, but I'd been holding onto that phone all night, ready for this moment, so I wasn't about to miss it.

I looked at my phone and read the text message that had been sent to me (Warren's chosen method of secret communication). The message simply stated: NEARLY THERE.

'They're on their way,' I told Billy.

'I'll go tell the DJ,' Billy said, hurrying away.

Just a few moments later, the music stopped, and the DJ announced that my parents would soon be arriving at the party.

As the lights dimmed and the party guests gathered by the entrance doors to the hall, ready to surprise my parents, I felt a tug on my arm. It was Cleo.

'Gracie, this is so exciting!' Cleo said, grinning.

'I feel sick,' I confided. 'Something's going to go wrong. I know it.'

'Don't be silly,' Cleo assured me. 'Nothing's going to go wrong. Unless, of course, you count that big stick I left on the floor for your mother to trip over in the dark...'

I looked at her, horrified.

'Cleo!' I cried loudly.

All I got in return was a huge 'SSSHHH!' noise from the gathered guests, and some giggling from Cleo.

'I'm just kidding!' Cleo said, then turned towards the doors. 'Look, they're coming!'

I turned to look, just in time to see my mother and father, followed by Warren, enter the pitch-black room.

'Are you sure we're in the right place?' I heard my mother ask.

Suddenly, all of the lights in the room were thrown on at once and, as one, all of the party guests – including myself – shouted: 'SURPRISE!'

My parents both reeled back in, well, surprise. Mother, ever the drama queen, put on a particularly impressive display – clutching onto my father's arm for support, her other hand flying up to cover her mouth as if she were totally speechless (that'd be a first). Though they both, I was pleased to see, looked suitably shocked.

'HAPPY ANNIVERSARY!' somebody shouted, as if to clarify exactly what the party was for.

And then everything happened in a blur. The party guests all surged forward, ready to congratulate my parents. I hugged my father, who rewarded me with a look of pride, and I hugged my mother (which was strange, as I hadn't done so in such a very long time), though she quickly moved to embrace the next person in the queue, without a glance like the one my father had afforded me with. And then my parents did a lap of the room, hugging and kissing everyone in sight and thanking them for coming.

While all of this commotion was going on, I hung back out of the way, along with Billy and Cleo. Cleo, clearly, wasn't too keen on getting grabbed and kissed by my mother in all the confusion, and Billy seemed to think it safer to stick by my side. Meanwhile, poor Gretchen and Robert, I noticed, had already gotten caught up in the tangled web of party guests surrounding my parents.

Eventually though, with their mingling complete, my parents returned to me.

'Gracie, did you do all of this?' Mum asked.

'Well, I had a little help,' I told her, smiling at Billy and Cleo.

'It was my idea,' Warren protested, suddenly appearing next to me.

'Yes, dear,' Mum sighed, placating him. 'We've already picked out a car for your eighteenth, don't worry.'

'Really?!' Warren grinned. 'Thanks Mum!' And, seeing as he'd gotten what he wanted, Warren promptly disappeared.

I was tempted to protest about my brother being handed such a lavish gift for his eighteenth birthday, but found myself just too amused by the way my mother had so successfully summed up his motives to be angry.

Besides, Mum spoke again before I had the chance to say anything. 'Darling,' she said to me, 'you look lovely tonight.'

'Thanks,' I said, a little concerned by her uncharacteristic flattery.

Luckily, I had more important things to worry about. 'There's someone I want you to meet,' I said, addressing both my parents. 'Well, actually, Dad,' I said, looking at my father, 'you've already met him.'

I took Billy's arm and gently tugged him towards my mum and dad. 'This is Billy Ramsden,' I announced, before turning to Billy. 'Billy, you've already met my dad, Richard.'

'Good to see you again,' Billy smiled. He held out a hand, which my father politely shook.

'Yes,' my father replied, loud enough so I could hear. 'I thought we'd be seeing each other again soon.'

After casting a reproving look in my father's direction,

I pointed Billy towards my mother. 'And this is my mother, Ellen,' I told him. 'Mum, this is Billy.'

'That's nice, dear,' Mum said, before Billy had even had a chance to greet her. She turned to look at me imploringly, apparently oblivious to her own rudeness. 'But where's Roman?' she asked me. 'I was looking forward to seeing him again!'

'Roman's not here,' I told her.

'Don't tell me you didn't invite your own boyfriend to the party?' Mum asked incredulously.

'Mum,' I said. 'I already told you. Roman is *not* my boyfriend.'

'Of course he is,' my mother said. 'Don't be silly, darling.'

I was getting more and more exasperated by the minute – with my mother's attitude; with the way she'd just treated Billy; and with an incessant tapping on my shoulder.

'WHAT?' I shouted, spinning around.

But apparently, over the beat of the music that was throbbing through the hall once again, my yelling had gone unnoticed. Abigail and Martin Stewart stood smiling at me, Abigail lowering the hand she'd been tapping me with.

'Gracie!' Abigail cooed. 'How are you? You look lovely by the way.'

'Thanks,' I replied, through gritted teeth, annoyed at their interruption. 'What do you want?'

'We were just wondering where Roman was,' Martin Stewart told me, with a sickly grin.

'Roman is not here!' I yelled.

This really was the final straw.

'Didn't you bring him?' Abigail asked.

'No,' I said. 'I didn't bring him.'

'Why ever not?' Abigail asked, looking terribly confused.

'Because –' I began, then stopped, realising my efforts were futile. 'Oh, forget it,' I told Abigail and Martin.

I had to end this speculation once and for all. It really was driving me insane.

'Excuse me,' I said, pushing past Abigail and Martin. Then, without looking back for fear of what I might see, I made my way directly to the stage where the DJ was spinning his tunes. I had to do this quickly or I wouldn't do it at all.

'Stop the music,' I ordered the bewildered DJ, as I sidled up next to him.

'What?' he asked, clearly taken aback.

'Stop the music,' I told him again, more firmly this time.

Faced with this apparently-insane young woman, the DJ (not surprisingly) did as he was told. The music stopped, the hall fell silent – and everyone turned to look at me. There was a hush around the room as I grabbed the DJ's microphone and raised it to my mouth.

'Okay, listen up everyone,' I said into the microphone, trying not to look too closely at the dozens of people who were now all staring up at me.

And I was just about to speak again, when somebody beat me to it.

'Speech!' a voice called, from the side of the stage.

I looked over to see Warren standing there, grinning at me wickedly. Amy was by his side, looking suitably bemused (no doubt wondering what kind of family she'd gotten herself involved with).

Ignoring my brother, I turned back to address the masses.

'There's something I have to say,' I told the gathered party guests. 'And I want you all to listen very carefully.'

I looked around the room to check everyone was listening. They were. Good. This was something I definitely didn't want to say twice.

Taking a deep breath, I continued. 'I am *not* dating Roman Pearson,' I told them. 'I have never been dating Roman Pearson. In fact,' I added quickly, 'I'm not even really his PA. All I do is open his fan mail.'

A little gasp went up around the room at that statement, which caused me to falter, almost expecting to be pelted with rotten vegetables at any moment. Luckily, among the crowd, I spotted Gretchen. She flashed me an encouraging smile, which spurred me on to continue.

'And I'm sorry if I let you all believe those things were true,' I told them. 'I should have told the truth way before now. But I didn't – because I was so afraid of what you all might think. You see, I wanted you all to like me. And I wanted you to think I was a success.'

I was really on a roll now. 'But you know what?' I asked the crowd. 'I don't care what you think anymore. It doesn't matter.' I paused, smiling at Billy and Cleo. 'Because my true friends know who I really am,' I continued. 'And they love me for who I am. And they're the people who really count.'

I stopped then and looked around the room. I was all out of things to say. And so I added the only thing I could think of.

'Thank you,' I told the party guests.

For a moment, there was silence. Then I heard someone clapping. Everyone turned to look, including me. It was Billy. He was clapping my speech in a show of support. Then the clapping got louder, and I realised Cleo had joined in with him, a huge, goofy grin on her face. Soon, someone else's applause was added to the mix, and I turned to find that Gretchen was clapping my performance too, Robert not far behind her in joining in with the applause.

A few more people then joined in with them, including a snickering Warren and, I was delighted to see, my father.

And everyone else? Well, everyone else just stared, mouths wide open in disbelief. They certainly hadn't been expecting *that* tonight.

'Well, okay then,' the DJ said, cautiously taking his microphone back from me. 'Let's play some music, shall we?'

And I exited the stage to the sounds of a Kylie Minogue remix.

The song, quite appropriately, was called 'Shocked'.

❄ ❄ ❄

I was making my way towards Billy and Cleo, through the crowds of guests who were already back on the dance floor (apparently they hadn't been *that* shocked by my big announcement after all), when I was suddenly intercepted by my mother. She grabbed my arm, leading me over to the function hall's entrance way, where the music wasn't quite so loud.

'Mum, before you say anything,' I got in, before she

could speak, 'I'm sorry if that embarrassed you. But,' I added, 'it had to be said.'

'Darling, why didn't you tell me you weren't dating Roman?' Mum asked. To my surprise, she sounded calm – not at all angry, as I'd expected.

'I did,' I reminded her. 'Several times.'

'This is such good news!' Mum cried.

'It is?' I asked her, confused. And there I was thinking that my dating Roman Pearson was my mother's life dream. 'But I thought –'

'This works out very nicely,' my mother continued, as if I wasn't even there. She seemed to be off in her own little world right now, daydreaming away. The only question was – about what?

'How exactly?' I asked her.

Mum looked at me, and for the first time seemed aware of the fact that I was standing in front of her.

'Now you can get back together with David!' she exclaimed excitedly.

That was it. My mother had finally cracked up. It must've been my speech – it had pushed her over the edge.

'Um, newsflash,' I said, trying to get through to her. 'David is getting married to Lorna Spence. I told you that, remember?'

'He *was* getting married to Lorna Spence,' Mum smiled. 'But not anymore.'

'What are you talking about?' I asked her.

'David caught Lorna cheating on him with another man,' Mum explained. 'And it was all because of you, Gracie.'

'Me?' I asked. 'How do I fit into this?'

'You sowed the seeds of doubt in his mind,' Mum said proudly, 'when you met him that day and told him what Lorna had said to you.'

'How do you know about that?!' I spluttered.

I hadn't mentioned my encounter with David to my mother, I was sure of it. And I'd only given my father the most basic of details, which I was confident he'd known better than to repeat to anyone – most especially my mother.

'Oh, David told me all about it,' Mum said.

Mystery solved.

'You've been talking to David?' I asked her.

'We've been in touch,' Mum replied. 'Anyway, after you warned him about Lorna, David decided to test her. So he told Lorna he was going to be working late, but really he came home early – where he found her in bed with another man!'

'What a shocker,' I said sarcastically.

Was I supposed to be surprised by this? After all, it was bound to have happened sooner or later. It was inevitable.

'Don't you see?' Mum said happily. 'Now you can get back together with David! It's the way things were meant to be.'

'Do you really think things are that simple?' I asked her, taken aback.

Oh sure, David's a free agent and I'm not dating Roman, so that obviously equals a reunion. My mother's thinking baffled me sometimes.

'He still loves you,' Mum said. 'He told me.'

'Mum –' I began, but was interrupted.

'And now he can tell you himself,' she smiled, nodding over my shoulder.

I turned around to see who my mother was nodding at, and received perhaps the biggest shock of my life. David – my ex-fiancé David – had just walked into the function hall.

'Hi, Gracie,' he said, with a smile.

'David?' I asked dumbly, though I was in no doubt it was he. 'But –' I turned back to my mother – she just *had* to have had some hand in this. 'Mum?' I asked her. 'What is he doing here?'

'I invited him,' Mum said.

'You can't have done!' I protested. 'This was a surprise party! You didn't even know it was happening!'

'Oh, Abigail Stewart let slip about the party weeks ago,' Mum told me. 'She just can't keep a secret, you know.'

'You knew?!' I asked her, more astonished than upset. 'But you looked so surprised! Genuinely surprised!'

'Yes, didn't I play it well?' my mother asked with delight. 'I could've had a career in acting, you know,' she told me. 'Do you think Roman knows anyone who could help me get a foot in the door?'

'Mum!' I practically yelled. I couldn't believe she was babbling on about her chances of an acting career at a time like this.

'No need to shout,' she scolded me. 'Now why don't I leave you two alone so you can talk?'

And she walked away then – but not before giving me a little shove towards David.

'Gracie, I hope you don't mind –' David began immediately.

'David, what are you doing here?' I interrupted, determined to get this over and done with as soon as possible.

'I came to see you,' he told me.

'Why?' I asked him. 'You couldn't get away from me quick enough last time.'

'I'm sorry about that,' David said. 'I should have listened to you.'

'Yes,' I told him. 'You should have.'

'Gracie, can we talk?' he asked me.

'We *are* talking.'

'No,' he said, shaking his head. 'Can we talk properly? Outside?'

'I don't think that's such a good idea,' I told him honestly.

'Please?' he pleaded, in that annoyingly imploring way of his. I could feel my resolve weakening.

'Okay,' I finally sighed in agreement, 'but just for a minute.'

I led the way outside, letting David follow me. As soon as we'd stepped over the threshold, I turned to look at him. 'Go on then,' I instructed him. 'Say whatever it is you have to say.'

David took a deep breath before speaking. 'Gracie, I still love you,' he told me. 'I've always loved you.'

'Really?' I asked him. 'Even when you were sleeping with Lorna Spence?'

'That was a mistake,' David said quickly. 'A big, huge mistake. A terrible mistake. Haven't you ever made a mistake before, Gracie?'

'I think you're getting off the point,' I told him.

After all, what did *my* mistakes have to do with anything?

'Yes,' he agreed. 'I am. Gracie, I still love you,' he said again. 'And I want to be with you. I want back what we had.'

'It's too late for that,' I told him, surprised to find my eyes welling with tears as I spoke those words.

'Why is it too late?' David asked. He moved closer to me, taking my hands in his. 'Gracie, we had something special,' he continued. 'And I ruined it – I know that. But I'd do anything to save what we had. And there must be a way to save it. There must be.'

'I'm not sure there is,' I told him sadly.

'It's up to you, Gracie,' David told me. 'All you have to do is say the words and we can have it all back again. Please don't throw this away,' he pleaded. 'Think about what we had – what we can still have.'

I looked into his face then; into his eyes. He looked so sincere, so truthful – so desperate to have me in his life again. And in that moment, with my hands joined with his, I realised how much I'd missed him. And how lost I had been without him.

'This is so sudden,' I told him. 'I need –'

'Time to think,' he interrupted, 'I know.' Then he smiled at me. 'But at least let me give you something to think about.'

And then he kissed me.

And as he did so, all the memories of our time together came flooding back. All of the happiness we'd shared. All of the love.

And I found myself kissing him back – forgetting the bad and remembering only the good. And David had always been a good kisser.

But when we finally parted, the kiss ended, I suddenly realised David and I were no longer alone. There was somebody standing in the doorway of the function hall, looking out at us in silence.

And that somebody was Billy.

❄ ❄ ❄

'Billy!' I cried. 'Wait!'

After witnessing the kiss shared between me and David, Billy had disappeared back into the function hall without saying a word. I'd immediately chased after him, even though he was obviously doing his very best to avoid me, plunging into the crowd of people on the dance floor in a deliberate attempt to shake me off. But I'd also thrown myself into the midst of the dancing dozens and had finally caught up with him.

I grabbed his arm now in an attempt to stop his flight. 'Billy!' I called again. He spun around to face me, but didn't say a word. 'I'm sorry!' I told him.

'Sorry for what?' Billy asked, having to yell above the beat of the music to be heard. 'Sorry you did it, or sorry you got caught?'

The thing was, Billy was yelling a little *too* loudly. I cringed in embarrassment as everyone in the room turned to stare at me for the second time that night.

'The last one!' I said, in a complete panic. 'No, wait,

both. No –' I threw my hands in the air in frustration. 'I don't know!'

'No,' Billy agreed. 'You don't know much, do you? You keep chopping and changing your mind – and you forget that you're playing around with other people's feelings while you do it!'

'Billy, I –' I began, shocked by his outburst.

'Just make up your mind, Gracie!' Billy ordered me. 'Decide what you want and go with it – because I'm sick of being stuck in the middle!'

And with that, he was off – storming off the dance floor away from me, and out of the function hall doors.

And this time, I didn't follow him.

Chapter Seventeen

'You know, Gracie, when you throw a party, you really throw a party!' Cleo grinned. 'That's the most excitement I've had in ages!'

She was trying to cheer me up, I knew, but I just couldn't be happy right now. The party had come to an end, the guests had dispersed back to their homes – and I'd been left with clearing-up duties.

Warren, amazingly, had managed to make yet another great escape, sneaking out along with the other party guests. I'd seen him disappearing outside at the end of the evening, holding hands with Amy, and I'd moved to stop him. However, Warren had seen my approach and, as if silently pleading with me not to come after him, had mouthed the words 'true love' at me, while pointing at himself and Amy.

True love? The romantic in me wanted to believe him but, knowing Warren, he and Amy would've gotten together and broken up again by this time next week. Still, it had been enough for me to let them go. The last thing I wanted to do tonight was ruin yet another budding romance.

And I'd ordered my parents home as well, if only to

end my mother's constant questioning about David and me. David, meanwhile, had also exited at my insistence – but not before eliciting a promise from me that I would call him and arrange a time and a place for us to meet, to discuss the implications of his break-up with Lorna and *that* kiss.

So that just left me and Cleo to make a final sweep of the room and check that everything was in order.

'You're thinking about David, aren't you?' Cleo asked me, breaking into my thoughts.

'Maybe a little,' I admitted. 'Why? Do you think that's completely insane?'

'Completely,' Cleo said. And from the look on her face, I could tell she wasn't joking. 'Are you actually considering taking him back?' she asked, sounding annoyed. 'After all he put you through?'

'That was a long time ago,' I pointed out to her.

'So?' she said, completely unmoved.

I had to smile. 'You don't believe in forgiving and forgetting?' I asked her.

'Not where David McAllister's concerned,' Cleo replied.

'Anyone would think he cheated on *you*,' I told her.

'No, he cheated on *you*,' Cleo reminded me. 'So why would you want to forgive him?'

'Maybe I still love him.'

'Maybe?' Cleo asked, eyebrows raised.

'I don't know!' I cried, for what seemed like the hundredth time that evening. Why did people have to ask such difficult questions? 'It's just that it might be nice to have my old life back, you know?' I told her. 'I liked that life.'

'Your old life was boring,' Cleo told me bluntly.

'Thanks a lot!' I cried.

'You know what I mean,' Cleo said. 'The life you have now – it's so much better than what you had before. *You're* better.'

'I'm better?'

'You're different, Gracie,' Cleo explained. 'You've changed – for the better. You've really come alive since then. You'd be mad to go back.'

'Maybe I'd be mad not to?' I suggested.

Cleo ignored this. 'What about Billy?' she asked.

'What about him?'

'Don't you think you should've gone after him?'

'No!' I said. 'He humiliated me in front of everyone! I wasn't going to go chasing after him!'

'No offence, Gracie,' Cleo said, choosing her words carefully, 'but Billy was right. What he said to you was spot on.'

'Oh, well thanks for taking my side!' I protested.

'This isn't about sides,' Cleo told me. 'This is about you. Gracie, you have to make a choice. You have to decide what you want.'

'Before it's too late?' I filled in for her.

'Before you don't have any choices left,' Cleo finished ominously.

❄ ❄ ❄

Despite Cleo's urging, I still hadn't made any decisions by the time Monday morning came around again (oh why do the weekends always seem to go so fast?). And so I'd trudged into work, hoping that a few of Roman's fan letters would help me forget the burden of choices weighing me down.

I'd been surprised by the fact that the office was empty on my arrival – Olivia was nowhere to be found. But that was explained in a telephone call soon afterwards, when Olivia rang to tell me she had an emergency dental appointment and wouldn't be coming into work that morning.

But she had, she'd told me, great faith in me. She knew I could hold down the fort while she was out of the office. And I'd thanked Olivia for that, despite my shock at hearing such complimentary words pop out of my co-worker's mouth.

What this meant, however, was that I'd been left all alone in the office – with nothing to do but think (never a good thing where I was concerned) or read Roman's fan mail. I'd chosen the latter.

I'd already read and replied to six letters and was picking my seventh from the post sack, when I clumsily dropped the envelope I'd chosen. The envelope fluttered to the floor underneath my desk. I was tempted to leave it where it was but, realising that it needed to be retrieved sooner or later, I instead climbed from my chair, got down on my hands and knees, and crawled under my desk to collect it.

While I was under the desk, I heard the office door open.

'Gracie?' a man's voice asked.

'Billy?' I said out loud, as that was my instinctive thought.

My instinctive action, meanwhile, was to try and get out from under the desk as soon as possible. However, I attempted that far too soon and ended up banging my head rather painfully on the top of the desk as a result.

'Ow!' I cried and, having learnt my lesson, attempted to manoeuvre my way out much more carefully the second time around. I climbed out from under the desk, rubbing my sore head, and stood up, ready to greet Billy eagerly.

Only it wasn't Billy standing there. It was Roman.

'It's just me,' Roman said apologetically. I wasn't sure if he was apologising for not being Billy, or because he'd caused me to bang my head. 'Are you okay?' he asked, nodding to my head.

Oh, well that cleared that one up then.

'Yeah, I'm okay, thanks,' I told him, a little embarrassed he'd caught me in such a state. 'What are you doing here?'

'I came to apologise,' he told me. 'For...well, for a number of things.'

'You don't have anything to apologise for,' I told him, sitting back down on my chair.

Which was true, in my opinion. Anything Roman had done wrong was long forgotten after what had happened at my parents' party.

'Yes,' he said, 'I think I do. I behaved terribly at your friend's wedding. I've been thinking about it, over and over, and I realise now you were trying to warn me what I was doing – but I just didn't listen. That should've been your friend's big day but I charged in there and took all the attention away from her.'

'It was my fault,' I told him firmly. 'I should've known that would happen. I should never have invited you in the first place.'

'No,' Roman said, perching himself on the edge of my desk – the spot where Billy usually sat. 'You shouldn't have. You should have invited Billy. He's who you wanted to invite, right?'

'How did you –' I began.

'How did I know that?' Roman laughed. 'Well, it took me a while to work it out, but I got there eventually. I should've known something was going on between you and Billy though,' he grinned. 'Every time I mentioned you, Billy got that look about him. You know, like a little love-sick puppy?'

'He did?' I asked, not quite being able to picture it.

'Plus, he was getting really cranky with me,' Roman continued, not answering my question. 'And I wondered why, but I didn't think...well, I guess that's just me. I don't think.'

'That makes two of us then,' I told him glumly.

'Listen, I know Billy said some things to you,' Roman told me. 'But he only said what he did because he cares about you.'

'Yeah, but did he have to say it in front of quite so many people?' I asked, questioning myself more than Roman.

'I know you're mad at Billy right now,' Roman said, displaying completely unexpected insight, 'and probably mad at yourself too – but there's something you should realise about Billy.' Roman checked he had my attention before continuing. 'Billy's not like me,' he explained. 'He's one of the good guys. And let me tell you something – however great you think that guy David is, I guarantee you Billy is ten times better. No, one hundred times better.'

'I don't need you to convince me how great Billy is,' I told Roman. 'I already know how great he is.'

'Good!' Roman cried. 'Well then it's simple, isn't it?'

'No,' I told him. 'It's not. It's never that simple. Not for me.'

'You like Billy, he likes you,' Roman pointed out. 'What's the problem?'

'There are just so many people's feelings to consider,' I told him.

'Gracie,' Roman said, leaning towards me. 'The only person's feelings that actually count are yours. How do *you* feel? What do you want?'

I thought for a moment, but found things still weren't any clearer. 'I don't know!' I cried. 'It's all so confusing!'

'But you know you don't want me?' Roman asked, after a moment.

'What?' I asked him, completely taken aback.

'Well, I just wanted to check,' Roman said. 'You know, that you're *really* not interested in me?'

I couldn't help but smile at Roman's dogged persistence. 'I'm not,' I told him firmly.

'Mmm,' he said, 'okay.' Then he thought for a moment. 'Well,' he said, as if taking it all in, '*that's* never happened to me before.'

'I don't suppose it'll become the norm,' I reassured him with a smile.

❄ ❄ ❄

It wasn't until I stepped through the front door that night, and smelled the familiar odours of my mother's cooking wafting out from the kitchen, that I remembered it was once again dinner party time in the Parker house.

'Gracie, is that you?' my mother called, hearing me close the front door.

'Yes, Mum, it's me!' I called back, taking off my jacket and hanging it up.

As I did so, Gretchen appeared from the dining room and hurried towards me. Gretchen, along with Robert, was one of tonight's 'lucky' dinner guests. Gretchen's parents had also been invited, and were no doubt already sitting in the dining room, waiting to be served. Mother never allowed dinner guests access to the kitchen while she was preparing their food (which kind of made me wonder what she was feeding them).

'Gracie!' Gretchen said, in a hushed tone. 'There's something you should know before you go in there.'

'What's up?' I asked her, already making my way towards the dining room.

After all, there was no point in delaying the inevitable, was there? I'd already admitted defeat in trying to make myself scarce for Mother's dinner parties, because the ploy simply never worked. It was easier just to accept my fate.

'Gracie, wait!' Gretchen said urgently, grabbing my arm before I could enter the dining room.

'Gretchen!' I cried. Her fingers were digging into my arm. 'What is it?!'

'It's –' Gretchen began, then suddenly stopped.

'Gracie!' a voice behind me said. 'You're here!'

With Gretchen looking on worriedly, I turned around – to find David smiling fondly at me.

'David?' I asked, shocked. 'What – what are you doing here?'

Just then, my mother emerged from the kitchen, her arms laden with plates of food. 'Oh, Gracie!' she smiled. 'There you are! I hope you don't mind, but I invited David to dinner.' Before I even had a chance to reply, she moved towards the dining room. David took a step towards her.

'Ellen!' he said sternly. 'Let me help you with those!'

He took some plates from my mother, lightening her load, and they made their way into the dining room together.

'Mind?' I muttered to myself, as they disappeared. 'Why should I mind?'

'I tried to tell you!' Gretchen said, a little nervously, before disappearing into the dining room herself.

Obviously Gretchen was a little worried about what was to come.

As was I.

❄ ❄ ❄

Dinner had so far been horrendous. And, no, I don't mean

the food. The food had been great, but the conversation less so.

My mother, as ever, had completely dominated proceedings. And by the time she had brought in dessert, it had become clear to me that she'd organised this dinner party purely for her own manipulative purposes. In other words, to do her very best to ensure David and I were reunited.

The evening had so far consisted of a dissection of the three years that David and I had been together (concentrating on the happy times, of course). And it seemed Mother wasn't finished with her reminiscing just yet.

'Do you remember,' Mum said, between mouthfuls of orange pavlova, 'about two years ago when Gracie saw that movie – *Strictly Ballroom*, I think it was called – and decided she wanted to take up ballroom dancing?'

She aimed her question at David, which was no great surprise. Most of the evening's conversation had been bounced between the two of them.

'I remember,' David chuckled, looking at me. 'Gracie dragged me along to those ballroom dancing classes and I thought I was going to hate every minute of it. But I guess I should've been more open-minded, as I really enjoyed myself.'

'You didn't enjoy it!' I corrected David. 'You hated it. We only went to three classes!'

'Yes, because you got bored of it so quickly,' David replied (which wasn't true, by the way – we quit ballroom dancing class because David said he couldn't spare the time off work). He smiled at me affectionately. 'Typical Gracie – always wanting to run off and try something different.'

'Well, she's always been a rather flighty girl,' my mother said, before I could respond in my defence. 'Even when she was little – always running from one thing to the next.'

'I don't think Gracie's flighty,' Gretchen said.

At least someone was on my side. Unfortunately, my mother completely ignored Gretchen's comment.

'Still, hopefully now you two are back together, Gracie will settle down,' my mother said, patting David on the hand.

'MUM!' I yelled.

Everyone seated around the table, including my father, Gretchen's parents, and Robert – who'd so far all been politely finishing off their desserts in silence – looked up in startled shock.

'David and I are *not* back together,' I reminded my mother, through gritted teeth.

'Yes, dear,' Mum said, waving away my protests, 'but it's only a matter of time, isn't it?'

'Is it?' I asked her. 'Because I don't remember saying anything about getting back together with David. I hadn't even decided whether I should meet with him and discuss it yet.'

'Yes, well, you never *were* any good at making decisions, were you?' my mother asked, in a disapproving tone. 'So I thought I'd give you a helping hand.'

At that point, she turned her attention back to David, seemingly satisfied her point had been made. 'Now, your job *is* still secure after all that nasty business with that horrible girl at work, isn't it?' she asked him.

'Yes, it's quite secure,' David laughed, apparently finding my mother's reference to Lorna quite amusing.

Like it didn't take two to tango.

'No need to worry, Ellen,' he said. 'I'll be able to provide for Gracie quite nicely.'

Provide for me? What the hell did he mean, provide for me?! Like I was some little woman who needed to be looked after!

I was approaching boiling point, almost ready to explode due to David's condescending attitude, when my mother smiled and said: 'I'm glad to hear that. Because I can't wait much longer to be a grandmother, you know!'

And then I exploded.

'That's it!' I yelled, scraping back my chair and standing up. 'I can't listen to anymore of this!'

'Gracie!' my mother said, looking up at me reprovingly. 'Sit down.'

'No,' I told her firmly. 'I won't sit down. I've had enough. I've been sitting here all evening, listening to you plan my life for me, and I've had enough!'

'Gracie!' Mum cried, clearly shocked.

'I've heard you tell David that I'll get back together with him,' I continued, undeterred, 'even though I've said no such thing. And now you're talking about us having children together! I bet you've even encouraged him to propose to me again, haven't you?!'

'Gracie, it seems to me that you're angry with me, not your mother –' David began.

'Yes!' I said, turning on him. 'I *am* angry with you. Why did you come here? You knew I wanted time to think, so why did you come here and try to push me into getting back together with you?!'

'I thought –' David started.

'No!' I interrupted. 'You didn't think! Not about me anyway. Because if you *had* thought, you would've realised this was the last thing you should have done.'

I looked from David to my mother. 'Thank you for reminding me exactly why my old life was so terrible,' I told them. 'You've both been a big help.' And with that, I quickly left the table and made my way towards the door.

'Gracie!' my mother wailed. 'Where are you going?!'

'I'm going to try and salvage my new life,' I said, turning to face her. Then I looked at my ex-fiancé. 'David,' I told him, 'I don't love you. I don't even like you very much anymore. And I should never have kissed you at the party. That was the second-biggest mistake of my life.'

'What was the first?' Gretchen's father asked, completely engrossed in the scene playing out in front of him. His wife elbowed him in the side, indicating that he should shut up. But I didn't mind the question.

'The biggest mistake of my life,' I told them, 'was letting the man I love walk away without trying to stop him.'

'Billy,' Gretchen smiled at me.

I nodded.

'Billy?' my mother asked, confused. 'Who's Billy?'

'I have to see him,' I said, at the exact moment that I realised this. 'I have to go now. Gretchen,' I said, turning to my friend, 'I know you probably need it to get home and all, but do you think I could borrow your car?'

'Sure,' Gretchen agreed, with a laugh.

'No need for that,' I heard my father say. I turned to look at him, and found he was smiling at me proudly. 'You can borrow my car,' he said. 'In fact,' he continued, standing up, 'I'll drive you there myself.'

'Richard!' my mother cried, horrified. 'Don't encourage her!'

'Do you want to leave right now?' my father asked, ignoring my mother's comment.

'Yes,' I told him, as he made his way over to join me by the door.

'Then let's go,' he said, sounding rather excited.

'Great,' I told him. 'Just let me get something from upstairs first, okay?'

'Okay,' my father agreed.

As I made my way out of the dining room and up the stairs, I couldn't help but overhear my mother's wailing and protesting at my actions. Usually, this sort of thing would've bothered me, but right now I didn't have a care in the world.

I was going to tell Billy that I loved him. And everything was going to work out fine.

Or at least, I sure hoped it would.

❄ ❄ ❄

'Do you want me to wait?' my father asked, as he stopped the car outside Billy's apartment block.

I had to smile. It seemed as if my father had been having the time of his life this evening – what with standing up to my mother and then running off on this big adventure with me. Clearly he didn't want it to end.

'No,' I told him gently. 'Don't wait. I could be a while.'

Seeing the rather knowing look my father gave me, I thought it better to clarify that statement. 'Billy and I will have a lot to talk about,' I told him.

'Of course,' he nodded in agreement, though I wondered if he really believed me.

Unclipping my seat belt, I climbed out of the car. 'Good luck,' my father called after me. I looked back in the car at him and smiled.

'Thanks for the lift, Dad,' I told him, and I leaned back in and kissed him quickly on the cheek before shutting the car door.

I heard my father drive away as I approached Billy's building. This was it – there was no going back now.

Gathering my courage, I prepared to press the intercom for Billy's apartment, keeping my fingers crossed that he would actually let me in. Then, to my surprise, the doors to the apartment building opened and a man in his early fifties came out. Rather than let the door slam shut, he held it open for me.

'Going in?' he asked.

'Yes,' I said, stepping away from the intercom and taking the door from him. 'Thanks.' And thanks to that man's politeness, I thought, as I made my way into the building and up the stairs to the first floor – where Billy's apartment was located – I was going to be able to surprise Billy, face to face. He'd have no choice but to speak to me now.

Reaching Billy's apartment, I knocked politely on the door, then waited for it to open. Except nothing happened. Frowning, I knocked again – harder this time. But still, no answer.

I looked around for a doorbell to press instead, but found none. What I did notice, however, was a little peephole in the door which, had Billy used it, would have revealed to him exactly who was standing outside his front door.

I knocked again, even louder still, and again received no answer.

So that was it, was it? Billy was still mad at me and was going to ignore me, pretending he wasn't home? Well, I wasn't about to go away that easily.

'Billy!' I shouted, banging on the door again. 'Billy, I know you're in there!'

I stopped and waited, but received no response. 'Billy!' I yelled at the door. 'Just come out and talk to me! Please?'

'He's not home,' I heard a voice say.

I stepped away from Billy's front door and looked at the speaker – a woman who (quite obviously) was at least in her sixties, but who was dressed as if she were only twenty-one, in a little baby doll nightdress.

'What?' I asked her.

'He's not home,' the woman said again. 'That's why he's not answering the door. He can't hear you yelling. I heard you though,' she added.

Which was when I realised the woman was standing in the open doorway of the apartment next to Billy's. She was Billy's next-door neighbour.

'Oh,' I said. 'I'm sorry. I didn't mean to wake you.'

They were the first words to pop out of my mouth due to the time of night (it was just after eleven, after all), though apparently I'd assumed too much.

'I wasn't asleep,' the woman said. And then, as if to illustrate her point, a man – in his sixties probably – appeared from inside her apartment.

'Lola?' he asked the woman. 'Are you coming back to bed?'

'In a minute, Frank,' she placated him, waving him back inside. Then she turned back to me. 'My boyfriend, Frank,' she explained.

I tried not to grimace at the thought of Lola and Frank joining each other in bed, as Lola smiled at me. 'You're a very pretty girl,' she told me. 'Are you Billy's girlfriend?'

'Not exactly,' I replied, though smiling my thanks for the compliment. 'Do you know where Billy is?' I asked her.

'He's gone away for a couple of days,' Lola said. 'Something to do with his paintings, I think. He asked me to look out for his place while he was gone.'

'Oh,' I said, disappointment washing over me as I realised my impromptu pilgrimage to Billy's apartment had all been for nothing.

'He'll be back tomorrow though,' Lola added, apparently sensing my dismay. 'Early he said.'

'Okay,' I said, smiling gratefully at her for the information. 'Thanks.'

'Lola!' a man's voice called.

'Coming, Frank!' Lola called into her apartment, before turning back to me. 'Are you okay, darling?' she asked me. 'Do you need anything?'

'No,' I told her. 'I'm fine, thank you.'

And with a final smile at me, Lola disappeared back

into her apartment – leaving me alone on the landing outside.

With no way of getting home.

I cursed myself for being stupid enough to send my father away before I'd even checked Billy was home, let alone that he'd see me. And I'd been in such a hurry to get to Billy's apartment, I hadn't even thought to bring my mobile phone with me, so I had no way of calling for either a lift from Gretchen or a taxi home.

I supposed I could always knock and ask to borrow Lola's phone, but I really didn't want to interrupt whatever it was Lola and Frank were doing in there. I didn't even have any money with me, I realised. In fact, the only thing I'd brought with me was...well, that didn't matter anymore, did it? Billy wasn't home and that was that.

Except that Lola had said Billy would be home early the next morning.

An idea started to form in my head. Not one of my better ideas, admittedly, but perhaps one of my most adventurous. I had no desire to return home tonight – especially with no good news to tell. So the answer was simple. I would wait here for Billy to return. However long that might take.

My mind made up, I sat down outside Billy's front door. The floor, I noticed immediately, was hard – and cold. But I could put up with it for one night.

I rested my head against Billy's front door and prepared myself for a long wait. All I had to do was stay awake.

And that was something I was certain I could manage.

❄ ❄ ❄

'Gracie!' I heard a voice calling me. The voice echoed all around my head. And then somebody was shaking me. 'Gracie!' the voice said again.

I opened my eyes – to find myself looking up into the face of the man I loved. Billy. 'Are you okay?' he asked me.

Suddenly, everything came rushing back to me – the excitement of hurrying to Billy's apartment; the anticipation of what would happen; the disappointment of Billy being away; the coldness of the floor.

'What time is it?' I groaned.

Probably not the most romantic of greetings, but I was still sleepy – and I ached all over from my stint in Billy's doorway.

'It's seven in the morning,' Billy said, without needing to check his watch. 'Gracie, what are you doing here?'

'I fell asleep,' I told him apologetically, not answering his question. 'I didn't mean to fall asleep.'

'Are you trying to tell me you spent the night on my doorstep?' Billy asked incredulously.

'It's true,' a voice said.

Billy turned to look at the speaker, and I (with great effort) stood up so I could do the same. It was Lola, outside her apartment again. 'She came to see you last night, but I told her you wouldn't be back until morning,' Lola told Billy. 'So she must have waited all night for you on your doorstep. How romantic!' she sighed.

Billy shot a questioning look in my direction, as if to determine the truth of Lola's statement. I just shrugged.

What else could I do? I was suddenly aware of how totally ridiculous this whole plan of mine had been.

'Gracie, I don't know why you're here,' Billy said, 'but I haven't had much sleep. I'm tired – I don't have time for games.'

Okay. Not quite the reaction I'd been looking for.

Manoeuvring around me, Billy unlocked and opened his front door before I could stop him.

'Billy, wait!' I protested. 'I have to talk to you!'

'And what would you say?' Billy asked me. 'Sorry for leading you on, but I've decided to get back together with my lying, cheating, ex-boyfriend after all? I don't want to hear it, Gracie.'

'Wait!' I said again, trying to block his way into the apartment. 'Please – let me explain!'

'Yeah!' a voice said. 'Let her explain!'

Billy and I both turned to look in astonishment – at Frank, who'd come out of Lola's apartment to support my cause. Now Lola and Frank were both watching Billy and me in anticipation. It was a totally bizarre situation – but even if every single one of Billy's neighbours came out to watch, I wouldn't have cared. I just wanted Billy to listen to me.

'Billy,' I said, turning back to face him. 'I know what you think – but David and I aren't back together. We never were. And we never will be.'

'For two people who aren't together, you looked pretty cosy at your parents' party,' Billy commented.

'That was a mistake,' I insisted. 'A huge mistake. The second-biggest mistake of my life,' I told him, repeating my words of the previous evening.

I'd hoped Billy would respond to my statement in the same way as Gretchen's father, but sadly that was not to be.

'Only the second-biggest?' Billy asked, clearly not expecting a reply.

'You're supposed to ask me what the biggest mistake of my life was,' I complained.

'What was the biggest mistake of your life?' Billy asked, finally playing along – though not looking too happy about it.

'The biggest mistake of my life,' I told him, 'was not going after you when you left the party.'

'Oh,' Billy said, clearly a little stunned.

'The truth,' I told him, 'is that I don't love David – because I'm in love with someone else.'

I took a deep breath before finally saying what I'd come all the way to Billy's apartment, and slept on his doorstep, to say.

'I love you.'

'Are you sure?' Billy asked me, after an excruciatingly long moment of silence. 'Because you never seem sure about anything, Gracie.'

'I'm sure about this,' I promised him. 'And I can prove it.'

I rummaged around in my jacket pocket until I found what I was looking for – the thing I'd made a detour upstairs to collect before leaving home.

My engagement ring from David.

'Here,' I said. 'I want you to have this.'

I pulled one of Billy's hands forward, opened his fingers, and placed the ring gently in his palm.

'This is –' Billy began.

'My engagement ring,' I told him. 'The one David gave me.'

'And you're giving this to me because?'

Billy looked confused. But I'd thought about this moment long and hard during the drive to his apartment, and was prepared for his question.

'Think of it as a symbol of my old life,' I told him. 'It represents everything I used to have – and everything I no longer want. And I'm giving this ring to you, and you can do what you like with it. Because I don't want it anymore – I don't want my old life anymore.' I looked deep into his eyes. 'All I want is you, Billy.'

That was it. I was done. All I could do now was wait for Billy's reaction.

I held my breath in anticipation as Billy looked from what I hoped was my most earnest face, to the ring sitting in his hand. After what seemed like hours, he closed his hand around the ring and looked up at me.

And then, in the best traditions of all those old romantic movies they show on TV on rainy Sunday afternoons, Billy suddenly grabbed me – scooping me up in his arms and carrying me over the threshold of his apartment, shutting the door behind us with his foot.

As he gently placed me back on my own two feet, I found myself too surprised to speak. Luckily, Billy spoke enough for the both of us.

'This didn't feel right with Lola and Frank watching,' he said, smiling.

And then he kissed me. And I kissed him back, finally sure I had found what I was looking for.

Epilogue

'Okay, I think that's the last one,' Billy said, breathing a sigh of relief as he put the big cardboard box he was carrying down on the living room floor. 'You know, you sure have a lot of stuff,' he added, smiling at me affectionately.

'And I can't wait to see it again,' I told him. 'There wasn't much room for it all at Mum and Dad's, so it's been stuck up in the attic for months now.'

'Well now there's plenty of room for it,' Billy said, looking around.

'Yes,' I said, joining him in looking happily around my new home, 'there really is.'

I smiled at Billy. 'Did I thank you yet for finding me this apartment?' I asked him.

'A number of times,' Billy said. 'But I can't take all the credit, now can I? After all, Lola was the one who told me this place was being rented out again. I think she likes you – she was really keen for you to move into the building.'

'I was really keen to move into the building,' I admitted. 'I like that you're just downstairs if I need you.'

'You know, you could've just moved in with me,' Billy

said, putting his arms around my waist and pulling me to him.

'I know,' I told him. 'But this just feels right at the moment.'

'Okay,' he smiled, kissing me quickly on the lips, 'as long as you're happy.'

'I am,' I smiled back at him.

'Um, could someone help me with this please?' a voice asked, interrupting our romantic moment.

Billy and I both turned to look at the sound of the voice, to find that Cleo had entered the apartment, her arms piled high with so many boxes she couldn't see over the top of them.

'Cleo!' I scolded, as Billy and I went to assist her. 'Why didn't you wait for Billy to come back down?' Billy and I each took a box from Cleo's arms, allowing her to emerge from behind them.

'Because,' Cleo explained, putting down the rest of the boxes, 'I wanted to grab the best bedroom before you bagged it for yourself.' She looked from Billy to me, and then grinned mischievously. 'Which I can see you were just about to do...'

I rolled my eyes at Cleo's insinuation, doing my best to ignore it.

'Is that the last of your stuff?' I asked her.

'Yep, that's all of it,' Cleo said. 'I can't believe we're moving in together, Gracie! Isn't this exciting?'

'I think I'll leave you two to get settled in,' Billy smiled at me, making his way out of the apartment. I followed him to the door to see him off.

'Are you visiting Roman today?' I asked him, as he stepped outside.

'Yes,' Billy laughed. 'He practically begged me to come down. Olivia's invited herself onto the set and I don't think he wants to be left alone with her!'

'Olivia's okay,' I told him. 'Once you get to know her.'

And I'd actually gotten to know Olivia quite well over the past two months. Ever since Roman's last day as a member of the *Hearts & Minds* cast, Olivia and I had been pooling our ideas and thoughts together, working as a team to find Roman work elsewhere.

And we'd succeeded; securing Roman the lead role in a highly anticipated new film, which was to mark the directorial debut of Roman's good friend, Toby Swann.

Now Roman was back in the celebrity loop again (and so much the happier for it). Meanwhile, my employment had become much more pleasant and interesting. Oh, and did I mention that I'd also satisfied my mother's acting ambitions for the time being, by getting her a walk-on part in Roman's new movie?

Suddenly, Mum was a lot more accepting of my new career and (especially after discovering his family connection to Roman) my romance with Billy.

So things seemed to be working out for the best.

'Told you so,' Billy teased. He was as pleased as anyone that Olivia and I were finally getting along.

'Don't you get sick of being right all the time?' I asked him.

'Never,' he replied with a smile, before kissing me

goodbye. 'I'll be back later for the house-warming!' he called, as he disappeared down the stairs.

Once Billy had gone, I turned to help Cleo with the unpacking – only to find she was already rummaging through boxes, pulling things out.

'So did you choose your bedroom yet?' I asked her, amused.

'They're both exactly the same!' Cleo complained, stopping what she was doing to look at me.

'I know,' I grinned at her. 'I already checked!'

I moved to help Cleo, picking out a couple of boxes and opening them up.

'So do you think you made the right decision moving in here?' Cleo asked me, before I could begin sorting through my boxes.

'Definitely,' I replied, without hesitation. 'I mean, don't get me wrong, I love Billy. But having him just downstairs is close enough at the moment. And there's no way I could've stayed at home for even one more week. I've just got to accept it; my mother and I get on far better when we're living under different roofs!'

I studied Cleo's reaction to this. 'What about you?' I asked her. 'Aren't you going to miss Trott?'

'Oh, I'm going to miss *her*,' Cleo smiled. 'I'm just not sure if she'll miss me! She practically ordered me out of the house this morning when I asked if she was sure she'd be okay living alone. Said she was perfectly capable of looking after herself and didn't need me fussing over her anymore.'

'That sounds like Trott,' I commented.

'Yeah, well she doesn't get rid of me that easily,' Cleo

smiled. 'I'm taking Jason over there to meet her next week. I think she's quite excited about it really.'

'I'm sure she is,' I agreed. 'But how excited is Jason?'

'Oh, he doesn't mind,' Cleo said. 'After meeting my mum, he thinks Trott will be a piece of cake. Little does he know!' she grinned.

'Poor guy,' I smiled.

'Yeah, but he has to do as I say,' Cleo smiled. 'Now I'm a manager and all.'

'So you still don't regret taking on Penny's old job?' I asked her.

Cleo had been doing the managerial thing for just over a month now and was still wildly enthusiastic about the whole experience. It was strange. I wasn't used to seeing Cleo so excited about anything. Well, apart from the obvious, that is.

'No!' Cleo said. 'Of course I don't regret it! There's so much more to do – it's really interesting. Plus, I'm pretty much in charge of the office while Jane's away, so I can get up to all sorts of mischief now. With Jason and without, if you know what I mean.'

'Yes,' I told her. 'I *always* know what you mean.'

'I'm so glad we're moving in together!' Cleo said, hugging me. 'It's like a brand new start.'

'Yes,' I agreed, hugging her back. 'It really is.'

For it truly was a brand new start for me. My old life had gone out of the window (quite literally, actually, as that was exactly where Billy had thrown my engagement ring from David), and I now had a chance to build something new – something better.

And life didn't get much better than this. I had my own apartment, a job I enjoyed, a great best friend, and a wonderful boyfriend.

And I was finally happy just being me.

Gracie Parker.

About The Author

Lisa Jane Weller was born in 1980 in Woolwich, London, but spent most of her childhood in Bexley, Kent. There she studied at Townley Grammar School for Girls and Orpington College of Further Education. English Language was her favourite subject at school, as it allowed her to indulge her growing passion for writing.

Lisa wrote her first short story at the age of eight and continued to write creatively throughout her time in education. Since then, she's penned numerous short stories and screenplays of many different genres. *Amazing Gracie* is her first full-length novel.

When she's not writing, Lisa enjoys reading, watching cult television shows, and cheering on her favourite football team, Blackburn Rovers. She is currently hard at work writing her second novel, an intriguing fantasy/horror/chick-lit hybrid.

Find out more about Lisa Jane Weller by visiting the Troll Boy Books website: www.trollboybooks.com